THE
TRUNK

DECEIT AND INTRIGUE IN THE LAST DESPERATE
DAYS OF THE NAZI THIRD REICH

DALE ROLLINGS

For my Family … for encouraging me.

CONTENTS

PROLOGUE

South St. Louis is a giant neighborhood stretching from Old US 66 on the north, in a giant arc to Broadway on the south and east. It is, above all things, a German community. From the earliest settlers in the Nineteenth Century the Germans found comfort in the jobs and employment in that part of St. Louis. The City's massive beer industry with breweries like Lemp, Anheuser-Busch and Griesiedieck Brothers provided familiar employment for arrivals from Mid-Germany and Austria. Other industries like baking, food processing, trucking and shipping all found a welcome labor force in the South St. Louis German Community.

A new wave of German immigrants came after World War I and infused the neighborhood with a fresh connection with "The Old Country." At the time of our story many "southsiders" were only one, or less, generation removed from Germany. It made for mixed feelings about the rise of a Militant Germany in the Thirties. It was against this backdrop that our characters, Frieda and Hugo Jurgens found themselves torn between the wants and desires of a new marriage, a growing family, and the dark magnetism of Nazi Germany.

As this story began to unfold I asked myself several times: "*What would I have done under similar circumstances?*" A deep economic depression was still gripping the nation; money was hard to come by. Times were hard. Would I have committed the unspeakable acts that Frieda and Hugo planned…, even for a huge sum of money?

And what about their only son, Donald? What would have been my reaction if I found out that my parents were Nazi spies, and the horrible atrocity my parents had planned? Were Donald and Connie's reactions what I would have felt if I found out what my parents had really planned? I, honestly, don't know…

This book, like most others, went through several rewrites. Not because of the technical exactness that writing requires, but because I was ambivalent about how I felt about the characters. I really could not reconcile what my feelings would have been if I had discovered what Don and Connie found out about his mother and father. On some days I found them just an ordinary couple trying to get by in a difficult time – doing what they had to do to get by; on others I judged them to be despicable traitors without sympathy or excuse.

Today, I do not know how I feel. Let me tell you the story, and you decide. I suspect you will have the same problems I did.

1
CHAPTER
FUNERAL

The funeral concluded with the customary dinner at an Italian restaurant on the Hill. Don't ask where that custom began - it just did, and it's been going on after every family funeral for thirty years. After a funeral in the Jurgens family pasta always seems to somehow assuage the grief. It could be spaghetti and meatballs or mostaccioli. It didn't matter as long as it was red sauce. Not that this was the saddest funeral on earth. Sure, we would miss him, but the death of Hugo Jurgens did not come as much of a surprise. At eighty-nine he had spent a long and healthy life with us. It is pretty hard to be critical of such a long run on this earth.

Reverend Luther Twiehaus, a stoic and forever-somber icon of a Lutheran minister, had read the 23rd Psalm. He made the mandatory remarks about Hugo Jurgens and, his beloved wife, Frieda, who had preceded him in death some six years before, and me, his only son, Donald.

We were going to miss Dad. We loved him. My wife, Connie, and I and our children loved and respected his quiet solid understanding and guidance. One never comes to a funeral prepared to say farewell forever. Death for an eighty-nine-year-old is just as unwanted as for a thirty-nine-year-old. The difference is in the expectations. After eighty-nine good years you cannot claim surprise. Death did not cheat us. We have had had full measure. He had been healthy most of his life right up until the end when he had a heart attack. Still, it was hard to turn him loose.

Hugo Jurgens was the son of immigrants who came to these shores from central Germany in 1884. He was born in 1901 in an area of St. Louis now called "Soulard." His father, Heinrich, was a farmer in Germany who had a working knowledge of barley and hops. It made him very employable in Saint Louis' growing beer industry. I don't remember much about Grandfather Heinrich, since he died when I was very young, but everyone tells me he was quite a fellow. He kept the traditions of Middle Germany and saw himself as the repository of all German culture that would be passed down in the transplanted Jurgens family tree. "The branches," he said, "might be in America, but the roots are still in Germany." Never mind that he had immigrated, Grandpa would never let the culture of the Fatherland die. I only remember him as would a three-year old; a mustached, slightly rotund little man with stories and quips that made me laugh. Those aren't bad memories of your grandfather.

My father, Hugo, never quite got the hang of German culture. While both his father and mother were German-born immigrants, he was born an American. He was not much different than most first-generation Americans, and his German heritage was soon forgotten. He was responsible for removing the umlaut from the name Jürgens, and his father never forgave him for it! He entered the Moler Barber College in St. Louis the year after his graduation from high school, and his course in history was set. It was 1918. America was on the rise. The Roaring Twenties lay ahead, and a good trade was something no one could take away from you. Barbering seemed as good a trade as any. Hugo embraced it totally, and he was a pretty good barber. Barbering was nominally rewarding. A busy barber could support his family well, although you would never get rich, and you got to meet lots of people who depended on you. It was a good choice, and one that Hugo Jurgens embraced with gusto. When you are eighteen the world is a big ball at your feet. All you need to do is pick it up and punt. Becoming a barber was my father's way of punting.

Dad loved sports. He followed the St. Louis Browns and the Cardinals. He listened to the games on an old Philco upright radio console in the living room, and when television came along it was as though the heavens had opened up.

He was also a tinkerer. There wasn't anything he could not fix. Clocks, radios, small appliances were challenges for him, and when they went on the blink they would wind up downstairs on his workbench where he would methodically disassemble them, diagnose the problem and proceed to remedy the defect like a surgeon. The truth was that he was very talented in that area. I even saw him fix a pocket watch one time. How he got it apart and back together, and all of the parts back into the case is still a mystery to me.

Dad was one of nine children. Grandpa and grandma Jurgens never got birth control right! Seven of their children were born in six years, and not one of them was a twin. Dad was the second oldest of five boys and four girls. Of the nine, only four outlived Dad. All four attended the funeral.

Under the direction of George Mapplethorpe and Sons, Funeral Directors to the Jurgens family for over fifty years, the funeral arrangements had been carried out to perfection. From the first time a visitor to the wake drove into the parking lot of the Mapplethorpe Funeral Home, a dark-suited Funeral Director would direct you to a parking space, take your coat, ask you, in hushed tones, what family you were here to pay respects to and stand by the Memorial book while you signed your name and address. Before the book was delivered to the family after the funeral it was photocopied, and the names and addresses added to the mailing list of the Mapplethorpe Funeral Home. George Mapplethorpe had long ago passed, but his two sons maintained the proper decorum through the wake, and then orchestrated the funeral service itself the next day.

The Lutheran church rewards its faithful with a good funeral service. An eleven-voice choir backed up a soloist in a respectable version of *How Great Thou Art*, and concluded with *In the Garden*.

There were a few damp eyes, many handkerchiefs and some sniffles at the end of the solo, but generally those assembled in the sanctuary of the Salem Lutheran Church on Gravois this cold January morning in 1990 managed the loss of one of their own pretty well. It was a good crowd – a proper measure of one's stature in the community. Hugo had made a lot of friends on his life's journey. Several came to see him off, and they were genuinely sad to see him go.

At the wake the night before the funeral service one of my father's brothers had inquired if I was going to say a few words in the service? He was incredulous when I said that I had not planned to. He could not understand why Hugo's only son was not going to deliver some sort of a eulogy. It was quite a guilt trip. I heard him telling his wife that I was not going to speak.

What would I say? What do you say about your father? That he was a nice guy? A good father? Brought up his only son right? Paid his bills? It all sounded a little self-serving to me. Later in the evening I was approached by my dad's sister, my aunt Mildred, a hawkish little runt of a woman in her early seventies who always seemed to assume that she knew the best for the family. In fact, I think it was her who started the pasta-eating-after-family-funerals-ritual years ago when her first husband died from a fall from the roof. I still believe he jumped! Mildred was always dressed in clothes that looked like they were in style about fifteen years ago.

You might get the impression that I did not like Mildred. That's not entirely true, but I had learned that she was a cunning, dominant woman who wanted her way, and usually got it. I just learned to steer clear of her. So did the rest of the family when she was on a terror. My feelings about Mildred go back to when I was three years old in 1944. My father contracted Tuberculosis and spent a month in a sanitarium in Arkansas. My mother could not handle me alone and work too, so they deposited me with Aunt Mildred. My recollection of my extended visit is a little vague, but I remember that I was glad to get back to Mom and Dad when it was over. She was domineering, a strict disciplinarian who zealously endorsed corporeal punishment - and she scared me to death.

"Donald," she intoned in that look-down-your-nose demeaning voice that she managed to evoke anytime something did not suit her. I knew I was in trouble when she called me 'Donald' instead of Don."

"You really should say something at your father's funeral tomorrow. It *is* your father, and, after all, you *are* his only son."

To my horror all conversation in Mapplethorpe's little visitation parlor had stopped. Each surviving relative was looking at me. Mildred had clearly orchestrated the event. I half expected my father to sit up and listen, too. It was a "look-what-this-young-punk-is -going-to-do-to-our-family" scene. I looked around the room. The average age had to be eighty. At forty-nine, I was one of the youngest people at the wake. Glassy eyes peered at me over cheeks with too much rouge and powder. Canes and a few walkers were shuffled as frail hunchbacked bodies turned to face me as if on cue. Chins were lowered so that elderly eyes could peer over reading glasses at the little bastard who was not going to deliver a eulogy at his own father's funeral!

"Mildred, I don't know what to say." It already sounded like a pathetic defense. "We all loved Dad. Everyone who knew him liked him. I never knew him to have an enemy, but that does not convert to a good eulogy. Besides, I am a mathematician, not a public speaker. What would I say?"

Mildred fumbled for her handbag, an immense green Naugahyde blob that looked like it came out of the Fifties. It had a big Bakelite twist clasp on the top, and she had trouble twisting it open with her arthritic claws. It finally yielded, and the yawning hinges flopped open to provide access to the cavernous interior. She reached in and plucked out an outline written in pencil on green Spiral notebook paper. It was one page, but written on both sides in very small tidy words closely spaced on the printed lines."

"Here. Take this," she rasped. "I've done it for you."

I hesitated.

The room continued to glare.

"Take it. Deliver it tomorrow." She turned on her little black lacquered cane and headed for the door. The last I saw of her that night was her gray hair bun disappearing into the crowd of family.

I stood there like an idiot reading the notes. The conversations began to reassert themselves around me. It was as if Mildred had delivered a final edict. I was going to deliver a eulogy, and that was that. I stuck the notes in my pocket and continued shaking arthritic hands clasping damp handkerchiefs.

Connie had seen the whole episode. In the car on the way home she could smell my guilt.

"Are you going to do it?"

"Huh? Do what?" I was deep in thought. I loved my dad and the real shock of losing him was just sinking in.

"Deliver the eulogy."

"Connie, I feel really bad about it. Should I do it?"

If Connie has added anything to my life, except two boys and twenty-eight years of a good marriage, it is balance. She had a good sense of what battles to fight and which ones to leave alone.

"I think you should do it. What will it hurt? Besides, you are not *only* the only *son*; you are the *only* child. God forbid that morbid Mildred gives a eulogy. Obviously, she has thought about it with that outline in her purse."

I gave in immediately. I could see that Connie thought it was a good idea. She was not as close to it as I was. Maybe her judgment on the subject should be heeded.

"OK, I'll tell Reverend Twiehaus. I guess he'll just work me into the service.

"I saw you reading the outline at the funeral home. I mean, is it what you would say if you had written it?"

"To tell you the truth, I looked at it, but I really did not read it. I felt like I was standing in that room naked. I looked at it, but I did not see. I'll read it when we get home."

Connie slipped across the front seat against me and put her arm under mine. It was a cold night. The February wind buffeted the car as we headed up Rock Hill Avenue. It was a statement by Connie. She was saying *I'm your wife. I understand your pain. I'll be here if you want me, but you really should do it.* She did not have to say a word. I got the message.

We drove the rest of the way home in silence.

I was up early. One does not sleep well the night before one buries one's father. The sky had turned steel-gray and come closer to earth. Snow was predicted. I thought I saw a few flurries against the dark barren trees in the back yard as I made coffee in my robe. Connie and the boys were still asleep. The boys had come home from college for the funeral. It was Saturday. I wouldn't be teaching today.

At times like this it is easy to reflect on one's life. When you lose a parent it's as though a little part of you dies, too. My Dad had been a force in my life. He helped me through high school, attended all my Little League games, and took out a loan to help me with tuition at the University of Missouri. More importantly, he and Mom set a moral tone and encouraged me to follow it. They were good people – active in the church, in the community and in the life of their son – "their Pride and Joy" – me. When mathematics emerged as one of my strong suits they encouraged me, and again loaned me money (I think they borrowed it, too) for college, then graduate school, and a resulting PhD in mathematics at Washington University in St. Louis.

Twenty-two years ago, when I received an appointment as Assistant Professor of Mathematics at my Alma Mater, Washington University, my dad was the proudest person on Earth. He was so proud of me that he and Mom refused to let me pay them back for the loans they had floated to get me through. "Put it down on a house, son," he said "It'll get you and Connie started right."

I built a fire in the stone fireplace in the den. It just seemed like the thing to do. The morning paper had not even come yet, and I did not feel like reading it anyway. Mildred's eulogy outline was still in the jacket pocket of the suit I had on the night before. I tiptoed upstairs to the bedroom and plucked it from the inside pocket. On the way back to the big winged-back chair in front of the now-blazing fire I poured a cup of steaming coffee and sat down to read the outline.

The handwriting was a little creaky. The letters were well formed and printed as if the writer had intended to make sure they could be read. An occasional shake of the hand betrayed the age of the author. It was not very original. It started by talking about my dad's boyhood, his father and mother, brothers and sisters enumerating each who had died before. It went on to talk about how Hugo put himself through barber school, opened a shop and had become prosperous (at least for a barber). It detailed his good works, his dedication to his church and friends, his loving wife, Frieda, who he had buried six years before.

Nothing very imaginative. Just the straight stuff. Hugo Jurgens was a straight man.

She mentioned his love for the outdoors, how he loved to hike, hunt and fish even right up to the last. She talked about the many friends who he had made through the many social and cultural organizations to which he belonged.

"Social and cultural organizations?" It was a strange reference. Dad never got involved in many social or cultural organizations. He wasn't much of a joiner. Mildred was getting carried away.

I read on.

She talked about the twenties, when dad was a single fellow, a dapper dresser, man about town in his Whippet Coupe. I had always heard that he was quite a fashion plate. I had seen pictures of him and that car. He was usually decked out with spats and a straw skimmer, fresh starched shirts and a puff of handkerchief in the breast pocket. He must have been quite the lady-killer.

Mildred's outline carried on about the Thirties, the hard times of the Depression, and the difficult financial times that followed Dad's marriage to Mom. Money was scarce, but even so it seems Dad did what he could for others. He was active in the Black Forest Society and the Turners and ...

I knew what the Turners were, but *The Black Forest Society*? I never heard of it. Funny, I thought I knew almost everything there was to know about Dad. We talked a lot, particularly after Mom died. Dad liked to tell stories about south Saint Louis. He never mentioned the Black Forest Society.

Connie came downstairs in a chenille robe rubbing her eyes and poured herself a cup of coffee. It was just getting light outside.

"Can't sleep, huh?" she said.

"I just thought I would check over Mildred's outline."

"And?"

"And, it's OK. Nothing special, but probably better than I could do. Very organized."

"Well, then use it." She sat down on the arm of the big chair and sipped her coffee. Connie was so practical.

"Connie. Did you ever hear of the Black Forest Society?"

"No, I don't think so. What is it?"

"Damned if I know. Mildred has it in her outline. Says my dad was a member of it in the Thirties."

"Probably some South Saint Louis social club. With all of the German immigrants down there the area was full of them. I hear there used to be over a hundred breweries in that part of town alone. I'll bet it was a drinking and dancing club. If the stories about your dad are true, it was probably one of the best. Didn't he meet your mom in a club?"

"He told you that story?"

"Twice. Those two must have cut some swath in their younger days. You want some Waffles?"

"I'm really not very hungry."

"Why don't you ask Mildred about the Black Forest Society? She seems to know a lot about it."

Connie knew I wouldn't ask Mildred.

The funeral started promptly at ten. It was Saturday morning. The boys fidgeted in their seats, tugged at their ties and watched the increasing cadence of the snowflakes through the tall windows of the Salem Lutheran Church. I knew they would rather be back a school at the University of Missouri.

Mildred asked again on the way into the service if I was going to give the eulogy. She seemed genuinely pleased when I said I would. Her sharp-beaked nose looked even more pointed. She had her hair pulled back from her face and tucked into the ever-present bun at the nape of her neck. Her high forehead was accentuated by pulling back the hair. God, she was ugly! I always had the impression that the clothes she wore were borrowed from the Goodwill – they probably had to be back in the morning! Her shoes looked like military issue. On the hook of her arm was the same mammoth dark green Naugahyde purse.

I struggled valiantly through the eulogy. Public speaking is not my forte', I teach mathematics. I can talk to a class of graduate students, but public speaking to strangers does not come easily. I followed Mildred's outline, even to the part about the Black Forest Society about which I knew nothing. I consoled myself that it was my duty. After all, I *was* his only child.

At the close of the service we all filed by the open casket for the last time and went out into the falling snow while one of the Mapplethorpe boys closed the lid. Six pall-bearers loaded the casket into the hearse under the watchful eye of Reverend Twiehaus and the other Mapplethorpe.

The church had been full, but only about a third of the people went in procession to the cemetery. The snow had scared them off. The weather had turned really foul. A nasty North wind was now whipping the increasing flakes into a blizzard. The prediction was for six to eight inches.

It was two o'clock before we got to Pepino's Authentic Italian Restaurant. Pepino had a downstairs room that he rented for weddings, banquets and funerals. It was to Pepino's that the Jurgens family had adjourned for the last two generations to console themselves over the death of their own and to eat a pasta meal and drink beer and wine. Germans will never admit it, but they love Italian food more than their own. For wines they still prefer Auslase and Piesporter to Chianti and Pino Grigio but watch them order food. They'll take carbonara over potato dumplings any day. Besides, pasta is cheaper than schnitzel!

I didn't make the arrangements at Pepino's. I guessed that Mildred did. She ordered everyone to attend after the committal ceremony at the cemetery. She kept giving orders to the waiters and was conferring with Antonio Pepino about seating and other necessary arrangements when we arrived. I resigned myself to the reality that I was probably supposed to pay for this orgy, but after that I had a pretty good time with the assembled relatives many of whom had come a long way. I suspected that the incentive might have been the meal rather than the funeral! All told there were forty-four people present, many of whom I had not seen since the last Jurgens family funeral, my uncle's, three years before.

The banquet tables were set up in an open horseshoe shape. The shape dictated that the end table was, *de facto*, the head table. Mildred pointed Connie and me to it. The boys were left to themselves. What an honor. You get married or your father dies, and you get to sit at the head table. Mildred parked herself next to me. She had no children and had outlived three husbands, so she reserved herself only one chair by hanging the mammoth purse over the back. No one dared transgress the staked-out territory. She moved through the room sort of like a macabre Martha Stewart stopping at selected tables, greeting guests and coming to light on my right at the head table.

She tapped her spoon on a water glass. "Now that everyone is seated," she began, "Reverend Twiehaus will give the blessing."

The good Reverend Twiehaus, already uncomfortable at being the only non-family member at the gathering, rose and gave a somber and short benediction that began with the mandatory "Shall we bow our heads..."

Thankfully the Benediction was short, and bowls of steaming pasta were produced. Steins of beer and carafes of wine and pitchers of beer flowed freely. Hugo Jurgens was soon but a memory - and fading fast.

I had pretty-well forgotten to ask Mildred about the Black Forest Society. Connie reminded me after we sat down to eat, and I leaned over to Mildred.

"Mildred, what is the Black Forest Society?"

"You father never told you?" she replied looking straight ahead and not batting an eye.

"No. Should he have?" She continued to look straight ahead, avoiding my eyes and my question. "Have you found the trunk?" Her voice was flat. The irascible cackle was gone. The question bore no emotion. It was an interrogatory.

"Trunk? What trunk?"

Mildred rose abruptly and dabbed her lips. "Excuse me Donald, I must go. Pepino will present you with the check."

"Aunt Mildred, for God's sake..."

She had turned and was heading for the door. She stopped only to take her unfashionable black wool coat and cap from the coat rack.

Connie had heard only part of my conversation with Mildred. She had noticed her leave abruptly.

"Donald, what did you say to her?"

"Connie, I didn't say anything."

"You must have. Why would she leave so quickly? Were you rude to her? She's just a crotchety old woman. You don't have to treat her rudely."

"Connie, I..." It was not much use. What had happened? It made no sense. It made even less sense to try to explain it. I tried, but I couldn't.

We drove back to our home in University City in silence.

2
CHAPTER
THE ATTIC

Our Sony MusicCube LED clock-radio cast a green glow over the bedroom. Connie's eyes were so bad that she always kept the display on "bright" so she could read it in the night. I had awakened with a start. Don't ask me what woke me. I had fallen asleep quickly, but it was a troubled sleep. I could tell that I had tossed and turned. The fitted sheet had been pulled off the corners of the mattress. The Sony display read *2:19.* I tossed and rolled to my side. The snow was still popping against the windowpane. A gray glow had settled in over the yard and reflected through the window. Our white painted walls took on a gray patina from the snow.

"What was that thing with Mildred all about?" I asked myself. "What was she talking about? The trunk?"

There was something vaguely disconcerting about her reference to a trunk. Something deep in my memory stirred but could not be identified. It was related to the trunk. I shifted my pillow and rolled to my other side. Connie was snoring that little purr-like sound she emits when she is flat on her back and sleeping soundly - not a snore really, rather more like a cat humming on your lap in deep slumber.

The trunk? What about the trunk?

I threw off the comforter and wandered into the bathroom. I really didn't need to pee but did it anyway. The snow continued to pelt the windowpanes. The street was illuminated by the streetlight out front, and I could see that at least six inches of the white fluffy stuff had fallen. A single set of tire tracks in the street were rapidly being covered by the snow.

I crawled back into bed and pulled up the comforter. I lay on my back looking at the ceiling in the green-gray glow. It hit me like a ton of bricks. It all came rushing back so suddenly that I sat up straight in bed. Seven years ago, about a year before my mother's death, she called me up and asked me to come over for dinner. A cook she was not. Dinner consisted of three Swanson TV dinners in aluminum serving trays heated in a toaster oven. Iced tea was served in red plastic Solo cups from 7-11.

Mom had wanted to show me a trunk in which she had placed the family archives. It was not a very auspicious occasion, and I had forgotten all about it. She had, on at least three other occasions, made the same effort to show me pictures, newspaper articles and other memorabilia that she had archived in photo albums through the years. I had not seen the trunk for a long time. Mom was a self-styled chronicler of our family. Maintenance of a photo record of the events of a lifetime was her personal quest. She had old photographs that she had collected over many years with which she filled vinyl covered photo albums. As each album had been filled she orchestrated a little presentation ceremony and entrusted them to me for safekeeping. She didn't really give them to me. Each time she prefaced her presentation with "I want you to have this after I am gone..." Then she flipped through them, explained them in detail and put them away. But she felt like she was giving them to me.

There was nothing new or special here. Mom always had some grand idea that my need to connect with my ancestors through photographs, newspaper articles and church bulletins was greater than it was. I couldn't care less, but I recognized her need to collect these archival items. So, I feigned sincere appreciation. Don't get me wrong, I believe that a family should preserve its history, and old photos and historical items are important. I just do not live my every waking hour in pursuit of archiving my family's history. The fact that my uncle Teddy had an affair with a woman in a traveling show was interesting but hardly worthy of a photo essay. I just couldn't get that enthused.

Mom was just the opposite. Her last years were spent organizing and chronicling the history of her and my father's family into scrapbooks, photo albums and binders which she presented to me with much pomp and circumstance. Nothing would do but that we sat on the sofa and went through each page and item so that she could explain to me what it was. Each photo had a story, and Mom knew them all. Never mind that each had been labeled with a small, typed cut-out label pasted on the bottom of each photo or article giving the basic reference as to time and place. Each had to be explained and discussed. No detail was omitted, No fact was left undiscussed.

As each scrapbook was finished, I received an invitation to come over and eat TV dinners, after which I was escorted to the velour-covered sofa in the living room to sit through Mom's explanation of her latest masterpiece of Jurgens family history. Dad was left to finish his dinner, which usually meant he was going to have a dessert – something my Mom rarely did. I had long ago recognized the importance of these evenings to her. I endured them for her sake, feigning interest, asking questions, studying articles and photographs. She was delighted. I was a good son.

On this particular evening, after we had scraped the mashed potatoes out of the aluminum trays and drank the last of the iced tea, we adjourned to the living room for Mom's latest completed adventure into the bowels of the family tree. I was dreading every moment, and Mom did not disappoint me. On this occasion, however, she had a trunk she wanted to show me.

The trunk itself was dark brown with little brass rivets holding the panels together. It had wooden strips along the side to slide it and to protect it. It has sort of a domed top right out of the Thirties. She reminded me every time that it had been my grandfathers, and he had brought it from Germany. I had remembered it from my childhood days and knew that it had been in the family for years. On the corners were little brass corner pieces, and in the back three brass hinges held the lid. The front had one of those flat round brass latches that never work.

Mom produced the key from her apron and told dad to do the dishes. He obeyed and began to clear the aluminum trays from the dining room table.

"Get that," she ordered, gesturing to the trunk that had been slid under the coffee table in front of the living room couch. I knelt and pulled the trunk from under the table. It slid across the rug but was quite heavy. She inserted the key into the cheap lock. It popped open and flapped down against the front of the trunk. She lifted the creaky lid.

The interior of the trunk was paperboard. Little line-drawings, clowns and balloons, dotted the pale blue liner in the lid and covered the tray that formed the top shelf. The tray had an outside rim around it and fit nicely onto a ridge on the side of the trunk so that it only dropped about one-fourth of the way into the interior. A label from the trunk-maker was pasted on the underside of the lid immediately caught my eye. A divider in the middle of the tray separated it into two equal sections. Stacked neatly on their sides in these two top compartments were packs of photographs, bundled in shoestring ties each bearing a paper label as to date and subject. Some of the packets were as thin as two or three photos while others were an inch or two thick.

I reached in and picked up a labeled package, the label read: "Florida, New Year's, 1949 - 1950." Mother was delighted at my interest and began to recite factual data about a driving trip we took to Florida over the New Year's holiday of '49-50' for which I had only a vague recollection. I would have been less than ten years old.

On the shelf of the trunk there had to be a thousand photos, all bunched and tied by date and subject and stacked neatly on their sides like bricks. I never got past the shelf. Whatever was below it, more photos I guessed, but she never got to it.

"I want you to have them," she said, waving her hand over the trunk in a grand gesture. She had designated me as the repository of this excessive photo history of the Jurgens family. I feigned interest. I wish I could have been more excited.

"Mom, what am I going to do with all of these photos? You must have a thousand of them in there."

"Not now. When I'm gone. I'm not giving them to you now. You'll have to wait until your father and I are both gone. You'll cherish these the same way I do."

I could see this trunk full of photos meant a lot to her. Mom had always taken lots of pictures. She had a Brownie box camera in her hand in one of my first memories of her. It had to be in the Forties. The trunk represented her treasure trove of photos. I never got past the top tray. I speculated that if we went through them this evening we would be up until dawn. If the rest of the trunk was packed as densely as the top tray there had to be thousands of photos.

"This trunk contains a living chronology of our family," she went on. "You are the only heir, and it's your duty to preserve our family's heritage. When your father and I are gone you should have the trunk. We can't leave you much money, but we can leave you our heritage."

She slammed the lid shut and locked it with the small flat key. Reaching for my hand she dropped the key into my palm and rolled my fingers shut. She gave a little squeeze for good measure. "There are two keys," she said. "You have one and I have the other."

Dad had finished the dishes and had parked himself on the Laz-E-Boy recliner. across from the sofa. It was clear that something was on his mind.

There was a long silence.

"Your mother has cancer, son," he said, rather flatly. The statement seemed so out of context, but looking back on that night, the reason for the invitation to receive the trunk was now apparent.

"The doctor gives her about a year."

"Mom is that true?" I was incredulous. I knew she had not been looking well, but I never suspected anything terminal. Everything else paled in the light of the disclosure. I remembered the evening for the revelation of my mother's illness. The trunk became a non-event and I soon forgot it. The thought of Mom's cancer and the inevitable end outweighed everything else. I never thought of the key, or where I put it, and, to my knowledge, I do not remember seeing it again after that night.

Mom died a year later. The service, by the same funeral director, with the same casket, and with most of the same people who attended Dad's funeral yesterday was held at the same church with Reverend Twiehaus presiding.

I had never thought again about the trunk after that night. The news of Mom's terminal illness completely overshadowed her revelation about the trunk and its contents. Until Mildred had mentioned it, the trunk had been completely out of my mind.

"Connie!" I shook her. She snorted and rolled over on her side putting her back to me. I shook her again.

"Connie, I know what Mildred was talking about."

"Huh? What?" Connie rubbed her eyes, raised her head and squinted at me. "What are you talking about?"

"The trunk. It has to be the trunk that Mom showed me before she died."

"Donald, that was years ago."

"Sure, but what else could Mildred be talking about? What else could she mean?"

"Maybe she didn't mean anything, Maybe Mildred is senile, or a little bit nuts, like all the rest of your family. Maybe she is just wacko! Connie was in no mood to be shaken awake.

"Donald, it's the middle of the night. For God's sake go back to sleep." She rolled back over on her side, put her back to me and pulled the covers over her head.

I was left alone to bask in the green Sony glow. Connie clearly did not intend to discuss it. More snow beat against the windowpane. The dark pin oaks in the yard scratched against the house. I tried to remember what was in the trunk. Photographs, some newspaper articles in plastic sleeve binders. Nothing memorable. Nothing remarkable.

I couldn't go back to sleep. I lay on my back, then on each side. I got up again and paced around the house looking out at the accumulating snow. I turned on KMOX radio and listened to some other creatures of the night call in and vent their frustrations at an equally frustrated host of an all-night talk show.

Why would Mildred want to know if I had found the trunk?

Dawn brought a tapering off of the snow. A gray morning lit a fresh eight-inch snowfall. I had seen it uncovered from a blanket of darkness by the softly encroaching light of dawn. I could not go back so sleep so I went downstairs and made coffee. The Mormon Tabernacle Choir greeted me from "The Crossroads of the West" through the little Panasonic on the kitchen counter. It was about as close to church as I cared to be this morning. Connie came down at 7:30.

"What's wrong with you? Couldn't you sleep?"

"No, but thanks for asking."

She walked around behind the chair in which I was sitting and put her hands on my shoulders. "Donald, it's not going to be easy. You've lost both of your parents. No one could ask for more, or better, years than they had - but it has to be hard. No one is ever prepared." She bent over and hugged me allowing her chestnut-brown hair fall over my forehead.

She was right. No matter how prepared you think you are, when you lose someone close to you there is a hollow loneliness that just takes time to heal.

"Thanks, Connie. You are a rock when I need it. But it's not just the death of Dad. I can't help thinking about Mildred and that damn trunk. What did she mean?"

"Donald, you know she is a screwball. Is that why you can't sleep? That's dumb. She probably doesn't mean anything. I'll bet she doesn't even remember what she said. She hits the bottle a little too, you know."

"Yes, but..."

"Hey. No 'buts' about it. Forget Mildred. Forget the trunk. She's a kook."

By ten o'clock that morning I was totally consumed with the idea of the trunk. After he died the thought of going over to Dad's place had not appealed to me. I had gone, but reluctantly. I knew that I would have to tackle the chore of cleaning out the house and selling it sooner or later, but I had really avoided the thought until now. By ten o'clock, I was putting on my boots and a parka for the second time this morning. I had thought shoveling the driveway would get my mind off the trunk. It didn't work. After breakfast I was determined to go find the trunk.

It took fifteen minutes to get to dad's place. Connie had decided to come with me. She, too, dreaded the big clean-out job that would inevitably have to be faced. For her, this was a reconnaissance job just to size up the effort that would be involved. She knew she would wind up supervising it – more accurately, probably doing the lion's share of it.

Dad and Mom had lived most of their married lives in a brick and white frame bungalow on Vienna Avenue in the Frances Park area of South Saint Louis. It was about three blocks off the park. The gabled roof, red brick bungalow was indistinguishable from its neighbors. Each was a "shotgun" of a house thirty feet wide and fifty feet deep separated by a sidewalk between the houses that provided access around the side of the house to the back yard. A small, grassy front and back yard were kept manicured to perfection right up to the yews that lined the house foundation in front and back. A detached garage was accessed through an alley in the back.

I parked the car in the street and slogged up the unshoveled walk to the front stoop. The key went in easily and the door swung back. I hesitated before entering. Connie put her hand on my shoulder.

After Mom had died dad lived here alone until five days before his death. He was a healthy fellow, at least until the last two years of his life, and he kept his house clean and neat inside and out. The Zoysia grass yard was always perfectly trimmed as were the evergreen shrubs along the foundation. The inside was just as neat and tidy. Dad lived his days up to the end the same way - neat and tidy. The barbershop where he spent forty years of his life until he retired, was always spick and span. His cars were always washed and shined. The basement was immaculate with everything in its place. You could eat off the floor.

The neighbors loved him. On summer evenings he could hardly work on his yard for people stopping by to chat. He got so that he did yard work in the morning so that the constant interruptions that would inevitably accompany afternoon and evening yard work could be accommodated. But he went out in the yard in the evening anyway just so that he could be interrupted. Dad helped people too, often to his own inconvenience. In his later years he was always taking something to a sick friend, or an invalid to the doctor. He worked in church activities and never missed a service. When there was a bar-b-que or a social he would always help set up the tables or haul chairs. Hugo Jurgens lived an exemplary life - a fact that had not escaped comment by Reverend Twiehaus in his funeral sermon.

Dad had lived quietly and comfortably in this house for six years after Mom died. He was lonely. He missed her, but he did not let his loneliness force him into a shell. In fact, he seemed even more visible after Mom died by increasing his activity. No one thought for a minute that Hugo Jurgens was not lonely. His love for Frieda was evident right up to the end. They were a pair. If you saw one, you saw the other. They were inseparable. Yes, everyone knew that Hugo missed Frieda, but they were awed by his efforts to overcome the pain.

Dad lived in this house until five days before he died. The heart attack had come without warning as he was ascending the front stoop steps after fetching the morning paper. A neighbor found him slumped on the top step and rushed him to the hospital. But the damage had been done. Five days later he was dead.

I was jolted by a rush of cold air as the front door swung back. That was odd. If anything, Dad and Mom kept the thermostat about ten degrees above where I was comfortable. The house was always toasty. Not today. I could see my breath against the darkness of the living room as I entered. It was cold inside.

My first thought was the furnace had gone out and I wondered if there were pipes frozen or about to burst. I had not been over to the house since the day dad went to the hospital. That was ten days ago. Frozen pipes can do a lot of damage in ten days.

I moved through the house turning on lights. Most of the drapes had been closed. I could still see my breath, but there were no frozen pipes. I noticed that the trunk was not under the coffee table where I had last seen it seven years ago when Mom showed me its contents. It could have been gone for years. I could not actually remember seeing it since that night seven years ago.

As I moved through the central hallway past the bedrooms to the kitchen in the back of the house I heard a dull thud. I stopped cold and listened. It had come from the vicinity of the kitchen. I heard it again.

Thud.

Connie, who had lingered in the living room, was now behind me. "What was that?"

"I don't know."

Thud.

"Listen, there it is again."

I'm not sure what made me do it, but I took a flying leap into the kitchen. Perhaps I thought surprise would give me some kind of advantage.

The back door into the kitchen had been smashed in. The complete door facing where the dead bolt had fitted into the jamb had been shattered. Someone had just kicked it in. It was swinging in the wind against the kitchen counter emitting an irregular "thud" as it contacted the Formica counter top. Cold air was rushing in with each swing of the door. So much for the broken furnace theory.

Connie and I looked at each other dumbfounded. I glanced around the kitchen. Everything was in place. No drawers were opened. No cabinets ajar. Everything seemed normal. Nothing missing.

I knew Dad kept his watch, wallet and jewelry in the top drawer of his dresser in the bedroom. I walked in and pulled the drawer open using a Kleenex tissue to hold the drawer pull. I saw the police do it that way on *NYPD Blue* - preserves fingerprints, I guess. The watch was there. So were the jewelry and the wallet where he had left them. Nothing was gone. We walked through the remainder of the house, including the basement. Everything was neat and tidy just as Dad would have wanted it. Nothing was missing.

"Who would smash in the back door and not take anything?"

"Beats me," said Connie. Do you think we should to call the police?"

"Probably. First let's take a look around outside. Anyone who has been around since last night would probably leave some tracks in the snow."

The snow leading up the back steps and across the porch was as smooth as glass. No one had been there since it had begun to snow last night. I looked carefully for tracks that had been covered. Perhaps a slight indentation would betray a burglar who had traversed the porch early last evening before the heaviest snowfall. Nothing. Whoever had been here had done it before the snow began to fall. It could have even been several days ago.

I had almost forgotten that our original mission was to find the trunk. Going to the police seemed less and less like a practical idea. Nothing was missing. Of course, someone had broken in the door, but they were long gone. I went to the basement to find a hammer and some nails to nail it shut. I found some on Dad's workbench and was returning up the stairs.

"The trunk! Where's the trunk?"

I took the last steps two at a time and came bounding out into the hall.

"Honey. The trunk! They could have been after the ..."

I stopped dead in the hall. Standing in the kitchen door silhouetted against the light of the broken door was Mildred.

"What the Hell are you doing here?" There was a clear edge on my voice. She was the last person I had expected to see. Connie came in from the living room.

"And how did you get in here?"

"I was passing by and saw your car out front. Donald, you look white as a sheet."

"I... I just didn't expect to see you here this morning."

"What happened to this door?" she said, eying the damage to the door frame.

"Someone tried to break in. Doesn't look like they took anything."

"Oh? Are you sure?"

"Pretty sure. We checked the whole house and can't find anything missing.

"What about the trunk?"

"What about it, Mildred? I turned squarely to face her. "What about the damn trunk!"

"Is it here?"

"Why? Why, Mildred, is that damn trunk so important to you?"

"Is it here?"

"I haven't seen it."

"You had better find it. That's all I can say. You better find it."

"Mildred, for God's sake! What is so friggin' important about a trunk full of pictures?"

"Pictures? You know what's in it?"

"Pictures! Pictures and clippings, Mildred! What the Hell do you think is in it - gold?" I'm sure I was screaming at her. She was so irritating; so persistent. God, she was a bitch!

"How do you know there are pictures in the trunk, Donald?" Her voice was icy cold, emotionless. Her steel blue eyes looked at me with a cold determination.

"I just know." I didn't want to tell her any more than I had to.

"Find the trunk, Donald." She turned and headed down the hall toward the front door pulling on the little wool skullcap she always wore in winter. The door slammed shut behind her.

Connie and I looked at each other for a few seconds, dumbfounded at what had just transpired. Almost as if to read each other's minds we turned and went room by room through the house and down into the basement to find the trunk. It took about thirty minutes. We ended our search back in the living room. There was no trunk. I got down on my hands and knees and examined the area under the coffee table where I had last recalled seeing the trunk seven years ago. I thought there might be fresh signs of its removal - a bent rug pile, a scrape of paint. Nothing. The trunk was not anywhere to be found.

We sat on the living room sofa, frustrated.

"Is there an attic?" inquired Connie, somewhat absentmindedly.

"Attic?"

"Sure, an attic. Every house in South St. Louis has an attic."

She was right. There had to be an attic. The house had a single gable roof running front to back. There had to be an attic. But I had been raised here, and I never saw an attic.

"You're right. There has to be an attic." I looked up at the ceiling as if to see through it.

Connie was already up and walking down the hall. "Sometimes you access it with one of those stairways that fold down. They are usually in the hallway," she said. She was looking up. I don't see one in the hall. She paused. What's that set of louvers in the hall ceiling?"

"An attic fan. You use it in the summer. Draws cool air in through the windows and sucks it up and out vents in the eaves."

We walked back through the house looking at the ceiling of every room. There was no sign of an attic access or pull-down stairway.

"Remember that house where Mrs. Hofstra used to live? You got into the attic using a ladder that went up through an opening in the ceiling of one of the closets?"

We went back through the house opening closet doors and peering up at the ceiling.

"Bingo!" I had found a framed hatch in the closet of the master bedroom. A panel of painted plywood rested in the frame. I took a broomstick and pushed it upward and to the side. It moved easily.

The first thing I could see was a block and tackle on a sturdy hook bolted to a roof rafter straight above the opening. The hook was hanging from a large eye screwed into the roof rafter and braced on either side. From it a pulley dangled on dusty ropes that were tied off to a nail in an adjoining rafter. Its function was clear: to lift heavy objects from the bedroom below up to the attic through the opening in the closet ceiling.

We brought a white metal kitchen step stool and I climbed into the hatch pushing the little plywood hatch door completely to one side. A folding ladder-stair lay against the floor. It was on a hinge with a rope so that when pulled over the opening it opened and extended down to the floor of the closet. I was sure that I would need a flashlight, but at the top of the folding stairs the string of a bare ceiling light bulb dragged against my neck. I reached up and pulled it on.

The dark little attic was immediately flooded with light. Dad didn't like dark spaces, so he had hooked up three one-hundred-watt bulbs in porcelain sockets on a parallel circuit all along the center roofline. When you pulled on the middle one over the hatch, they all came on.

I stood on the second-from-the-top rung of the ladder-stairs and looked in a full circle. It was the prototype of all attics - discarded lamps, boxes of clothes, old furniture.

We climbed into the attic.

"Look at that pile of old clothes," said Connie. On the floor there was a stack of old clothes four feet high. "Your mother never threw away a thing. Some of that stuff looks like it goes back to the thirties." She kicked at the edge of the pile. Dust rose from the pile of stiff old clothes. "We should tell Mildred," Connie said, "These might be unstylish enough for her to wear!" We both laughed.

At the far end of the attic, back under slope of the eaves, was the trunk. It had a thin mantle of dust.

It was quite a task to drag the trunk across the attic floor and load it down through the little ladder-stair hatch into the closet. We didn't use the hoist above the opening. It wasn't that heavy. I didn't have a key, so we couldn't open the trunk in the attic. I got below it on the ladder and Connie held it from above by one of the end handles, and we lowered it to the bedroom. We got it down the ladder-stairs with much difficulty without using the rope and pulley. I had long since misplaced the key that Mom so ceremoniously gave me, so we were going to have to force the lock. That was best done in the living room with a hammer and a large screwdriver brought from Dad's workbench in the basement. The trunk was bulky, and it was quite a chore to lug it from the closet into the living room.

Connie sat on the sofa while I positioned myself over the trunk with the tools. The flimsy lock yielded with the first blow. It flapped open and fell down against the front of the trunk with a thud. I lifted the lid.

"Look at all of those pictures," Connie exclaimed. "There must be a thousand of them."

"Wonder why Mildred was so excited? Maybe one of them is of her in the nude!"

Connie chuckled. "What a horrible thought!"

We thumbed through the neat, dated and tied packets of photos on the top tray of the trunk. Both of us made a conscious effort not to displace the little typewritten labels mom had so laboriously affixed to each packet with the year typed on in faded ink.

"They seem to go back into the early Thirties," said Connie as she picked her way through a pack of black and white photographs with serrated edges and yellowing white borders. "Maybe even the Twenties. Is this whole trunk full of photos?"

"I don't know." I stood up to grasp the top tray by the little twisted rope loops that served as handles on each end of the top paperboard tray. It was wedged tight. I had to wiggle it a little. It gave way and slid upward, lighter than I had thought it would be.

We stood dumbfounded for several seconds looking down into the trunk.

"Jesus Christ! Do you see what I see?"

"Donald, I see it, but I'm not sure what I am looking at."

Neatly folded so that it fit squarely into the trunk covering its contents was a dark olive-green Army blanket; one of World War II vintage, the scratchy wool kind. Lying neatly side-by-side on the blanket was a packet of passports bound in the same shoestring ribbon that bound the packets of photos. I had never known my mother and father to travel outside the United States. Why would they have passports?

It was what was lying next to the passports that got, and held, our attention - a blue-black German Luger and two leather pouches shaped like small wallets.

The Luger, wallets and packet of passports on the blanket were pressed into it from the pressure of the photo shelf above, leaving their exact outline in the blanket when we picked them up. Connie picked up the packet of passports. I examined the Luger. The clip was full. The safety was on.

"Connie, I..." I turned to Connie. She was a white as a sheet.

"Donald, look at this." She had opened the ribbon on the package of passports and she was holding them like a deck of cards. There were two blue United States passports - one with the name *Hugo Jurgens* and the other *Frieda Jurgens*. But it was the black passports that held her attention.

"Your mother and father had German Passports?"

"No way," I said, incredulous.

Connie dropped the two blue United States passports to the coffee table and handed me the black leather passport folders.

"Here," she said. "believe."

I took the black shiny passports, almost afraid to touch them. Each had a little glassine window that held a slide-in typewritten card. One Read Frieda Jurgens; the other Hugo Jurgens. Above the little windows was embossed a stylized Eagle with its wings spread and its claws embracing a globe of the world. It was the unmistakable emblem of the Third Reich!

I thumbed through the pages somewhat numbly. They had yellowed slightly, but the typewritten information, and red inked entry and visa stamps were clearly visible. From the first pages of each a black and white photograph of a much younger Hugo and Frieda Jurgens looked back at me. The stamps bore dates in 1944.

But the strangest items of all were the little leather pouches. They were about four inches across and folded over like a wallet with a tab that slid into a stitched hole to receive the strap. I opened one of

them. Into my hand fell an iron cross. Not just *any* iron cross – *the*
Iron Cross, the four-bladed Prussian Cross, and at its center a ceramic
swastika. It was the highest civilian award of the Nazi Empire! Folded
neatly behind the medal was a red ribbon with a small hook clasp. I
stared at the grey metal cross. My mind had no questions - let alone
answers.

Nothing fit. Mom and Dad had never been east of Cleveland,
Ohio, let alone Germany. Dad had even told me years ago that he
would like to visit Europe sometime. Traveling far from home was
not in their blood. Mom feared airplanes and thieves. She hated to
travel. Nothing made sense. What the hell were my father and mother
doing with a German Luger and German passports? For that matter
what were they doing with a United States passport if they never went
outside the country? More important, what were they doing with
Nazi Iron Crosses?

Connie bent over the open trunk and lifted the corner of the
stiff blanket. It had stuck in places to the paper liner of the trunk as
though it had been in place for a long time. It crinkled and made a
scratching sound as Connie lifted it from the trunk.

Neatly packed along the bottom of the trunk were seventeen
notebooks. They were the black simulated leather kind that you can
buy in any dime store with blank pages and a red band around the
spine. Each had a label, inked onto a stick-on paper label, which bore
a year. The first was 1932. The last was 1945.

The rest of the trunk was filled with more photos.

I reached in and pulled out the furthest notebook to the left. It
was sandwiched between the left side of the trunk and the book next
to it. The cover had stuck to the lining paper on the inside of the
trunk. It took some effort to break it free. 1932 was inked into its label.

Connie got up from the couch and looked over my shoulder as I
flipped through the pages. They were entirely handwritten, mostly
in ink, but there were a few pencil-written pages. The handwriting
was my mother's - laborious, neat. Stuck to the marbleized interior of
the binding page was a price label that read "F.W. Woolworth," and
below it on the label the price, $.49.

"Do you think she wrote them all?"

"I don't know." I pulled out several more notebooks randomly from the line of diaries and flipped through the pages. It was Mom's handwriting all the way. They were written in a narrative style. I never really saw her write that way, but the handwriting was unquestionably my Mother's.

Connie picked up the first notebook and returned to the couch. I plopped down beside her. Connie began to read.

3
CHAPTER
NOTEBOOK ONE

"January 13, 1932

I remember it as if it were yesterday. It was just a little over three years ago. The exact date is etched on my brain. It was August 23rd of 1929 - the first time I saw Hugo. He was standing in the shadows to the left of the bar leaning against a mirrored post in the Casa Loma Ballroom on Cherokee street. The Casa Loma was a "Gentleman's Club" in those days. Oh, women could come in, but it just seemed better to call it a "gentleman's club." Each Saturday night there was a dance. They had some great bands. Most of the men came with their ladies, but several men and women were always there stag, and it was a good place to meet eligible bachelors if one was inclined to that sort of thing. I was occasionally so inclined.

My, he did look dapper! I think it was the cream-colored spats that first caught my eye. He had on a pair of burgundy striped suspenders over a vertical striped broadcloth shirt with a coordinating burgundy tie. He wore cream woolen trousers with a crease so sharp it would cut you. Brown and white tasseled loafers rounded out the outfit. A thin cheroot dangled casually from his lips, and he occasionally removed it and blew a tight ring of smoke up into the air. His toe was tapping to the strains of the Jimmy Flowers orchestra. He was some looker, that Hugo Jurgens, with those big steel blue eyes. Trouble was, he wasn't looking at me.

I had come to the Casa Loma with two friends, Ruby Breakers and Ethel Mayer. It was one of those things you do on a summer Saturday night with girlfriends when you don't have anything else to do - or a man to do it with. We had eaten chicken fried steaks at a diner up near Grand and Cherokee. Ethel suggested that we go down to the Casa Loma and see what was going on. After all, it was Saturday night. Little did I know that night would change my life forever.

Hugo was alone. That was evident when I saw him go over to a table on the other side of the big mirrored ballroom and ask one of the girls to dance. It was a Charleston. Nobody could play a Charleston like Jimmie Flowers. The girl he asked to dance was a twerpy little blond in a shimmy flapper. I had seen her before. She was a show-offy little thing with one of those "hey, hey, look at me" smiles - the kind that men fall for every time. She put her hand to her flat chest when he asked her to dance feigning surprise that fooled no one. I knew she would dance with him. He was the best-looking guy in the place.

Boy, could he dance. She bounced around like a rubber ball so that the fringe on her flapper was going in three directions to impress Hugo. He would have nothing of it. He suavely ignored her gyrations and glided around her as if he were on ice skates. He was a great dancer. Very smooth. It really made her look pretty stupid.

When the dance was over he walked her back to the table. I couldn't hear what he said, but it must have been flattering as it titillated the little bitch into a phony giggle. He bowed courteously and excused himself. He was easy to admire. He didn't ask her to dance again. Hugo knew a fraud when he saw one.

I noticed that he was very selective. He wasn't going to dance with just any of the eligibles. He didn't ask miss shimmy-tits to dance again either. All evening he never came near our table. I thought my chances were about zero by eleven o'clock. Ruby, Ethel and I were on our third beer of the evening when suddenly from behind me I heard a mellow courteous: "Would you join me for this dance?" I turned and looked up into the most beautiful set of steel blues I have ever seen. Ruby and Ethel were incredulous. What was I to do, but accept? I took his extended hand and thus began a romance that resulted in our marriage two years later.

Don't ask me why I am writing all of this down. I never kept a diary as a little girl. I always thought it was kind of silly - writing down your thoughts and experiences in a diary. Why I am starting now is as much a mystery to me as the moon and the stars. I just decided to do it. Maybe it's because I am so happy that I started to write down my thoughts. But mostly it's because I want to make a record of my happiness. We will have children, Hugo and me, and I want them to know what I think when I am thinking it. I have always wondered what it would be like - writing a diary, but I finally got around to taking pen in hand and writing my first page. That's the hardest part - starting. I think a description of the time I met Hugo, my husband, my children's father-to-be, is a good start. Good or bad, it's where I will begin. And don't expect me to write in it every day. That would be the most boring thing on earth! When I have something to write I'll put it down.

They say that once you form the habit of writing you will miss it if you don't keep it up. I don't know if that is true, but I hope to find out. I think that regular writing is like any other habit, like brushing your teeth or cleaning your ears. If you do it long enough and regular enough it becomes a part of you. For me, it sort of clears up my mind. Maybe it just puts things in perspective if I write them down. I don't know, but I like it already.

We danced until one in the morning, Hugo and me. Ruby and Ethel went home at Midnight. Hugo agreed to see me back to the four-family flat I shared on Pestalozzi Street with Lillian Pearlstein. It wasn't far. In fact, I could have walked. But Hugo, honorable gentleman as he was, offered to take me home in his car.

Do you believe in love at first sight? I'm not sure I do, but when I got home that night if I had been keeping this diary I would have written in it that Hugo Jurgens was the man I was going to marry someday. We talked through every dance. I had to concentrate to talk while I danced. He didn't. He was a good conversationalist and a great dancer. Both came naturally to him. Hugo was easy to talk to and I found myself telling him more about myself than I had told any man in my life. He was charming and courteous. He went to the bar and brought us Alpen Braus in big steins. He was careful not to drink too much. He had a car he had to drive and didn't want to wreck it.

After the first dance that night he gave me his card. It said "Hugo Jurgens, Barber." His address was the Statler Hotel, downtown - some address! I was impressed, but I should have known even then - Hugo was the one. His nails were manicured to perfection, his pants' creases would cut butter, and his haircut was immaculate in the style of the day. He told me that he liked working in the Statler Hotel Barbershop, but he wanted to buy his own shop. After six years in the employ of the Statler Barbershop, he had saved enough for a year's rent and shop equipment. If everything went right a year from now, he would have his own shop. Little did he know that the stock market would crash in a couple of months and the Great Depression would set in. He had already begun to look for a location. Hugo was true to his word. One year later, depression or not, he opened his own shop.

Hugo was twenty-seven, two years older than me. He wasn't like the other fellows who prowled the clubs and ballrooms looking for girls. He professed a sincerity that I had not before seen. He was honest with me, without pretense or arrogance. That he had his own car was something, but to Hugo, it was just a goal that he had set and had worked for. Your own car, though, and at twenty-seven was something. Wow! I was impressed.

On that first night, he walked me to the door of my walk up flat. My roommate, Lillian, had long since hit the bed and was snoring wildly in the front bedroom. You could hear her through the screens all the way out on the front stoop. Sounds travel easily in the stillness of a hot August night, especially with the windows open.

Hugo shook my hand warmly at the door and thanked me for a wonderful evening. Then he squeezed my shoulders with both hands and bounded off of the porch toward the idling Whippet Coupe waiting at the curb. I thought it was a perfect gesture to leave his car idling at the curb. It removed all speculation about his intentions. That Hugo Jurgens was very thoughtful; very thoughtful, indeed.

Dating Hugo Jurgens was like living a fairy tale. When I was growing up my mother told me that I would know when I met the right one. She also told me that all men were animals who would spread my legs and do horrible things to me only to leave me for their beer-drinking buddies at the drop of a hat. After I left home and entered Miss Hickey's School for Secretaries I began to form opinions of my own. After eight years of being single and on my own I had come to believe that my mother had told me only a little part of the story. Not that what she told me was all wrong - she just left out a few parts! I had begun to fill in the missing links. Hugo helped me fill in some more.

Hugo worked hard six days a week, so we never saw much of each other except on weekends. On Fridays, he almost always worked until near eight o'clock. When he got off was determined by how many customers were in the waiting chairs when the manager locked the barbershop door at six o'clock. If you were in by six they cut your hair. Sometimes there were six or eight customers waiting at six o'clock. It took a couple of hours to finish up. If you didn't make it in by six you had to come back the next morning at eight. But on Friday night the weekend officially began. Never mind that Hugo had to work on Saturday. On Friday night the party began.

On Fridays, Hugo would go home and bathe after work. He was immaculate about himself. He always kept himself clean as a pin. He smelled good too. There was this particular brand of Bay Rum that he wore - *Shillington's*. I can smell it now. He still wears it, especially in the summer. It made him smell fresh. I loved it. I would put my nose up to him right behind his ear, close my eyes and drink in the aroma.

We would head out on Fridays in the Whippet. It had a fold-back top and a rumble seat. Hugo bought it used from the wife of a client of the Statler barbershop that he had served for over five years, which was almost the whole time he was barbering. When the fellow died his wife asked Hugo if he wanted to buy the Whippet? It was less than a year old. Want to buy it! Hugo couldn't wait to get his hands on it. There was only one problem - he didn't have the money. The old lady was sympathetic to Hugo's plight. The truth was she liked for him to come over to her house and cut the old boy's hair before he died. Hugo never gave me the details, but I always suspected there was more to the story than that. In any event, she offered to sell it to him for five hundred dollars. If he would put down seventy dollars, she would finance the rest. The Whippet was immaculate - just like Hugo. He kept it shined and sparkling with Carnauba wax. The seats were burnished brown cowhide and he kept them supple with saddle soap and neat's foot oil. The Whippet looked and smelled like it had just rolled out of the showroom.

We'd usually stop for a bite to eat at the Bevo Mill or drive out to Schober's on Lindbergh. Hugo liked schnitzel and sauerkraut. If it was a good night, sometimes we'd put the top back and drive out Highway 30 to Affton and eat at one of the bar-b-que stands that smoked their own pork.

After dinner, we would wind up at one of the beer gardens on Cherokee Street near the Casa Loma or over at Little Bavaria. I liked the outdoor gardens in the warm weather. Our favorite was the Black Forest on Gravois. They usually had a polka band and we would dance until one in the morning. Even during Prohibition, the beer gardens in South Saint Louis had beer. The big breweries had to close down, but there were plenty of small ones that could keep the supplies flowing. Some of it was manufactured in bathrooms and basements just a few blocks away. Americans are very enterprising when it comes to meeting a demand with a supply. Beer was no different. OK, so it was bootleg. In South Saint Louis where three-fourths of the population is German, and only half of them are even one generation removed from immigrant status, you aren't going to be able to legislate beer out of their lives from Washington. To them, Prohibition was just a suggestion – in most cases disregarded. The Black Forest and the other beer gardens in south Saint Louis never missed a draught. I knew Prohibition would be a flop.

The Black Forest Inn is an outdoor beer garden on Gravois just east of Kingshighway. It had an indoor bar that was packed in the winter, but when the good weather of spring came everyone moved out of doors under the big trees in back. The owner had strung lights between the boughs of the big dark Mulberry trees and filled the sockets with colored bulbs. Whitewashed picnic tables were spread around the graveled grounds and a little bandstand held a six-piece German band that usually played in lederhosen. Most of the time it was Franz Bacher and his Orchestra, but occasionally on weekends Buddy Kaufman and the Polka Dots held forth. There was an Oak dance floor that management never seemed to varnish, wax, or even take inside during winter. It had been rubbed to a white patina by thousands of dancing feet over the years. Its bleached white surface was covered on weekend nights with waltzers, polkaers, and the occasional traditional Bavarian who insisted that he demonstrate something from the Old Country.

I loved to go to the Black Forest in warm weather. Even in fall when the nights got chilly, they built a big bonfire and we all stood around and sang drinking songs, some in German, toasting each other with grand steins of beer while huge logs crackled. Hugo had a good voice and we sang until we were hoarse in the crisp fall air.

Hugo would hold me close during the slow dances, and he was as light as a feather during the waltzes. He was not just a good dancer, he was a great dancer! The difference between a good dancer and a great one is that the great dancer makes his partner look good. I wasn't as good a dancer as Hugo, but when I was in his arms, he fairly made me float. When people said we were a good dancing couple Hugo would blush and give me all of the credit. He was quite the gentleman.

I loved those nights. For the first six months, we dated he would take me out on Friday and we would look into each other's eyes and talk about the past, present, and future as if it was a script that we were to follow. He would make me laugh with his jokes. Sometimes he would make me cry with his serious side. Oh, Hugo had a serious side. He worried about little children who did not have enough to eat. He had read stories about children in China and Africa who had no shoes or clothes and it troubled him. He was sensitive to social injustices and governments that betrayed their people. I found out he had a sensitive and very compassionate side. I suspected that inside that good-looking body a fire burned.

We argued politics, too. Despite his concerns for social justice, Hugo was very conservative. President Wilson was a great disappointment to him. Roosevelt scared him to death. He sure hoped that Roosevelt never got elected. I stayed away from politics. It wasn't my cup of tea, but I did relate to his concern for children with no shoes or food.

On Saturdays, he almost always got off work early. A downtown hotel barber shop does most of its business during the week. Saturday is a slow day. There were five working chairs in the Statler shop. Most of their clientele was downtown businessmen and business travelers. They just weren't around on Saturday. The management had some kind of a requirement from the hotel that the shop would keep open on Saturdays - for travelers, I guess. Hugo told me that it was not unusual for them to have only three or four customers among them all afternoon. As the result, they had a system of rotating early departures. If there was no business by three, one of the barbers would go home. If, by four there was still no business another would leave. Almost always they were all out by six o'clock. I could usually count on Hugo being free by late afternoon.

Saturdays were always special. We'd plan a special evening. Sometimes we would have the entire next weekend planned the week before. Occasionally a reservation was needed. If so, I would make it. One of our favorite places was the Arcadia Ballroom on Olive Street. It was the "in" place in St. Louis if you were into dancing and the latest music. There wasn't so much German music there as jazz and they played some of the hot new tunes. We would Charleston and Fox Trot until the wee hours after a dinner at one of the little side tables. I always tried to get one near the dance floor, but half the time we wound up way in the back. It didn't matter. I was with Hugo.

Sometimes we went with a couple that Hugo knew, Lucian and Willamina, 'Willie', Schmitt. They were just married the year before, and Hugo knew Lucian from barber school. We all liked to dance, and we'd change partners all night. Lucian was a card. He always knew the latest jokes and Willie was a real cut-up. None of us was as good a dancer as Hugo, but we always had a good time dancing with each other.

The Arcadia had great jazz bands, too. My favorites were Bix Beiderbecke and Wingy Mannone. Hugo liked Pee Wee Russell. But when it came to dancing, the best dance band of them all was Frankie Trumbauer and his group.

Hugo told me the Arcadia got closed up during Prohibition but reopened several times until the Alcohol Agents discovered they were serving again. Then they got closed up again. Everyone knew it was just a matter of time before it would reopen under a new name. Hugo told me that the first time he had been there it was called *Dreamland*.

It was a time of discovery. I was really falling in love with the guy. In the first months of dating, he never kissed me except at New Year's 1929. Hugo never laid a hand on me. He was the perfect gentleman. At the end of the evening, he would take me to the door while the motor on the Whippet idled at the curb - a signal that no untoward advances were coming. It wasn't until we had dated for over six months, and had seen each other at least once on every weekend, that he kissed me good night for the first time.

He had brought me home. It was very cold. He left the Motor running as usual and walked me to the door. We both had on big puffy coats. I remember he had on a black woolen coat with a big beaver collar. I loved that coat. When we reached the door, he just said, "good night" and reached out and put his arms around me and pulled me to him. I really didn't expect it, but I was more than willing to cooperate. He gave me a big kiss right on the lips and squeezed me.

"Could we do that again sometime?" I said to him.

He got a big smile on his face. "Sure," he said and pulled me to him again. It was wonderful. We stood there freezing and kissing for ten minutes. That did it. I knew it was going to be Hugo forever.

August 29, 1933

It is Sunday afternoon. I am home alone in our flat on Hartford Street. It is a scorcher. They say that the temperature could reach one hundred today. Hugo is out in the park pitching horseshoes with some of his friends. Tower Grove Park is just a couple of blocks from our flat. You can get there in three minutes from our front door. Once a month on Sunday they all gather over at the park after church, bang a couple of iron stakes into the ground and pitch horseshoes. It's an all-afternoon affair. They drink a little beer, tell each other lies and have a good time. If this is what my mother was talking about when she said he would soon rather be with his beer-drinking buddies, I think I can handle it. About six o'clock the wives usually join them with picnic baskets and we'd sit around and talk until dusk when the mosquitoes drive us out. I look forward to the quiet time alone at home on Sundays. I also love the times we have with our friends now that we are married.

There are six couples of us that pal around together. All but two of the couples we knew before we were married. Two of the fellows are barbers. One is a mechanic. One works at the brewery and two of them work with me at the Marquardt Chemical Company. As of today, three of them have at least one child and one, my good friend, Margaret, is pregnant. She is due in late September. God, it would be terrible to be all bloated up like that in summer when the temperature is one hundred and the humidity is ninety- five.

Hugo and I talked about having children almost from the day we got married - even before. We wanted to have three. We've been trying to get me pregnant since our wedding night eleven months ago, but no luck yet. Tomorrow I am going to the doctor for an examination. We haven't even thought about taking any precautions for the last year, but I can't get pregnant. Maybe something's wrong with me. Maybe it's Hugo. We agreed we'd check me first. I've never been to see a doctor for a woman's physical. All of my girlfriends tell me you get used to it. I am going to see Doctor Wilhelm Hauser, my mother's female doctor. I mean, the doctor is not female, just his patients are. I figured if he had seen my mother's it wouldn't hurt for him to see mine. Actually, he is the doctor that delivered me. He even has the same offices on South Grand just a block from Saint Anthony's Hospital.

Hugo seemed a little nervous at breakfast today. I couldn't tell if he was upset with another man poking around in there or if he was concerned that the problem might be him rather than me. Oh well, tomorrow we'll find out.

August 30, 1933

Great! Just great! The doctor can't find anything wrong with me. He says I look normal. He should know, he poked around in there enough. Now I have to convince Hugo to go. That isn't going to be easy. I think he is nervous about going in for an exam. He has never said it right out loud, but just the little things he says tell me that he isn't going to like it. I know he's got a lot on his mind - the new business and all, but I want a baby! I think he does, too.

I have to admit that he has been everything I could ask in a husband. In the fall of last year, he got a lease on a building on Arsenal Street just down from its intersection with Grand Avenue in which to put his new barbershop. I love the location. It was just across Arsenal Street from Tower Grove Park. That area of South Saint Louis is a good solid middle-class neighborhood. It should be a good location for a barbershop. Streetcars run within a few feet of the front door along Arsenal Street and hundreds of commuters pass in front of the door on their way to the streetcar and connecting bus stops. Hugo had done his homework. He checked every location south of Forest Park. No neighborhood went unexamined. He had maps and demographic data. Some of it was so complicated I couldn't understand it. He settled on this location, and his reasons made lots of sense. There were lots of people who lived within a short distance. All basic services were present in the immediate neighborhood - bakeries, grocery stores, shops, bars, a doctor and a drug store, restaurants, butchers, but no barbershop.

It was perfect. The building was a red brick storefront with an alley in the back. It had two commercial spaces facing the street - a barbershop on one side and a beauty shop in the other. Upstairs was a large apartment that covered the whole top floor. It belonged to the proprietors of the beauty shop. They were twins named Morgantha and Arsenia Buchenwalder, "Morgie" and "Arsie" for short. I soon came to believe that they were a little strange, but they are great landlords. They keep the place spotless. I even saw them on their hands and knees using a scrub brush scrubbing the stone stoop that leads to the apartment stairs. No sir; no dirt for Morgie and Arsie.

The beauty shop had been started by their parents thirty years ago. They had been born there in that same apartment upstairs and had lived there all their lives. Their mother was in some kind of a rest home out on Manchester road. I never did know the details. Their father was dead. I guess with the life insurance money, income from the beauty shop and the rent from Hugo they lived pretty comfortably.

The area where Hugo's shop was had been a barbershop in the early Twenties. The owner had committed suicide and the shop had been vacant for eight years when Hugo found it. They said the old owner drank a lot. Morgie explained that they didn't want to rent it to just anybody. From their stories, I suspected that they had lots of problems with the prior tenant.

Hugo set about the renovation. He and a carpenter friend of his constructed a partition about two thirds of the way to the back of the space so as to divide off a back room. You could get in and out of the back room through a door that faced the alley without going through the shop. Hugo found a huge cache of mirrors in a barbershop in the Chase Hotel that was being remodeled. He bought them cheap and had them re-silvered by a man down on Bates Street named Hans Hudkin. They were huge plate glass affairs with beveled edges in ornate frames which had to be cut down to fit into the new shop. Hudkin was a master. He re-cut them, beveled the edges and replaced them in the great frames. When they were installed they went all the way around the shop reflecting and re-reflecting in all directions. What with the big plate glass window in the front the mirrors made the place as light as you could imagine. Every little ray of light was captured and bounced around the new shop. It made everything sparkle.

Even with the partition, the shop was big enough to handle three barber chairs. Hugo put in only one - right in the middle of the shop. His carpenter friend built him a long back bar the whole width of the shop and incorporated the huge mirrors into it above a real white marble slab that held the sinks. Hugo set it up to hold three chairs. He was optimistic about his growth and said that he would need space to expand. The floors were covered with high-grade linoleum with a good gloss so that they would sweep up easily. Hugo even built a little trap door under one of the window seats that opened to a chute to the basement. He could sweep hair into the trap door and it would fall into a big collection box in the basement for disposal. Hugo was very practical.

The cream de-la-cream were the ceiling fans and the lights. Hugo had seen a picture of Rockefeller Center in New York with its Art Deco architecture and fixtures. He wrote the building management and found out who had supplied the light fixtures. Then he ordered three special replica fan and light units that were just spectacular. They were black lacquered fans with Art Deco teardrop styled lights that fit right in the middle under the fans. Hugo was really good with electrical things. He installed them himself in a row over each spot where a barber chair would ultimately be installed. Their symmetry and the reflections of the milk glass and black light covers together with the slowly rotating fans was just something. Most people had never seen a fan and light combination before that. When he told them that they were just like those that were in the new Rockefeller Center they just looked at them gaga. Hugo had class, and so did his new shop.

The shop opened on January 2, 1932. I was as proud as he was. Hugo consulted me on many of the choices that had to be made when the shop was being planned and built. I picked out the cloth for the haircloths and sewed the snaps into them on black ribbon to match the art deco fixtures. He incorporated many of my ideas into the shop. For example, I told him that the northwest exposure of the big front plate glass windows would be perfect for growing plants. He took me up on it and put two big rubber tree plants in each window on either side of the door. As I predicted they did well. Both are sprouting new chutes.

The week before he opened Hugo put an ad in the *Saint Louis Star-Times* newspaper. It read:

> *Wanted - high-quality Negro*
> *to handle porter duties for new*
> *barbershop in return for place*
> *to operate shoe shine stand.*
> *Supplies furnished. South Side.*
> *Call PL 4793 after 6 P.M."*

He had over twenty phone calls the first day. Hugo set up interviews in the new shop the next Sunday afternoon and invited the candidates in for fifteen minutes. In all, he interviewed thirty-four men. He hired Crandall Watts, a thirty-four-year-old Negro who had two children and a wife, Samantha. Hugo purchased him a used shoe shine stand with a padded chair from a fixture house and set it into the corner of the shop. The deal was that Crandall Watts could shine shoes and keep all of the money from the shoeshine business. Hugo would buy the polish and supplies. In return, Crandall was to perform services for the customers like brush the hair off their backs when they got out of the chair and help them on with their jackets when they left or hang up their coats when they entered the shop. Crandall was also charged with sweeping the floor and keeping the shop clean. He was to arrive one-half hour before opening time and prepare the shaving mugs, sterilize the razors and the scissors and bring in the newspaper. But most important he was to take the little iron crank from the hook by the door each morning and evening and wind up the mechanism on the outside barber pole that made it turn.

A good wind would last about twelve hours. Crandall Watts was, in a word, the "Porter" of the Arsenal Barbershop, a position that he took very seriously. And, he built a good business shining shoes - and he got to keep the tips!"

Connie reached up and turned on the floor lamp above the chair. It was getting dark outside. The snow no longer reflecting light through the window.

"I'm getting dry from all this reading. You want a can of 7-Up?" She rose and headed for the kitchen. Dad always had a supply. The fridge still contained 7Ups, my dad's favorite drink.

"See if there is a Coke or something in the fridge."

I mused over what Connie had just read. It sure wasn't very exciting stuff. While it gave me some insight into my mother, it was a pretty poor diary if that is what she intended. There weren't even daily or weekly entries. It looked like she just sat down and wrote in the book every-once-in-a-while - just when she felt like it. Still, it was interesting to see my mother write. I never knew her to do so with such clarity.

"What do you think?" Connie had returned with the drinks.

"I think, if we are going to sit here and read these diaries it's going to be a long night. At this rate, we'll not finish by dawn."

Connie sat the can of Coca-Cola on the coffee table. "It's interesting how your mom and dad met, but there sure isn't anything here worth getting excited about. What's with Mildred? What is such a big deal about the trunk? Why, this stuff wouldn't even be interesting gossip at a quilting social."

I leaned forward and picked up a packet of photos from the trunk tray. It was marked 1942 with a grease marker. The ribbon had been tied into a bow and fell away when I pulled the loose end. The packet contained about twenty-four black and white photos. The first was of a grassy field with woods in the distance. A dirt road trailed off toward the woods. It was a clear well-focused photo but somewhat faded. I didn't recognize the subject and flipped it over. On the back was written "Weldon Spring - North area."

The rest of the pack was of similarly non-descript rural areas with fields, some woods, some wooden stakes, a trail, road and other pastoral scenes that held no interest to me. In one there appeared to be a foundation. It was marked on the back "Main Building??"

I tied them up and stuck them back into the sea of photos on the trunk tray. I tried to keep the packets in chronological order.

"Let's go home," I suggested. "I'd rather look at this junk in the comfort of my living room with a beer in my hand than over here."

"Agreed," said Connie. She drained her Coke like a tomboy chug-a-lugging a beer. "Put the tray back into the trunk and I'll help you lug it out to the car. It ought to fit into the trunk of the car. It'll take both of us to lift it in."

4

CHAPTER

DISTANT RUMBLINGS

It was three days before we got back to the trunk. We had lugged it home and stashed it in a corner of the family room next to the fireplace. Connie had become embroiled in some political issue over ward boundaries with a Councilman, and I had been immersed in a project at the university that kept me working overtime. Between all of our commitments and shoveling snow off the front walk, neither of us thought much about the diaries or the photos.

On Wednesday evening I left the office a little early and, being the master chef that I am, ordered out for Chinese food to pick up on the way home. It was a dreary, damp winter evening with the temperature hovering just above freezing. The headlights made fuzzy rings in the gathering mist as darkness descended around the car. It wasn't snowing, but the cold was bone chilling. I was glad to get home with my precious cargo of little white wire-bailed Chinese carryout cartons. I built a fire and reheated the egg foo young in the microwave. Connie poured two glasses of a mediocre Riesling, and we retreated to the fireplace with paper plates, wine and little wire-handled buckets of Chinese food.

I pulled the trunk out of the corner and flipped open the lid. After setting out the top tray of photographs I couldn't help stopping before

47

pulling back the Army blanket. The Luger, passports, and medals were still a mystery to me.

"The Luger bothers you doesn't it?" said Connie.

"Yeah. I never knew my dad to even own a gun. Maybe one of his customers at the shop gave it to him."

"Maybe." Connie was not convinced. Neither was I.

I set the blanket and its array of unexplained memorabilia on the floor and pulled out the second book. Its pages were yellowed. Age had not been kind to the glue of its binding. The writing was with a dip-pen. You remember the kind - that had to be continually dipped into the ink, and the words trailed off when the ink ran out of the pen.

I began to read:

"December 23, 1934

We could dance every polka or waltz with the best of them, and we usually did, at least one night a week. It was in our blood. A German can polka before he can walk. These songs are the heart and soul of South Saint Louis.

We could speak the language. Hugo's father had taught him, German. The old man insisted that it be spoken in his house. He and his wife could speak both English and German, but speaking German was their way of preserving the Trust. Hugo's parents were thankful to be in America, but heritage was important. The language was an integral part of the heritage. Even I learned a little. Hugo was pretty fluent.

This had been a good year. In the summer we fished in the Black River on several weekend excursions. We even took a driving trip up to Hannibal, Missouri to see the Mark Twain homestead. Life with Hugo included a large dose of exploration. Just sitting at home when he was not working at the shop was not in his blood. If he had nothing to do he would be dismantling a radio or an alarm clock down on his workbench or on the kitchen table. He was an inveterate tinkerer.

The old crowd at the Black Forest missed us on the Friday nights that we did not show up. They often commented that we were out "traveling the world." That was true if you call a motor trip in a Whippet Coupe out Highway 30 to Alley Springs to fish for trout a world tour. The ribbing was good natured and fine with us. We were all friends, and they loved to tease us.

Helga Thurman loved to sing the old German and Austrian songs with Hugo. They would harmonize on "Auf Weidersein" or belt a few stanzas of the "Beer Barrel Polka" while waiving steins of Alpen Brau or Hyde Park beer. It was impossible not to chime in. It was a time of friends, of camaraderie, and of idyllic moments in the sun.

I've been remiss in writing in my diary, but the time has gone so fast. This has been a great year.

Hugo says I'm a dreamer. I don't think so, at least any more than anyone else. Oh sure, I have my fantasies like any other young married woman. Well, maybe I do have this reoccurring dream: I'm sitting in a white painted lawn chair - You know the big Adirondack chairs with flat armrests and high backs. I have a Mint Julep in my hand - with a straw. I think it's in Key West. I'm looking out to sea towards Havana. I always dream of Havana. Someday I'll visit Havana. I have on a white chiffon dress - very filmy, and a big hat with a bow in the back. The sun is setting. It's warm, and the breeze is blowing the chiffon of my dress. I think it's January. A palm tree rustles in the light breeze as sailboats, far out on the horizon, beat against the wind. I wonder where they are going.

A man's hand caresses my shoulder. I take it and brush it against my cheek. His skin is dark, and he smells of tobacco and limes. He is tall, in a white suit, with a broad-brimmed Panama hat. His face is ruddy, and he has a bushy mustache. I take the hand, rise from the white painted chair and walk with him past Bougainvillea and Palmetto to a low white shuttered cottage at the edge of the beach.

We enter the cottage. A black woman - a maid I think - retires through a shuttered door. The dark man carefully removes the chiffon dress and places it neatly on the wicker chair near the bed. I fall onto the big feather bed and he comes to me. I hear myself screaming as he touches every part of me first with his hands and then with his tongue.

Then something happens. I don't know what. Everything goes white. I awake and find myself in bright sunlight. I don't know what has happened. The man is gone. I don't know who he was or where he came from or went. The dream is over. I'm Mrs. Hugo Jurgens again.

I'm not sure when the music began to change - probably in the second half of the year. It was subtle at first, but if you listened closely the change was there. The Black Forest, Little Bavaria, and the Neuschweinstein Inn always had a German band. You know the kind - where the tuba player wears the little lederhosen and they all have on those Bavarian hats with the big brush pins. I loved that music. So did Hugo. I think he got it from his father who insisted so strenuously that we honor the German traditions. There were drinking songs, and walking songs, and songs about love and life. There was even an occasional song that stirred the German soul. There were rousing songs meant for raising a stein of lager. There were love songs, and songs of the rivers, mountains and the flowers of Bavaria.

But sometime in the summer of 1934 new songs began to creep in that spoke of Germany as something else. One song called on Germans to unite; another was a stirring march. Nationalism is a characteristic of many songs from many countries, but there was something this summer that took Nationalism to a new high. We sang of Germany, all right, but the songs held hints of fair-haired Nordics and pure-blooded children of the Fatherland. There weren't that many. I didn't notice it at first, but when I think back on it they were there. I began to notice them and listen to the words. They were different. I noticed.

Other things had also begun to change. We noticed it in early October. In Europe, there had been some rumblings. The Bavarian government had come under the control of a group of right-wing radicals headed by Adolf Hitler. Debates about Fascist philosophies had begun to permeate conversation. The songs around the early fall campfires at the Black Forest began to take on a definitely nationalistic flavor - an occasional march or a beautiful melancholy rhapsody about the beauty of the Fatherland and the purity of its children. At first, I didn't pay much attention, but even the casual observer could see that the lighthearted drinking songs were interspersed with songs that rang of German Nationalism. The fervor with which they were sung permeated the Black Forest Inn. There was a reverence for them. It made me a little uncomfortable. Still, there was no need to complain. After all, we were all of a common bond. We were Germans. Germany was the homeland of our ancestors. Of course, we were Americans, but who would expect us to forget our heritage? Everyone in America was from somewhere else. What was to hurt if we all stood when the band played a chorus of Deutschland Uber Alles?

The songs didn't mean much to me. It was still Friday night. We went to have fun, relax and drink a few brews with our friends. I didn't have to work tomorrow. It was the end of the work week. My job at Marquardt Chemical kept me busy, and Friday was the day we could let down our hair. A working girl and her beau are entitled to a good time on a Friday night.

I had gone to work at Marquardt five years ago. After graduating from Miss Hickey's Secretarial School, I had been employed by a lawyer downtown in the Wainwright building. He was the best and the worst of employers. His practice consisted of two specialties: collecting debts and bringing suits against the Public Service Company for mostly trumped up injuries to bus passengers from bus accidents. The second: he spent his spare time trying to get me into bed with him. That I had told him "no" made no difference. It only seemed to intensify his efforts. In this endeavor, he was extremely resourceful despite the fact that I was only twenty-four and he was almost sixty. He even offered me twenty dollars to go to bed with him. That was more than I made in a month. I respectfully declined, but he was not easily diverted. Other attempts followed with equal lack of success. I thought he would get discouraged and give up. He didn't. Finally, he had a heart attack while shaving one morning and was permanently disabled. It fell on me to clean out the office and try to get other attorneys to take his cases. It was then I realized how sleazy he really was. Almost no respectable attorney would even look at his practice. I couldn't give it away. His files were worthless. He raged at me for not trying hard enough. I gave up in despair and began to seek employment somewhere else.

In 1928 the Marquardt Chemical Company began to do important research in several technical areas and put out a call for qualified chemists, researchers and laboratory personnel. I was none of those, but I was a good secretary. My shorthand and typing were second to none. So, I applied and was immediately hired at twelve dollars a week.

I worked as the secretary for several researchers. The terminology and the procedures became known to me although I did not understand it all. Much of it was in the area of x-rays and fluoroscopy, radiation conduction and related processes. By 1930 I had been promoted to secretary to the Assistant Director of Research. My salary had been increased to eighteen dollars a week and I got two weeks of paid vacation each year.

Thank goodness for my salary, because after the Crash of Twenty-Nine jobs were next to impossible to find. After our marriage, Hugo and I began to wonder if the opening of the new barbershop was a very good Idea. His business was flat and had been that way almost from the start. Haircuts were fifty cents; a shave was a quarter. It was not unusual for Hugo to gross twenty dollars in a whole week. The rent took over half of it and had to be paid.

This year things were looking up. A new Director of Research had taken over for the old. He was an Army man named Avril Hollenbeck. He came to Saint Louis from New Jersey. I found out that he really was a General but had retired from the Army to take over the position at Marquardt. He held a doctor's degree from MIT. Hollenbeck asked me to be his secretary. He said he had heard that I was very talented.

I was flattered, but what interested me the most was that the job meant a big raise - to twenty-six dollars a week. He said that I would have to have a security check. That meant nothing to me and I knew that I would be accepted. Marquardt was becoming more security conscious. I noticed that they seemed to be doing more Government jobs and I guessed that the security had to do with the Government.

I love working for Avril Hollenbeck. He was a big gentle rock of a man who seemed to know where he was going and just how to get there. You never have to guess what he is thinking. He tells you straight out in loud and clear terms. He is patient with me, and he has taught me a lot about the job of running a research department in a large chemical company. I noticed that he gets a lot of respect, and much of that respect rubbed off on me. When I make a call on General Hollenbeck's behalf I am almost immediately connected with the recipient of the call, and you know that the message is going to be given significant weight.

Many of Hollenbeck's contacts are in Washington and New York. I spend a lot of time putting through long-distance calls.

As Thanksgiving neared we noticed that Hugo's business was picking up. It seemed that more people wanted to come into the shop. Not that he was swamped. He still sat around a lot of the day reading the paper waiting for customers, but the customer count was a little better as the Holidays neared. It was at least enough to be encouraging.

Hugo was funny about the shop. It had to have a certain level of decorum. Did you ever go by a barbershop when the barbers weren't busy and see them sitting in the barber chairs? Well, not in Hugo's shop. He did not think that it was right for the barber to be sitting in the barber chair waiting for customers. Instead, he always sat in one of the waiting chairs.

He was very well read. You'd be well read too if you had as much time to read the paper each day. Hugo subscribed to the Star-Times, the morning newspaper, and the Post-Dispatch that came in the late afternoon. He always brought the Post home with him for me to read in the evening. By the time I saw it he had read every word.

I got along well with Hugo's family. His mother and father are good people and I enjoy our visits. His sister Mildred intimidates me. She is a small opinionated person, and she is so strong, so intense. Apparently, she had been married, but that did not work. Her husband left her after a couple of months. Big surprise! She seems to have a few friends, but most are women. I imagine that it would be very difficult to find a man who would put up with her. She is so "my-way-or-the-highway." He would either have to be a monster or a Casper Milquetoast.

By Christmas of 1934, Hugo had gotten very interested in the events that were happening in Europe. He kept up with the daily news via the newspapers and Edward R. Murrow reports and Charles Kaltenborn's Commentaries. He always had the radio on in the shop. On days when the subject of Europe had been a hot topic in the shop, he would relate the positions and arguments made by his various customers. Hugo's barbershop was beginning to be a place where you could expect a spirited debate on World Politics. It began to attract customers who liked that sort of thing.

I loved being Hugo's wife. He excited me. We talk of politics, finance (even though we had no money) and world affairs. We fantasized about the future and talked about children. By our third year of marriage, I was beginning to feel the peer pressure to have children. It was, after all, time.

My attempts at getting pregnant were to no avail. The doctor could not find anything wrong with me, and Hugo was not excited about going in for an examination. He said that he did not want to know if he was the one preventing me from conceiving. We didn't fight over it, but I was disappointed in his attitude. While I could not get pregnant, we sure had a great time trying. Hugo was a great lover. He was always gentle with me and there were nights we couldn't wait to get into bed with each other. He would have his trousers off before he got through the kitchen. Sometimes we would race to see who could get undressed first. He would always win until I started taking my underwear off before he got home and just slipping on a one-piece house dress. I usually got home just after six, so I had a little time to get ready. When he would start peeling off his clothes, I'd flip the house dress over my head, and presto! I was buck-naked and ready to go! The first time I did it Hugo was so surprised he couldn't stop laughing.

There was something about making love when you knew that you could not get pregnant - or didn't care. It removed all inhibitions. Hugo and I made love on every smooth surface in our upstairs flat. We had so many friends that were scared to death of getting pregnant. They count the days before and after periods, use diaphragms and spermicide creams, rubbers, and every other contraption just to keep those pesky little sperms away from those eggs. Not me and Hugo. We are all over each other inside and out. I wasn't getting pregnant, and neither of us cared if I got that way anyhow. It is a great time to be alive.

Just after we were married, we rented a flat on the second floor of a four family flat on Hartford Street. It was just a few blocks from Hugo's shop. He could walk to work. That was a saving as we could leave the Whippet in the garage. The flat didn't have its own garage, so Hugo made arrangements with an elderly gentleman who lives about halfway in between the flat and the shop, to rent his garage. The man does not have an automobile, and Hugo talked him into letting him use the garage in return for cutting his hair twice a month. The old guy bargained hard and got Hugo to throw in one shave a week. On that agreement, the deal was sealed, and we got a garage. Hugo was relieved. There was no way that his precious Whippet Coupe was going to sit outside on the street.

Our flat is spacious with two big bedrooms, a living room, dining room and a big sun porch on the back. The porch has big screens in the summer and we can sleep out there on hot nights with the fan blowing directly on us. In winter the porch has storm windows that can be put up to turn it into a glassed-in porch. It doesn't have any heat out there, but it is comfortable on all but the coldest days – particularly when the sun was shining. We put plants out there in winter and leave the back door cracked so that the heat can get to them. The plants do fine what with the bright winter light and all.

Our flat is heated by steam running through radiators from a boiler in the basement. Since there is only one boiler to serve all four of the living units no one could have their own thermostat. When winter comes, the landlord, who lives on the first floor, just turns on the heat. Never mind the temperature - "you can control it by opening windows," he says. Sometimes it gets a little warm but complaining is fruitless. He'll just say, "open the windows." You can't argue much with his logic.

This Christmas Hugo and I decided to get really practical. Rather than splurge on individual gifts, we decided to pool our money and buy a living room set. It's something we desperately need. We've been living in the flat for four years, ever since we got married, and we do not have any living room furniture. Besides the hardwood floors, which come with the flat, we have a Samsonite card table and four metal folding chairs we got as wedding presents - not much for a living room after four years.

We searched around for a month to find the right set for the living room. Hugo wants a sofa that is long enough to take a nap on. I want to be sure that we get at least two matching chairs and a coffee table. We found the living room set of our dreams at the Union May Stern furniture store on Union Boulevard. Finally, our apartment will be complete. They promised to deliver it by Christmas.

On the Friday before Christmas, we dropped into the Black Forest. It had been snowing, and quite a bit had been piled up along the streets and sidewalks. I snuggled deep into the armpits of Hugo's massive coat. The Black Forest would be fun tonight, just a few days before Christmas. The decorations had been up since Thanksgiving. There would be plenty of Christmas Carols and gehmulkheidt. It was packed with people when we got there. You could hardly get in the door. The husky barmaids were hauling three steins in each hand to an ever-increasing throng. The proprietor, Heinz Gunther Hobler, could hardly contain himself. The cash register was ringing off the shelf. He had brought in two bands so that one could play while the other took an intermission. The music was continuous.

The songs were boisterous, but there were not as many Christmas Carols as I had expected. There were more than the usual number of songs about "Germany, beautiful, Germany," and several marching songs that I had never heard. The trend continued.

Shortly after ten o'clock a tall man, whom I had seen once or twice around the bar stood on a table and clapped his hands for attention. The band, which had just finished a polka, blew a fanfare to help him silence the crowd. Most of the patrons had plenty to drink by now and the best that could be expected was to lower the din a few decibels. The man reached down a picked up a big stone stein raising it into a toast. He bellowed in a deep basso profundo voice: "I raise a toast to all of my German brothers and sisters. May this Season be of good cheer and may the New Year bring you happiness and prosperity."

The crowd applauded and most raised their glasses high in convivial agreement, toasting the thought. It was Christmas, and the toast was appropriate.

Then the man then did a strange thing. He transferred his glass to his left hand and lowered it to his side. He then raised his right hand above his head and held the palm outward. "To Germany, and the German people who have suffered too long at the feet of incompetent outside influences. May Germany rise again. Heil!"

The crowd fell silent. We were all stunned. Most of us had no idea what led him to do that. It was strange. Many of us looked at each other for an answer.

Then from somewhere in the back of the room came a reply, "To Germany! Heil!"

A few others, but not all, joined the toast.

"Heil to Germany!"

Every person in that room had some connection to Germany. Most of us were one or two generations removed from our family's immigration, and we all have a soft spot in our heart for the "Old

Country." The stranger only expressed a sentiment that we all could relate to. All of us had good feelings about Germany. Some of us spoke German. The stranger's toast was acceptable, comfortable, but when he raised his hand in the open-palmed salute it was strange - and, if the truth was known, just a little bit frightening.

On the way home that night the Whippet's heater was slow in warming up. I snuggled close to Hugo. We both had quite a bit to drink, but not enough to impair thought.

"Hugo," I asked, and pushed my hands deep into the folds of his big coat as he peered at the dark street ahead.

"Yes, my love"

"What did that man mean?"

"What man?"

"The man with the funny toast and the 'Heil Germanys'"

"Frieda, there are many people who agree with the Social Democrats that Germany has been kicked around too much since the end of the War."

"You mean the First World War?"

"Yes. A cruel and unfair disarmament treaty has been forced on Germany by England and France. Even the United States is a part of the oppression."

"But Hugo, you don't believe that, do you? I mean, Germany did start the war."

"I don't know what I feel about it. True, Germany was the aggressor, but when does the punishment stop? Let's face it, Germany lost, but that was twenty years ago. This generation of Germans should not have to pay for the sins of their fathers."

I didn't have an answer. I just looked into the light of the headlights as they poked out into the dark road ahead. I truly didn't know what I thought.

5
CHAPTER
"WHERE DO YOU STAND?"

"December 1, 1935

By last summer the debate between the National Socialists and the Moderates had become every day conversation in the German Community. You could hardly go to a church supper or a ball game with friends without someone bringing up the events in Germany and the activities of the National Socialist Worker's Party. To many of us it was just a series of events that were occurring "thousands of miles away" and did not hold too much meaning to us. After all, this was America. What real relevance could the activities of a group of Nazi and Fascist extremists eight thousand miles away mean to us anyway?

I had heard the rhetoric over and over of how the European powers that enforced the Treaty of Versailles on Germany after the First World War had taken advantage of Germany. Germany had lost its colonies and been forced to disarm. It could not even maintain a militia. "It was all so unfair," went the argument, "when France and England, Poland and all of the other European countries could arm themselves to the teeth." Germany was in danger of being overrun and without the ability to defend itself. Poor Germany!

Sometimes when you hear a story frequently enough you begin to believe it. In our circle of friends, those we saw at church, in the park, and on Friday nights, no one got too disturbed about Germany's plight. Some were even cynical about it.

"If Germany was in such bad shape," quipped Hans Klauber, "how come they are building such big airships and ocean-going vessels?" He was like many who just couldn't get too disturbed about what was going on in Germany.

But others were openly concerned. It was those who expressed concern that seemed to keep the debate alive. One night in August, Hugo and I were at the Black Forest. The weather had been stifling all week - a St. Louis summer specialty - temperature over ninety, humidity to match. On this August Friday afternoon a front had come through pushing both the humidity and the temperature downward. The heat wave had been broken. It would be a beautiful night to enjoy the beer garden of the Black Forest. After dinner at the Neuschweinstein Inn with Lucian and Willie Schmidt we dropped by the Black forest about ten. The night had taken on a fresh cool feeling, welcome after the sizzling week. Everyone seemed in good spirits. The music, the colored lights in the trees, the beer and the dark green branches of the Mulberry trees made for a perfect setting.

We had been there about thirty minutes when our little knot of friends was joined by Helga Thurmond and her boyfriend Klaus Rocher, and another man who looked very familiar. I knew the minute that he spoke that he was the man on the table who offered the strange toast last December. He was a big man, with broad shoulders. His head was almost bald, and I guessed him about forty-five. He had a booming voice and a broad smile. He was the kind of a person you could like instantly. He was introduced to Hugo and me as Eric Muller. He spoke with a deep creamy German accent.

We had not known him for fifteen minutes when he turned to Hugo and asked: "Where do you stand on the German Rearmament issue?"

"Stand?" Hugo was incredulous. "Why should I 'stand' for anything? That's Germany's problem."

"Oh, no, my friend," said Muller. "It is an ethical and social problem that affects us all."

"How so?" Hugo marched right in and gave Muller an opportunity.

"If the Moderate Democrats, the French Socialists, and all of the left-leaning governments of Eastern Europe can keep Germany subjected, they can continue to plunder the Continent economically and socially. Don't think for a minute they will be satisfied with a weakened Germany for long. They will covet the Ruhr, the Rhine and the rest of Germany with a pirate's eye."

Hugo looked at him skeptically. "So? What does all of that have to do with us?"

"We are Germans!" Muller's voice began to rise. "We are the natural inhabitants of the Fatherland. It will be up to us to protect it from those who covet its treasures, its resources, and its people! Are we going to stand around and allow the rape and pillage of our land by Slavs, Gypsies and Jews? If anyone will protect us it will only be those of us who know and love the Fatherland. We can, and will, be an industrial might. Germany is a natural resource bonanza. We are a land of pure Aryan people whose homeland is coveted by every other country in Europe."

Hugo's mouth was agape. So, I think, was mine. Muller had become so excited. He was a big man with steel gray eyes, and they were bulging out of their sockets. The veins in his neck were sticking out. He was glaring at Hugo. We could only look at each other in disbelief.

"So, my friend," Muller continued, getting right up into Hugo's face, "Where do you stand? Do you stand with those who would devour Germany and suck out its very soul, or with the National Socialists who stand against their tyranny?"

Muller's tirade had so embarrassed the rest of our friends that they had faded off into the crowd to leave Hugo and me to deal with this maniac. Hugo, always the diplomat, reached onto the bar, upon which he had been leaning during Muller's diatribe, and picked up his stone stein half full of beer. He pushed it into Muller's stein with a "click" in a half-toast that caught Muller somewhat by surprise.

"To Germany." said Hugo, gazing deep into Muller's blue eyes.

Muller raised his stein to drink. "To Germany," he repeated, not sure if he had gotten his message across to Hugo or not.

Hugo turned and winked at me and turned back to Muller.

"Nice meeting you," Hugo said to Muller, and steered me by the elbow toward our friends who had fallen back a safe distance to a table under one of the oaks.

The events of that August night were only indicative of what was really happening in the German community of Saint Louis in the mid-thirties. Pressures were beginning to build, subtly at first, but pressures just the same. People were being asked to take sides. More people were being asked "Where do you stand?" The question, casual at first, and without any threat or meaning, was becoming more intense, more menacing. An uneasiness has crept into conversations with friends.

It was a question that struck deep at the American isolationist philosophy. Much of America wanted nothing to do with the problems of Europe and felt that the United States should stay out of their problems. Some people even predicted war, but they were in the minority, but America they said, did not need to get involved with the centuries' old conflicts of Europe. We are protected from the problems of the "Old World" by two large and mighty oceans and we did not need to get back in to their problems. But here in South St. Louis most of the heritage was German, and isolationism did not come so readily. Our community was truly split, and those that supported Germany were far more vocal than in many parts of America.

I'm not sure where Hugo and I stood at that time. I admit that the case for Germany was compelling. Yet the militancy, the menacing nature, of the pro-Social Democrats scared me.

Hugo's business has again leveled off. The slight rise in traffic of just a couple of years ago was not continuing. America is still in the grip of a deep depression. The Crash of Twenty-Nine didn't mean anything to us when it happened. It was probably bad timing for Hugo to open the shop in 1932 right in the middle of the Depression, but we did it and we had to live with our decision. We were naive then, just going about our business; two newlyweds, why, we didn't even know what a depression was. We were free in the way that unattached people are - without cares. Without commitments. Without children. We owned no stocks or bonds - that was only for rich people. A stock market that crashed in New York might as well have been in New Delhi or Nairobi for all we cared. It made the headlines, but it really meant nothing to us in South Saint Louis.

That attitude changed as the Great Depression deepened. By 1935 its effects reached everyone, even in South Saint Louis. Many people were out of a job. Luxuries had to be forsaken. The essentials became more precious. Even things that are not luxuries have to be prioritized. We are seeing more bread lines and desperate people, once gainfully employed, on the streets. People cut their own hair - or they didn't cut it at all. They certainly don't get their hair cut by a barber. Fifty cents buys a lot of groceries. Given the choice between a haircut and a good meal, the haircut loses every time. Hugo has some weeks when he doesn't gross twelve dollars.

He tried everything. Specials, where if you got a haircut, you got another within a month for half price. The Barber's Union came down on him for that one. They said it was "cutting prices." Hugo did it anyway, but it didn't work.

He threw in a shoeshine with a haircut. Crandall Watts didn't like it since he was the one doing the shines, but he saw that something had to be done. Hugo reimbursed him for one half of the shoeshine price of the free shines. They gave away a few shoe shines, but it had no real effect on business.

Several people suggested that if Hugo would re-sole their shoes, he would really get the business. No one was buying new ones and shoe soles were wearing out. So, Hugo talked to a local shoe repair shop to see if he could give a coupon for resoling shoes with every three haircuts? The shoe repairman wouldn't participate. He had his own problems.

Hugo even upgraded his services. He offered a drop off point for laundry. People could leave their laundry at the shop and the laundry would pick it up and return it in two days washed, pressed and folded neatly into tissue bundles. People liked the service, but it really did little to increase business.

Hugo introduced the shoulder massage at the conclusion of a haircut or shave. He had learned it when he was working in the Statler Hotel shop but thought it a bit pretentious for a neighborhood shop when he opened. The Wahl Clipper Company made an electric vibrating massager that fit onto the back of the hand like a glove. The massage motor was on the back of the hand and you put your fingers through little fingerlets like a half-glove. It vibrated your whole hand with the most intense vibration being concentrated in the fingers. At the conclusion of a haircut Hugo gave a shoulder and neck massage with the vibrator. His customers loved it. You could see their eyes roll back in their heads as Hugo manipulated his hands around their necks, over the shoulders and onto their upper back. It was a great way to end a haircut! He got lots of complements. Still, it didn't increase business very much.

My job at Marquardt Chemical Company held. There were some layoffs as the Depression deepened, but it seems as long as Avril Hollenbeck's job was secure, so was mine. Some new projects were starting, and Hollenbeck was essential to everything that Marquardt was doing so the chances of him leaving were thin.

Hugo and I got to be pretty good friends with the Hollenbecks. They live in a nice, but not pretentious, home in the Saint Louis Hills area of the City. Hollenbeck likes to Bar-B-Q and has us over at least once or twice a summer on Sunday, for some Bar-B-Q steaks and baked beans. It is a real treat. Not everyone could afford steaks – including us. Hollenbeck's wife, Shirley, makes the best baked beans, all smothered in bacon and onions. Hugo loved them and lavishes praise on Shirley. It is embarrassing. Now she always makes too much when we come over. She puts the excess into a covered dish and offers it to us to take home. She didn't have to offer twice. Hugo accepted immediately. It has sort of become a ritual. Hugo praises her baked beans, and she makes too much knowing full well that we will accept her offer to take the excess home.

In return Hugo would take along his little black faux leather case of barber tools. He had made up this little traveling case in which he kept a set of combs, electric clippers, two pair of scissors, a hair brush, talc and a folded snapping hair cloth. By the end of summer of 1935, we had been to Hollenbecks for Bar-B-Q three times. Hugo would seat General Hollenbeck on a high stool in the backyard in the shade of the detached garage, drape the drop cloth around his neck, snap it, and the next thirty minutes would be spent cutting General Hollenbeck's hair and listening to the Cardinals on the radio. Sometimes Hugo would even trim Shirley's neck. Hollenbeck loved it. Hugo likes it too, especially when he knows that we would get an offer of excess baked beans to take home. I have to admit I enjoy it too.

On a beautiful crisp Sunday afternoon in September Hollenbeck was getting his hair cut while the steaks sizzled on the grill. I never knew where Hollenbeck got the steaks. He always seemed to have plenty of money although they did not live opulently. He was, after all, the number two man in the whole company. He slumped on the stool with his eyes closed while Hugo cut his hair. Hollenbeck always looked like he was dozing when he got his hair cut. He really wasn't and sometimes carried on a conversation with his eyes closed.

"Hugo," he began. "I know that times have been a little rough. Maybe I can help."

I was setting out plates on the picnic table that Hollenbecks had in the back yard. I couldn't help but overhear his statement.

Hollenbeck continued: "Aren't you closing on Wednesday afternoon like all of the other barber shops in town?"

"Yes." Hugo clearly did not know what was coming.

"Y'know, I've been looking for some good perks for my management people over at the plant. I'm trying to build a great team and I want to keep them happy. Would you be willing to come over and set up shop at the Labs on Wednesday afternoons and give haircuts?"

Hugo knew that he might as well be closed all day on Wednesday the way that business had been going. Hollenbeck's question caught him a little off guard. He didn't know if Hollenbeck was proposing to pay or not.

"Well, I never thought about ..."

Hollenbeck cut him off, sensing his hesitance. "This is a paying proposition, Hugo. What would you charge for a special in-plant haircut? What are haircuts going for these days? Fifty cents?"

"They are Fifty cents in the shop, sir."

"Well, if you could do ten or more haircuts at the plant on Wednesday afternoon, could you do 'em for fifty cents each?"

Hugo finally caught up with Hollenbeck. He realized that Hollenbeck thought the on-site haircuts were a luxury and would have expected to pay more. His offer of "ten or more" at fifty cents was Hollenbeck's way of getting a group rate at a discount. Hugo would have been willing to do ten or more in a single day for thirty-five cents each. He bit his tongue. Ten haircuts in a day at fifty-cents? That would be five dollars!

"What about shaves?" said Hugo.

"Can you give shaves, too?" Hollenbeck was incredulous.

"Sure, if you have a tilt back desk chair."

"We've got loads of 'em." Hollenbeck laughed at the idea of shaves in the office. "When do you want to start?"

"Is October first soon enough?"

"Done. We'll do it every other week on Wednesday afternoon. I'll have Frieda set up a schedule."

The in-plant haircuts and shaves were an instant hit. By the second visit Hugo was grossing an average of seven dollars per day. Shaves became as popular as haircuts and almost everyone who got a haircut got a shave. Hollenbeck even had a woman division manager who had Hugo crop her hair and bob it in the style of the day. I thought he was pretty good with women's hair, but Hugo steadfastly said he preferred to cut men.

I set up a little red appointment book and reserved time in half hour increments the first and third Wednesday afternoons. My appointment book is full for the next visit almost as soon as the previous Wednesday had passed. Hugo is pleased as punch. I love it, too. It gives me additional contact with some of the middle managers that I only rarely see. It was a real management boon for Hollenbeck, too. Even the President of the company signed up for Hugo to cut his hair.

Hugo normally held forth in a little empty office about four doors down the hall from mine. For the President he went up to his office on the second floor.

The haircuts were a tonic for Hugo and me. We needed the money. Up until then he was bringing home almost nothing from the shop after all of the expenses were paid. It all went to pay rent and buy supplies. We lived, bought groceries and paid our flat rent on my salary. That didn't leave much. We saved a dollar a week for weekend entertainment. We could muster one night out at the Black forest or forego a week and go out for dinner on three dollars. The Wednesday afternoon haircuts at Marquardt took the pressure off. We weren't flush, but it sure helped.

Wednesdays at Marquardt brought us into contact with new people. We met some new friends. While there might have been little opportunity to do so with just one of us there, we found that by me working there all of the time, and Hugo in on Wednesdays, we actually got to know some of the people better. We got to know some of the chemists, and scientists who we would never have come into contact otherwise. Our social life has improved, too. Occasionally we get invited out for an evening of pinochle. Hugo and I are even trying to learn bridge, but that's a story for another day.

We have retained a frugality that we learned from the first days of our marriage. There were fewer weekend trips to fish or explore sights in Missouri that we loved. Gasoline and the operating costs of the car were one of the luxuries we have had to do without. But the new income that Hugo got from the Marquardt job makes it easier now. By mid-fall the additional income had helped up clear up the account at the Kroger store, and we were looking forward to the Holidays.

Hugo and I have always been avid churchgoers. Except on those Sundays when we took a weekend jaunt you could always find us in the congregation of Messiah Lutheran Church. We participated in many church activities. I am in a Missionary Club that meets on Thursday evenings once a month and studies the activities of Lutheran missionaries around the world. Hugo is active in the Men's Club. It is the first step to becoming an Elder, but no one becomes an elder under age forty - at least not at Messiah. We know it won't happen for a while, but I imagine he will be named an Elder someday.

This Thanksgiving Hugo suggested that we begin a regular weekly offering to the Church. He allowed as how we had been so blessed, and that God had looked after us in hard times. We talked it over and agreed on a dollar a week. If a dollar was good enough for entertainment, we could do at least as good for the Church. Starting in November we made our weekly offering in a little white envelope that was dropped into the offering plate. Even if we could not attend, we vowed to send in the offering.

December 22, 1935

It is now year's end, and at least we have our bills paid. Things are looking pretty good. No baby is on the horizon. We've tried everything (and I have to admit it has been fun trying!), but I am as regular as a clock. Every twenty-eight days I am "out of commission" as Hugo calls it. At least we never have to guess if I am pregnant. We always know on the end of the twenty-eighth day!

In December I was three days late. Hugo bought a bottle of champagne. I really think he had traded a haircut for it and had kept it at the shop for quite some time waiting a special occasion. We chilled it down, popped the cork and drank to the probability of our new status of "parents." I started my period within an hour of finishing the bottle!

Making love to Hugo Jurgens is something special. He is an explorer. Every time we make love it is like a new adventure with him. He is like a wide-eyed teenager. Each time is as if it were his first. I'll never forget the first time we made love. It was in 1932. We were engaged to be married in three months. Hugo and I had decided that we would go on a fishing trip down to Arcadia Missouri. We sent a post card down to the Moonlight Cabins. We had seen the place advertised in the Star-Times newspaper on Sundays. Every Sunday there was the little ad that proclaimed it to be "a romantic hideaway right on the banks of the Black River," and it was right next door to a restaurant. In addition, they cleaned and iced the fish you caught. That assumed you caught some. I made the reservation knowing full well that it meant sleeping with Hugo. I told my mother and father that I was going to Saint Charles to spend the weekend with a friend who taught at Lindenwood Female College. Hugo closed the Shop Saturday night and put a little sign in the window that the shop would be closed on Monday for a "vacation day." By eight Saturday evening we were on our way to the Black River. The sun had set and left only an orange glow lit the western sky.

All the way down there we sang and talked, never once mentioning what was on both of our minds. We stopped just outside Saint Louis at Dohacks for dinner and ate catfish and onions. We both drank two beers. It was pitch dark when we returned to the road, and it took almost two more hours of driving.

I wondered how I was going to explain to Hugo that I was not a virgin. The thought had crossed my mind several times before. After tonight there would be no more secrets in that department. Oh, not that I had ever been with a man before, that wasn't the problem. In my case the truth was harder to explain. I know it sounds silly, but I lost my virginity to the fat end of a carrot when I was fifteen. Adolescent girls do strange things when the hormones begin to flow. My mother told me to save "it" for my husband. How did I know what "it" was? I guess I was a bit of an explorer, too. Of more concern to me was the explanation I was going to give to Hugo. How could I really expect him to believe that - a carrot!

We arrived at the Moonlight Cabins just before eleven. The check-in was amazing. We had registered as "Mr. and Mrs. Hugo Jurgens."

The night clerk, probably the owner since he appeared through split curtains from an apartment in the back, registered us gingerly and began to talk of fish and where they could, or could not, be caught. He offered to help us with our gear. We declined. I was sure he knew that we were not married. Desk clerks just know those things. I even made it a point to flash my engagement ring at him to be sure that he knew we were not just a couple who had met on the road. He gave us a key to cabin number four.

We were on the bed and into each other's arms before the door closed behind us. You would have thought that the world was going to end before midnight. That we were novices at lovemaking was immediately evident. Hugo had bought a box of rubbers at a Gasen Drug store far from his or my neighborhood to avoid detection. Neither of us knew how to put them on him. I had to admit the sight of his erect penis caused me to pause. It was a lot bigger than that carrot!

It was horrible! We must have torn the rubber. Hugo flooded me with semen and when he withdrew all that remained was the little ring of the rubber's collar about halfway down his penis. The rest of the rubber was in shards. We looked at each other in abject panic. I will cherish that moment forever - even though it was not so funny then. Instead of basking in the fine afterglow of our first orgasm together we stared at the little rubber ring that gripped his throbbing penis. We both could have cried. If we only knew then what we know now!

The thought of my pregnancy three months before our impending marriage didn't thrill either of us, but in a gesture, which has become somewhat symbolic of our marriage, we both reasoned that the damage, if indeed there was any damage, had already been done. Of course, there were things like vinegar douches, but in the middle of the Missouri Ozarks after midnight on Saturday night where were we going to find vinegar? If I was going to get pregnant tonight it was a done deal. We decided to enjoy the week-end. The rest is history.

We never put a worm on a hook the whole time we were there. It rained almost all weekend. I'm not sure how many times we made love. I quit counting at fifteen, and there was a whole day left. The desk clerk asked us if we had any luck fishing in the rain when we checked out on Monday. Neither of us knew it had rained. We hadn't been outside!

One thing I learned about Hugo Jurgens that weekend - he was a terrific lover. I have always said to myself that even if we had never married that weekend making love to Hugo would have been worth the price of admission. Oh, he made lots of mistakes. I never asked him if he had done it before and he never volunteered. It didn't matter. He never asked me about my virginity, so I didn't have to explain about the carrot. When I was in his arms I couldn't care less if there had been others. He was so tender, so respectful, while at the same time he was the consummate explorer. By Monday there was not a part of me, inside or out that he had not caressed, tongued, licked, bitten (but very gently), or sucked. He was like a kid looking for marbles in a sandbox. Every new discovery brought a look of joy to his face."

"God" said Connie. "It's like having a video camera in your parents' bedroom! Can you believe you mother wrote all of this down?"

I had to admit that I had been taken aback. Mom was never one to reveal her innermost thoughts. She was always a bit stoic on the subject of sex. Discussing her and Dad's sex life was completely out of character.

"In a word, no, Connie. I guess I never contemplated my parents actually coupling in their youth. My visions of them seemed to be tainted by recent memories. They were both in their eighties when they died. I never even pictured them as young enough to be sexually active - let alone erotic. Obviously, I was wrong."

Connie's eyes were sparkling, almost moist. She had that impish little grin she gets on her face when she wants to tease. "I thought the only time your Mom and Dad screwed was when you were conceived." She laughed.

"Shows how wrong you can be. They were apparently quite a number."

"A number? Sounds to me like they screwed like rabbits," she said. We both laughed.

Connie looked back as she headed for the kitchen. "Want a Scotch?"

"Thanks. If you are going to have one, I will too. Make it a light one."

I read the passage again about my mother and father's first liaison. It was like reading a dime novel. I couldn't believe it was them.

Connie returned from the kitchen with two Dewars and water in short fat glasses. She put them on the little side table and sat down on the floor at my feet.

"Read on," she said. "I can't wait to hear how this book ends."

April 26, 1936

"We are now in our sixth year of marriage and Hugo Jurgens is a better lover than when we started. Some of our friends have complained that after a few years of marriage that sex had become dull, flat, even boring. Not with Hugo.

In November Hugo did something I will remember until the day I die. It was common for us to make love three or four times a week, sometimes twice on Sundays. It was not unusual for us not to get dressed on Sunday morning until we went to church. We would run around the house nude as the day we were born. Sometimes I'd even fix breakfast *au natural.* It was a real panic if someone came to the door. Hugo would run for his pants and I would scramble for a chenille robe that I kept behind the bathroom door.

On Thanksgiving we decided that we would sleep in. We were invited to go over to my parent's house for an evening meal, so the day was uncommitted. A late sleep, a little love making, some coffee, a little more love making, read the paper. You get the picture.

Hugo really knows how to send me over the edge. He usually starts with a light kiss on the side of my neck and moves gently over my shoulder and down my arm. If I would lift my arm he will move to its soft underside and tongue his way down my ribs to the underside of my breast. By then there is no turning back. My nipples get as hard as a rock. Hugo takes full advantage by rolling them gently between his thumb and forefinger. I love to put both arms above my head. Hugo knows how to work my breasts like a master. I usually have an orgasm before he even gets to my waist.

But when he gets between my legs, he can do the most damage. He will deftly position himself between my knees and kiss the soft inside of my thighs trailing upward with his tongue. I get so wet that I think he would drown. His tongue parts me, and he will put its point on the end of my clitoris and press gently. It is wonderful! Hugo brings me to an orgasm every time. I'm not sure whether it is the anticipation or the act, but he knows just how to do it.

When Hugo gets me going, I spread myself so wide that I make my thighs sore. He says I am a screamer. I don't know. I just lose control. He enters me with the wide-eyed anticipation of a teenager and together we would roll around the bed like a couple of Eskimos only to fall into a heap when we both come together. That Hugo; he is really something!

On this Thanksgiving morning Hugo started with a kiss in my left ear quickly moving to the nape of my neck. I relaxed and welcomed his advance. He quickly moved to my right nipple. God, I love it when he massages my nipples. Then he moved down across my belly. If I say so myself, it is a flat belly. I don't have an ounce of fat on me.

Then he did something I never in my life expected. He had put the massage vibrator from the shop under the bed. He reached down and slipped it onto his right hand. I guess he had put it by the side of the bed the night before. He flipped on the switch. I almost sat up.

"Shhhh." He put his finger to his lips displaying the vibrating contraption on his hand. I had seen it before and Hugo had given me a back and neck massage just like he gave his customers. I recognized it immediately and fell back onto my back.

Hugo moved his hand across my belly and over the hairy knob that led to my vagina. He touched the entrance lightly. It was as if an electric current shot through me. I felt my back go rigid. He did it again. I responded the same way - automatically. He circled his hand parting the folds of skin with his vibrating fingers. I was in ecstasy. My back arched, and I spread my legs.

Without warning Hugo inserted his middle finger and enveloped my clitoris with the palm of his hand. I lost control. My back arched upward, and my legs flailed like a bicycle rider. I've never experienced anything like it before. I impaled myself on his vibrating hand. Juices dripped from me like a fountain. I even slobbered onto the pillow.

"Ohhhhh, God! Hugo. Ooooo...." My voice trailed off. I gripped the bed rail above my head and pushed myself against his vibrating hand. I was ensnared in spasms of ecstasy.

Even Hugo was startled by the reaction. For a second, I thought he almost withdrew his pleasure machine from me, but I pushed his hand on firmer. One orgasm followed another. I didn't want him to stop.

It must have really gotten him excited. He put the machine aside and climbed inside me. He came in just a few seconds. When he had finished and was resting inside me I had one more orgasm just for good luck.

Dad asked the blessing over Thanksgiving dinner that evening at my parent's house. In his prayer he thanked God for that day. Hugo looked at me over his folded hands and winked. I could not have agreed more!

6

THE BLACK FOREST SOCIETY

"August 17, 1936

Last week Hugo received an invitation to attend a lecture at the Carondelet YMCA on current events in Europe. We had seen a couple of flyers posted at the Neuschweinstein Inn. I had ignored them until last Tuesday night Hugo came home from the Shop with one in his hand. A fellow, whom I had never met, named Gunther Hoebel, had been a customer of Hugo's and had urged Hugo to attend. The program was sponsored by some social club that Gunther belonged to. The speaker was to be a noted expert on European affairs attached to the German Consulate in Chicago. There would be drinks and refreshments afterwards. Hugo thought that he might go and asked if I would be interested?

We had both been working a lot and normally stayed around the flat on Wednesdays, but what the heck? It might do us some good to get out. Hugo and I had bowled a couple of times with friends at the Carondelet Y, but that was the only time I had been down there. We decided to go.

The Carondelet Y was a dreary place. It had terribly institutional architecture and was painted drab green and tan colors inside. It smelled like moldy showers and urine. It has four bowling alleys in the basement. Upstairs the meeting room had large windows that reach toward the twelve-foot ceilings. The floors were covered with asphalt tiles that caused every sound to echo as if it were a tiled bathroom. The meeting room had folding chairs and two flags in front - one American and the other German. Gunther welcomed us, and Hugo introduced me to him. He was a pleasant, jovial fellow with a big red nose. I couldn't tell if it was just bulbous from size or a little too much sauce.

The speaker had arrived early and was mingling with the small crowd. Gunther and another fellow introduced people to the speaker as they arrived. He was a tall man with ice blue eyes and blond hair named Heinrich Bloch. He spoke with a German accent, but his English was impeccable - almost British sounding. He was very charming and took my hand. I almost expected him to kiss it, but he didn't. He held it for several seconds before releasing it.

"I am very pleased to make your acquaintance, Mrs. Jurgens," he said with a slight bow. "Gunther has told me about the two of you. He says that you are very well thought of people. I am very happy to meet you."

Hugo took immediate notice of Bloch's long handshake with me and extended his hand as if to cut it short. "Nice to meet you, too, Mr. Block."

Block released my hand ever so slowly and turned to Hugo. "I understand that you have a fine barber shop and are well respected in your community." He looked into Hugo's eyes.

"Gunther exaggerates. I am just a hard-working barber trying to get along."

"Oh, no, my friend," said Bloch. "You underestimate your standing in this community. To be a barber is a very noble calling. You are an essential ingredient in the personal hygiene of conscientious men. I'm sure that you daily see the leaders of your community when they call on you for personal service."

Hugo was not used to this kind of flattery. He really did not know how to react. "Well," he said, "maybe I do see a few good people now and then."

"I'll bet you know what is going on before anyone else. Every barber shop I have ever known that was worth its salt was a clearing house for news and information of what is going on in the community."

Bloch had hit a nerve with Hugo. If there was one rule that Hugo lived by it was that what he heard at the shop was not passed on. Truth is, that with the exception of a woman's beauty shop, a barbershop is truly the repository for every bit of gossip, true and false, that circulates in a community. Why, I could sit in there for ten minutes and pick up more dirt than I would hear anywhere else in a month. Hugo knew it too. But he reasoned that keeping your ears open and your mouth shut was good for business. He lived by the rule that "What you hear, leave it here."

"I usually don't talk about what I hea..."

"Of course, you don't," said Bloch, cutting Hugo off. "I wouldn't expect it to be any other way."

In a funny way Bloch had extracted an unusual concession out of Hugo. He had gotten him to admit that he really did have a lot of knowledge about what was going on in the community by saying that he did not want to talk about it. This Heinrich Bloch was a very clever man.

He also was a very convincing man, too. In his lecture he reviewed the history of Europe from the end of the First World War concentrating on the continuing instability in the Balkans. He discussed the Serbian and Croatian situation. He did not get into the start or causes of the War. He then moved to Poland and Czechoslovakia, Italy and France. He briefly touched on the civil strife in Spain. There was a strange edge to his lecture. I couldn't quite put my finger on it, but it seemed to insinuate that all of these countries had some wretched infirmity that prevented them from achieving greatness, self-government, and leadership in the European Community. He hinted that some flaw existed in the fabric of their being that kept them from uniting and giving direction to their potential. It was as if it would be impossible for them to achieve greatness under any ruler.

Finally, he got to Germany. He discussed the Kaiser, the history of the current German Republic and its emergence from World War One as a federation of states each of which was different, yet each possessing a common thread. "Germany, he said, "was not bound by the stigma of the other European countries. Deep within her are people and forces that have the ability to overcome the degenerative forces that restrain her neighbors."

I glanced over a Hugo. He was listening intently. I couldn't tell what he was thinking, but he was taking it all in. He didn't miss a word.

Bloch got to the events in Bavaria since the "Beer Hall Putsch," the emergence of the National Social Democratic Party under Hitler and its ideas of social and economic reform. "They are symbolic of the new Germany," he said, "and what will, in time, signal the rise of Germany as an industrial and political giant."

Bloch's voice rose slightly when he spoke of the "New Order" in Germany. It fell when he spoke of the repression of the German People by the Communists and the signatories to the Treaty of Versailles at the end of World War I, particularly England, France, Poland and Czechoslovakia. The audience was spellbound by his oratory. He even suggested that the United States had to share some of the guilt for the suppression of Germany. His criticism of the League of Nations as a tool of the enemies of Germany was scathing.

His words fell on mostly German ears. He had a sympathetic audience and he knew it. He played his audience like a fine musical instrument telling them what they wanted to hear, titillating them with intrigue and conspiracy, and swelling their breasts with nationalistic pride. Block was, indeed, an effective and powerful speaker. He was interrupted several times with applause from the thirty or so who had gathered in the dull antiseptic-smelling meeting room of the Carondelet YMCA.

Bloch concluded with a plea for all Germans to come to the aid of their homeland. "The Fatherland should not be forgotten but must always be the repository of all that is typically right," he said. "Let the seeds that have been sewn in Bavaria grow and prosper. Let the produce of the true Germany flower and multiply," he said. "Let the world know that deep within the Fatherland lies pure virtue, untainted, unadulterated and ready to spring forth."

He then faced the German flag and raised his right hand in the salute that I had seen two years before at Christmas in the Black Forest Inn, and said: "Germany, my Germany, may your Aryan heart be cleansed. May your sons retake their rightful place among the stars and purge their souls of all that reviles their true heritage."

He then turned to the audience and again raised his right hand in the salute. "Seig Heil!"

The audience didn't hesitate this time. Almost everyone rose and replicated the salute.

"Seig Heil!" "Seig Heil!" Seig Heil!"

Hugo and I did not know what to do. We were taken aback, dumbfounded. The audience broke into applause. We joined in. It was appropriate. Bloch had presented an interesting lecture. He had entertained in a disquieting way. But he was troubling. I could feel Hugo's unease. I knew I was uncomfortable.

After the meeting, in a small anteroom, in which small sandwiches, beer and snacks had been placed on a banquet table, we were immediately joined by Guenther Hoebel who had remained on the podium during the lecture after he introduced Bloch.

"I noticed that you did not return the salute," he said, in an inquiring kind of voice.

"Guenther," said Hugo, "this is America. Not Germany. Why should I get so worked up about what is happening in Germany? My life is here," Hugo replied.

"Aren't you concerned about the oppression of Germany by outsiders? Aren't you concerned that Germany cannot arm itself against outside aggression? Why, every country in Europe is fairly licking its chops over German territory, yet they keep us in chains with an unfair peace treaty that is obsolete and repressive."

Bloch had now joined Hoebel and was looking intently into Hugo's eyes with his steel blues. "And, my friends," injected Bloch, "you cannot disconnect yourselves from the events that affect your Homeland under the guise that they are events "over there." Bloch gestured towards the east. "They affect us all." He turned his gaze to me. "They even affect your job at Marquardt."

The statement - the way he said it - sent chills down my spine. How did he know about my job at Marquardt?

As if to drive the point home; as if to demonstrate his superior knowledge, he said: "You Frieda, have an important and sensitive job as the secretary to the Director of Research. Much of what we all do will someday be connected to the events in Europe. We must choose what sides we will be on. That choice will, someday, be important."

Hugo and I were silent. We were dumbfounded. How did he know I was the secretary of the Director of Research at Marquardt?

He reached for my hand. "I'm so glad that you could come. Think about what you have heard here tonight. I hope to see you again." He again bowed slightly and excused himself.

On the way home Hugo and I hardly spoke. Hugo was visibly upset. I couldn't tell if it was a twinge of jealousy, Bloch was unabashedly fascinated with me, or what he had said about choosing sides. In truth, it turned out to be a little of both.

We arrived home a little after ten. Hugo pulled a beer from the icebox and rummaged through the drawer for an opener.

"Want one?" he called to me from the kitchen.

"Sure. Sounds good."

He came out onto the porch with two Falstaffs in one hand and a packet of crackers in the other.

"Where does that guy get off with that kind of talk?" Hugo was seething.

"Honey, I think he is just too intense for either of us. You hear that kind of talk all day in the shop. Just forget it. Why should it bother us now?"

"I didn't like the way he was leering at you either. I caught him undressing you with his eyes."

"Hugo, I think you're jealous."

"I'm not jealous, but that big Fascist needs to keep his eyeballs in his head."

"Hugo, you *are* jealous." I couldn't resist. I have never seen Hugo react so violently towards someone as to Bloch. I'm no slouch when it comes to looks, but Hugo almost never gets upset when men make passes at me. He is a very confident and comfortable guy. Why would this Bloch upset him so? Maybe it was the message that came with the man.

"Don't tell me he didn't make you uncomfortable," retaliated Hugo. "That little remark about your work was out of line. How did he know what you did? What's he been doing, research?"

I had to admit his knowledge of what I did, even on our first meeting, made me very uneasy. Hugo was right; why did he know so much about me - and what I did?

October 4, 1936

Hugo and I had been out to dinner at the Bevo Mill. What with the Wednesday afternoon haircuts at my plant and another raise that I had in received in July we were occasionally hitting a good restaurant for a meal. Not frequently, mind you, maybe once a month. Tonight, we had gone to Bevo for some schnitzel and sauerkraut, and had stopped by the Black Forest for some late-night conviviality. They would have the fires lit in the beer garden. It was a beautiful crisp fall October night. A stein of lager under the big full moon would be a great way to top off a Saturday night on the town.

There had been lots of talk lately about Hitler and his rising Nazi party. Hugo had been very sullen since the lecture in August. He had not talked about it much even though I knew that he was hearing more and more of that kind of talk in the shop. Sides *were* being chosen, whether Hugo liked it or not. Even some of our friends were becoming more active in pro-German causes.

When we arrived at the Black Forest Hugo parked the car on the gravel lot and we walked around the building toward the entrance to the beer garden. As we approached the gate two young men in brown shirts and black trousers stepped into the path. The shortest one said: "Are you members?"

Hugo was a little surprised. "Members of what?"

"This is a private party. You can't come in unless you are a member."

"What do we have to be members of?" I asked.

"I'm sorry. If you do not know, then we are not at liberty to tell you."

"You mean we can't come in and have a beer?" asked Hugo incredulously.

"That's right. Now, if you'll just step back to your car ..." It was clear that he was not going to let us in.

Just then over the high wooden fence we could hear the strains of *The Horst Wessel Song* wafting through the trees. Voices were raised in a lusty ovation that permeated the grove of Oaks and Mulberries. Whoever was in the private party was singing with compassion. We listened for a moment and went back to the car. We wondered how many of our friends were in there. Both Hugo and I were disappointed that we could not go in.

December 5, 1936

Christmas was coming on fast. I had done little shopping. We had little money so shopping was academic. There would usually be one gift for Hugo and he would find one for me. I had hinted several times for a sewing machine, but the reality of it was that we could not afford it. I had my eye on a vest at Famous Barr that would just look great on Hugo. I had been saving from my grocery money for the past three months. If all went well, I would have enough money by the week of December 15th. I had sewn aprons for gifts for Hugo's mother and mine. It was the best we could do. Both of us were at a loss as to what to do for our fathers. Whatever it would be, it would have to be inexpensive.

Hugo and I never thought of ourselves as poor. I guess, in fact we weren't, but money was always a problem. Neither of us was extravagant, but we just had to budget tightly and watch what we did. We had enough to eek by, but that was about all. We had been married seven years now and our standard of living had not improved much. Oh yes, Hugo had gotten the shop going, but without the Wednesday shift at the chemical plant and my job we would not have been able to make ends meet.

December 18, 1936

Something happened yesterday that was very strange. Hugo came home from work at the usual time. I had gotten home about an hour earlier and had begun dinner. It was December and fresh vegetables were hard to get. After I left the streetcar, I had stopped by at the little fruit stand on Grand avenue, but nothing looked good. For sure nothing was very fresh. I went across the street to the Kroger and bought a can of green beans and three links of sausage. It would be a fine dinner. Total cost: seventy-six cents.

Hugo came in fuming. He stomped into the bedroom and took off his jacket and tie. He put on a sweater and hardly said a word - not even a kiss. That was not my Hugo.

"What's eating on you?" I asked, when he returned to the kitchen.

"You won't believe what happened today. Remember that Eric Muller? Well, he and Heinrich Bloch came into the shop today. They waited until everyone had gone out, just before lunch. I saw them drive by twice and look in to see if there was anyone there. Then they came in.

Bloch tried to make small talk. I thought it was unusual from the very first. The only time I ever met him was at the Carondelet YMCA.

Muller got into the chair for a haircut. Bloch sat in one of the waiting chairs. After a few minutes they asked me if I would like to join the Black Forest Society.

I didn't have the faintest idea what they were talking about. Eric Muller explained that it was a group of concerned Americans with German parentage who were following the events in Europe and how they would affect the future of Germany.

"What did you tell them?"

"I told them that I was having a tough time getting all worked up about Germany's plight in the scheme of things. I said that I was having enough trouble paying the bills - let alone worry about what was going on in Germany."

Then Bloch said that I had better be careful. That what went on in Europe was having an effect on what would happen here. I told him I didn't see how, and he said that we, you and I, had a debt to pay to the Fatherland. Just because we were living here, we could not escape our obligations to Germany. I said that he might sell that to my father, but I felt no connection to Germany.

Muller said that he understood how I felt but joining the Black forest Society. It would be an easy way to make friends, increase business, and even though I felt no connection to Germany, keep in touch with those who did. He said my father would be proud of me."

"So, did you agree to join?"

"Hell, no."

"Hugo, I bet that was what was going on at the Black Forest when went there last October. Remember when we couldn't get in?"

"So, what?"

"Hugo, it wouldn't hurt. It's just a bunch of 'old country' Germans who want to maintain the old ways. Maybe Eric Muller was right, your father would be proud of you. Maybe we would make some new friends. And it might be good for business."

"Frieda, you know I don't like to just join anything."

"C'mon Hugo. Wake up. You live and work in a German community. You are a German. Of course, you are an American, but you were a German first. It won't hurt. I'd love to do it. Can I join, too? It'll be good for both of us. We need the connections, the friends, and the camaraderie. Besides, you might be able to practice your German."

"I don't know Frieda. I ..."

"Are there dues or charges? Do we have to pay to belong?"

"Frieda, I haven't the slightest idea. I never got that far with them to ask."

7

A GROWING INTEREST IN EVENTS IN THE FATHERLAND

"Well," said Connie, taking a deep draw on her Scotch. "Now we know what the Black Forest Society is. But I still don't see what got Mildred so upset about it when you started asking questions."

I had to admit I didn't see the problem with a German Club sympathetic to the National Socialist Worker's Party. Let's face it, half of South Saint Louis was secretly pulling for the Nazis before and during World War II, at least until the atrocities began to be discovered.

I pondered the deteriorating paper cover of the next notebook. Its spine was coming unglued and the pages had yellow around the edges where the air had gotten to them. Saint Louis summers aren't kind to aging newsprint paper.

"I think Mildred is just a crazy old lady. She has got to be in her late seventies. She is as healthy as an ox, and about as strong, but I don't know about her mind. Maybe the way she sees things now is not really the way they were." I paused. Was I making excuses for her odd behavior?

"Maybe she is getting a little senile. Remember, towards the end, Dad's memory got a little off, too."

Connie flipped through a package of photos. One of them was of Mom and Dad standing in front of the Whippet Coupe.

"Y'know, they really were a handsome couple. Your mother was lovely in her day. Look at this photo." She handed the yellowed glossy black and white to me.

Mom had on a tight flapper with a scoop neck. She was really trim - svelte would be more descriptive. She had on one of those head-bands and carried a little sequined purse. Her hand was on her hip and her weight had been shifted to one leg in a seductive pose. She was really a sexy woman. Dad had on a light suit, almost white. It had a vest, and he wore a long watch chain. His shoes were covered with a dapper pair of spats, and in his hand, he held a wide brimmed Panama. He had one foot on the running board of the Whippet. On his face he had a broad smile - sort of an "ain't I got the world by the tail?" smile.

From the looks of the picture, he did.

"January 12, 1937

"We joined the Black Forest Society. Hugo called Eric Muller in the first week of January and told him we would be interested in joining. Muller was elated. He told us when the first meeting would be and offered to pick us up in his car. Last night we attended. It was exhilarating.

The meeting was held in an upstairs hall on south Grand avenue. It was on the corner upstairs over a drug store and across the street from Halbertshaw's Heating and Sheet Metal shop. About sixty people were in attendance. Everyone said it was a small meeting as we were told an average meeting was about one hundred.

There was a stirring pledge of allegiance to the United States followed by a pledge of loyalty to the German Republic. Hugo and I were introduced, and there was a rousing cheer and a song of welcome. Then followed an account of the progresses and failures of the new Bavarian Socialist Worker's Party and the National Socialist Worker's Party. A freckle faced young man read an essay on opportunities for youth and the benefits of health and exercise. Then a man in his sixties, white haired and slightly bent introduced an 8mm silent film of Germany which stressed Bavaria and the Alps, hiking and picnicking in the out of doors. It was the first color movie I had ever seen. I loved it.

There was a song about Germany, its beauty and its people. They passed out song sheets. A thin woman accompanied on the piano. Then a beautiful young woman, a tall blond, sang a solo about German heritage, its purity, its honor and glory. It ended in a rousing chorus in which most joined in. The song, in German, wasn't known to me although Hugo seemed to know some of the words. Everyone stood and raised their hands in the open-faced salute that I had seen Bloch use at the lecture. Afterwards we all drank beer and shook hands. Almost everyone in the room came around and introduced themselves. It was quite an experience. I could tell that even Hugo had enjoyed it.

On the way home Hugo asked me: "Do you really think that Germany is getting screwed over by the Allies? Is it time for Germany to assume its rightful place at the head of the European table?"

I was somewhat surprised by his question. Hugo had been a little bit cynical about the whole thing before the meeting. Now he was asking some interesting questions. Questions that indicated he was not so sure. Had he become a believer? It was hard for me to read him, but he was clearly doing some soul searching.

"May 19, 1937

It was Mother's Day and we had agreed to take both of the mothers out for lunch after church to a restaurant overlooking the Meramec River near Fenton. It was a glorious sunny spring day. The temperature was perfect with low humidity. We picked them up after church and all of us piled into the Whippet. That it was crowded was an understatement. Hugo's father said that it was like riding in a can of sardines. We all laughed. We put the top back. It would be a good day.

We hadn't missed a meeting of the Black Forest Society since joining. Hugo was anxious to tell his father. He was sure that he would be proud to know that his son had joined a club whose purpose was to further the heritage of his Homeland.

Lunch was at a big round table for six looking out through tall French windows onto a wide green lawn that led down to the Meramec River. Plates of biscuits and cornbread were passed followed by large tubs of freshly churned butter and strawberry jam. The meal was fried chicken, fresh corn, peas, beans, carrots, potatoes and topped off with cherry pie. On request they would add a dollop of fresh creamy ice cream to your pie. We ate like hogs.

About halfway through the dinner Hugo raised the issue. "Dad, you'll be happy to know that Frieda and I have joined a Society for the preservation of German ideals."

"Oh?" Hugo's father seemed somewhat perplexed. Perhaps he knew Hugo too well.

"Yes Dad. Have you heard of the Black Forest Society?"

"Can't say that I have," was the reply.

"It's been a real eye-opener for me. I've learned more about Germany than I ever knew."

"And what have you learned?" Hugo's father seemed suspicious.

"I have learned that there is no substitute for a strong Germany. I believe now that Germany can no longer rely on the benevolence of other European countries for its wellbeing."

"Sounds like Nazi drivel," said his father.

"So, what if the Nazis believe in it," said Hugo. They've Germany's best interests at heart."

"Be careful son. Being in love with Germany does not mean being in love with all of her ideologies. Germany is a country split with causes. Not all of them are noble or worthy of your support. Choose who, and what, you will support, very carefully. I fear that there are many changes ahead. It will be difficult to tell who is right and who is wrong in the battle for the hearts and minds of our homeland."

Hugo was stunned at his father's rebuff. He was sure that his dad would be pleased with our affiliation with the Black Forest Society. He was quiet for the rest of the day. For Hugo to have little to say is strange of itself. He is usually so outgoing. You could tell he was perplexed. He really did not know how to react to his father's caution.

"August 24, 1937

The summer of 1937 has been a hot one. Almost every day in August has been above ninety degrees. We've had six days over one hundred. Hugo and I are sleeping on the porch at night with the fan blowing directly on us. It seems to cool off just before dawn. Hugo and I often wake up and make love in the cool of the morning. We have a fold-out couch on the porch that creaks when he is on top of me. Hugo says I make too much noise when we make love, and that the combination of my groaning and the creaking bed will wake the neighbors downstairs. Sometimes we get to giggling when the bed creaks."

"Last week my boss, General Hollenbeck told me that he was going to be assigned additional responsibilities. A parade of Army brass had been in and out of the office for several months. I knew a little about what was going on through the correspondence that I was doing for Hollenbeck, but he never gave me too many details. I guess I could have figured it out if I tried. There is a plant in north Saint Louis that manufactures some kinds of small ammunition, shells I think. It's called the Army Ammunition Plant. General Hollenbeck is being assigned the responsibility of expanding it and making some conversions in the plant so that other small armaments can be manufactured. He'll be spending some of his time over there. So will I. Hollenbeck has set up an office up there and there is a place for me to work, too. He said a typewriter and telephones were being installed that day. Some of the plant managers and technicians will also be doing double duty at both places. He also said the main plant would be engaging in some new research. He was vague on the specifics.

Hollenbeck says the expansion and renovation of the plant will take over two years and several million dollars. Somehow, I suspect something big is going on and Hollenbeck hasn't told me all of the details. He says it's going to be a lot of work. I think the additional duties will be good for me. It doesn't mean any more pay, but a change of scene will be good. You need something like that once in a while. The good part is that it virtually guarantees me employment for two or three years at the least.

I'm not sure what this means for Hugo's Wednesday afternoon appointments for haircuts at the main plant? Some of the people whose hair he cuts will be affected by the transfers. As the planning progresses most of them might even be moved over there. The changes will begin in September, right after the Labor Day holiday.

"September 6, 1937

Hugo and I have been very active in the Black Forest Society - at least as active as new members can be. We enjoy the meetings and the camaraderie of meeting the members. At least one of us has attended every meeting since we were inducted. I noticed there seems to be a 'club within a club'. It's not exactly like they are cliquish, but rather there is an inner circle of men who seem to control everything that goes on. I hear that they meet weekly. Only one report of the 'Committee' is ever read at the regular monthly meeting. It usually is related to finances. Their meetings must be very dull.

The Black Forest Society is very pro-National Socialist Worker's Party. In fact, some of the locals refer to it as a Nazi organization. It is affiliated with the *Auslandsorganisation* – sort of an overseas German support organization. What's wrong with that? Many countries have home-based support organizations for groups of native citizens living abroad. Just because something is pro-Germany doesn't make it Pro-Hitler. I have even come to believe that some of his ideas are right, but I'm not the fanatic some people are. To some you would think that he was the savior of the world. But it's hard to argue with some of his ideas. He wants Germans and Germany to stand up and be counted. It's difficult to find fault with that.

I really enjoy the activities of the Society. I think Hugo does too, but he has been so busy. Sometimes I have to go by myself. I have to tell him what goes on at the meetings if he cannot attend. We are going to organize a leaflet distribution at the Thanksgiving parade in downtown Saint Louis for the Friday after Thanksgiving. I am more than willing to participate in that type of activity. The Committee is drafting the pamphlet. A first draft was presented at the meeting last week. It is a good position paper on where America should stand with respect to the New Germany. Americans need to know. I'm going to work on the corner of Sixth and Olive. I hope it is not too cold."

November 1, 1937

"The changes in the plant have been monumental - all in the past few months. My job has changed considerably. I spend about three days a week at the Chemical plant and at least two days at the Small Arms Plant. General Hollenbeck has given me the responsibility to set up a shipping and invoicing system for the small arms that are being manufactured here. What is manufactured at the main plant and at the new plant are shipped to a lot of different locations in the United States. Most are military bases. I had to integrate all the shipping into one system. It is quite challenging. The amount of work has grown so much that I've even been given an assistant. I'm now sometimes working on Saturday mornings. I don't mind it since Hugo has always worked on Saturdays. Hollenbeck says that I can expect a big raise at the beginning of the New Year. Apparently, it's contingent on some budget approvals, but he says it is a sure thing.

The Small Arms plant manufactures several types of pistols and ammunition. We also make some parts for machine guns and rifles, but they are not all completely manufactured here. Some items are shipped elsewhere for assembly. A new line is being set up to manufacture shell casings and cartridges. Already 9mm shells are made here and 35mm shells are assembled into machine gun bands.

We've been required to take an oath of secrecy about what goes on at the plants. I'm not so sure what we do is so secret. Everybody in this part of town knows about it, but the rules are the rules. There seem to be so many new ones… I'm probably breaking the rules by just writing down what we do in this diary.

Even Hugo has benefited by the plant expansion. Several of "Hollenbeck's boys" as the middle management team is called, complained about being over at Small Arms on Wednesdays when they had their haircut appointments. They were not able to keep their appointments with Hugo. For the first week it cut down on the number of haircuts and shaves that Hugo was able to give. Both of us were concerned that it would affect Hugo's income. It didn't take long for the word to get around that there were some vacancies so others who had been bumped by some of their seniors signed up. After only one week the schedule was full again.

I guess Hollenbeck was feeling a lot of pressure, so he called Hugo and asked him if he could spare another half day each month to come over to the Small Arms plant and cut hair? Hollenbeck was good about taking care of his team. Hugo decided that Wednesday was shot anyway so he started closing the shop all day on Wednesday and spending the morning at Small Arms and the afternoon at the chemical plant. After just two weeks he had a fully booked all day schedule with an hour in between to travel from one to the other and grab a bite to eat. Hugo scheduled ten hours of haircuts and shaves on Wednesdays and would average two customers per hour. Haircuts were rumored to be going up to seventy-five cents or a dollar. If that happened Hugo would earn twenty dollars on Wednesday. That paid our rent for a month at both the shop and the flat. Still, there was just enough to go around. The raise hadn't happened yet. Going into November haircuts were still fifty cents.

Avril Hollenbeck is a hard-working man. He is one of those guys who always wore an affable smile even when he is working sixteen hours a day. He's in the office before six each morning and he is frequently there at six in the evening when I leave. He has a lot of responsibility. He's already managing over three hundred researchers, technicians and production personnel at two locations. He takes his job very seriously, but never seriously enough to be unfriendly or uncaring to the people who work for him. The General is well liked and runs his office like a team with everyone on the team knowing what their responsibilities are. I really like working for him. Oh, he can be a tyrant if he has to be. I've heard him cuss out people on the telephone using words that I never even knew. If you cross him, or lie to him, or do something intentional to hurt or delay one of the programs he will come down on you like a ton of bricks. I saw him fire three production workers on the spot one day when he caught them loafing. He hates loafers.

Hollenbeck is known for delivering on schedule. Whether it was research or a production item, he has it when he says he will have it. The Army knows it, too. The Department of the Army is always sending some bigwig around to study how he does it. He jokingly tells them there are two secrets to delivering on time: one, set the delivery date far enough ahead that it is easy to make, and two, reward the people who deliver the goods on time. One day a visiting General asked what he said to the people if they did not make the deadline? Hollenbeck replied, "I don't remember what I say, but neither do they because they are not here anymore." Everyone thought that was funny, but we all knew it is the truth.

"December 22, 1937

By early December it was clear that something was happening over at the main plant. Things had changed. The fluoroscopy and x-ray research had continued, but the company has taken a direction that is a little different. They've started some research that is somehow related to the X-ray and fluoroscopy research, but not exactly the same. I don't know the details. Hollenbeck set up a special research wing to work in one of the out buildings away from the main plant and research facility. I didn't handle the paperwork for the setup of that group. They cleared Building D in late November and Hollenbeck said it would take six months to gear it up and staff the project. I did some ordering at the outset, but once they were established, they became a completely self-contained unit. Hollenbeck didn't say much about it either. He was busy, and so was I, but I got the impression he didn't want many people to know what it was about. I was spending more and more time over at the Small Arms Plant, so I didn't have time to spend worrying about what some of the brain boys at Marquardt Research were doing. Hugo cuts the hair of a few of them, but generally they keep pretty well to themselves and don't say much about what they're doing."

"Christmas Day, December 25, 1937

On December 23, it began to snow. Dawn brought light flurries so fine you could hardly see them. They gathered in little wrinkles in my black coat and stuck to the band of Hugo's hat. By noon it was looking like it could really come down. The sky had turned ashen gray and a light cover of snow had begun to affix to the streets and sidewalks. The grass on the lawns had already taken and held about an inch. I went to work, but Hollenbeck ordered both plants closed at three because of the snow. By then it had now accumulated to over six inches.

Hugo closed the shop early. The last customer had come in about three o'clock and Hugo had sat around for about an hour before deciding to call it a day. He wasn't in the door five minutes when our landlord came up and asked if Hugo would shovel the front walk. They were nice elderly people who had been good to us and didn't crab too much if the rent was late. Hugo would usually do the walks when it snowed for fear that the old man would have a heart attack when shoveling.

We had found a good Christmas tree that was over seven feet tall and just fit under the eight-foot ceiling when it was in the stand. It cost us a dollar eighty-five cents, but it was worth it. We had looked forward to this evening as we had invited some friends over to help us trim it. Hugo was changing from his snow boots and I joined him in the bedroom. It had already gotten dark.

"Merry Christmas," I said as I put my arms around his neck. He was standing there in his shorts and still had on his white shirt. I gave him a kiss on the cheek.

"My, you are in good spirits." He gave me a squeeze around the waist.

"Why not? It's Christmas. It is snowing. I love the snow. Aren't you in the Christmas spirit?"

"I guess." His reply was a little tentative. He managed a smile.

"What's wrong with you? Have a bad day?"

Hugo pulled away. "Oh no, nothing like that. I guess I'm just a little down. It's Christmas and sometimes I get to wondering just where we are going."

"What's that supposed to mean?"

"It's not you. I mean, we're almost thirty. We can't seem to have any kids. I'm working every day, but it all seems to go to the rent and for groceries. There are just lots of things I would like to buy you for Christmas that we just can't afford. You know, I just get down sometimes."

"It's really the baby thing isn't it?' I mean it really gets to you at this time of the year. I know what you mean. Christmas is for kids. When I see the other couples and their kids at the stores all dressed up in their Sunday best with their eyes sparkling I wish we had one, or two. It would be great."

"Frieda, I didn't mean to make you sad. I know how much you want a child. I'm sorry. I don't want to spoil the evening. We have both been looking forward to it."

I got up off of the side of the bed where I had been sitting and went to him. He folded me into his arms and held me tight. It was one of the only times in our marriage that I had seen Hugo really down. I assumed it was the baby thing although I knew he was always concerned about having enough money to get along.

Hugo wasn't a greedy man. Neither was he one of those people who have money on their minds all of the time, but he did worry. I think he genuinely wanted to make a good life for him and me and would see himself as a failure if he could not do it.

I rolled in his arms and looked out of the window at the snow piling up on the ledge. Hugo's arms still encircled me. I was very content to be right there, snuggled in his arms, watching the snow fall out through the venetian blinds. I'd put on a sweatshirt when I arrived home. Hugo put his hands up under the shirt and fondled me. It wasn't a sexual thing at all. It was a caring caress. He just held me for a few seconds and we swayed back and forth gently. I knew that this man would do anything in the world for me. I'd probably do the same."

8

CHAPTER

CONFLICT

"January 2, 1938

I decided that I was going to make a New Year's resolution. I was troubled by all of the talk going around about the National Socialists, the Communists, the Social Democrats, oppression of Germany and all of the other factional conversation that seemed to be springing up everywhere we went. The crusher had been at our tree trimming party on December 24. We had invited four couples to join us for refreshments and to trim the tree. Every one of the girls would bring a snack tray of some kind and Hugo and I were to supply the beer. Before he left for the office that morning Hugo had put two cases of Alpen Brau on the back steps to cool. He had pulled a washtub to fill with ice out of the basement. When he came home from the barbershop he stopped by the Saint Louis Ice Company and brought home a five-cent block.

Everyone had arrived and was in good spirits. Lucian and Willie Schmidt arrived first. Willie had made a platter of Christmas cookies and I had put together little finger sandwiches. Hans Klauber and his bride of four months, Rosie got there last. The girls migrated into the kitchen while the guys wound up in the living room to put the lights on the tree. There was sort of an unstated rule that it was the job of the men to put on the lights and the girls would join in when it was time to put on the ornaments and tinsel.

The tree light project was going slowly. All of a sudden Lucian and Hans began shouting at each other. They'd been in a discussion about recent events in Europe and particularly Austria. Klauber had expressed concern over the actions of Hitler and his National Socialist Worker's Party. Lucian took immediate issue. He was an active advocate of a strong Germany and began shouting at Hans. Hugo had tried to intervene and calm him down when Lucian told Hugo to shut up, that he didn't know anything about what was going on in Germany. Hugo really got mad when Lucian called Hugo a pussy foot for not standing up for his heritage. The thing really degenerated after that.

"Heritage? Listen asshole, whose heritage are you challenging? I've got more German blood in my little finger than you have in your whole body."

Everyone knew that was not true, but Hugo was really offended. He got red in the face and lost his temper. It was one of the few times I have ever seen him fighting mad. By this time all of us girls had joined them to see what the ruckus was all about. Hugo was almost ready to throw a punch.

"Who are you calling an asshole? Not in this house. You can take yourself and that stupid bitch you call a wife and get the Hell out of here. Go on! Get out!" Hugo gestured for the door.

"You don't call my wife a 'bitch'," said Lucian. This time he headed for Hugo. Hugo stood his ground. Hans grabbed Lucian and wrestled him to the floor.

Willie had grabbed their coats from the bedroom and was helping get Lucian out the door.

"Fucking Nazi," said Hans as Lucian and Willie headed down the steps.

We all stared at each other when the door closed behind them. I'm sure that our faces registered the shock of what had happened. We'd all been such good friends for so long. How could this happen?

Hans and Rosie said they'd better be leaving. Truth was, the evening had been ruined for all of us. Hugo went into the bathroom and washed his face with a cold washrag. He too, had been shocked by the events.

Everyone left by nine o'clock. We looked at the untouched plates of food and the undecorated tree. It looked so naked with its half-strung strands of lights. The flat seemed empty. It was. I began to cry. Hugo looked and felt like a heel.

"What's wrong with us?" he said. "Why is this political thing eating away at us?"

"I don't know." I was still sobbing. The tree decorations would have to wait until Christmas day. The food would keep in waxed paper in the icebox. We were both miserable.

The incident before Christmas seemed to harden Hugo. Not that he became unreasonable, but it seemed to give him some direction. He talked more freely now about Germany, the National Socialist Worker's Party. He seemed to identify more readily with the Nazis and what they were trying to accomplish. For the first time I heard him say that he thought Hitler was doing the right thing for Germany. In a funny way I thought he might just admire Lucian a little for his strong views.

I thought Hugo would try to make amends with Lucian and Willie. After all, we'd all had a few beers. They were our oldest friends. It could easily be explained away. We all say things we don't mean when we drink too much. But he didn't. Instead he told me several times over Christmas week that Lucian owed the two of us a big apology, and that until he apologized for making such a big scene in our house he was out of our lives.

"Pussy mouthed shit," is what Hugo calls Lucian. That is the label that he has affixed to him. It should be obvious why I am making a New Year's resolution not to get into political discussions with our friends.

June 17, 1938

Every day now the newspapers have some article on the rearming of Germany. Everyone knows it is in defiance of the Treaty of Versailles, but nobody seems to want to do anything about it.

Hitler and the New Germany had begun to rearm and forge a strong military. The Treaty forbids Germany from having more than 100,000 in the military and required it to demilitarize the total left bank of the Rhine. Germany had repudiated the treaty under a claim that it was signed under duress and had begun to conscript large numbers of young Germans into the Army. The formation of the German-Fascist Axis with Italy only seemed to confirm that trouble was ahead in Europe. Germany had even gotten involved in the Spanish Civil war on behalf of the Royalist Forces of General Francisco Franco. There was even talk of annexing Austria.

I had to admit that the events were troubling. Germany had announced that it would annex Sudetenland, a part of Czechoslovakia. More important to me was the open support that Hugo was now voicing for the Nazis. He seemed supportive of almost everything that Germany did under Hitler. He studied the National Socialist's "New Order" and its avowed goals of eliminating unemployment. I remember one night in early May he was reading an article in the *Star Times*. Hugo looked up at me and said, "The United States could take a few lessons from the Germans. They are bringing Germany out of the Depression a lot faster than Roosevelt and his New Deal."

Hugo never used to talk like that. Before that I only heard praise of the United States from him. He was the original skeptic about events in Germany. A year earlier he couldn't have cared less about what was happening over there. Now he seemed to hang on every word. He reads accounts of what was happening on a daily basis. Before he had only been an observer to the debates down at the shop. Now he was a participant, taking sides and advocating positions–mostly pro-German.

October 12, 1938

The year is wearing on. Hugo and I are talking politics more and more. It seemed as if we have nothing else to talk about. He gets so riled up. I almost have to hold him back when he gets started on the stupidity of Britain and its policies toward Germany. I wonder how he gets anything done at the shop if he gets so embroiled in the arguments.

At the same time, he has gotten more morose. He even makes me morose. He thinks a lot about us not having any children. He won't talk about it, but I think it bothers him. He asks a lot of questions now about us, our future, where we are going to be twenty years from now. He ruminates about money, or rather the lack of it. We are making ends meet, but that is about all. He knows I would love to buy a house, and he almost apologizes because we can't afford it. He even went down to the savings and loan on Grand avenue and talked to them about what it would take to buy a house. When they said he would have to have 20% down to get a loan it only made him more morose.

"We'll never get it," he said.

At night we have long conversations about the future; what will it will be like when we're old; what kind of a world it will be? I don't mind these imponderable questions. In fact, speculating on what life will be like is sort of fun. I enjoy talking about us and where we want to be years from now; but sometime Hugo goes into deep depression. He has even put his head in my lap and wept because he cannot guarantee us the future we both want. The shop just will not produce the kind of money we need. If I really did get pregnant, we both worry about how we will pay the bills without my salary.

October 30, 1938

Last night we were involved in an automobile accident. The Whippet was badly damaged. We had been to a Halloween party at Schober's Wine Restaurant out on Lindbergh. We had ridden with our friends, Hans and Rosie Klauber. The Whippet had been left at their apartment, and we went in their car. Just after midnight we returned to their apartment and picked up the car. Hugo and I had both had a little to drink, but neither of us was drunk. I can't say that for the guy in the Nash who plowed into the side of us. He didn't see the red light and came right out into the intersection without even putting his foot on the brake. The Nash hit us so hard we were actually tipped onto two wheels. Our car went out of control and smashed into a fire hydrant. Both the side and the front of the Whippet were badly damaged. In Fact, Hugo thinks it could be a total loss. He says the frame is bent and the car can never be aligned again. They towed it to an auto wrecking yard on Gravois. An adjuster from the insurance company is going to come out tomorrow after they look at it. About the last thing we can afford right now is a new car.

November 12, 1938

The Nash owner's insurance company denied our claim flat. They said that Hugo had the last chance to avoid the accident even though the guy ran a stop sign and was cited for drunken driving. Can you believe that? I didn't even see him until he hit us! Neither did Hugo. How could Hugo have avoided the collision if he didn't even see him? It was ludicrous. Hugo was enraged. I thought was going to bust a gut. I have never seen him so mad as when he got the letter from the adjuster for the insurance company. He threatened to go down to their office and crack his skull. I pointed out to him that the letter had come from Kansas City.

"This wouldn't happen in Germany!" he bellowed. "If we had a system of laws that treated the little man fairly no damn insurance company would treat us like that."

I told him that I really didn't think that kind of talk did any good.

"Why the Hell not?" he blurted. Hugo was so out of control that his face had turned beet red. He was sweating profusely. I never saw him this way before.

"The big insurance companies just run this country. They just screw over anyone they want, when they want! Hitler wouldn't let that happen."

I tried to reason with him. "Don't we have our own collision insurance?"

"Of course, we do. Why the Hell should we have to pay the hundred-dollar deductible? Why should we endure the claim and foul up our record? It's not fair. That asshole ran the light and wrecked our car. Why should we have to pay to invoke our coverage? It'll just result in our premiums going higher. Why doesn't his cover it. Those bastards!"

I was really worried about Hugo. I actually worried that he would have a stroke. The accident and the denial of the claim ate on him. Like acid it would gnaw at him until he could not think about anything else. It was all he could think or talk about for the next two weeks.

The truth of the matter was that we didn't even have the one hundred dollars so that we could make the claim with our own insurance company. More than once I suspected that Hugo was too proud or too embarrassed to admit that we could not even afford the deductible.

November 22, 1938

I finally convinced Hugo to make a claim on our insurance. It became perfectly clear that the other insurance company was not going to pay the claim. I had talked to one of the lawyers at the plant and he said that the only way to make them pay was with a lawsuit. That would take months. We had to have an automobile. I used the Christmas money that I had been saving for the deductible.

The adjuster for our insurer went over to the auto salvage yard to look at the remains of the Whippet. It was, as feared, badly damaged, but repairable. Our policy would pay nine hundred dollars, the depreciated value of the Whippet. Hugo was despondent. He swore all night and didn't sleep a wink."

It was after midnight. Connie got up from the big overstuffed chair from which she had been reading aloud.

"Y'know, your parents were really concerned about what was going on in the world. Much more so than you and I."

Reading about the times in the notebooks sort of detached me from them. It is as if I was reading about two fictional characters. It was hard to picture them as my mother and father. Connie was right, they seemed so involved with what was happening - almost paranoid. I was also troubled about the change that had come over them even just in the time covered by the notebooks.

"Connie, we have the advantage of hindsight. We sit here in the comfort of our living room, and review entries in a diary knowing what is going to happen. History is laid out for us in a panorama. My mother did not know what was going to happen when she wrote this stuff. She did not have clairvoyance, yet she seemed strangely perceptive."

"What about your father? He seems like he is going over the edge. He seems marginal. His interest in the Nazis is sort of scary. It's a little strange."

"In all my years he never mentioned Hitler, the Nazis or any of this stuff. It's as if I am reading about a total stranger. God, I wish he had talked about it."

"Can you imagine those times? They had to be difficult. Your dad certainly had become a sympathizer if not a full-fledged Nazi?

"I think that's a little strong, Connie. I mean, Dad a Nazi? It just doesn't make any sense. I don't even know how he voted in presidential elections, let alone his political leanings in the thirties."

"But you have to concede ..."

"Yes, it looks like he was at least a sympathizer. I've heard there were lots of them in South Saint Louis in those days."

Connie picked up the glasses from the table by the big chair. "I'm going to bed."

"I'm right behind you." I had to lock the doors and let the dog out to do his business.

I climbed into bed. I couldn't sleep. I stared at the ceiling for over an hour. How could my father be so strong a sympathizer with the National Socialist Worker's Party? Couldn't he see Hitler and his cronies for what they were? I had to remind myself that I had the advantage of hindsight. Maybe I was rationalizing.

There is no sympathy in my generation for Hitler and his ideals. History has branded him a "monster"; but back then? Was it the same? Was it possible to see? Was Dad duped? Couldn't he see the forest for the trees?

Connie sensed that I was not falling asleep. She had quickly slipped into that quiet murmur that I call a snore. I was left alone with my thoughts. Sleep would not come easily this night.

The green eye of the Sony told me that it was after two.

"Hey big fella." It was Connie. "Can't sleep, huh?"

"I know. I know."

"Look, that is pretty interesting reading. For the only son of a guy who you saw as a stanch Lutheran, conservative to the core and absolutely non-political, it's probably a shock. It has to be a little disturbing. I don't know how I would feel if I was reading the same thing about my parents."

"Connie, I have a bad feeling. I think that there's something in the diaries that is very bad. Otherwise why would Mildred be so upset about them?"

"What do you mean?"

"Connie, everything we have read about my parents is exactly the opposite of how I perceived them. I'm afraid of what is in those diaries. If my parent's life on the outside was exemplary, I'm afraid to find out what is on the inside. It might be inherently evil."

"There's only one was to find out, you know."

"I know. Read them all. But what if I don't want to read them all? What if I want to throw them in the trash? I happen to cherish the memories I have of my parents. I loved them the way I remembered them. What if those memories are destroyed? I have this bad feeling that reading the diaries is going to destroy my feelings for my parents. Maybe they are not the people that I thought they were."

Connie sat up in bed and propped herself on one arm. The moonlight was pouring in through the Venetian blinds and made little stripes across the bed. I could see her clearly above me. Even at fifty she was a beautiful woman. She slept in the nude and her large breasts were inches from my face. She was my lover and my friend. My confident. She was a rock, and she knew me well.

"Listen dip shit," she said. "You cannot change life. Your parents were what they were. They had all of the problems - money and all - that we had when we were first married. Look at it this way; you have the unique opportunity to look back through the diaries and see the times through their eyes. That's pretty unusual. Not many people get that chance. Not all of us have the opportunity to look into the window of their parent's lives through a set of diaries like your mother wrote. She was an amazing woman, and the fact that she took the time to record her thoughts and the events of the day is really unique. The facts are the facts, and you can't change them. You have to come to grips with them. You might choose to live your life remembering them as you did. But if your recollection is not an accurate picture, you have to be prepared to accept the truth."

"What is the truth? What my mother wrote? I mean, c'mon, Connie, I lived in that house for nineteen years. I should know. My parents never discussed politics let alone supported Nazi causes. My dad even took time off work to go vote on Election Day. He was an exemplary citizen. Now I find out I knew nothing!"

"You should know, but it's obvious that you did not know."

Connie laid back down and looked up at the ceiling resting her hands behind her head. God she was beautiful!

"Donald, the truth is that the diaries paint a picture of your parents that is different from your recollection. Did you ever think that it may be your recollection that is flawed? Remember you were not even born when this stuff was written."

I did not like what I was hearing or what I was feeling. Connie was right. Mom wrote these diaries before I was born. Maybe things changed. Maybe when I was born they went in a different direction. Maybe their lives changed after I was born. Let's face it. Children often cause parents to change.

It was three weeks before I returned to the diaries. Connie had gone to her mother's in Chicago for the week-end and I was left alone, at home, with the dog. I actually liked the break. I'm sure she did, too. The house was quiet.

On Saturday night I picked up the volume we were reading and opened it to the page that I had folded down when we had stopped three weeks ago. We were still in the volume marked "1938."

November 29, 1938

Hugo came home from a meeting of the Black Forest Society with a copy of *Mein Kampf*. I hated even the sight of it in our flat. I told Hugo that I thought that it had no place in our lives. "What are you doing with that thing?" I said. "It is just the memoirs of a man in jail. You'd do better to read the United States Constitution."

Hugo looked at me with a blank stare. "What's wrong with you?" he retorted, scowling at me. "Why can't you read important works with an open mind? This book is the philosophy of a whole nation - a nation from whence your roots sprang. Why can't you read it like I do, and try to understand the struggle that is going on in Europe?"

"All I see is a nation caught up in itself. A nation that seems to use its subjugation as an excuse for aggression. Yes, Hugo, I am German, but I am not proud of what's happening. Hitler is doing things that I do not approve of. I am an American. So, it seems, were you, until you got caught up in this wave of emotionalism toward Germany."

Hugo slammed the book on the table. "You are narrow minded, Frieda. You don't have the will to read and decipher the truth. I don't know if this book represents truth or not, but I'm going to read it!"

He stomped out of the room.

December 28, 1938

By the end of December, the Army Ordinance Plant had become a reality. Additional acreage had been acquired and plans were made for the construction of several new buildings on a site off Goodfellow Boulevard in North Saint Louis. An appropriation by Congress was all that was needed to make the plans, and my raise, a reality. Hollenbeck said it would be a sure thing.

9
CHAPTER
THE COMMITTEE

"January 29, 1939

I'm not quite sure how the invitation to join the "Committee" came to Hugo. All I know is that one night late in January he came home and sat with the evening paper at the kitchen table reading intently while I washed up the supper dishes. It was as if he wanted to talk, but used the paper to conveniently distract himself, so he didn't have to.

He was intently studying the front page, but I suspected he wasn't reading it. He would look up from time to time. I was at the sink washing dishes. Suddenly he was behind me and his hands enfolded my waist.

"Guess what?" he whispered into my ear.

"What yourself?"

"I got a rather exclusive invitation."

"What kind of invitation?"

"To join the Steering Committee of the Black Forest Society."

I turned to him. He was grinning from ear to ear. "Hugo that's wonderful. Do you want to accept?"

"Want to? I'd love to accept. Frieda this is really big. It's a great opportunity. Of course, I'm going to accept."

Hugo was ecstatic over the invitation. He had mentioned the Committee several times. By now everyone knew it was the brains of the Society. Most of the major issues of the Black Forest Society were decided in The Committee. Everyone also knew that its members were hard-core Nazi sympathizers.

I hugged him around the neck. Hugo clearly wanted it. I wanted him to have it. For myself, I wasn't so sure.

"Hugo, what about your politics? Do you think you have the same level of commitment? I mean, let's face it. Those guys are pretty dyed-in-the-wool Nazis."

"Frieda, Frieda." He stroked the hair out of my face and kissed me on the forehead. "You worry too much about me and my politics."

"I worry about you generally."

He held me away and looked into my eyes. "What's that supposed to mean?"

"Hugo, the world is coming apart at the seams. Europe is a tinderbox. All it's going to take is one spark and the whole thing is going to go up. We're safe here. Europe is a long, long way away. We don't have to be involved. We can live our lives and not get involved in that mess. This is the middle of America. We are buffered - protected. We don't have to get into the fight if we don't want to."

He looked at me blankly. "And when it's over?"

I mocked his prior question: "What's that supposed to mean?"

"When it's over where will we be?"

"Safe?"

"I doubt it."

Sometimes Hugo scares me. I did not know what he was talking about. It must have shone on my face.

"When all of the dust settles there will be a New World Order. The old ways will not suffice. The strong will survive and the weak will be subjugated. Hitler knows that. The Germans know that. They are making ready. I want to be a part of that future. I want to be ready for the New Order."

"And you think that being a member of the Committee will help you?"

"Frieda, don't you see? The Committee is the pipeline. It's the direct connection into the New Order. It's the extension of the new and risen Germany."

"Hugo, sometimes you scare me."

Hugo reached around my waist and pulled me to him. "There's no need to be afraid. The family, our relationship, our ultimate children are all consistent with the future. The Party encourages us. It asks us to participate. A family unit is the strongest of its links. You, Frieda, can be a part of it too."

"Hugo, I want to be. I want so much what you want." I was sobbing. I knew it. The tears ran down my cheeks and onto Hugo's shoulders. Why was I afraid? He scared me so.

Hugo's induction into the committee took place on the first of March at a Committee meeting upstairs in a two-story building on South Grand Avenue. The hall was small and adjacent to an apartment occupied by Otto Schmidt, the Secretary. The building was a part of a block that held a Woolworth's, a jewelry store and a Velvet Freeze ice cream store. You entered through a side door and took a flight of stairs to the hall on the second floor. The door was marked "Eagles Hall." The room had a table and eight chairs. A single light was suspended over the table with a shade the directed the light downward onto the table. Large windows faced out on Grand Avenue. During the day the room was very bright. At night the only light was the single shaded bulb suspended over the table.

Hugo told me something that surprised me: He revealed that his sister, Mildred, was on the Committee. She was the only single person who had ever been asked. It explained some things, though. Maybe it was Mildred who was instrumental in extending the invitation to Hugo.

I was not invited to that meeting. Why should I be? I was not the one being inducted. I was not a member of the Committee. I only knew what went on that night from Hugo's accounts. I suspect that he did not tell me everything.

There was to be a meeting with all of the spouses present a few days later. To my surprise I was invited to join him. Hugo told me that all of the spouses would be there. The Committee, it seems, wants all of the families of its members to be supportive of their efforts. The meeting would be on Friday at seven o'clock. Then we would all have dinner. I went out of a sense of duty. I had promised Hugo that I would support him. I was not without apprehension.

The room was as Hugo had described it - a bare room with a long table and eight chairs. Several couples had already arrived and were chatting quietly when we got there. I was introduced to each member of the Committee by Otto Schmitt's wife. Hugo was introduced to the wives of the Committee members by Otto Schmitt. I got the impression Hugo had already met some of them before. Mildred was there. She wasn't with anyone. There were no absentees. When all seven couples and Mildred had arrived, we were invited to sit. Each committee member held a chair for his wife and the women were given the chairs at the table. Each man stood behind his spouse. Mildred remained standing. Eric Muller, the Chairman, stood at one end and Otto Schmidt and his wife were at the other. They reminded me of bookends. Both were big men with broad shoulders and doughy faces. I guessed them about thirty-five or forty. Their wives were chunky and dressed in unstylish clothing. It was then that I noticed that both Muller and Schmidt had donned black patent belts with shoulder straps and black arm bands. Eric Muller spoke first.

"Each of you is here because your spouse has chosen to become a part of the Struggle. Each of you has a vested interest in the success of our fight. You are the mothers of our children both born and unborn. We are committed to you, the sanctity of your purity, and the produce of your loins."

I leaned back against Hugo to be sure he was still behind me. I found Muller's words disquieting. I pushed the back of my head into Hugo's stomach. He was right behind my chair.

Schmidt continued: "As we have nothing short of our absolute commitment to you, so too, must we have your absolute commitment

113

to us. Each of us has taken a solemn oath. That oath is to the Fatherland - to Germany and its new leaders. We are the outriggers of the New Reich. We are the emissaries of the New Germany. It is our sworn duty to support the Fuhrer even though we are thousands of miles away. You, our wives are a part of us. You have joined in union with us physically. Now you must join us spiritually and philosophically. You must commit yourselves to the Cause."

The room was silent.

Muller spoke. "Ladies."

With that every lady at the table got up and moved to leave the room. Every lady, that is, except me. I started to get up. Hugo kept his hands on my shoulders. His grip was firm, and he simply prevented me from rising with the rest. I got the idea - The others had already been brought into the circle. I was to stay.

Eric Muller moved around the table and took the seat across the table opposite me. His big gray eyes were piercing. As he moved to a spot under the single light from the shadows I could see a scar on his cheek. He looked at me for several seconds. Then he said:

"The others have made their commitment. They have embraced the Cause. It is time for you to do so now."

I thought it was a little dramatic. Nevertheless, I was uneasy - bordering on scared.

"Look, I just..."

He raised his hand. I stopped.

"There is nothing in between. There is no Gray. You either commit to the Cause or you don't. If you do, we accept your undivided loyalty. We treat your word as a solemn bond. You become one of us - united in our bond to the Fatherland. If you do not - you may go with no recriminations."

I thought Hugo was still behind me. I was sure I could hear him breathing. The only other sound was a streetcar going by on the street below scratching its electric boom on the wires above. All of the others had stepped back into the shadows behind the range of the solitary light. It was just Muller and me. Hugo was only a witness.

I moved my hand from my side and dropped it down to feel behind me. I had to know Hugo was there. I brushed his pant leg just above the calf. Then, Hugo did something that startled me - he stepped back - he pulled away! I was alone. Just me and those steel grey eyes of Eric Muller. He had not taken his eyes off of me. He never blinked.

I was so scared. What was I doing? What was I being asked to commit to? I was just Hugo Jurgens' wife. I didn't want to get involved in the Nazi Party. I just wanted to go home. I started to get up. "Hugo…?" No. It wasn't Hugo. Big doughy hands pushed me down from the shoulders. I pulled my hand back. It wasn't Hugo. Schmidt was behind me, his hands on my shoulders, holding me in my seat.

His hands moved from my shoulders to the base of my neck. Muller never took his eyes off me. There was a bead of sweat on my back. It ran down under my dress. I know I was screaming, but I did not hear a sound. Schmidt's massive hands moved inward from my shoulders. My eyes were as big as saucers. My mouth went dry and contorted into a silent scream. The big hands closed gently around my neck. I couldn't move. I couldn't talk. Where was Hugo? Schmidt didn't squeeze my neck. Rather, his fingers expertly found my Carotid artery, my windpipe, my spine all in quick and efficient succession. It was as if he could touch, or tear, any part of me at will. His hands were huge, his movements quick, sure, solid and menacing. He instilled in me absolute terror.

Schmidt's calloused hands moved up my neck to the side of my head. He never applied pressure, but just moved my head slightly the way a barber does when he wants to reposition it. The message was clear - crystal clear - he could snap it any time he felt like it.

I knew I was sobbing. I could feel tears dripping from my cheeks onto my blouse. Muller handed me a handkerchief.

"Your commitment, Frieda. Do we have it?" Muller's voice was cold, unwavering.

I couldn't answer. The room was silent.

"Frieda?"

There was a long silence.

"Yes." The word stuck in my throat.

"Clearly Frieda, so that we all can hear you. We are all here. We are all beneficiaries of the bond that we now create. We must all hear your commitment.

"Yes. You have my commitment."

The room burst into applause. They had been there all along. I only wondered if they had endured the same terror when they "committed"? Hugo hugged me from behind as if he had been there all the time.

Had he?

Each woman returned to her place at the table. The men of the Committee stepped in behind them. Schmidt and Muller resumed their places at the ends of the table.

"We are now one, said Eric Muller.

He raised his hand. "Seig Heil!"

"Seig Heil!" came the unanimous reply from each of the standing members of the Committee.

"Seig Heil!"

"Seig Heil!" I repeated. And for the first time in my life I raised my right hand open-palmed.

When we had adjourned each woman came around the table and hugged me. Each, in her own way expressed her joy at having Hugo and I join them. They reeked of sincerity. My knees were weak. I just wanted to leave.

We went out and down the street to Lemmon's Restaurant - just friends out on the town on a Friday night - socializing, having a good time after a hard week. We were friends, united in our friendship. We were a bund. I couldn't comprehend what it all meant. I was in a daze. We were Nazis.

I remember that the talk at dinner was of Germany's annexation of Austria. It was the right thing to do, they all agreed. Austria was a natural part of Germany, an extension of its being. It had a historical significance - there was precedent. The language of Austria was German. The customs were German. The government was a remnant of the Hapsburgs. The heritage was German. Yes sir, it was the right thing to do. Everyone concurred.

"God damn you, Hugo!" I was screaming. The mantle clock was chiming midnight. We didn't have a mantle, but we had a mantle clock. It sat on the big Zenith console radio in the living room of the flat.

"Damn you, Hugo Jurgens." I was pounding on his chest. He held me at the waist. I was furious. Hugo was unaffected.

"Frieda. What are you talking about?

"What was that all about, Hugo? I felt like that big ape was raping me!"

"Take it easy, Frieda. I told you it would take a commitment. We had to be sure."

"Sure? Sure, of what? That you were going to terrorize me into peeing in my pants? You didn't need to let him do that. You consigned me to him. I felt like you turned me over to him even if it was just for a few minutes."

"Frieda, I did no such thing. I was there all of the time - right behind you."

"Hugo, all you have to do is ask. I'll follow you anywhere; but don't send that big gorilla to threaten me."

Hugo looked down at me and brushed away a lock of hair that had fallen across my face. It was a tender gesture. I was trembling. I had been crying I was so mad. I squeezed him. He knew how to get to me. I couldn't be mad at him. I would follow this man anywhere. Still, the events at the Committee meeting had unnerved me.

"Frieda, what do you say we talk? Just like we used to do when we first met. Remember? How about a beer on the porch?" He smiled that Hugoesque smile; he knew I could not resist.

"There's some Falstaff in the fridge."

"I'll get us one. You slip into a robe."

Hugo knew I hated to sit around the house in a dress. I had an old chenille robe that was like an old friend. I went to the bedroom and put it on. Hugo met me on the porch. He had taken off his white shirt and tie. He wore an undershirt and slacks.

"Frieda," he said as he handed me a bottle of Falstaff beer. "I feel good about myself. I believe in something."

"What do you mean, Hugo?" I really did not know what he was driving at.

"For years I have just been a little guy trying to make a buck and make ends meet. I've got a great wife, no kids, a car and a flat full of furniture. I've got nothing else."

"Hugo, I think that is a little simplistic."

"No, it isn't. What do I stand for? Where do I fall when they take the count?"

"What are you talking about, Hugo?"

Hugo was not acting despondent. He was, in fact, very rational. He had only two beers all night. He had clearly been contemplating the question.

"I'm talking about casting my lot with something that will make a difference. I'm talking about looking into the crystal ball of the future and seeing where it is all going."

"Hugo, if you mean the Black forest Society and the Nazi party, we've had this conversation."

"That's only part of it, Frieda. Don't you see? We are all going to have to choose – and soon. The world is going to force us all to make a choice."

"Between what Hugo, what are we going to have to choose between?"

"Between the continued drift of a world whose ideals, morals, economics, and governments are all slipping. You know it and so do I. They are eroding, slowly, surely. Anarchy and chaos will soon follow."

"Hugo, I think you are over dramatizing."

"Am I? Frieda, read *Mein Kampf*, you'll be hard pressed to disagree.

I got up and paced back and forth. Hugo got me upset when he talked like that.

"Hugo, listen to me. You are mesmerized by the events in Europe. You spend your day reading accounts of what is going on in Germany. You are infatuated with the Third Reich.

The truth is, Hugo, that even if Hitler and his National Socialist Worker's Party are right, they are not going to affect you and me. Look at us. We are in the middle of America. We are in Saint Louis, Missouri, U.S.A. What goes on over there cannot reach us. We are insulated. We don't have to get into it. We have the option to live our lives without getting involved in that mess. Europe may be in turmoil - it usually is, but we don't have to get involved. We have the luxury of staying out of the fray. It's eight thousand miles away."

"You still don't understand, do you, Frieda?"

"I guess I don't."

"Frieda, I *want* to get involved. I want to stand for something. All I ask is your support. I want to help the country of my ancestors, but more important I believe in the New Order. I believe Germany will change the world. I believe that the German Ideal is right. I believe the discipline of the German Ideal is the only way to stop the erosion. Without commitment we are going to lose our world, our society, ourselves for future generations."

I could only look at Hugo with dismay. He was so committed, so intense - so fanatical. He was so taken with his ideologies that I felt he could not see the forest for the trees.

But when it all came down to the end of the day - I loved him. I would go to the ends of the earth for him. If he had to meet with a group of toy Nazis a couple of times a month, I'd support that too. After all, our neighbor puts on a little red fez and goes to a Shriner's meeting where they have this silly ritual and chant. What's the difference? I could put up with Hugo and his Nazi friends.

"Hugo, you tell that big galoot, Schmidt, to keep his hands off me and I'll follow you anywhere."

Hugo smiled. He knew I would. He knew he really didn't need to win me over. Like a faithful puppy, I would follow.

10

CHAPTER

A VISIT FROM HERR BLOCH

"August 20, 1939

It's been quite a summer so far. The social and political activities of the Society have increased. We see Black Forest Society members at least once a week. Sometimes there are social events, even an occasional cultural event. In June they staged a Wagner concert under the big trees at the Black Forest Inn. I hated it. Wagner is really boring. There were two soloists who sang songs from Wagner operas. Everyone had drunk some beer and by the end of the third song you could hear a few snores. I had been working long hours at the Army Ammunition Plant and I made it to the fourth aria. I started dozing. Hugo punched me. Despite his feigned attentiveness I could tell he was not so enthused about Wagner either.

Hugo attended the Committee meetings once a week. Mostly they were held at the hall on Grand by Schmidt's apartment. In July they were held in the Rathskeller room of the Bevo Mill. After the July meeting all of the wives joined the Committee members for a dinner in the upstairs hall. It was very enjoyable. I even got along with Eric Muller and Schmidt. I still don't like Schmidt, but we are civil to each other. At nine o'clock a little band with a singer that sounded just like Vera Lynn began to play and we danced until almost midnight."

September 26, 1939

I can't really believe what happened last night. It started with the monthly meeting of the Committee the second week in September. Hugo came home and said that Eric Muller and his wife, Loretta, wanted us to join them for dinner some time later in the month. Hugo accepted without even talking to me. I wasn't really upset, only I wish he would just talk to me before he starts making plans. The Mullers had suggested we do it last night. Eric said that he had heard of a new bar-b-que restaurant way out on Lindbergh. The weather was still warm and eating bar-b-que out under the stars would be just the thing. It would be a great Saturday night. Muller said he would pick Hugo and I up in his car about seven thirty after Hugo got home from the shop.

On Wednesday evening Eric Muller called and said that he had an additional guest who was in town and would like to join us. Muller was in the machine shop business and always seemed to have a customer or a supplier in town that he had to entertain. He said that the man was single, and would I mind if he joined us for bar-b-que on Saturday. I didn't mind. Neither did Hugo.

Muller pulled up right at seven thirty. Hugo had gotten home with ample time to take a bath. The weather was warm, but without humidity. The sky had cleared from a rain earlier in the day. I was looking forward to a beautiful evening. I was anxious to get to know Eric and Loretta Muller better.

As I dashed down the front steps, I was ahead of Hugo who had stopped to lock the door of the flat. Eric Muller got out of the car and opened the back door. His guest stepped out. He was a tall man. I stopped short. I knew that I had met him before. I couldn't place where.

"Frieda, I'd like to present Heinrich Bloch."

I now recognized him. Bloch was the speaker from the German Consulate in Chicago we had heard at the Carondelet YMCA several years ago. He was the lecherous creep with the sweaty palms and the long handshakes that Hugo had mistrusted from the start.

"I believe we have met," Bloch said to Muller. He turned to me. "Hello, Frieda. It is good to see you again. You look lovely in that print dress."

I remembered Bloch, the Flatterer.

Hugo had come to the car. He recognized Bloch instantly; although I am not sure he recalled his name. I could see him tense the minute he stepped off the final step.

"Hugo, this is Heinrich Bloch," said Muller.

"I've met Mister Bloch," said Hugo.

"You have?" Muller was incredulous.

"Yes. It's been some time ago."

"Herr Bloch is visiting from Washington, DC," said Muller, not picking up on Hugo's invitation to ask where.

"Washington? Sounds like you have gotten a promotion since we last met," said Hugo.

"Not really. I'm just a servant of the Fatherland," said Bloch. "I go where they ask me to go."

"A career bureaucrat, eh?" injected Hugo. He just couldn't resist the jab. He did not like Bloch at all. It showed.

"You might say that," said Bloch. "What do you say we go?" He held the car's door open and gestured for Hugo and me to get in. We all got into Muller's big DeSoto. Muller and Loretta were in the front. Bloch, Hugo and I were in the back. I was in the middle.

I found Bloch's last remark very interesting. He suggested that we go. Muller, without hesitation held the doors and went to his position behind the wheel. It was Muller's car, Muller's event, but Bloch sure seemed to be in charge.

Eckert's Orchard is a beautiful place out on Lindbergh. Big Black Oaks spread their branches over a large graveled area where wooden tables and benches had been scattered. A German band played selections from *Der Fledermaus*. As the evening wore on, they moved into lively polkas. We sat on a whitewashed bench on the edge of the gravel pad near the back of the little park-like restaurant and drank beer from steins. The big moon had risen above the evergreens in the east and was casting a pale glow on the Bavarian styled stucco buildings that housed the main part of the restaurant. The bar-b-q was as good as it had been billed. Hugo had a full side of ribs and I had a smoked pork cutlet with applesauce. Several times during the evening I had to brush Bloch's hand off my leg. He was unabashed in his attempts to put his hands on me. One time he got up to go to the rest room and put his hand on my shoulder.

"Would you like another beer?" he asked as his hand slid off the front of my shoulder. I honestly thought he was going to put it on one of my breasts. Hugo did not see Bloch's move, but I did. He was repulsive.

"No, thank you," said Loretta.

Bloch looked at her funny. He wasn't even talking to her.

By ten o'clock the little band had switched to dance music exclusively. Eric and Loretta got up to dance. Now that I look back on the evening, I see that their dance was pre-arranged. Bloch moved across the table from Hugo and me. He clearly wanted to talk to us alone.

"I suppose you wonder why I am here this evening?"

It had occurred to both Hugo and I that his presence was not an accident.

"We didn't think it was a coincidence," said Hugo.

"I am here on a mission for the Fatherland," said Bloch. "It is a mission of ultra-secrecy and confidentiality." He looked to either side to be sure that no one was within earshot. Satisfied he continued. "Not even Eric and Loretta Muller know of what we are about to speak."

"What if the music stops and they come over?" I asked. It seemed a simple enough question.

"The musicians are on their third set of the evening. Their sets last for forty minutes. Eric has been instructed to continue dancing until I put my hand to the top of my head. He will then rejoin us. We have enough time."

"Time for what?"

"Mister and Mrs. Jurgens, you are reported to me to be very reliable people. People of conscience and conviction."

Hugo looked at me quizzically. Bloch continued: "I am here on a mission for the Reich. I seek your help. I will ask for it in the most straightforward and businesslike way I know how. Your decision is not for me. You should not to consider your feelings for me as a person. It is unimportant whether you like me or not." Bloch paused. It was clear he knew that neither Hugo nor I cared very much for him. "Rather, I am an emissary for the Fatherland - Germany. The country of your heritage asks you for your help."

"What kind of help?"

"You possess information that is important to Germany. Information that is invaluable, that can mean life and death to those who are committed to the New Order."

Bloch paused again to let this sink in. He talked cautiously, deliberately. He was choosing his words carefully.

"Information? We don't have any information," said Hugo.

"Perhaps I should be more succinct. Frieda possesses information or at least she has access to it. You, Hugo, might have some ancillary or back up information, but Frieda is the one who has the information we seek."

"What the Hell are you talking about?" I was on my feet.

"Please sit down, Frieda." Bloch was cool. He hardly raised his voice above a whisper. I was agitated.

"Do not do that again. If you do, I will have to terminate this conversation," said Bloch.

"Then maybe you'd better terminate it." It was Hugo, and he was getting red.

"Do not be upset. Hear me out before you make a judgment. Hear all that I have to say. Then you may judge."

"What do you want?" I said. My voice was sharp. I'm sure he caught the edge.

"What I want is the shipping information on arms shipments from the Army Ammunition Plant."

I looked at Hugo. The shipping information! Why would Bloch want the shipping information? What good would it do Germany?

"How do you know I even have access to it?"

"I know that you have access to the reports. You set up the program. You supervise it. Each week the shipments go out there is an invoice and a bill of lading generated. All I want is the information contained on those documents."

"And what information is that?"

"A description of the goods, the quantity, and the destination. It's all very simple."

"Why would I ..."

"Ah, my friends hear me out." Bloch lifted his hands like a traffic policeman. "I am willing to pay you fifty dollars for each report. I believe that there is at least one production report, sometimes two, each week. Four or more reports a month. That amounts to over two hundred dollars each month."

"No way," said Hugo. "We are not interested."

"Do not be hasty. Think it over. You can let me know in a week or so."

"Forget it. We aren't going to play."

Bloch would not be deterred. "I'll call you, say, in a week or so? Think it over. You can give me your answer then. If you say no, I'll understand. But if you say, yes, we'll begin the payments on the first delivery. It will be very easy money. Think about it."

Bloch put his hand on his head and Eric and Loretta broke from the dance floor and rejoined us at the table.

"So, what a lovely evening," said Bloch. "Frieda, would you honor me with a dance?"

September 30, 1939

Hugo and I had talked all around the subject for four days. It was difficult to confront. Hugo saw it in black and white.

"Frieda, you are talking about a crime. You know that there is a security issue involving the work you do. You even said so yourself. If Hollenbeck knew what we were talking about he would fire you even if you didn't turn over a single report."

"I know, Hugo, but fifty dollars just for a little information? This stuff can't be Top Secret. Anyone in the shipping department could get it. Any clerk who types up the invoices or the bills of lading could get to it."

"Yeah, then why isn't Bloch trying to get it from them?" It was a fair question. I didn't know the answer.

"Hugo, I don't want to do it, but it would be really simple. I do see the invoices and the shipping reports every week. Bloch is right, we have a weekly invoice and an overall bill of lading that summarizes the shipments and their destinations. There is even a carbon copy that gets thrown away. We grind it. It would be a cinch to get it out."

"Frieda, for God's sake! You are talking about spying!"

"No, I'm not, Hugo. Think of it as an easy way to double our income. The two of us together hardly make two hundred dollars a month."

Hugo sulked around for a couple of days. I was sure that I hadn't convinced him that it was really simple to get the information out. There was no risk. In fact, I could probably memorize the information without even pinching the extra carbon. It wasn't difficult. There are only a handful of destinations and about a half dozen products - mainly shells. I could even commit them to memory in just a few seconds and get the information out in my head. It would be the easiest two hundred dollars anyone had ever earned.

By Thursday evening Hugo had to return to the subject. I could see it was eating at him. We had finished dinner. It was after eight o'clock.

"Frieda, do you know what he is asking?" he said out of the blue. There was no doubt what he was asking about.

"I know exactly what he is asking. He wants us to deliver classified information to him. It's as simple as that."

"Frieda, that's a crime. You... we could go ...."

"Listen to me, Hugo." I got up from the kitchen chair and carried a dirty plate to the sink. I know my voice turned stern. I could feel it. I turned from the sink and picked up a towel. When I turned to Hugo he was staring at me. His eyes were wide in anticipation. "I want you to think for a moment about who you are, where you are, and what we are talking about."

Hugo looked at me incredulously.

"Yes?" His voice was tentative.

For the last ten years you and I have worked and loved together. It's been good, but it's been hard. We haven't always known how the bills were going to be paid, but we've made it."

"So?"

"So, Hugo, the next ten years hold more of the same. We work our fingers to the bone, maybe have a buck to go to the Black Forest for a beer on Friday, but not much more."

I began wiping a dish. "Well, I want more than that. I deserve more than that and so do you, Hugo"

"What are you talking about, Frieda?"

"Hugo be realistic. Have you ever met a rich barber? Have you ever met a barber who even drove a Packard?"

"No, and you never will."

"Frieda, all I want is ..."

"Well I want more. Hugo; don't you ever dream of sitting on a porch smoking a rum soaked cheroot in New Orleans or Havana while a dark woman serves you oranges and Bourbon in little wicker-covered glasses? Don't you know that there are places out there named Rio, Paris and Monte Carlo? Haven't you ever wanted to sleep late by an open window with chintz curtains near the sea in the South of France?" I paused. Hugo was looking down. I could almost see those places, feel that breeze.

"Well, I have."

Hugo looked up and stared at me.

"Hugo, I love my city, where I grew up. Saint Louis is a good place to live, I suppose. But there is a big world out there, and I want to see it, too. I do not want the next ten years go by with only rent receipts to show for it."

"And you think that delivering classified information for fifty bucks a pop is the way to do it? Frieda, you are nuts."

"Hugo, I'm not nuts. If they offer fifty bucks, they'll pay a hundred. Do that four times a month and we have more than doubled our combined incomes. We could trade in the old Whippet."

"Frieda we'd be criminals."

I had to look at Hugo with dismay. I couldn't help it. "You really don't understand, do you, Hugo?"

"What's there to understand? You want to trade military information for money. Any schoolboy can understand."

"Hugo, you don't see the big picture. Listen to me. There is going to be a war in Europe. It may spread to other places. You and your neo-Nazi friends can debate the politics of the National Socialist Worker's Party from now 'till Hell freezes over. You can go to your secret meetings, your rallies, wear your armbands and debate the reforms in your barbershop - I don't care. But when it all shakes out - when it is all said and done there is going to be a war."

"I don't know that it will come to that, but ..."

I interrupted him, "And if there is a war there will only be three kinds of people - those who will fight it, those who will be trampled in the fray, and those who are smart enough to profit from it. Do you think that Krupp or Schlinegen, Henry Ford or General Motors gives a rat's ass if there is a war? They'll only emerge bigger, richer, and more powerful. The same holds true for individuals who are smart enough to see war as an opportunity to profit. Hugo, profit comes in many ways.

If war comes, I have no idea how long it will last - a year, five years, ten? Whatever time it takes, I guarantee you that when it is over there will be more, bigger, fatter bank accounts in Switzerland than when it started. Those who see the opportunity will profit. Those who do not see it get trampled.

Hugo, I see the opportunity. I intend to seize it."

Hugo was stunned. He looked at me without speaking. There was a kind of panic in his eyes. Then he said, "You really mean it don't you?"

"Every word, Hugo. I want to play. You can't win if you don't play."

I had been reading Mom's diary in the living room. Connie was still in Chicago. She had called this morning and said she was driving home this afternoon. I thumbed through the faded pages of the old notebook half reading, half dazed. I couldn't believe what I had just read. My mother, the woman that had always been the maternal rock in my life, an anchor of the family, a Christian, and my Father, stoic, hardworking pillar of the community, now an Elder of the Lutheran Church, were considering treason?

Impossible.

It had to be a trick, some kind of a hoax. I engaged in all sorts of rationalizations. My mother was always a practical joker. She had a strange sense of humor. This had to be a trick. She did this as a joke.

None of the rationalizations played. This was no joke. They were about to sell out to a Nazi spy! *They* were about to become Nazi spies! It made me sick.

I had closed the book. It rested on my lap. This notebook was finished, but I felt as if I did not want to touch it. It was dirty; horrible vibrations emanated from it. It was vile. I threw it back into the trunk and headed for the kitchen for a Scotch. It was one-thirty on a Sunday afternoon - a little early for Scotch, but I needed it.

Connie trundled in about four o'clock, shopping bags in hand. I helped her unload the Crate and Barrel Bags and the cartons and bags bearing labels from other Michigan Avenue shops. She did this to me about once a year. She said she needed the space. It was her way of cornering a little bit of sanity for herself. I didn't begrudge it, but I usually jabbed her about paying off the charges sometime in the next six months. It didn't faze her. In fact, she had come to expect it.

The drive from Chicago had been a bore. You can take only so much corn before you realize that there is nothing between St. Louis and Chicago but corn!

We fixed dinner – toasted cheese sandwiches, Caesar salad and a beer. Over dinner I briefed Connie about the approach to Mom and Dad by Bloch and told her that I thought they were going to do it. Connie was intrigued and said that she wanted to read the part about Bloch's approach and Frieda's arguments for getting involved. She couldn't believe that they would do it, either.

November 1, 1939

Hugo continued to maintain his activities in the Black Forest Society. Muller apparently didn't know about the arrangement we had with Bloch - at least he never let on if he did. The talk about Germany continued. Tensions in Europe continued to rise. Germany was rattling sabers now with regularity.

Hugo and I resumed a regular social life. Fridays at the Black Forest or Neuschweinstein Inn; perhaps Saturday dinner at Bevo Mill or Schober's, Sunday in the park; an occasional meeting of the Society, Committee meetings in the little upstairs hall on Grand Avenue. We were careful not to spend too much money. Hugo continued to argue politics and social issues in the shop, and I was diligently caring out the directives of my boss, Avril Hollenbeck."

February 22, 1940

We began to pass information - pretty innocuous stuff at first. I would summarize bills of lading for the shipment of ammunition. We sent only a few destinations, but we were paid one hundred dollars for each envelope of information.

The procedure was established in a meeting with Bloch right after the Holidays: A drop site was chosen so as to be close to our neighborhood so if we were ever watched we would not be frequenting an unusual place. A place we would naturally pass by when heading to and from our flat from the bus stop. Tower Grove Park occupies a large rectangle approximately a mile long and half a mile wide between Kingshighway on the west and Grand Avenue on the east. Hugo's barbershop was on Arsenal facing the park on the south side toward the east end. Arsenal is the street forming the southern border of the park. His shop faced north across the street from the park within a couple of blocks of Grand Avenue.

The park is comprised of gently rolling terrain laced with a road and path system that carries vehicles, walkers and bike riders around tree-shaded courses past picnic pavilions and over cast-iron bridges. There is a shallow man-made lake with fountains and rock sculptures in the middle of the park where kids often float model sailboats. On hot summer days local children wade in the lake.

The pavilions are very unique. Some are oriental; some are reminiscent of India and others are just plain old gabled shelters with picnic tables under them. One of the pavilions has an onion dome and is surrounded by a ring consisting of busts of composers sitting on pedestals about eight feet high. Interspersed between the pedestals are benches facing outward. A concrete sidewalk rings the outside of the circle. Block instructed me to sit on one of the benches opposite the bust of Beethoven and wait for a contact.

Right on time a man showed up and sat down at the other end of the bench. I had never met or seen him before. He pointed out a large crack in the base of one of the pedestals – Beethoven's. The block at the base of the pedestal had separated and there was enough space in the cracked base to slide a full-sized manila envelope completely in.

"Here," he said, "is where you will place your envelope. But first you will sit on the bench opposite the Beethoven statute for at least fifteen minutes – no less – to be sure there is no one watching you or in close proximity. Bring a sandwich, smoke a cigarette or eat a candy bar. If anyone appears, or if you see someone watching you move on without putting the envelope in the crevasse." I asked him how they would know when I had put an envelope in the crevasse?

The man continued: "Hugo has an "OPEN" sign that he puts in the corner of the barbershop window. It has 'CLOSED" lettered on the back-side. Hugo always puts it in the lower right-hand corner of the shop's front window. When there is a pick-up to be made he was instructed to put it in the lower *left* corner of the window. Our contact will drive by the shop, and if the sign is in the lower left corner of the window we will go retrieve the envelope. If it's in the right side, we'll simply pass. We'll drive by every day and check."

"I understand. And our money?"

"It will be in an envelope in the same place on Friday at 5 PM after we pick up an envelope anytime that week."

And with that he rose and strolled off.

Two weeks later we placed the first envelope with the shipping information, and on Friday an envelope with two fifty-dollar bills was in the crevasse.

Hugo was delighted with the simplicity and the efficiency with which the information was transferred, and the payment made. But it raised a question. We banked at the Southwest Bank on Kingshighway. If we started putting one hundred dollar deposits in our account, it may raise some suspicions. After all, we had banked there for several years and the most our account ever got deposited in it in a whole month was a total of a couple of hundred dollars, and that was in several much smaller deposits.

Hugo and I devised a plan to deposit the money in several banks, and never to make more than a couple of deposits a month in either one of them. The money would be put in safe deposit boxes rather than deposited in bank accounts. There was no record of safe deposit cash. We made a list of banks on the streetcar lines that ran along Grand, Kingshighway and Arsenal. We located six banks and opened safe deposit boxes in our names, some in Hugo's name and some in mine. All were easily reached by streetcar, and the furthest was on north Grand Avenue up near Sportsman's Park. It took twenty-five minutes to ride up there, but it was a straight shot on the Grand Avenue streetcar without a transfer. We methodically began making the deposits as we got payments. Sometimes I would even make deposits on my way home from work.

August 18, 1940

General Hollenbeck was working more hours than ever. It seemed that he never left the office. He was there in the morning when I arrived and was there well after I left. A "secure" Telex had been installed in the anteroom off his office. It seemed to be busy most of the time. I had access to it, but he was in the habit of ripping off the typewritten messages as fast as they came in so I read few of them. Most of those I did see I didn't understand. They were mostly technical, and they dealt with subjects far beyond ammunition.

This morning I was in General Hollenbeck's office. We were going over some cost estimates for one of the new production lines. The Telex started to clatter. He paid no attention and finished going through the numbers before handing them to me for checking. He got up and ripped off the Telex sheet. Whatever he was reading disturbed him. A deep furrow appeared on his brow. He read it again. He was clearly upset by whatever it was. He wadded it up and threw it into the wastebasket beside his desk. It was the wastebasket destined for the shredder.

"Shit!" he exclaimed. "Shit! Shit! Shit!"

I didn't know what to say or do. "What's the matter Sir?" I asked.

"Nothing, Frieda. Nothing."

I knew better. 'Nothing', doesn't make you curse like that. I knew better than to push. He would tell me if he wanted me to know. I finished up and went out to my office.

Hollenbeck left about fifteen minutes later. I knew that he had to go out to a heavy equipment yard in Lemay and would be gone the rest of the day. My curiosity got the best of me. I had access to his office. I was in there a lot. I went to the waste basket and pulled out the crumpled Telex. It made no sense to me. It read:

"Intelligence determined that Otto Hahn and Fritz Strassman, in Berlin, confirm Fermi work. Used uranium - bombarded with neutrons. Have split atom. Fission possible. Need you to come to Washington for meeting next week, August 24."

I had no idea what it meant. I only knew that it upset Hollenbeck.

August 19, 1940

General Hollenbeck has begun to make arrangements to go to Washington for a meeting to be held next Thursday. This morning he called me into the office and gave me several instructions about the plant that he wanted carried out while he was gone. He said he did not know how long he would be gone. He was making a list of things that he would take. Several items were files that he kept in a secure filing cabinet that only he had access to. Even though he was not going to leave until Monday there seemed to be a sense of urgency in his preparations.

Hollenbeck's wife had gone to Holland, Michigan for the month of August. She did this every summer. They had a big white frame house right on the lake up there. He planned to join her this weekend for a couple of weeks, but the Washington meeting took priority. It really must've been something urgent. Hollenbeck always looked forward to a summer vacation in Michigan. He asked me if I would drive him in his car to Union Station on Tuesday to catch the train. He preferred to leave his car in the plant lot rather than at the railroad station. I agreed.

August 23, 1940

I took General Hollenbeck to Union Station on Tuesday. His train left just past noon. He would arrive in Washington on Wednesday evening. Apparently, the meeting was going to be at the Department of the Army Headquarters in the Pentagon. Hollenbeck did not say much about the subject. A Telex came in last Friday with details of the meeting. It contained a list of all who would attend. I didn't recognize any of the names. I noted the meeting would be chaired by a Brigadier General Leslie R. Groves of the Corps of Engineers. An adviser to President Roosevelt named Alexander Sachs was to be there. They apparently had brought together a big group of heavies for this one. General Hollenbeck was in the company of some big players.

For the first time I wondered how much Bloch would pay for this kind of information? If there was a high-level meeting called in the Pentagon involving the head of our plant wouldn't that be as important as ammunition production information? Probably not if I couldn't deliver the reason for the meeting. I dismissed the idea, but it had some merit. The idea kept coming back to me. If I had the meeting agenda and the list of participants would this be a two-hundred-dollar piece of information? Three hundred? Five hundred...?

August 30, 1940

Hollenbeck is back. He seems somehow distant. One of his first acts upon arriving was to call a staff meeting of all of his department heads. He informed them that he would be doing some reorganizing of the management and control of production, research and development at the main plant. The "object of the reorganization," he said "was to make the plant more self-sufficient, more decentralized in its management, more responsive to its department heads." Almost everyone found that quite odd since Hollenbeck was a hands-on sort of a guy. He delegated, but only while he watched the delegatee very closely. He always kept the leash short. How was it he was now telling everyone that he was going to loosen up - especially with production pressures to produce more products.

I watched Hollenbeck for the first day or two that he was back in the office. He acted a little different. It was as if he was preoccupied with something else. He seemed to have his mind on something other than day-to-day production problems of the plant.

One thing that he changed immediately was security. Hollenbeck started establishing new security measures almost the first day back. Areas were designated as "Restricted." He asked me for a list of employees with access to various areas of the plant. He said that he intended to establish a hierarchy of access ranging from high to low, for certain information - records and data.

Then he shocked me. He called me into his office.

"Frieda, I want you to submit to a security check. You are going to be handling Top Secret documents and I must put you through security scrutiny of the highest level. I have arranged for an Army Security Specialist to come down from Chicago next Monday to initiate the check."

"I don't know what to say, sir." In truth, I was scared to death. My palms were wet. I tried not to show it.

"Well, you don't have anything to hide, do you? You are not a spy, or something are you?" Hollenbeck laughed that big laugh he has when he thinks he says something funny.

October 1, 1940

I received a *Top Secret* clearance. I had passed the scrutiny of the Army intelligence officers. It has been seven weeks since I was walked into a room with two somber thin men from the Army Intelligence Office in Chicago. They asked me questions for three hours. The questions were so stupid.

"What were the full names of my mother, father, grandmother and grandfather?"

"Do I gamble?"

"Does my husband?"

"Do we have a good marriage?"

"If so, why don't we have children?"

"Have my husband or I ever been arrested?"

On and on they went. I thought they were going to lift up my skirt and poke around. And some of the questions were really personal:

"Did I manage to keep control when I got my period?"

"Had I had any affairs during my marriage?"

"Had I ever been treated by a psychiatrist?"

"When was the last time I saw a doctor?"

"What for?"

One question almost made me laugh. They asked me if I had ever taken anything out of the office without the permission of General Hollenbeck?

"No," I told them. "Why would I do anything like that?" They wrote down the answer with all of the others.

Well, shows how smart they are! I now am cleared for Top Secret documents. Hugo and I got a good laugh on that one. We now have almost four thousand dollars in the bank. We are considering renting another safe deposit box in a seventh bank.

October 18, 1940

I had been thinking about it for some time. Hugo and I talked it over. There had to be much more money for information if we let them know I had a Top-Secret clearance. Hugo reminded me that the instructions that we had received the first night by telephone said that no information other than shipping records was to be included in the drops. We were not to contact them in any way. I knew of no way to contact them at all except by including something in the weekly report envelope. We had no name except Bloch in Chicago. We had no phone or address.

We decided to put a note in the next drop.

"Have just received Top Secret clearance. Can we do any more business?"

The note went in with the Friday evening drop about six thirty. Then Hugo and I went out on the town. I had never seen *Gone with the Wind.* It was playing at the Loews Orpheum Theater. Hugo promised he would take me if he got off in time. We caught the Seven o'clock show, stopped by the Black Forest Inn for some refreshment at about ten and got home at midnight. The phone was ringing as we came through the door.

"Mrs. Jurgens?"

"Yes."

"Are you alone?"

"No. My husband is here."

"Good. I wish to speak with you both."

"Is this Herr Bloch?" I couldn't tell from the voice on the phone. We hadn't talked to Bloch in a long time. The voice had an accent. It sounded like him.

"I cannot confirm who I am."

"Then I cannot speak with you."

The voice ignored me. "We have your note."

"So?"

"So, you may have something to discuss with us. However, we cannot talk on the phone. Can we meet you on Sunday?"

"Not unless you tell us who 'we' is?"

"Mrs. Jurgens, please do not be tedious. If you did not want to talk you would not have contacted us."

"Get to the point."

"We want you to meet us at the Westlake Amusement Park. Do you know it?"

"Of course, but why in the heck do you want to go all the way out there? It's miles from here."

"Yes, I know. It offers certain facilities that we can use to our advantage."

"What facilities?"

"There is a fun house with a large Tunnel of Love. Have you been there?"

I hadn't been there in many years, in fact,

I had only been there once. It was before I met Hugo. I went into the Tunnel of Love, and the creep I was with tried to put his hand down my dress. How well I remember the Tunnel of Love.

"I know it." I said.

"Each little boat is in the shape of a swan. Each has a double seat in front and a double seat in back with a partition in the middle. Only four can ride. There are numerous swan boats, but only one pink one. Arrive at two o'clock. The first time the pink swan-boat goes by after two o'clock get in the front seat. We will join you. Do you understand?"

"Sunday at two. Tunnel of love. Pink swan-boat. I understand."

"Good. Then you'll be there?"

"We will be there."

11

CHAPTER

THE TUNNEL OF LOVE

"October 21, 1940

The Sunday Sermon was on Cain and Able. Hugo dozed for most of
the eleven o'clock service. Church let out at twelve fifteen.

We went out Olive Street to Lindbergh and north to Saint Charles
Rock road. The old Whippet was on its last legs. It coughed and
wheezed all the way to the city limits, then ran smoothly for several
miles before lapsing into a chugging beast whose every gasp seemed
to be its last. We arrived at Westlake Park at One-thirty and paid the
five-cent parking fee. Hugo pointed the Whippet toward a grassy
parking lot near the base of the towering roller coaster. I'm a little
afraid of roller coasters. I've only seen two in my life – this one, and
the roller coaster at the Forest Park Highlands. They scared me. Hugo
loves to ride them. He does it without me.

We pulled into the grass-covered lot. Above us the clanking of
the chain ratchet that pulled the roller coaster up the first and highest
grade made its whirring sound. Hugo parked in the shade of the
monstrous wooden structure.

"Could we have lemonade?" I asked. "We have time."

"Sure," just make sure that you don't have to go pee at two o'clock. We have to be on time." Hugo sounded irritable. He really didn't want to drive all of the way out here.

"Oh Hugo, you worry too much. We have plenty of time."

"Look, we can play all we want to after the meeting. I could use a hot dog, but it'll have to wait until we are finished." He paced off toward the midway. Hugo could be so serious at times.

We paid the ten cents admission to the park. That got you in. Westlake was a big permanent amusement park with every conceivable ride, game and amusement. You paid extra for tickets to get onto the rides. The place stretched for blocks along a semi-midway. At the far end was a huge white clapboard three-story fun house.

The fun house made liberal use of running water. I guess it was pumped over falls, through troughs and into swirling streams that siphoned out the bottom, only to be recycled by some gargantuan underground pumps. Inside there was a giant three- story slide, a polished wooden saucer that spun while you tried to stay on, games and slot machines. In the bowels of the building, beneath the towering waterfall was the Tunnel of Love.

Hugo led me down the steps into the chasm between the mighty waterfalls. It was cool and humid in the lower level where you went out on a platform to enter the little two-seated swans that came out of the oval tunnel. The little boats would disgorge their passengers, only to be refilled with other giggling riders by the attendant and again disappear into the dark round-topped tunnel.

Even though it was October, it was a warm sunny day. The temperature had to be in the low eighties. The coolness of the platform where the little swan-boats came through for reloading was moist and humid. Hugo held my hand as we descended the wooden stairs to the platform. Mist boiled up from the dark waters below where the falls plunged into the frothy pool. There were few people in line. It was two o'clock. Recorded organ music played in the background adding certain garishness to the scene. Little swan boats of various colors came out from the tunnel behind us. None were pink.

We waited in line until we were first. The next boat was purple. Our instructions were to wait for the first pink boat after two o'clock. A red boat came through. The attendant motioned for us to get in. We held back and let the couple behind us get in. Another couple joined them. The boat departed. The next boat was red. We held back again to let couples behind us get in. The attendant yelled at us.

A pink boat emerged from the tunnel. It was the only one. We jumped in ahead of the couple behind us who had anticipated that we would again let them in. Then, a strange thing happened. The couple started to get into the seat at the rear of the boat behind us. The attendant waived them off. The chain in the water below caught our boat, and we glided off - the boat's only occupants.

The Tunnel of Love is entered through a round-topped tunnel entrance with roses and cupids painted over the arch. The boat glides on underwater belts or chains until it is almost to the entrance. Then a current created by large pumps catches the boat and it's floated through the arch into the dark interior. A rubber railing bumps the boat along while the current keeps it moving. Once spaced, the boats maintain the approximate spacing through the dark and twisting tunnel of water.

The interior was cool, dark and damp. The only sound was the fading sound of the waterfall's roar that seemed to be magnified in the round-topped tunnel. The loud organ music from the exterior faded behind us as we entered total darkness. The boat turned right following the narrow tunnel.

Suddenly we felt someone get into the boat behind us. Their weight changed the boat's attitude, and the swan on the front rose in response to the added weight in the rear behind us.

"Good afternoon Mister and Mrs. Jurgens. Thank you for coming. Please do not turn around." The voice was definitely not Bloch or the voice on the phone. It had a creamy German accent - clear, soft and a little menacing. "We received your message and we want to discuss the possibilities of an exchange of additional information with you."

"Go ahead," said Hugo. "Discuss."

"With your new status we believe that you would have access to virtually every part of the Army Ammunition Plant and the chemical plant. Is that correct?"

"I might have access, but I do not routinely visit, or have contact with all parts of the plants."

"Yes, but those areas restricted to Top Secret clearance are generally familiar to you. Correct?"

"Not all. Remember I am classified as a secretary to the plant superintendent. Geographically, I do not move around a lot."

"But you do have access..."

"I have some access to some areas. Not all. What are you looking for? What do you want?"

"Your superior, Avril Hollenbeck is in the inner circle of a group of men in Washington who hold the key to the development of American war making technology."

"So?"

"We don't know what Hollenbeck and his circle of friends are up to. We don't know if they plan development of strategic weapons or are just a bureaucratic committee that meets irregularly to justify their jobs. We want to know what they do. You can help."

"How?"

"Just keep us informed about who Hollenbeck meets with; where he goes; what projects he is working on, and of course, what his communications say. You have access to his communications, don't you?"

"Some I do. Some I don't."

Hugo interjected: "What if we do. What if we have information for you? What's in it for us?"

"What do you want?" The inquiry was flat, unemotional.

"Money, of course. What do you think we do this for? Thrills?"

The second voice chimed in. It was the voice of the telephone - no accent, detached, unemotional. "For every delivery that we deem important we will pay you one-hundred dollars."

"Whaddya mean 'you' deem important? You mean we deliver the goods and you decide if you pay for them? No thanks."

"You are not capable of deciphering much of the information that Mrs. Jurgens has access to. You cannot tell what is important and what is not most of the time. We can."

"Well, la dee dah!" exclaimed Hugo. "And maybe if we're lucky we get paid?"

"That depends entirely on the quality of the information you deliver."

"That's it? That's the offer?" Hugo sounded offended.

The boat bumped around a curve. To our right a diorama portrayed John Smith and Pocahontas in each other's arms at the mouth of a cave. In another time I might have thought of it as romantic. Today it looked simply grotesque.

"Listen you guys. We might not have the ability to interpret the information we bring out. But one-hundred dollars to carry Top Secret stuff is not enough."

"We asked you what you wanted. You did not give us a reply. We could only assume that ..."

"No deal, Hermann. You know what the first three letters of assume are. If we are going to smuggle out Top Secret information, it's going to cost you one hundred fifty dollars a pop regardless of the information. Each carry - one hundred fifty. Got it?"

"That's very expensive for ..."

"We got it," said the creamy German accent, cutting off the telephone voice. "But we'll expect a delivery every week."

"It's a deal, Hermann," said Hugo. I found his use of the word 'Hermann' in the familiar very offensive. I'm sure the passengers in the back seat did too. I think Hugo intended it that way.

"Once a week. And where do you want it - on the marquee of the Ambassador Theater?"

"The same time, same place will do fine."

"Done. Expect the first delivery next week," Said Hugo without even consulting me. After all, I was the one who was going to get the information out.

"We should establish another drop location, if we have to change, or the Tower Grove Park drop site becomes hazardous."

"What did you have in mind?" Hugo had suddenly become the chief negotiator.

"The Granada Theater on Gravois has an alcove on the right side of the mezzanine level. It contains only three short rows of seats. Lovers use it when they want to be alone. They tend to stick to the seats near the walls of the alcove so no one sits next to them. The second seat in the second row is almost never occupied. The cushions can be lifted up and an envelope of almost any size inserted between the metal seat bottom and the cushion. It will be an alternative drop if a smudge appears on the pedestal of Beethoven."

We passed another diorama; this time of Romeo and Juliet. The little swan bumped to the left and around another curve. A third diorama came into view. It was Clark gable and Vivian Leigh at the foot of the great staircase of Tara Plantation. He had swooped her into his arms and was about to turn to go up the stairs. A recording on a repeating belt or tape kept saying every five seconds "Frankly my dear I don't give a damn." I had seen the movie. He was walking out the door when he said it, not carrying her up the stairs!

The phrase was repeated on a five second delay. Every boat that passed in front of the diorama was treated to about six of the repeated phrases. It was absurd.

"Here, take this" A sleeveless arm reached around the partition and poked me in the shoulder. It held a folded note.

"What is it?"

"Instructions, Mrs. Jurgens"

I took it. The arm retracted to the back seat.

"It's a pleasure to see you Mister and Mrs. Jurgens," said the German accent."

"Likewise," chimed in the non-accent.

"We look forward to your first delivery."

A light appeared in the distance, and the little swan moved ever steadily on its faux current toward the tunnel's exit. The tenants of the rear seats jumped ship onto a concrete walkway that paralleled the flowing channel just before the boat reached the tunnel exit and were gone.

12

THE MYSTERY OF WELDON SPRING

I was despondent after Connie and I had read the last notebook last Sunday. I had been sick to my stomach all week. Normally, I'm not a depressed person, but I clearly had begun to sink into a state of depression. Connie spotted it immediately and rendered a diagnosis:

"Donald. Snap out of it. You have been depressed all week."

She was right. It had been a week. I couldn't get it out of my mind. My mother and father were passing military secrets to the Nazis. It wasn't even an ideological thing. They were doing it for money!

"I'm sorry. I'm not dealing with this very well, am I?"

"That's an understatement." Connie walked around to the other side of the bed and turned her back for me to zip up the back of her dress. Connie has a great back. I could see all the way down, and it excited me. We were getting dressed on Saturday night for a fundraiser for Multiple Sclerosis downtown at the Hyatt at Union Station. "Donald, it's only information. You don't have to bear the shame. Frankly, I don't see why you even have to say a word to anyone about it. It has been a well-kept secret up until now. Why should it get out? No one needs to know if you don't want them to."

"I'd like to see the way you'd handle it if it were your parents," I said crabbily. I didn't need to say that. I regretted it the minute it was out.

"I'll ignore that," said Connie, "but I might suggest something."

"What?"

"Reserve judgment until you have finished all of the diaries. Frankly, I find them fascinating. Maybe there's something in them that will restore your faith in your mom and dad."

"What if there isn't?"

"Well. You aren't going to feel much worse than you do now. Maybe there's a silver lining. If I were you, I would want to know, regardless of the facts."

"That's easy for you to say."

"Think about it, Don. You didn't find these diaries by accident. Your mother wanted you to find them. Did it ever occur to you that she had some reason for showing this trunk to you? She could have destroyed the photos and the diaries just as easily. She has to have had a reason that she wanted you to find them. Remember they didn't have to tell you at all. They kept it a secret from you during their lifetimes. For some reason they wanted you to know. You might as well finish the diaries to get the whole picture."

Connie was putting on her earrings - the last act in her ritual of getting ready to go out. She really looked good in the black dinner dress that clung so well to her trim shape. It was a welcome change from the blue jeans she wore so frequently.

"God, I love this woman," I said to myself.

"Hurry up and put on your shoes," she said as she headed out the bedroom door. "It's not often I am ready before you." She pointed at my neck. "And straighten your bow tie - it's crooked."

I looked into the mirror. She was right; it was crooked.

On Sunday afternoon we got back to the diaries. I was now reading a chapter ahead of Connie. She is a rapid reader and was usually waiting for me to finish so that she could devour the notebook I had been reading.

January 9, 1944

After the meeting in the Fun House I wondered how we were going to obtain enough information to make a weekly drop in addition to the shipping documents? Hugo, the great negotiator, had made us this sweet deal, but I worried how we could deliver.

I voiced my concerns to Hugo.

"Make it up," was Hugo's reply.

"What?"

"Make it up. How are they going to know what is real and what is phony?"

"Hugo, you are crazy."

"You think so? Well, I've got news for you. Those guys in the middle that are talking to us are just a bunch of carrier pigeons for someone else higher up. That someone else, whoever it is, is putting the pressure on them to deliver information. They are in the hot seat. We are their out. They need us, and they depend on us, but when you think about it - they have no way of checking out what we give them. So, we give them a little fluff and collect a few extra bucks."

"Hugo that's dishonest..." I caught myself.

"Dishonest?" Boy was that an incredible thing to say. We were in up to our eyeballs selling classified secrets. Since when did honesty play a part in the transaction?

"Listen, Frieda. If you don't believe me. I can show you."

Hugo was suggesting that we simply slip a couple of dummy manifests into the Friday envelopes if we didn't have an actual shipping report. Making up shipping information was easy to do. We had just to make up a load, quantity and destination. I could make up shipping information by memory. I saw so much of it. If, by any remote chance, we got caught all we had to do was explain it by saying that there was a last-minute change. Other classified material was not so easy, particularly since I didn't understand most of it. But Hollenbeck was always going to Chicago, New York or Washington. Relaying his schedule would be an easy filler even if we could not surmise the reasons for his trips. The trips to Oak Ridge, Tennessee would be the toughest to explain. What was going on down there?

"It's a great way to keep the funds flowing," said Hugo. We've had only had a couple of weeks without a shipment, but each one of them we missed cost us a hundred bucks. If we had a dummy manifest, we could just slip it in and get our money. No one's the wiser. Now they want more, and we can deliver it – all for an increased payment"

Hugo was right. It was easy. Last week there was no shipment, so we slipped in a dummy manifest. Poof! There was the payment. Sure enough, slipping in phony information would be a snap.

The first week in December I made the first drop of classified information other than shipping manifests. I really didn't know what to deliver. Some of the stuff in Hollenbeck's office is so mundane I doubted whether it would have any value. Hugo didn't like to deliver information "on approval" as he called it. "How are we to know?" he argued, we could give them the keys to the city, and if they didn't like it we were just out in the cold.

We decided that the first information would be a copy of the memo and date, time and place of the Washington meeting that had been held in such a rush on August 23. I didn't know what that meeting was about, but it clearly had something to with defense and weapons. The news was a little old, maybe stale, but if they had the information from another source it would confirm our credibility. Secretly I hoped they had already had the information because it would establish us as a reliable source.

The only problem I had was making a copy. We did not have any copying equipment that I could use. The duplicators all had an operator and I just couldn't hand it to one of them and say, 'Make me a copy I want to deliver it to our German friends'.

I decided to re-type the letter verbatim. I had plenty of time to do it. Hollenbeck was not in town. I made no carbons. When it was finished, I tucked it into my bra and went home. Hugo had purchased a packet of large letter-sized brown manila envelopes. I put the typed copy into the envelope and followed the instructions on the little slip of paper that we had been given us in the Fun House. I unfolded it and read the hand printed page:

"Call FL 3856 and let it ring three times. Hang up.
Call again and let it ring four times. No one will answer.
Hang up. On the same day that you call
go to the assigned place at the
beginning of the 7 PM movie. Place the information
under the seat and leave after the first intermission."

We followed the instructions. The drop went without a hitch. I even enjoyed the show, an Audie Murphy western, Hugo didn't want to leave after the first intermission.

Three days later the phone rang. It was the Creamy German voice.

"Congratulations. The product you delivered was received with much favor. It has been helpful."

"What does that mean?" said Hugo.

"It means we pay you the next time you make a drop. It is accepted."

"You mean we have to deliver additional information before we get paid even if you have accepted it and are satisfied?"

"That is correct."

"Listen, Hermann. That's not the deal. You said that if it was accepted...."

"That IS the deal! There will be no further negotiations, Mister Jurgens." The voice had turned short - curt. "We will await your next contact."

Hugo was furious. His face was beet red. He didn't like to be treated that way. He slammed down the phone.

January 27, 1941

By the last of January, I was pretty sure. I missed my December period; and my next one, which should have been in late January appeared late. We had been so busy through the Christmas Holidays that we didn't pay much attention even though missing a period was pretty unusual.

At Thanksgiving we had taken a trip over to the baths at Okawville, Illinois. We decided to enjoy some of the fruits of our labors and treat ourselves to a train ride over to luxuriate in the hot steamy natural mineral baths. Both of us had been reluctant to spend much of the new money that was now rapidly accumulating in our separate safe deposit boxes. We stayed in the big gingerbread hotel in Okawville and slept late. It is a great place to relax, eat good meals and fall asleep on the chintz covered four-poster bed in our big room. In between we would go down to the bowels of the bathhouse and get a private bathroom with a big double tub. We'd soap ourselves up in the tile-lined chamber and sink into the hot steamy pool only to fuck ourselves into limpness before crawling back upstairs to our room. I don't know how many times that week end we did it, but I'm betting that's when I got pregnant.

It was a big event. Hugo was so excited when I told him what I suspected. I had not confirmed it, but that would have to wait for an appointment with Doctor Luther which would not come for another week. In the meantime, we just had to live on my diagnosis. I was right, though. I knew it. Women know those things.

We began to make the plans that all parents worldwide have made from the beginning of time. Where would we find the space? What would we name him or her? Did we have enough money to have a child? Hugo mused that the latter was really a rhetorical question. It did no good to speculate on whether you had enough money after you were pregnant.

He treated me like a queen. Hugo was so happy to be an almost-father. When the doctor confirmed it he brought me a big bouquet of yellow roses and took me out to dinner at the Rathskeller of the Lenox Hotel. We had champagne and toasted our new addition.

Early on my pregnancy posed some difficult questions. When would I tell Hollenbeck? The company had a policy that discouraged pregnant women from working past the fifth month and absolutely forbade it past the seventh month. How would we get the data out? Would Hollenbeck make an exception? He really relied on me. Would I go back to work after it was born?

We decided not to tell Hollenbeck until I really could hide it no longer. Then I was going to implore him to let me work at least until my eighth month, longer if possible. After all, I would reason, my work is not strenuous. There was really no reason I could not work until the day I delivered. That would be a hard sell.

February 6, 1941

I had been working in Hollenbeck's office all day. Most of his files were in disarray when he left for a two-day trip to Chicago by train. I set about cleaning out the old closed files and replacing them with current files for which we had previously had little space.

It was the red expandable Red Robe folder with an over-flap and a tie string that caught my eye. Mostly our files were tan-colored manila and had typed labels with a file number that matched an index card for easy reference. This one had a hand-lettered label. I had not prepared it. I recognized Hollenbeck's handwriting. It said, "WELDON SPRING PROJECT."

I had never seen it before. That, of itself, was strange because I knew most of the operational files. There might be few personal files in his cabinet, but ....

I took the red folder from the cabinet and laid it on Hollenbeck's desk. Out of an abundance of caution I went to his door and closed it turning the bolt to lock it. First, I thumbed through the documents without taking them out of the folder to be sure that I knew the sequence and the order that they had been placed inside. I removed them keeping them in the same order, and sat down at the desk and began to read:

The first item was a little index. The first document listed was a memorandum Dated August 24, 1940 - the date of the Washington meeting. It was on stationery of the U.S Army Corps of Engineers and it bore the signature of Brigadier General Leslie R. Groves. The letter was an authorization to proceed with the "Weldon Spring Project." It was part letter of introduction and part authorization to proceed. It was clearly designed to be shown to anyone who Hollenbeck would need to convince that he was proceeding with authority from Washington. It did not, however, explain what the "Weldon Spring" project was.

The next item on the list was actually three items consisting of folded maps and plats. Hollenbeck had drawn boundary sketches on them and the notation "25,000 acres?" in pencil.

Finally, there were some lists with names on them. I read them carefully not recognizing any of the names. There were no addresses or other notations.

I went back to the maps.

I spread all three of them on the big work table that Hollenbeck had moved into his office next to his desk. I laid them side by side. They did not match up so I concluded that they were not intended to be one single map which was to be hooked together. There was nothing I could match to get a reference. No landmarks were familiar. No roads were designated. It had topographical lines on it and I could tell that it was sort of hilly. In the corner there was a wavy line that had the word "river" penciled over it. I turned the maps on their side - nothing.

Finally, I folded them back up and put them back into the Red Robe binder making sure that they were put in the same sequence as before and facing the same way. I tied the ribbon in the same bow and returned the folder to the drawer.

In order to let me know if the file had been opened by Hollenbeck I pushed it all the way to the right side of the file drawer. Most of the files were fairly centered in the file cabinet drawer. There was about an inch of space on both sides of the files. I was in this drawer frequently on other matters. Hollenbeck would never notice if it was pushed against the right side. When he took it out and replaced it he would put it casually into the center like all the rest of the files. That way I would know immediately without taking it out of the drawer if he had been in it.

I was anxious to talk to Hugo. I had no idea what "Weldon Spring" was. Maybe he had heard of it. It looked like a place, but that was just a hunch. I kept racking my brain all the way home on the streetcar. It sounded familiar. Something about the words "Weldon Spring" rang a bell, but I could not bring it up.

Hugo got home after seven. He was in a good mood. He had been walking on air since the doctor confirmed my pregnancy. He patted me on the fanny and gave me a long languid kiss. I could tell something was on his mind. It didn't take long.

"Frieda, I have an idea whose time has come," he announced as I was putting dinner on the table. He had parked himself at the kitchen table and was grinning at me.

"What's on your mind, Big Boy."

"Frieda, I think it's time that we had a house." He watched me for a reaction.

"Sure, Hugo. Where are we going to get a house? More important, how are we going to pay for it?"

"You know how we have been wrestling with the space issues in this flat and all. What with the baby the space in here is going to get awfully small. I think we should consider buying a house. We can get a loan."

"Getting a loan may be easy. It's paying it off that bothers me."

"Listen, we have almost four thousand dollars in the safe deposit boxes. I haven't priced any specific houses, but I hear that some good ones can be bought for under ten thousand dollars."

"How much would that be in payments each month?"

"I dunno, but with a four thousand dollar down payment, it ought to be manageable."

"Hugo, it's manageable only if I can keep delivering the goods. I'm pregnant in case you hadn't noticed. It's all going to come to a halt when I have to start the laying in."

"We can manage for a few months. You'll just have to go back to work after the baby is born."

Hugo had diverted me with the house idea. I would love to have a house with a yard for the baby to play in. I'd love to paint it and make little curtains for the kitchen and bath. Truth was I'd sell my soul for a house, but was it practical? Was it feasible? Would it betray Hugo and me for what we were doing? I did not have any clear answers. I was confused. It was a great idea, but it had all come on so quick.

We ate dinner. I had fried some chicken, and he ate it voraciously. I love to watch Hugo when he gets something he really likes to eat. The joy of it consumes him. He even helped me with the dishes.

"Hugo, I said. I was lying on my back on our bed naked. I was looking for a bulge in my belly. I saw none. "Am I beginning to show?"

Hugo was undressing for bed. He looked languidly over my body as if he were unwrapping a banana. "Looks pretty good to me," he said.

"C'mon Hugo. You know what I mean."

"Of course, I do." He looked again. "I can't tell a thing. Of course, you'll look the same when you are six months when you are laying on your back like that."

"You mean I'm showing when I stand up?"

"Not really. I haven't noticed you showing at all, but you show faster when you are standing than lying on your back."

I had to admit I was a little nervous. There were suddenly a lot of unanswered questions. I really did not know how Hollenbeck would react. I didn't know if he would even offer me my job back after the baby was born. After all, he didn't have to.

"Hugo, did you ever hear of Weldon Spring?"

"Sure, it's that little town out Highway Forty just past the Missouri River. About thirty-five miles from here. Why?"

"Hollenbeck's got a file in his office marked "Weldon Spring Project." I haven't the faintest idea what it is all about."

"So, what's the problem?"

"I mean, he's been so mysterious. He hasn't mentioned it to me, and he keeps it in his personal drawer."

"Maybe he is buying a farm out there. It's really pretty out there with rolling hills and woods. It's near the bluffs overlooking the Missouri River."

"How do you know it so well?"

"I don't know it so well, but you have been out there with me. Remember a few years ago we went for that Sunday ride in the fall out along the river to Saint Charles County and down Highway 94? We turned off at Weldon Spring."

I honestly did not remember the area. I guess it just underlines the difference between men and women. Men remember those things. Hugo remembered it so well.

"What do you think? Do you think that Hollenbeck is doing something we ought to report?"

"Frieda, I don't think that a file with the name Weldon Spring Project" on it is going to get us any money in the envelope. Let's just forget it."

Hugo was right. There was far more important information to pass on. I had received a message on the Telex this morning about a meeting at the University of Chicago next month. It was from Groves. Nothing else was in the Telex except the time and place and a request that Hollenbeck confirm his availability. I thought that it might be something like the Washington meeting of last August. I would keep an eye out for more information, an agenda perhaps, or a list of participants. That would get us a payment. Heaven knows with the baby coming on a few good bonus payments in addition to the weekly shipping report payments would be helpful.

February 28, 1941

I had kept an eye on the Weldon Spring folder for three weeks. Each time I was filing in the drawer I checked on it to see if Hollenbeck had pulled it out. He had done so at least three times this month. The first time I noticed it had been filed in the Middle, I waited until he was gone for the day, and I pulled it. Everything had been in the same order and nothing had been added or subtracted. I figured that he had merely re-read it, or had pulled it out, intending to do something but got diverted. Nothing had changed.

On February 18th the file had been pulled again. I got in early one morning and casually checked the drawer. Sure enough, it was filed in the middle of the drawer. I pulled it. There was a carbon copy of a handwritten memo. It had been addressed to a Major General Alexander Harter in the Corps of Engineers at the same address in Washington where I had seen communications addressed to General Groves. It was Hollenbeck's handwriting and read:

"Have engaged attorneys in Saint Charles to act as straw parties in the acquisition. They, in turn, will hire land agents who will act for undisclosed principals to acquire land. Major push for completion in 90 days. Any land not optioned in 90 days will be considered for condemnation.

Will notify U.S. Attorney, but not until absolutely necessary. Not satisfied with security in U.S. Attorney office.

You will need to shake loose funds for land acquisition and to pay attorneys. Attorneys will pay land agents, divorcing us from all purchases. Attorneys to receive 10% commission on all acquisitions. Will need to access funds on short notice. Please advise of procedure."

Clearly Hollenbeck was not buying a farm - not using U.S. funds anyway, and the power of condemnation if the landowners did not want to sell? I thought of making a copy of the letter, but in reality, it contained very little information. I just decided to tuck the information away and look for more.

It came one week later.

The file was again moved. I looked at it over the lunch hour when I knew that Hollenbeck was out of the plant on a working lunch.

There was another letter from the Corps of Engineers signed by Alexander Harter:

"Avril, you are authorized to draw drafts on special account Continental Bank, Chicago. Use standard form draw. Further authorized to grant attorney in Saint Charles draft authorization to further insulate Corps of Engineers from project. Please advise of name of attorney authorized so that we can flag account.

Have you confirmed availability of water supply? Will have need for at least 1,000,000 gallons per day. Are well sites sufficiently defined that drilling for water can commence immediately on acquisition? Geology must be reviewed. Water quantity is absolutely critical."

One million gallons of water a day! What the heck were they going to do with that kind of water? And if they needed that much water why didn't they just take it out of the Missouri River? It was within a few thousand yards. Why did they need well water? And why did the Corps of Engineers want to be insulated from the project? What were they doing that they didn't want the public to attach to the Corps?

I memorized the note. Then I memorized the one of a week ago, too. On my lunch hour I wrote out the notes word for word from memory.

At dinner I told Hugo to make the call tomorrow. We were going to turn in the information. Neither of us knew what it meant, but we both agreed that something was going on. We also agreed that it would probably yield dividends in the form of a cash payment. It was Wednesday.

This evening on my Friday drop off of information about shipments there was a note tucked into the envelope with the one hundred dollars. It simply said:

"Get more information on Weldon Spring."

There was one hundred and fifty dollars in the envelope.

Hugo laughed when I brought it home. "Do they think that we have information that we are not passing along?"

I laughed, too. But there was a hint of sadness about our joy. We were being controlled, instructed to obtain specific information. Sure, there would be payment, but there were now orders emanating from someone instructing us to get more and specific data. I had a bad feeling.

I needed a beer.

March 12, 1941

It was one of those tantalizing early spring days, when the sky clears, and the temperature warms prematurely to the middle seventies. No trees were out yet, but the forsythia was showing some tinges of yellow. The grass had greened, and Hugo suggested that we take a ride after church.

"Where?"

"How about we go out to Weldon Spring and look around," said Hugo nonchalantly.

"It's a great day to be out. Sounds like a good idea. I'll pack a picnic lunch."

"Don't go overboard. Just some sandwiches will do. Got any of that Auslase that I liked so much?"

"I think I can find a bottle if you haven't hidden it too deep." Hugo and I had been buying some wine. Not much, just a bottle or two here and there. It was our splurge. We liked German wines. We had probably accumulated half a case in the kitchen pantry.

After church we returned home, and I finished packing the wicker basket with the picnic lunch.

"Put on some tough pants and shoes," said Hugo. "We might like to take a hike."

I was beginning to get the picture. Hugo wanted to look around Weldon Spring. He had slipped into a pair of moleskin hunting trousers that he wore when he went out to the country. This trip to the country had a purpose.

Weldon Spring is about twenty miles west of St. Louis on US Highway 40. From our house in South Saint Louis the most direct route was out Gravois to Lindbergh. Then north on Lindbergh to US 40; then west on US 40 across the Missouri River Bridge to its intersection with Missouri Highway 94.

The highway sign announced that we had arrived. "WELDON SPRING, Population 49 - unincorporated." Another sign announced the intersection of Highway 94 and had an arrow pointing south with the notation, 'Hamburg 4 mi'. We turned north toward a filling station.

There were a few houses along the highway, a feed and grain store, and a filling station combination grocery and hardware store. We pulled into the filling station. Two round Texaco pumps guarded the wooden porch on each end - one for regular and the other for Ethyl. On the porch sat a man in overalls basking in the early spring sunshine. Hugo pulled up to the pump and asked him to fill up the Whippet.

"Car's getting' to be almost an antique," he says and puts his hands into the pockets of his overalls as he eyed the Whippet. "How's it run?"

"Pretty good for a twelve-year-old car." Hugo is good at passing time with strangers. He has a good gift of gab.

The old gentleman was wiping off the windshield with a red rag, and whistling.

"Any property for sale around here?" Hugo looked off at the horizon as he finished the question.

"Whaddya lookin' for?"

"Oh, I just thought I might try to find me some acreage out here in the country. The city gets a little hectic you know."

"I know what you mean" He finished wiping the windshield and looked at Hugo sort of half-cocked out of the side of his eye. "You're a little late. Been a bunch of guys runnin' 'round here trying to buy up land the past few weeks."

"Ya don't say?" Hugo was beginning to sound like him. I couldn't keep from smiling.

"Yep. You'd think there was oil under these hills. Some guys - some lawyers out of Saint Charles are trying to buy up a whole bunch of land. Say they want to build a huntin' reserve."

"A hunting reserve?" Hugo seemed taken aback with that one. "Out here?"

"Hey mister, I am just telling you what I hear. I ain't vouchin' for its truthfulness."

"Where are they buying the land?"

"Down there." He pointed south, toward Highway 40. "South of 40 and all back down in there. He swept his hand in a broad arc toward the south. "Offered some pretty good prices for it seein' it's just scrub-oak and timber land."

"Is that all that's there?" said Hugo.

"Well, there's a few ponds and natural ravines in there. Not much else."

"Sounds like pretty poor land."

"Don't think it'll grow much if that's what you mean. But they are buyin' down in the river bottom too."

"Where's that?"

"Across on the East side of Highway 94 from Hamburg all the way down to the River. There's some good farmland down there. Can't see how it fits in with a hunting preserve." The old man took off his hat and scratched his head with the same hand. He pulled the nozzle out of the gas filler tube and capped it.

"That's twelve gallons. Two dollars and forty cents."

Hugo paid him. "Thanks for the gas and the information. I think we'll just drive around and get familiar with the area."

"Yep. You do that. See ya again." He waived as we drove off. He seemed sort of sad to see us leave.

Hugo drove back south across Highway 40 and south on State Highway 94. It was a gravel road south of Highway 40. It bore slightly left along a ridge of fields then swung back right and into the woods. Both sides were lined with Oak and Hickory. None of the trees were very big. Hugo remarked that he thought the land might have been logged in the past. There was an occasional farmhouse. Nothing out of the ordinary.

We rounded a bend and caught a glimpse of the Missouri river. Hugo suddenly hit the brakes.

"Look," he said pointing into the woods.

I didn't see a thing. "Where?"

"Over there. It's a surveyor's stake. See the little white ribbon on it. They use wooden stakes with different colored ribbons on them.

I saw it. It was a wooden stake about one hundred feet into the woods. It was easy to see with the leaves off. The breeze fluttered the little ribbon.

Hugo stopped the car. "Come on," he said "bring the picnic basket."

We walked into the woods over to the little stake. Hugo started looking around. "There." He pointed off into the woods. Sure enough, there was another stake. He headed off in the direction of the second stake. I tagged behind with the basket.

From the second we spotted the third, and from the third - the fourth. It was easy. The stakes were placed at varying distances apart, but always within sight. You just had to look around. Some were just a hundred or so feet away. Others were several hundred feet to the next. We trailed off into the woods following the stakes, linking them together.

After about thirty minutes Hugo stopped. "Frieda, these stakes are trailing off in a long line that does not seem to close. I think they are the boundary of a very big area."

I saw what Hugo meant. The stakes did not appear to form corners but rather a large sweeping arch that led deep into the woods. We had been walking a half an hour and had spotted twenty-six stakes. Not one of them seemed to form a corner. We kept going.

I felt we had gone over a mile and were still on the same boundary line. Still there was no corner.

"Hugo, if we are right this boundary encircles thousands of acres."

"Frieda, remember the notation on the plat "25,000" acres?" "Do you think this is it?"

"From the boundary it looks ..." Hugo froze. "Shhh!"

I didn't hear anything.

"Listen."

"I don't hear any ...." I heard it. Then again. It sounded like someone, or something, walking through the dried leaves of the forest floor. I could hear twigs snapping.

"Get down." Hugo pushed me toward a little ditch that wound its way between the trees. It looked like it held water when it rained, but it was dry now. We dropped over the edge and lay on our bellies. I almost dropped the picnic basket. The noise was coming closer.

Hugo looked up over the edge of the dirt embankment. He motioned for me to join him. I slid to the top and peered over.

A hundred yards away heading right toward us were two men on horses. They wore army fatigues with their pants tucked into riding boots. Each carried a rifle. They were following the stakes with the white flags.

Hugo pushed me down to the bottom of the little creek bed and slid down beside me.

"Shhh! Not a word."

We laid there for several minutes. The horses with their riders came closer and closer. The steep embankment would hide us from anyone near the stakes unless they came over and looked in. It seemed like an eternity. We could hear them talking as they got closer. The footsteps stopped. My heart was racing. One of them must have lit a cigarette. I got a faint whiff of toasted tobacco. They started moving again. We laid there long after their sounds had faded away; then we headed back for the car. My hands were wringing wet. I could hardly grip the unopened picnic basket. Sweat had run down the back of my neck and wilted my collar.

Whatever is going on at Weldon Spring, the Army doesn't want anyone to know about it.

When we got back to the car Hugo took out my camera and shot a picture of the area. There wasn't much to see. We drove off. In about a mile the road flattened. Hugo stopped but did not get out. Look. It looks like something has been going in and out of the woods here.

There were mud tracks onto the gravel roadway. While there didn't seem to be a road cleared into the woods something had been going in and out. Perhaps a truck? It was the area that they were using as the entrance to the woods. Hugo called it the 'main gate'. He took another picture.

March 27, 1941

The pictures took a week to get developed. When we got them back we put them into the envelope with an explanation and called up our contact to pick them up from the Granada Theater. There had been no new entries in Hollenbeck's file. I wrote a narrative about what we had seen and put it in with the photos. I marked each photo on the back with some description.

We were rewarded on Friday with a full payment along with the hundred for the shipping data. The envelope contained another note.

"Need higher grade photographs. Use better camera. Please purchase high resolution 35mm camera. Do not develop film. Send exposed roll. We will develop."

Connie had been looking through my mother's photographs. She had replaced the photos in the trunk tray after inspecting each neatly tied pack.

"That explains it." She said.

"Explains what?"

"Remember the pack with the photographs of Weldon Spring?"

"Oh yeah. But there were just two or three photos - not much to see." I really did not see what Connie was driving at.

"Those were developed by your mother and father locally. It was their earlier rolls taken on their camera. Then their controllers instructed them not to do that anymore, but rather to send the exposed roll without processing it."

I saw her point. It explained why there were no more photographs of the Weldon Spring project. They were delivering the rolls directly for developing.

"Why do you think they wanted to develop the rolls themselves?" asked Connie. "Do you think it was for security purposes?

"I don't know. That could be it. Maybe they did not want to have these photos in Mom and Dad's possession – particularly if they got caught.

I remember my mother telling me once that she had a friend that took some nude pictures and had them developed at a Gasen Drug store. When she went to pick them up the druggist told them that they would not develop that kind of pictures, and they had confiscated the developed film. Maybe they might have been afraid of someone seeing what they were photographing."

"Those pictures are pretty innocuous. Just some woods and a drive way."

"Yes, but whoever was controlling them must have known they were on to something. There would have to be more to come. Unless...."

"Unless what?"

"Unless they wanted to develop them to a certain high quality to get details that might not be evident in drug store developed photos."

"That has to be it, Don!" Connie was clearly excited. God, something else just crossed my mind."

"What are you thinking?"

"What if the instructions to purchase high resolution camera was for some other purpose?"

"Like what?"

"Almost any camera is good outside in daylight. A Brownie Box will take great pictures outside - and sharp too.

"So?"

"So, what if the better camera was for photographing documents?"

"Something that would photograph in low light?"

"Don, this is really getting dangerous. You and I both know what went on at Weldon Spring and Marquardt during the War."

"I don't believe it."

"You better believe it honey. Your mama and daddy were passing secrets. The Nazis wanted better-and-better quality photos. What we don't know is how much, and what, they got out."

April 23, 1941

I have been watching the Weldon Spring file in Hollenbeck's office. There had been and increasing amount of activity. Memos, plans and sketches are now beginning to appear. The file has now expanded to occupy an accordion file about seven inches thick. As each new item is added we photograph it and pass it along and are amply rewarded for each drop. There was not much in it, however, that explained what Weldon Spring was or what was the object of all of the activity. There was some correspondence about the Atlas Powder Company of New York and an "Operating Agreement."

But what were they operating?

So, land was being acquired, accesses being developed, structures being designed. I even saw a reference to a water plant that would have over a million gallons of water per day capacity. But why?

Last week Hollenbeck called me into this office.

"Frieda, you've probably noticed the Weldon Spring folder by now."

The question scared me. Did he know I had been into it? I tried not to react.

"I've seen it, General Hollenbeck." I didn't lie.

"I want you to clean out the whole file drawer and make room for more of that file. It's expanding pretty fast, and there'll be lots more."

"Yes, sir."

"And Frieda, I want you to put a label on the front of the drawer that says it is Top Secret. The only people to have access to that drawer are you and I."

"I'll take care of it General." I got up to leave. As I headed for the door I stopped. This was as good a time as any. I couldn't hide my pregnancy much longer. Summer was coming. Until now I could hide it under sweaters and full skirts.

"General, can I talk to you for a minute?"

"Sure Frieda. What's the matter? You sound serious."

"General Hollenbeck, I probably should have told you by now, but I'm expecting."

"Expecting?" Hollenbeck was incredulous. "A baby?" Hollenbeck was genuinely shocked.

"I thought you would have noticed by now, but I am about four months pregnant."

Hollenbeck's face was ashen. "Frieda, what am I going to do without you? You are my right hand. I will have trouble functioning without you here. And I trust you."

It was the last thing he said that really got to me. 'I trust you,' he said.

"General, I want to work as long as you will let me. I know that we have rules that say that..."

"Damn the rules. I want you to work as long as you can. Then I want you back as quick as you can get back. Frieda, you are indispensable. If we have to set up a delivery room in the plant, we will do it. Just don't leave till you are ready and come back as soon as you can."

It was frightening. He was saying just what I would have wanted him to say, but I didn't know if I could do it. I didn't know how long I could work, and I didn't know how quick I could come back. This was my first child. It was clear that the laying in would be a short one - just long enough to have the baby, if Hollenbeck had anything to say about it.

Hugo received Hollenbeck's reaction with great glee. He could hardly contain himself when I told him that he wanted me to work as long as possible and come back immediately after the baby was born. We talked about the hardship of the schedule. I was not so sure. Hugo, and I were both motivated by the money. He urged me onward.

The barbershop business had been increasing, not spectacularly, but steadily. Still, the income from the information exchanges had already exceeded the monthly net of the shop and was pulling away. There were at least two drops every week now in excess of the weekly drop of shipping invoices. We had opened two other bank deposit boxes, and all were swelling nicely, just like my belly.

Hugo suggested that we turn our attention to the task of finding a house. Hollenbeck's attitude about me remaining as long as possible and returning as soon as possible after the baby was born seemed to remove the last obstacle to the house decision. We started looking in earnest.

July 4, 1941

Hugo is still sleeping. We are exhausted. We found the house by June 1st and got title and possession to it on June 25th. It was on Vienna Avenue just off Frances Park in Southwest St. Louis. We painted for five days (and most of the nights). The last four days have been spent moving in. Cardboard boxes are everywhere. Our friends, Hans and Rosie helped us move. Hans had access to a truck from his work, and we moved a lot of the little things ourselves in the Whippet. The last load out of the flat came over at eleven o'clock last night. We fell into bed tired to the bone. I was so excited I could not sleep. Hugo passed out like a light and hasn't stirred since. I'm in the kitchen. The day is going to be hot. Sun is streaming in the curtain-less window over the sink. I can see our garage out back and the yard where our child will play.

August 15, 1941

We have been invited to Mildred's house for bar-b-q this evening. I really don't care if we go or not. She might be Hugo's sister, but she is such a weirdo, and the friends she will have over there will be just as weird. I suppose some of the members of the Committee will be there. It will be boring. I'll be uncomfortable. I'm big as a house. But she's Hugo's sister, and I guess a little family socializing once a year won't hurt me.

August 19, 1941

Donald Hugo Jurgens came into the world yesterday. He was a big nine-pound boy with fat cheeks and his father's eyes. He got my fair skin and both of our parents are claiming that he looks like their side of the family. I am so happy. Hugo is like a little kid. I will have to spend about six days in the hospital, and I do not know if I can stand it. He and I go down to the nursery and look at Donald through the glass. The nurse holds him up and Hugo goes nuts making faces and funny baby sounds. He is almost embarrassing.

War has broken out in Europe. In early May Hitler sent the armies of Germany into Belgium and Holland. Hitler's antagonism and outright disregard for Britain left little doubt that Britain would be next. Rommel drove the German Panzer units deep into Belgium without much resistance, and by the 18th of May had reached the Meuse River. Queen Wilhelmina has fled Holland. The disaster of Dunkirk had shocked the world. The newsreels carried pictures of British troops being evacuated from Dunkirk's desolate beaches. The British were being run off of the Continent. The British, seemingly the only real defenders against the German armies, appear defenseless to stop them. America remains neural.

By the end of May Rommel had penetrated fifty miles into France near Sedan. With the Dunkirk perimeter secure Hitler could release his forces for the push across France. Paris became his next objective.

Germany was confident, and rightfully so. Holland and Belgium were now fully in German control. By early June the scent of total victory in Europe for Germany was in the air. France was an easy, tantalizing and obvious target.

By the first of July it was all over. France had fallen.

Hugo was impressed with the efficiency of the German Armies. He had frequently expressed his admiration for Field Marshall Rommel and the other German Generals who had conducted the conquest of Europe. The talk at the Committee meetings and in the beer halls of South Saint Louis was tainted with a German bias. The forces of the Third Reich had a significant cadre of sympathizers in the German community in the heartland of America.

I, too, felt admiration for Germany. But deep inside, I wondered where it all ended? Did it stop at the coast of the European continent? Would Hitler go after England? We did not have to wait long for the answer to that question.

On August 17th the news carried stories of an attack by German fighters on a British plane over England, and bombings of plants and factories in England began. The war had crossed the English Channel. In the south the Italians attacked Gibraltar and Berber, the capital of British Somaliland.

September 19, 1941

We listened to the news on the radio in wonder. Every day brings a story of a new German or Italian conquest. Last week the Italians crossed the Libyan border into Egypt and the British were on the defensive in North Africa.

There were stories of many deaths. The bombings of England had continued. In one week in August over 1400 British civilians were killed in the bombings, mostly around London.

The British had struck back. They were now bombing Berlin from bases in the UK. Almost every night British bombers rained bombs on the German capital. It was a brutal blood bath. The Germans bombed England - England bombed Germany. Many civilians were dying on each side.

October 30, 1941

Italy invaded Greece from Albania. It was a bungled invasion from the beginning with the Italians able to advance only a fraction of what they had hoped, and the Greeks pinning them down in every rock and ravine in that mountainous country. In a funny way I was pulling for the Greeks. The Italians were so incompetent, so bungling. Hugo had said several times that Italy was a poor imitator of the Third Reich and was just trying to ride on Germany's coattails. We both predicted that Germany would have to take over for the Italians to finish the Greek invasion.

December 26, 1941

It's been a disquieting year. Hugo and I have settled into a life that does not seem to concern itself with monetary issues. Our standard of living had not changed much. We have fixed up the house so that it is almost the way we want it. Our son, Donald, has become the focus of our lives. Hugo and I both get up each morning and go to work. We found someone in the next block willing to keep him during the day for five dollars a week. The first one of us home in the evening would pick him up. It is usually me. I went back to work exactly five weeks after Donald was born. Avril Hollenbeck was ecstatic.

We still work hard, and long hours have become a way of life. But we enjoy it more now. Donald has brought a new dimension to our family. We had embarked on his first Christmas with a new and different feeling about life. While we did not go to any lavish extremes with Christmas presents, we celebrated the Holidays with a feeling that our lives have been expanded.

We continued our deliveries of classified information.

We stash our cash in safe deposit boxes and do not live pretentiously. Hugo is very concerned that we do not call attention to ourselves. We made the old Whippet last a few more miles, although I confess, we have done a little thinking about a new car. An occasional good meal, a little trip out of town for the weekend, or perhaps a better than average bottle of wine to celebrate a birthday or anniversary, was all that we allowed ourselves. The new house on Vienna Street just off Frances Park is the only visible sign of our newfound wealth. It has been a year to remember.

In Europe nine countries had been invaded without warning in less than fourteen months. Poland, Finland, Denmark, Norway, Holland, Belgium, Luxembourg, France and Greece were now under Nazi rule.

I have only one New Year's wish. I would like for things to stay the way they are. I have this bad feeling, and I am fearful that the war in Europe is going to affect us somehow. I cannot foresee how, but there is this nagging in the pit of my stomach. It has already resulted in shortages, rationing and War Effort propaganda.

At some point I guess the income that we derive from the information that we pass from Hollenbeck's office will dry up. I'll get transferred, or Hollenbeck will move on, or something else will happen, but for now if it can just continue, we can keep building our stash money and planning for a better future. It is so nice not to have the money worries that Hugo and I had when we first got married.

13
CHAPTER
AN INTEREST IN PHOTOGRAPHY

I could not get comfortable with the thought that my parents were Nazi spies. The very thought made me cringe, and I felt somehow dirtied, tainted by association. Connie was astute enough to recognize the guilt I felt, and she was caring enough to help me work through it. By now I was sleeping better and, despite my deep-seated feelings, could read the diaries with a more objective attitude than when I was first presented with the idea that my parents were committing treason. I think I had just become numb.

I took some time off from the University. I took a sabbatical from teaching to work on some special projects. I was pretty much my own boss until the fall semester. Tenure is a marvelous thing, and I had Tenure.

When we first began working through the notebooks it was in the evenings and on weekends. I couldn't read more than four or five pages at a time both because of the time required to decipher my mother's handwriting and the emotional torture the revelations each page brought. I believed that it was time to put the historical data into context. I had come accept Connie's theory that reading the dairies to a conclusion was the only way to do it. The disjointed herky-jerky of reading just a chapter at a time was not working. I had trouble grasping the magnitude of the events my mother was describing. I took a month off. I convinced myself the sabbatical would be well spent.

My first act, on a Saturday afternoon, was to return to the photos in the trunk. I noticed that the photographs that bore dates before the fall of 1940 were of a lesser quality than those that began to appear after that time. They had clearly heeded the instructions to purchase a better camera. The clarity and crispness of the photos changed in late September. It troubled me that if Mom and Dad were taking photos according to the instructions and sending in the undeveloped film then there should be no photos in the trunk other than personal photos. I was right. Their controllers were smart; there were no photos and no negatives to betray them. They were delivering the exposed film. Nothing was left in their possession that would, if they were caught, disclose what they had been doing.

Indeed, the photos in the trunk tray after the fall of 1940 were very innocuous - innocent. Nothing there revealed what they were really doing. Mom obviously liked photographing family, scenery, and events. That had long been evident from the wealth of photos that existed from the early thirties to 1940. She was pretty good at it, too. The subjects were framed well in the borders of the print, and the exposures were crisp and centered.

I spent all of Saturday afternoon going through the photos my mom had so neatly labeled, dated and tied in bunches. I took a methodical approach and started with the first ones in the upper left-hand corner of the tray working down each row of packets. The earliest photos were dated "1928" and were faded and yellowed black and whites. There were pictures of my grandmother and grandfather, cousins, relatives known to me only by their names and the descriptions my mother had given me. Mom took photos of everything - holidays, friends, family. Their funny faces, outrageous hats and outdated clothing portrayed an era known to me only by the stories that my mother had told me. I found what I believe to be the first picture of my dad. He was standing in front of a doorway with a big grin on his face holding a dog. I never knew them to own a dog, but there he was, looking in his twenties, and for the entire world as if he had not a care - grinning from ear to ear. He was a handsome fellow in his day. It's easy to see how my mom fell for him.

By Saturday evening I had gotten through the first three rows and was approaching the packet with the pictures of Weldon Spring. That packet was, somehow, a watershed. It was tangible evidence of what they were doing. It also represented a turning point after which precautions were being taken to make sure that Mom and Dad didn't have photos or negatives that would incriminate them if caught. Someone was being very smart - very careful. The photos of Weldon Spring, innocuous as they might have seemed to the casual observer, were also tangible evidence of what my Mother and Father were doing. There was only one packet. It was their first photos of the area. They kept the film and developed it. Apparently, they had made a second set of prints- one for themselves and one for their controllers. But they were proof-positive of the facts I refused to acknowledge from the manuscripts.

If what we now know about Weldon Spring is true, those photos and the information within the Weldon Spring file in Hollenbeck's office were the mother lode of information about Project Manhattan.

It was Saturday evening. Connie had made a big pot of chili. It was cold outside, pushing zero tonight. She had not spent much time with me today, instead busying herself with housework and some shopping. She had been far ahead of me in looking through the photos and had even pushed ahead deeper in to the tray several days before. I was trying to catch up.

We scooped out big steaming bowls of the dark chili and cut some sourdough bread baguettes into pieces. Connie poured a bottle of Cakebread Zinfandel and we settled onto the sofa in front of the roaring fire to read. Mom answered some of my questions in the first paragraph of the next book.

January 11, 1941

We had purchased a Nikon SLR from the Saint Louis Photo Company last fall after the instructions to get a better camera. I have always liked photography, and I had heard that Nikon made one of the best, but we never had the inclination or the money to buy one. This one cost forty dollars and had a 50mm lens that focused right through the aperture, so you could see what you were photographing before you snapped the shutter. Hugo and I studied the instruction book over and over to make sure that we could get a good photo every time. Hugo shot the first roll of the baby with the new camera. We had them developed and they came out very good - except for the one where Hugo had his thumb in front of the lens!

By the end of last year there was activity on the Weldon Spring Project file several times a week. I was filing in the drawer almost every other day. I noticed from one of the memos that the law firm in Saint Charles and its agents had succeeded in acquiring almost all of the acreage that was to be included, and that steps were being taken to obtain the rest through condemnation of the remaining property owners that wouldn't sell voluntarily. I got the impression that very little condemnation would be needed. They even took most of the houses in the little town of Hamburg because it was right in the middle of the target 25,000 acres.

This morning a little article appeared in the *Saint Louis Star Times*. It was on the last page of the first section and referred to a press release from Washington. The article carried a headline that read "Government plans expansion of munitions plant to Saint Charles County." The few short paragraphs that followed explained the expansion of the Army Ammunition plant to a site at Weldon Spring in Saint Charles County. There was not much detail, just an announcement of the plans to construct additional production facilities out there.

"So that is what they are up to," said Hugo. He had read the article at the shop and brought it home for me to see. "Not much there to get excited about."

"Hugo, it doesn't make any sense. I know what with the War and all the St. Louis Ammunition plant is being expanded rapidly, but what about the water? What are they going to do with all of that water capacity they are building?"

Hugo thought for a moment. I could tell that he, too, could not understand the connection between the need for water and the expansion of the plant. The existing plant in north St. Louis used water, but not quantities even approaching the amounts that they were talking about out at Weldon Spring.

We assumed that if the story was on the wire that it would be picked up by someone else, but we clipped the story and passed it on anyway. Hugo and I both had a penchant for detail. This story did not jibe, but we felt it should be passed on anyway. It wasn't our job to interpret it. Besides it yielded us another $100.

Lest history record me as less than a worthy mother by my omission of references to our new arrival from these notes, I have to record the joy that he has brought to our lives. Donald Hugo Jurgens has been a healthy, happy boy since his birth on September 16th. He sleeps almost all night. I breastfed him for the five weeks I was at home, and then put him on a bottle of whole milk and went back to work. He took to the bottle like a duck to water and grows daily. Some say that he is a little pudgy. I think he is just right. His cheeks are rosey and his skin is as fair as the milk for which he is so fond.

Hugo is an absolute convert to the position of father. He spends his every spare moment walking him around the house in his arms and talking to him. Hugo has even been helpful with the diapers and the washing. Right after Donald was born Hugo went out and bought a Norge washer with an auto-wringer. It makes short work of the diapers.

Five weeks at home was enough for me, and I was bored. I was anxious to get back to work and General Hollenbeck was glad to have me back. Hugo and I were able to find a lady who took care of infant children in her home just two blocks from our new house, and

I returned to work on November 4th. Within one week I was ready to pass along more information."

"Hugo and I are making regular trips out to Weldon Spring now. Activity has certainly picked up in the area. Highway 94 south of highway 40 is now asphalted and dirt covered in many places where vehicles have been entering and exiting the highway. Entrance points are no longer confined to the one driveway we had first spotted last year. Several more stakes are clearly visible from the road. Hugo and I couldn't make them out nor could we tell to what they referred. The stakes were on both sides of the road now.

We're afraid to stop, especially to take pictures. We have seen patrol cars on highway 94 and I'm terrified of being caught out there with a camera. Hugo will drive slowly, and I would snap quick photos of stakes, road entrances and signs warning trespassers to stay out.

Last week we almost got caught. Hugo was driving slowly down the road about five miles south of highway 40 at a point where the road begins to drop off the high ground. The woods are thick there and neither of us had seen anyone around. I was photographing a row of stakes that led up toward west. All of a sudden out of a little side road on the east side of the highway came a Jeep with two MP's carrying Carbine rifles. They caught up to us and flagged us down. I was petrified. I pushed the camera under Donald who was in a basket in the front seat between us praying that they had not seen me taking pictures.

The tall one walked around to Hugo's side of the car and Hugo rolled down the window. He was dressed in Army fatigues and had on boots.

"You folks are driving awfully slow," said the lanky soldier in a southern drawl. "Didn't you see that sign back there that says, 'No slowing or stopping next 6 miles'"?

I thought Hugo was going to choke. "No sir. I didn't see it," said Hugo. He lied.

The other MP had come around to the other side of the car and was peering into the back seat. I could feel him there even though it was January, cold and the window was rolled up. He walked into my field of vision and looked into the front seat. Donald slept innocently between us.

"You folks live around here?"

"We live in Saint Louis; just out for a Sunday drive after Church," said Hugo.

The lanky soldier peered into the car at Donald. I had this horrible feeling.

"Sure, is a cute little fellow you have there. It is a fellow isn't it?"

"Yes," said Hugo. "It's a boy."

"Mind if I hold him?"

If we picked up Donald they would see the camera. It was just tucked under the end of the blanket at his feet.

"He is a light sleeper," I said. "He has been a colicky baby and we have to drive him around in the car to get him to go to sleep. I really would prefer to let him sleep if you don't mind." It was the first words I had spoken.

"Yeah, sure Ma'am. I know the problem." The tall MP tipped his hat. "I've got one just like that back home in Louisiana. Have to take him for a ride at night just to get him to go to sleep. It's miserable, that colic."

"Sure is," chimed in Hugo, "especially if you are a working man."

The lanky MP stepped back from the car. "Well, you folks have a nice Sunday. Just keep moving through here. You are not supposed to stop or drive slow."

"We'll remember that," said Hugo. "So long." Hugo dropped the car into first gear.

I had never felt such terror in my life. Hugo rolled up the window and we headed off down 94 toward Defiance, a little town near the Missouri River, where we stopped and got a soda at a general store. We decided to drive on west and cross the Missouri river at Washington, Missouri rather than return back through Weldon spring on 94. It took all of the rest of the day, but we had no intention of passing back through the construction area.

I made the film drop on Tuesday.

179

March 3, 1941

Hollenbeck received a Telex this morning that referred to a meeting at the University of Chicago. I had no idea what the meeting was about or what it related to. It gave the time and place and who would attend. I would pass it on when Hollenbeck left. Hollenbeck frequency went to Chicago for various reasons, and I did not think too much of the Telex except that the meeting had been called for this Friday - just two days away. It was awfully short notice for a trip to Chicago.

Hollenbeck was not in the office when the Telex came in, and there were several that morning, so I thought it would be a good idea to call it to his attention upon his arrival. He got in just after eleven. He looked like he had been hunting and wore rough wool trousers and a down filled green bush jacket. His pants were speckled with burrs and his boots had mud on them.

News of the Chicago meeting disturbed him. It was not so much the short notice that seemed to bother him, but rather the content of the meeting. I asked if I could help him.

"I appreciate your offer, Frieda," he said, "but you really wouldn't understand."

"Try me," I said somewhat indignantly. I really didn't intend to be arrogant, but I didn't care for his condescending attitude about my knowledge about what was going on. "After all," I said, "I am your secretary. How can I help you if you won't tell me what's happening?"

Avril Hollenbeck was a forceful, intelligent man. He was also sensitive. I believe he regretted instantly any inference that I was not bright enough to understand something. He began to apologize immediately.

"Frieda, I don't mean to imply that you are some kind of a dummy. I'm sorry. I didn't mean that. It's just that with all of the security and what we are doing I can't tell you everything. Please don't think that..."

"General, I've been with you for twelve years. If you can't trust me who can you trust?"

His big sad eyes softened. He had been standing behind the desk in his rough clothes. For the life of me I could not get the image of Ernest Hemingway out of my mind. He leaned on the back of his chair, and a painful look crossed his face.

"Sit down Frieda." He pulled out the big leather chair behind his desk and slowly eased himself into it without taking his eyes off me. I had no idea what was coming.

Hollenbeck paused for what seemed an eternity, looking at his fingernails. He seemed torn between telling me something and pleading for my understanding. Apparently, he opted to talk to me.

"Frieda. I need your help. There are only a handful of people here that know what is going on, but I need someone in my office that I can rely on."

"Sir, I have a Top-Secret clearance. What more can I offer you?"

"I know. I know," said Hollenbeck raising his palms in mock protest. "Maybe it's me. Maybe I am too cautious. I just can't rely on someone's clearance. I have to know."

"Know what?"

"I have to know that the person with whom I am speaking is absolutely trustworthy."

"Sir, you've known Hugo and me for..."

"Long enough," Hollenbeck interrupted me. He looked down at the desk.

"Yes sir. Long enough." I shamed him. I couldn't believe my own ears. I shamed him and made him regret that he did not trust me.

"Frieda," he began, "we're doing something here that has never been done before, at least not in the way we are going to do it."

"I don't understand."

Hollenbeck paused before answering.

"Frieda, did you ever hear of Uranium?"

"What?"

"Uranium."

"No sir. What is Uranium?"

"Frieda, Uranium is the heaviest metal known to man. We're going to refine it."

"Why sir?"

"I can't tell you that, Frieda. Please don't ask me to give you any further explanation. I can't do it."

"But sir, I thought that our emphasis has been on lighter metals. I mean, those experiments with titanium and aluminum and ..."

"Frieda, stop. Don't ask any more. I've told you all that I can. You must respect me on this. I have told you more than you should know, but only because I need you to help me with the project. I need someone in my office that I can rely on to take some of the everyday administrative burdens off of me."

"What's all of this got to do with the plant expansion to Weldon Spring?"

"That's what we are going to do out there. It has to be kept top secret."

"Refining this Uranium?"

"Yes, Frieda. Refining Uranium."

"But you can't tell me why."

Hollenbeck looked down, dejected, exasperated. "I can't tell you why, Frieda."

I summarized my conversation with Hollenbeck on a single sheet with a Smith Corona typewriter that I kept at home. It was an old model that had been cast off from the plant several years ago. I confiscated it when it was on its way to the trash heap and paid a man down on Washington Street four dollars to recondition it. As far as I was concerned it worked like new. I lead off my synopsis with the statement that 'The story on the wire service about expanding the production capacity of the Saint Louis Army Ammunition Plant' was a decoy, a cover-up to decoy what was really happening at Weldon Spring. I repeated the conversation with Hollenbeck verbatim so as not to add or subtract anything. I wasn't fully aware of the implications surrounding the refining of Uranium. I tried for absolute accuracy.

Forty-eight hours after the note was passed I received a call at home from a man who identified himself as "Mister Graff." Hugo wasn't at home. I didn't recognize the voice.

"Mrs. Jurgens," he said flatly. "You have been placed in my charge. You are to have no contact with anyone else. Do you understand?"

"No, I really don't. I don't hear from you or anyone else for months. I pass information without incident. Then you call and identify yourself, and say I am to answer to you. I never heard of you."

"Of course, you have never heard of me. But I know very much about you, Hugo and your lovely son, Donald," Graff said, menacingly. "From now on I will be your contact. You will speak only to me."

I didn't like this man. I had never met him, but I knew when I did I would not like him.

"Listen carefully, Mrs. Jurgens. I will not repeat these instructions: On Saturday morning you are to go to Union Station. Directly in front of train track 12 there is a row of two- sided benches. Arrive at 11 AM and take the third bench from the track and sit down. You may bring Hugo or not. You will be contacted. Just sit there until you are. We will know you so there is no need for you to recognize us."

"Will you be coming, Mister Graff?"

The phone went dead.

I told Hugo of the conversation with Graff when he got home. He was strangely unmoved. Something had happened at the shop that had distracted him.

"Frieda, I had a man in the shop today who is a surveyor for one of the big engineering firms downtown."

"So?"

"He says they have a contract with the Army Corps of Engineers to do engineering work out at Weldon Spring."

"Well, that's certainly a coincidence."

"How so?"

"It seems our communication about the Uranium on Tuesday has certainly piqued the interest of our contacts. A man named Graff called me today. He wants a meeting on Saturday at Union Station."

"Really?" Hugo was now interested. He rubbed his chin and tried to put the pieces of the puzzle together.

"Anyway, the fellow in the shop, his name is Shanahan, says that they are engineering two big water plants that will take water from deep wells down near the Missouri river and process it for use in a huge plant that is located up in the center of the property."

"Do you think that is what all of the activity on the east side of highway 94 is all about? Remember those stakes that led down toward the river that we could not figure out?"

"Here's the interesting part," continued Hugo. There is going to be a railroad spur brought in there from the Missouri-Kansas-Texas Railroad that runs along the river. It is being designed to be protected by anti-bomb devices, and it's to be designed to specifications that anticipate extremely heavy weights."

"What does that mean?"

"I think it means that whatever they anticipate hauling in and out of there will be very valuable, probably critical to the War effort, and will weigh a tremendous amount."

I thought about Hollenbeck's statement that Uranium was the heaviest of all metals.

"Hugo, is this information reliable? I mean is something we should pass on? Can we be assured that it is true?"

"The guy had no reason to lie. Frankly, I thought him a little boasting, but I believe him. Everything he says connects with what we know. I think we should pass it on."

On Friday I prepared another typewritten summary of the information that Hugo had picked up in the shop. Hugo made the drop and retrieved the envelope with the cash on Friday evening.

I had to do the weekly shopping.

We sat in the third bench in front of track 12. Union Station was a busy place. Uniforms were everywhere - Army, Navy. You'd think something special was happening, but it was like that every day in Union Station. A long row of side-by-side tracks backed up to a huge concourse that was packed with people coming and going. Track 12 was roughly in the middle. Steam rose from the brakes and coupler pipes and filled the air with a wet carnival smell. Soldiers and sailors left and boarded train after train that backed into the huge station only to exchange their passengers and leave again. Porters hauled bags and baggage on carts. You could watch them walk along the concourse skillfully weaving through the crowds with their little handcarts only to dart between the trains with their cargo. Passengers followed gingerly behind. Union Station was a busy, noisy place.

We had come to track 12 and sought out the bench directly in front of the train for Memphis that had been backed into the track against the big bumper. The bench contained seven sections. We chose the third as we had been instructed.

The bench was constructed of oak slats on a steel frame. It had two slatted benches back-to-back. Each side was contoured to fit the body with each back abutted against the other. Brass balled posts separated the sections along with a brass armrest. We sat down at five minutes to eleven. Hugo smoked a Camel.

Just past eleven, a man in a Gray sweater smoking a pipe sat down on the bench across from us. He watched us closely but made no move to come closer. About three minutes later a little man sat down on the bench behind us. He had a folded newspaper under his arm. I saw him coming across the station. He made no hesitation before sitting down directly behind us on the abutting bench. I speculated that he had been watching us from some vantage point. He was short, only about five feet three or four, had on a suit and vest, and walked with a slight limp favoring his right leg. He had a little mustache and a big black hat that he held in his hand, and I thought he might be Jewish. He sat on the bench directly behind us.

"Good morning Herr Jurgens, Frau Jurgens." The accent was guttural German. I guessed from the north of Germany, but what did I know?

"We are here. What do you want?" said Hugo.

He got right to the point. "You have passed to us information that is very important. I suspect that you do not know of its significance."

"All I know is it involves something I do not know about nor understand," I said.

"I thought so," he said. "It is important, however that the information continue."

"I'll do my best, but since I don't understand exactly what the information is about I cannot guarantee that …."

"You don't understand, Frau Jurgens. We will be the arbiters of the relevance and quality of what you pass us. Your job is to continue to pass everything from the Weldon Spring files. These files are of extreme interest to Germany. Do you understand?"

Hugo turned toward the little man. He made no effort to hide his identity. "I understand you like what we are sending you. Right Hermann? But do you understand the risk of what we are doing? In case you haven't read the newspapers Germany is at war with most of America's European allies. Have you ever thought to think about what that means?"

"Of course. It means tha…."

Hugo was not going to be deterred. He cut him off. "It means that in times of war, spies like us get shot."

"That is a risk of our profession."

"Bullshit," said Hugo. It is a risk that must be compensated. If we are going to risk our necks, then you are going to pay dearly for the information. Got it?"

"On the contrary, Herr Jurgens, we…"

"Don't call me 'Herr'," said Hugo.

"OK, *Mister* Jurgens," Graff's voice dripped with sarcasm, "but you had better listen to me."

Hugo didn't respond. I did not like the way this conversation was going.

"We'll pay you the same - no more - no less. In fact, if we decide to pay you less we can do so. Whatever we offer you will take. If you don't like it all we have to do is expose Frieda as a mole in Hollenbeck's office and you as her accomplice. The game will end. It would be a pity to see Frieda tied to a stake and shot through the heart. You'd probably get life. It's easy. All we have to do is send an anonymous letter to Hollenbeck with samples of the Weldon Spring file that Frieda provided. The *Top-Secret* Weldon Spring file. It is so simple. I'm sure you understand how it would work."

The little man squared around so that he could see both of us. "In the meantime, the remuneration for the information will remain the same."

Hugo was silent.

"Listen carefully. You will report to me. I am known as Graff. You will continue the delivery of information as before, but we shall have more meetings. I will notify you tomorrow of three more drop points. The Granada Theater is over-used. The park is still a safe drop. It is important that you focus on relevant information. There is much that is useless. I will increase your efficiency. Your value to the Reich will increase concurrent with the quality of your information. You will obey my instructions to the last detail."

"And if we don't," said Hugo.

"They say a shot through the heart is painless," said Graff. He rose, folded the newspaper that he had spread on the seat beside him, and strolled into the crowd toward the east end of the concourse. The man seated across from us was gone, too.

June 23, 1941

This morning we awoke to news accounts of Hitler's invasion of Russia. The war had seemed to widen. Germany had swept through Yugoslavia, Romania and Bulgaria already this year. Crete had fallen. There were daily news reports of battles in North Africa.

We had continued to pass information in the usual manner without incident. For the last few months we have been dropping information at least weekly. In some weeks we had as many as three drops. We utilized the new dead drops that Graff had instituted, the Tivoli Theater in the Delmar Loop, a gatehouse on Westmoreland place at its intersection with Kingshighway, and a Statute in Francis Park not far from our new house.

Each drop point has been given a number a number 1, 2, 3, or 4. The Granada was number one; the Tivoli was number two and so on. If the drop was at number one we followed the same telephone procedure, but after making the contact call and waiting for the ring, we were told to hang up, call again, and let the phone ring the number of rings to correspond with the number of the drop point. Graff instructed us not to use the same point twice in one week. We hadn't had to with four drops. The signal to pick up the information was still the "OPEN" sign in the corner of the barbershop window.

The Weldon Spring files now occupy a full file drawer in Hollenbeck's office and have spilled over into a second. Many of the documents are lengthy and contain material that I cannot comprehend. Hugo, who has a good mind for things mechanical, was at a loss when I tried to explain the contents. I wasn't sure of myself and had little confidence in my ability to retain and interpret the information. I couldn't make copies of the documents. In fact, many of the documents contained a "DO NOT COPY" stamp that would have been trouble if I even tried.

I had always believed that the more complex documents could be photographed. But to bring my big camera into the plant and use flash bulbs to get a clear picture in the subdued light would have been suicidal. The flashes would be a dead giveaway.

Hugo had heard of miniature cameras that could handle fast film that could be used to photograph documents in low light. I thought they were just in the Dick Tracy comics.

Last Saturday we went down to Saint Louis Photo Company on the bus. We had some shopping to do downtown. Donald was growing out of his clothes faster than we had ever imagined he would. Hugo went with me so that we could go look for a camera - a special camera.

Saint Louis Photo occupies a large ground floor space with every kind of camera equipment imaginable. Clerks in little waist-length smocks wait on customers from behind glass counters. I was fascinated by all of the gadgetry. Hugo was in heaven. He loves little mechanical things.

"May I help you?" asked the youngish blond-haired clerk leaning on the counter with both hands.

"Er.,. No thank you. We're just looking," said Hugo.

"How are we going to find what we want in here without telling someone," I said to Hugo under my breath.

Hugo whispered into my ear. "What did you have in mind? Perhaps we should just ask for a small camera that we could use to photograph military secrets!"

I saw his point. How do you ask for a camera that will photograph data without looking suspicious?

The clerk was watching us. It was as if he had been assigned to follow us around the store. We browsed through the section of developing equipment, chemicals and paper, and moved on towards tripods and reflecting umbrellas. The clerk remained a few steps behind.

Finally, Hugo turned to him and said, "We are doing some research for the Archdiocese. Much of it is in the archives of the Old Cathedral and out at Saint Louis University library. Is there anything that you have that you can recommend for photographing old Church records?"

"Of course," said the young man. He turned and motioned for us to follow. "Follow me."

He led us into their camera area, and to a small locked glass case in an alcove slightly away from the big cases that held the 35mm cameras. He stepped behind the counter and took out a key. Reaching under the first glass shelf he grasped a small object that looked like a pencil box. It was about four inches long and rounded on the ends. When he got it to the top of the counter he held it with both hands and pulled it. It slid open to a length of about five inches and revealed a lens and viewfinder. He pushed it together and pulled it apart again.

"That's the way you wind the film. Push it together and pull apart. It's very quick and easy."

"What kind of camera is it?"

"It's a Minox. Made in Germany. Probably for spy work."

Hugo about choked. He coughed and put his hand to his mouth. "What kind of film does it use?"

"It's a very fast film. Specially made for the Minox. It's only about an inch wide.

Hugo rolled the little camera around in his hand admiring its brushed silver stainless steel case.

"It has a very short focal plane from less than a meter to infinity."

Hugo pushed it together and pulled it apart exposing its lens and the camera trigger.

"It's pretty pricey, but it is for low light conditions. You can only get the film in black and white. None of the new color films will fit it. I hope that you do not want to photograph any colorful manuscripts?"

I looked at Hugo. He was forcing back a grin. "Oh, no. Almost all of the Church records are in black and white.

"How much does it cost?" asked Hugo.

"Let's see here." The clerk fished for the box in a drawer under the cabinet. He found it and held it up to read the price on the bottom. "One hundred and five dollars."

"One hundred five dollars!" repeated Hugo. "What's it made of, gold?"

"Well, not exactly, but it is excellent German craftsmanship - and look at its size. It would fit into the palm of your hand, and it has a Leica lens." The clerk held up the camera so we could see the lens.

"We can't afford one hundred five dollars," said Hugo. "We'll have to think about it some more."

The clerk replaced the camera in the cabinet. "My name's Jack. If you decide to buy, please ask for me. I am on a commission."

"Yeah, sure, Jack. Thanks." Hugo took me by the arm and hustled me out the door.

At the bus stop I could tell that Hugo was up to something. He had that faraway look that told me that his mind was somewhere else.

"Hugo, what are you thinking?"

Hugo shuffled. It was a warm day and he was perspiring a little. "What do you say if we ask old Graff to buy the camera? After all, they want the secrets. They want the detail. They should pay for it."

"Let's ask him."

We left Graff a note in the next pick-up, and told him what we wanted. We even gave him the name and where he could buy it. To our surprise Graff responded that he was familiar with both Saint Louis Photo Company and the Minox camera. One week later it arrived in a brown paper package delivered by a courier riding a bicycle just as we were arriving home from an afternoon at the plant. Hugo had been cutting hair and I had waited for him to finish the schedule of plant foremen, so we could ride home together. It was after seven when we got home.

The package contained the camera and twelve rolls of film with twelve exposures each - 144 photographs.

"Let's try a roll to see what we get," said Hugo.

"Do you think that's wise? I mean the price of film and all. We could..."

"Nonsense," said Hugo. "What we need to do is try to duplicate the lighting conditions that exist in your office. Then we take some photos and see how they come out."

It sounded like a good idea. Hollenbeck's office is not exactly bright, but it is not fair to say that it's a dungeon, either. It's on the north side of the building so there is never any direct sunlight. He has two large floor lamps at the end of a large sofa, and a big gooseneck lamp on his desk for close up bright work. In the ceiling there are three milk glass globe fixtures that provide general light. Over the big conference table is a three-bulb chandelier that has shades that cast the light right straight down. Hugo began moving lights and screwing in and taking out bulbs until I said it looked about right. Changing our living room to a lighting twin of Hollenbeck's office was a wild shot at best. Finally, I thought it was close.

"Hugo, that looks about right. If I can put the documents on the conference table directly under the light, I can get pretty good light on them."

"Hugo pulled over a little side table and positioned it under the living room chandelier.

"Like this?" he said, gesturing to the surface of the little table.

"Approximately."

"Good. Now hand me that newspaper."

Hugo spread the newspaper on the little table. "Looks about right?"

"You are going to photograph the newspaper?"

"Sure. It's a good test. Lots of words. Closely spaced. It'll be a good test." He picked up the little camera and began walking around the open newspaper. He snapped off a shot and wound the film. Then he moved back a little and snapped off another. Then he handed it to me, and I did the same. We shot up the whole roll. Each position was different. He moved in close and then further away. We photographed into the light's glare and away from it. It took us less than ten minutes.

Gasen's drug store down on Morganford would not take the film. "Never heard of that kind of film," said the snotty clerk. "You'll have to take it to a specialty shop."

"Like where?" said Hugo.

"Like Saint Louis Photo or one of those places that specialize in photography and developing. We don't do it."

We took the film back to Saint Louis Photo hoping to avoid Jack. He probably didn't get the commission if Graff bought the camera. Indeed, we wondered if the camera had even been bought there. We really didn't want to have to explain. Hugo took it in. I waited in the car. He didn't encounter Jack.

It took two weeks to get the film back. The results were astounding. The pictures were crisp, and the newspaper was very readable on the prints using a magnifying glass. The only thing we had to watch was exceeding the focal length of the lens. When we held it at too much of an angle to the printed page the print on the far end, toward the top, got blurry. It was easily remedied by getting more directly above the page being photographed and shooting straight down.

We tried a second roll. Hugo had even laid the newspaper on the floor and stood on a chair to shoot down on it. He thought it might be a good way to photograph the big maps, plats and flow charts that I had described to him. Some of the larger items in the file had to be folded up, and I even noticed that there were two sets of plans that were rolled and were leaning against the back of the file cabinet. He simulated the big plats by opening the newspaper to its fullest and trying to photograph the whole thing. We got the prints two weeks later. They came out crisp just like the ones we took on top of the table.

The next day after we shot the second roll we got a phone call from Graff. He wanted to know when we were going to send some photographs of documents?

"Be patient," said Hugo. "We just had to try out the camera to get it right. Hold on. Your patience will be rewarded."

Indeed, it was. Hollenbeck was to go out of town to the University of Chicago for most of the week. It would be the perfect opportunity. I practiced using the camera without film to get the document in the viewfinder. Hugo suggested that I might lay four documents on the table at once if they were regular letter size. Then each frame of film could contain four documents and the photographing would be more efficient. I tried it on our dining room table. Using this method, I could get 48 pages on a roll of twelve frames.

In the first photo session in Hollenbeck's office I shot up two rolls and got in ninety-six pages of documents. I decided to photograph the whole file drawer from front to back in order. Filings in the drawer were made in separate folders but the most recent was always on top since we filed chronologically. I started in the front of the drawer and worked back.

The film was passed on the evening it was taken. I would call Hugo and give him a "Hello." It was a signal. We had worked out a set of code words so that I could tell Hugo that we would have a drop that evening. I would tell him: "I'm bringing something home for the baby." That was his signal to call Graff and arrange a drop at one of the locations using the phone code. That way I did not have to run the risk of making the call from the plant. Hugo would then move the "Open" sign.

September 12, 1941

I had finished photographing the complete file drawer. All that was left were the big rolls of plans. In just over two months I had taken up sixty rolls of film - over six hundred photographs. When we would run low on film Graff would send the messenger over with another brown package with another dozen rolls. He must have been counting. When we would deliver roll number nine back to him for developing we could expect another delivery of a dozen rolls within a couple of days.

Graff and his superiors must have been delighted. They increased the payments to us by fifty dollars each. Hugo didn't even have to fight with them to get the increase. Although Graff never told us what exactly was so important about the information that we were transmitting, it was clear that we had hit the jackpot. Graff called us almost every week to encourage us and to tell us how sharp and clear that the photographs were.

It is strange, though. We never saw one of the photos that I took. Once we delivered the exposed film they were gone forever.

December 2, 1941

Something important was brewing. For the last three weeks there had been Telexes and telephone calls about a meeting that would take place in Washington on December 6th. I tried to keep up with the activity, but some of it related to phone conversations to which I was not a party. All I could do was monitor written communications. General Hollenbeck told me last week that he would be attending.

Various names and places began to creep into the correspondence and Telexes whom I didn't recognize. Dr. Edward Teller, Arthur H. Compton, Oak Ridge, Tennessee. They were somehow connected to what we were doing at Weldon Spring. I noticed that many of the communications came from the University of Chicago.

December 8, 1941

I guess I'll remember last night as long as I live. We were on our way to Hugo's mother and father's house for dinner. They often had us over on Sunday night for dinner. The baby was asleep in a bassinet in the back seat. Hugo and I were going down Kingshighway talking about what we were going to do about Christmas presents. The car radio was on KMOX. The announcer cut into the mystery program with a bulletin:

"We interrupt this program for a special news bulletin: The United States Naval Base at Pearl Harbor, Hawaii was attacked this morning by planes of the Republic of Japan. The U.S.S. Arizona has been sunk and several other American naval vessels are badly damaged. Casualties are not yet determined, but are expected to exceed one thousand Americans killed or wounded. The attack occurred shortly after dawn this morning, Hawaii Time. Stay tuned to this station for further bulletins."

Hugo was silent for a long time. Neither of us spoke. The magnitude of the event just seemed to overwhelm us, and nothing seemed appropriate. The United States, our country, had been attacked. Neither of us could foresee what lie ahead. Deep within us was the realization that we were betraying our country weekly, yet the attack by the Japanese sickened us. For a fleeting moment I felt ashamed for the first time. I couldn't reconcile my feelings. On one hand, I was swept up into the torrent of emotion that every other American who heard that bulletin must have felt; on the other, I knew we could not stop now. We were in too deep; the money was too good; the life too well lived on the spoils of the information we provided.

We were frozen in time that Sunday evening. Thoughts and words came slowly, awkwardly. I can't even tell you what the rest of the evening was about, and it was just last night."

14
CHAPTER
AN INVITATION
TO TRAVEL

"February 14, 1942

Hugo is so romantic. He bought me a dozen red roses. They cost ten cents apiece and were grown in a hot house. They came with a big ribbon tied on them from the flower shop on South Grand. The note read: "To my Valentine. Will you be mine forever?" "Love Hugo"

Little Donald is walking and getting into everything. He likes to get into the pots and pans and pull them out to play with them. I have to keep the kitchen cabinets tied shut with a cord. Hugo takes him for walks in Frances Park even on the coldest days. The two of them are inseparable. I can hardly wait until he is big enough to throw a baseball. Hugo will probably have him down in the basement pitching before he's five.

It's interesting being the only woman in a house with two males. I never thought that I would feel like the odd man out, but sometimes I do. It's not that there is anything wrong, but I often wonder if it would be different if Donald had turned out to be a girl?

The project out at Weldon Spring has turned out to be huge. We would drive out from time to time making sure we didn't drive too slowly. From the road we can see massive construction. A large main building is being built on a spot in about the center of the property. In the winter with the leaves off you can see it as you drive by. It is rising well above the trees. There are other massive construction projects going on further down the road. I presume some of them have to do with the large water plants being built. A large set of pipes is being laid under highway 94 and down to what appears to be wells near the River. Hollenbeck goes out there now almost once each week - sometimes twice.

The Weldon Spring files now occupy a full filing cabinet consisting of four drawers in the rear of Hollenbeck's office. The two rolls of plans have expanded so that we had to order a plan cabinet with 48 drawer compartments in it to hold them. While I had no training in engineering or drafting, I am getting good enough to recognize some of the schematics. Some of them are plant designs and building specifications. Others are schematics of production components. All were photographed by me using the Minox camera and the fast film within a few days after they came in. I have lots of time alone in Hollenbeck's office nowadays as he is away about as much as he is there."

Connie had found a peculiar fascination with the photographs in the tray of the trunk. She kept going back and forth through them. Several times we had expressed wonderment that there was a whole block of photographs that Mother referred to about the Weldon Spring file that were not included in the trunk. The photos that Connie perused were the usual photos of a happy family - a mother, a father, a new child, and walks in the park, first steps, picnics and all of the other things of family life. Yet they masked the person behind the camera. She was my mother, a Nazi spy, stealthily committing treason by photographing America's secrets and selling them to the Nazis for money. It made me sick.

It was Sunday afternoon.

"Connie, what do you say we take a ride out to St. Charles County?"

"You mean to Weldon Spring?"

"Yeah. It's been a long time since I've been out there. I think we went by there when we went to a winery out at Augusta a few years ago didn't we?"

"Yes," said Connie, "but I think I might see it differently now. Don't you?"

It was cold. The Interstate got us to the Missouri River in no time and we crossed into St. Charles County rising into the rolling hills on the west side of the Missouri river.

"Isn't this the place they have been hassling over a plan to clean up the radioactive contamination?" said Connie.

We both had recalled there had been some controversy over the dismantling of the buildings and cleanup of the area. Something about a "Superfund site." Apparently, it was a real "hot" zone. As I recalled there had been millions involved.

"There was fear that the ground water has been contaminated or something like that," as I remembered.

State Road 94, a two-lane asphalt roadway, loops south from Highway 40 just like Mom described it - only fully paved now. We passed a sign that announced, "Busch Wildlife Area" and another that indicated that there were fishing lakes. The area was thickly wooded, with oak and hickory forests. We could see a lake. It looked natural. A few fields dotted the east side of the road, but soon gave way to the woods.

"Look" said Connie, pointing at a large group of buildings on the right side of the road. "It looks like a school. It is a school - Francis Howell High School."

"It's right where the plant should be." We drove past the sprawling high school with its modern gymnasium and glass and brick classrooms. Tennis courts faced the road.

The road began to bend to the left. "It sure doesn't look like Mom described it. Where is the plant that was so ..."

"Look at that." Connie saw it first looming up through the trees.

"That must be it." I slowed to a crawl. No signs told us not to stop or slow. We encountered a high chain link fence along the right side of the road with razor wire on the top. The fence stretched for over a mile. Set back from the road was a massive industrial building, dark, brooding and apparently vacant against the western sky. It was the monster factory that my Mother had described as Weldon Spring.

About halfway down the fence at an entrance driveway was a guardhouse and signs that prohibited entry without a pass. The guardhouse was manned. We drove slowly and peered through the fence. There were no signs that prohibited us from looking. Driving slowly didn't seem to be a crime, and there were no cars behind us, but we noticed that the guard in the guardhouse did write down our license number as we passed.

"That place is huge," said Connie.

The road began to loop along the ridge of the hill through deep forests.

"I'll bet it was around here that Mom and Dad got stopped when they were taking photographs."

"Sure matches her descriptions, doesn't it?"

"Look. There's the railroad track." A pair of tracks paralleled the roadway for several hundred yards and then crossed the road and dropped off to the east. The tracks had been removed across the roadway, but the blacktop surface was still rough where the tracks had crossed the road.

As we topped a hill, we could see a massive concrete building atop another hill further to the south. It had a big dome and large square piers that held up a large square tank. "What do you think that is?"

"I'll bet it's one of the water plants. See the big tank?" Connie pointed at the square structure alongside the main building.

"You're probably right. It's constructed on one of the highest points. Probably to enhance the pressure."

As we got closer the water plant appeared more ominous, dark and menacing, against the southern sky. All of its windows had been broken out. Its gray concrete had stains all over it and bore the weathered look of an old bunker. Graffiti had been sprayed on the concrete walls.

Chain link fences now stretched along both sides of the road. Every few feet were the familiar radioactive hazard warning signs with their universal skull and crossbones. The signs appeared alternately with "Keep out - U.S. Government property."

Connie and I drove home in silence.

"March 8, 1942

General Hollenbeck told me that he would be establishing another office out at Weldon Spring. I didn't know what that would mean. He was a little vague. I couldn't tell if he was going to move out there permanently, or if it would be a satellite office as he had done when we had moved from the main plant in St. Louis over to the Goodfellow Street plant. Few answers were forthcoming. I was nervous I would not have access to the information that was coming through our office in the St. Louis Plant. What if Hollenbeck was planning on moving out there and leaving me behind? The move had all kinds of financial implications to Hugo and me.

"You have got to make arrangements to be transferred with him if he is really moving out there," said Hugo.

"How do I go about doing that? I mean, he makes those decisions, not me."

"First, you need to find out what he really has in mind. Make sure you keep your ear to the ground to find out what's really afoot."

"What if he really is going to move the whole office out there?"

"Then you'll have to tell him you are ready to go with him."

"Hugo, that's impossible. How will I get there? How will we...."

"Listen Frieda, It's a Hell of a lot more important that you stay with Hollenbeck. We'll manage. We'll even move out there if we have to, but what's important now is that you keep your job. It's our future. It's our income."

I looked at Hugo over the dinner that we were eating in the kitchen. I'm sure that I had that same doleful look he did. It approached panic. We thought we were about to be cut off from our source of income. We were hooked. Even though we were not spending the money or living high - we were hooked. We wanted and needed the money more than we knew. We were willing to do anything to keep it flowing. It scared me. I know it scared Hugo, but we just couldn't shake it. We were earning over a thousand dollars a month passing secrets. That was three times more than Hugo earned in the shop. I hated myself for it, but I put the fear and self-loathing into the dark corners of my mind where the light could not shine on them. I put them out of my mind. Seeing Hugo's face; his fear of losing the income; it all came rushing back. We were spies. We were doing the villainous work of espionage for money. I didn't even have an ideological affinity for the cause. I could care less about the National Socialist Worker's Party. The Nazis were nothing to me. I'm not sure about Hugo. We were spying for money - plain and simple - money!

"Hugo. This is our chance. We have made enough. Besides, we always have got the chance of getting caught. Let's get out. If Hollenbeck moves, let's get out."

"No, Frieda. Things are going too good. If we can keep this up for another year, or so, we'll be set. Our life will be made much easier if we can put away another year. We shouldn't quit now."

"Hugo, my poor Hugo. Look at us. We are both scared to death. We can't sleep. We are both smoking like a chimney. Sure, we can always use more money, but it'll always be that way. We can always use more money; it's the nature of life, but I'm not sure we can take it much longer."

Hugo paused and looked at me for a long time. "You *really are* scared, aren't you?"

"I'm scared sick. Our country is at war. It's getting too risky. Hugo, this is a chance to turn it off without any ramifications. We both need it. It's been good, but it is too risky to continue. We've got twenty-seven thousand dollars in the bank. That's enough. Let's get out."

Hugo reached over the table and took my hand. His eyes were wet. I couldn't tell if he was crying or if he was just relieved.

"You're right Frieda. Let's get out."

July 30, 1942

The plans for the move of Hollenbeck's office out to the Weldon springs plant developed slowly. It turned out he was not going to move everything out to Weldon Spring, but rather a contingent of scientists that would be more closely connected with the mission of the plant would be relocated. Hollenbeck wouldn't manage them directly - a new scientific manager would arrive from Oak Ridge, Tennessee to do that. What they were doing was out of Hollenbeck's league. He was a production specialist and not a pure scientist. Hollenbeck's main office would remain at the plant in St. Louis. I would remain as his assistant with full access to his files. Without a move by Hollenbeck the opportunity for continued transfer of information was probable.

Hugo and I had talked several times of our decision to cut the umbilical cord and call it quits. Despite Hollenbeck's decision to keep the St. Louis Plant as his headquarters with me having full and continued access to the files, Hugo and I had decided to press forward with our withdrawal.

We considered it thoroughly. You don't just walk away from three years of delivering secrets. Hugo and I discussed it from every angle. We thought of the ramifications if we were threatened. We continued to deliver the information weekly. One week in August we even had three deliveries, but we vowed not to let our controllers know what we were thinking until we were ready to tell them.

We reasoned that there was little threat of them outing us to Hollenbeck or anyone else if the information we had passed was so darned important. Hollenbeck, and therefore the United States, never suspected a thing. To tell on us would be to tip the U.S. government that the Nazis knew about the mole in the Weldon Spring Plant.

August,1942

Hollenbeck asked me to make travel arrangements for him to travel to San Francisco in September. He never told me what the trip was about but in making arrangements I discovered that he was going to stay at a place Called "Bohemian Grove." I had no idea where Bohemian Grove was or how to get there, and I asked the General what he needed to get from San Francisco to there?

"I'll take care of it. Don't worry. Just get me to San Francisco" He said. He never gave me any more information, and I knew better than to ask.

He was there for several days.

When he returned something had changed. He was more serious, more determined. Things seemed more urgent to him, and he spoke even less about what he was doing. I only got information by perusing letters, memos and documents in his office when he was away. But there were lots of opportunities.

October 30, 1942

In the two years since our first meeting at Union Station we had many contacts with Graff. He was careful not to be seen with us, but meetings on park benches, train stations, and in theaters were common. His telephone conversations were always brief but encouraging. We learned to read Graff like a book. If he didn't tell you how he felt, you could read it in his voice. When we produced a particularly interesting or vital piece of information he would always call to congratulate us urging us onward to bigger and better accomplishments. He was a loyal soldier toiling in the fields, planting, harvesting, but always for someone else.

I never quite understood the information we were passing. It was mostly letters, drawings and memos of a technical nature, but certain words were frequently repeated, and caught my eye. Words like "Tubealloy" and "U-235" meant nothing to me. Names like Groves, Compton, Oppenheimer were often repeated, and I assumed they had something to do with the "project." There were several references to a place called Oak Ridge, Tennessee, but when I looked it up in the Atlas at the St. Louis Library I couldn't find it. It certainly was not on any of the Tennessee maps that I saw. I just passed the information on in the usual manner and got paid for it. Gathering and transmitting the information was easy, but nerve-racking. Both Hugo and I knew that it would be easy to slip up and get caught, no matter what precautions we took. It was unnerving, and our only tangible consolation was the payments that we dutifully stashed away in our bank safe-deposit boxes.

Graff never gave us an address where he could be contacted. If we wanted to talk to him we were to slip a note into one of the drops. He would call - usually within hours. On Thursday we had put such a note in the drop with shipping information on a load of mortar shells destined for New Jersey. The note simply read:

"Important we talk to you. Please call."

There was no signature. There never were any signatures on any of our communications with Graff. At eight o'clock on Saturday morning the phone rang.

"Got your note," said Graff. "Will you meet me at the zoo in front of the large birdcage? There is a bench there. Five o'clock tonight. Will you both be coming?"

"Yes. We'll see you there. Five o'clock," said Hugo and hung up the phone. Graff conducted no business on the phone.

It was a hot August evening. Hugo parked the car and we walked a block or so to get to the big black iron birdcage. It is a domed affair, bigger than a house, built during the 1904 World's Fair. Birds were squawking from within the vast interior. We walked around the end and there was Graff sitting on a bench in a suit feeding popcorn to pigeons from a paper sack. Several had gathered around his feet. He did not look up at our approach.

"What is so important?" he inquired in a matter of fact voice.

"We're pulling back, Graff."

"Oh, what does that mean?"

"It means that it's getting a little too hot. Frieda almost got caught the other day. I think they may be suspecting us." Hugo and I had made up the story. As far as we knew, no one at the plant had the slightest idea of what we had been doing. We needed a reason to tell Graff that we were quitting. "We'll start again if things cool off, but right now it is too dangerous."

"That's interesting," said Graff. "How do I know that I should believe you?"

"Believe us?" I said, "Why *shouldn't* you believe us?"

"Well, you could have found another buyer, or something like that."

"Hugo was incredulous. "What the Hell are you talking about, Graff? Who would buy this stuff except you? What do you think we are doing, putting an ad in the paper? You are nuts."

"Maybe. Maybe not." Graff was nonplussed. "I have heard nothing of your, so called, close call."

"Graff, how are you going to hear about it anyway? Have you got someone else in the plant?"

"That is for me to know," said Graff, stroking his chin. He flipped some more popcorn out for the pigeons. They fought each other for the kernels.

"You're bluffing, Graff. Next Friday will be our last delivery. That's the way it is." Hugo held his ground.

"You know all that I have to do is leak the information that you have given us and you are finished," said Graff, flatly.

We were prepared for this. Graff had made that threat before. I met it head on. "Yes, you can do that, but if you do you will tip off the Army as to what you have obtained. To my knowledge they don't even know that you have the information we have passed. Second, even though we're going to have to shut down we're still a resource. If the storm passes we may be able to get more out to you." I threw in the last item in the hopes that Graff and his controllers would be interested in keeping us available.

Graff was unimpressed. "We shall see. I think there is more here than meets the eye. I shall see what my superiors have to say about it."

December 13, 1942

It has been over a month since we made the last delivery. I had made it a point not to go near any of the old drop places. Slowly our life had begun to return to normal. I guess that we had never realized the amount of pressure that accompanied what we were doing. It had been four years. Spying, and I was now able to recognize it for what it was, had become a way of life. We had lost all moral concerns for what we were doing. Our inhibitions were completely overcome by the money. Now we had washed our hands of it. We had gotten out without even a close call. It was over. Hugo and I decided to celebrate with a week-end in Okawville to take in the hot baths. The weather had begun to break. The evenings were cold. Okawville would be just right. We would go the last weekend in December.

December 19, 1942

We returned home last night. Our house had been broken into. Someone had gone completely through everything, but they had not ransacked it. Nothing was destroyed; nothing was strewn about as could have easily been the case. But everything had been searched. I wanted to call the police. Hugo would not let me. We observed that nothing appeared to be missing. Hugo thought it might have some connection to Graff. No need to bring in the police if nothing was missing. In fact, that might be all the more reason not to call them. What kind of a burglar searches everything and takes nothing? It would be hard to explain. In fact, we had no explanation. What were they looking for? Hugo speculated that they might be searching for some evidence that we had not told Graff the truth, or that we really did have something else going. We even laughed again at Graff's speculation that we might be selling the secrets to someone else. Who could he have been referring to?

We put the house back together. It didn't take much, but I couldn't sleep. Who had been here? What were they looking for? I felt like I had been violated. I was dirty.

September 12, 1943

The break-in of our house was a signature event - a milestone. Despite its ominous connotations we haven't heard from Graff or any of his cronies for nine months. The further we got away from the break-in date the more we believed that we were out of the loop. Whatever they were looking for, they never found. Maybe finding nothing was only proof we were acting in good faith when we told them we were out.

This year has been a good one. Hugo worries that he might be called in the Draft, but to date they are only taking younger men. Donald continues to grow. He is a little boy now - and is a "terrible-two-year-old." We enjoy him so much. We have even talked of trying for another. I don't know what the odds are of me getting pregnant again. It took a long time the first time.

In all honesty, our sex life has been pretty poor. I guess the pressure of delivering the classified information took its toll. I know that Hugo and I have talked frequently about how the pressure affected us. We are just beginning to feel that we are in the clear, but because there is no finality; no termination point, we still worry.

We reasoned that if the Nazis were going to turn us in they would have done so by now. Maybe they bought the idea of 'holding us in reserve'. We still worry that the phone is going to ring, and it is going to be Graff – or worse the FBI. Any call in the night scares me to death.

October 10, 1943

"Good evening Mrs. Jurgens." The accent was unmistakable. It was Graff. I had answered the phone. Hugo was fixing the radio again. He had dismantled it and it was spread out on a newspaper on the kitchen table. Apparently, several tubes had gone out, and he was trying to figure out which ones were good and bad. Hugo had a little tester, and was fitting each tube into it and watching for the light go on. He stopped and looked up when I said, "Hello Graff."

"I want you to meet with us next week," said Graff, without hesitating at my chilly response.

"I don't think so. We are out of the game, Graff."

"No one is out of the game," Graff said impatiently. "I suggest you meet with us next Thursday evening."

"Who is 'us'?"

"An old friend."

"Who?"

"Heinrich Bloch. He is anxious to meet with you."

"Graff, for the last time. We are not going to meet with you or Bloch. We are finished. We can't get any more secrets out."

"We could always pay another visit to you home. Maybe we will not be so careful the next time."

"So, it *was* you. We thought so. You didn't find anything, did you Graff? Why won't you believe us? We are out."

"We have something for you that will interest you very much. I think you should meet us. It has nothing to do with your prior activities."

"What are you talking about?"

"We cannot discuss it on the telephone. Meet us next Thursday at eight o'clock."

"Where?"

"Could we interest you in a fine dinner?"

"What are you talking about?"

"The Mayfair Hotel. They have an excellent restaurant – German cuisine, of course. It's on the top floor. Will you be our guests? Eight o'clock."

I sighed, the deep exasperated sigh of a tired, worn out person. "We'll be there."

"Good. Eight o'clock" The phone went dead.

October 16, 1943

We had not seen Heinrich Bloch since the evening with the Mullers in which he had recruited us to pass on classified information. He appeared thinner, gaunter. Hugo remarked under this breath that he appeared ill. He was his usual charming self- quite to the contrast of Graff who purveyed his sour attitude and lifeless personality. They were some combination - not exactly the pair you would choose as dinner partners for a cheery evening! It was the first meal we had ever had with Graff. That was fine with me. I didn't like him from the first, even though we had many dealings with him to exchange information. I imagined his manners would be crude. He did not disappoint me. I anticipated that Bloch would try to put his hand on my leg under the table. He did – right on schedule.

They were at the table when we arrived. Both rose and greeted us warmly - old friends, out for an evening on the town. Naturally Bloch held the chair for me to sit next to him. Hugo almost laughed out loud. Bloch was so obvious.

Neither Hugo nor I had ever been to the Mayfair dining room. It is a beautiful dark oak paneled room with a magnificent silver service in the middle where chefs in white hats carve meats and prepare flaming dishes at a round counter. Large dark wood carved buffets and German sideboards line the walls, and tuxedoed waiters glide between the tables of well-dressed guests. Hugo and I felt a little out of our element.

Bloch was quite complementary of our work and appeared to have a working knowledge of all of the information we had gotten out. He was quite impressed with our consistency and offered his congratulations. He said that the photographs of the files were technically superb and were well received by his superiors. He never said who his superiors were.

With the pleasantries behind and dinner ordered Bloch got to the point. "I hope that this evening is a major event in your lives," he began. "I have come down from Chicago to offer you a single opportunity that will change your lives forever."

"Bloch, you have already done that once," said Hugo. "I'm not sure that my life can stand many more of these meetings." It was a weak attempt at humor. Bloch paused and smiled patiently, condescendingly.

"You are about to be offered an opportunity to become rich beyond your wildest dreams." Bloch paused again, looking first at Hugo, then at me, for a reaction. There was none. We were skeptics.

He continued, "We have a single task for you to perform. It's the single most important thing that you will do in your lifetime." He again paused. No reaction.

"If you will do it we will pay you five hundred thousand dollars."

Hugo blinked.

I blinked.

"Half a million dollars?" said Hugo.

"That's correct. Five hundred thousand dollars," he said, as if to correct our characterization of it as a half-million.

"What do we have to do, rob a bank?" said Hugo.

"Nothing like that." Bloch managed a condescending laugh and leaned forward. "But you will have to go to Germany," he said almost in a whisper.

"Germany?"

"Berlin, to be more specific." His big gray eyes searched Hugo, then me for a reaction.

"Come on, Bloch." It was Hugo. "Get with the details. What the Hell are you talking about. You can't expect us to believe that's all there is to it"

"No, that's not all there is to it, but that's all I can tell you."

"What do you mean 'that's all you can tell us'?" Hugo was irritated. "You want us to go to Germany for a half-million dollars, and that is all you can tell us? Get serious, Bloch."

"Hugo and Frieda, I know that it might seem preposterous, but I have never lied to you, nor have I ever let you down. When we made a deal, I stuck by it. You know that."

"OK, so you have nev..."

"Let me finish." Bloch put his hand up in mock protest. "Hugo and Frieda, if you do not know the esteem in which you are held by me and those to whom I answer, it is important that I tell you. You are a legend. Your information has been consistent, vital, accurate and timely. Most important you have not been compromised. We do not think the US government has any idea what you have been doing. J. Edgar Hoover and his thugs know almost all of our agents in North America except you. You are an untapped, reliable resource. You have proven yourselves good to your word in every respect. It is for that reason that I am authorized to offer you this opportunity." He paused, letting it sink in.

"Don't let us down. Don't let yourselves down." Bloch said, unemotionally.

"But go to Berlin on just what you have told us? Why, we haven't the slightest idea what will be demanded of us. What if you get us over there and ask us to do something that we can't do?" Hugo shook his head. "It's impossible."

Hugo paused for a moment. You could tell he was thinking. I had to ask: "For a half million dollars you are going to ask a lot, aren't you?" I was shaking.

Bloch turned to face me. He put on his sincerest face. "Frieda, we are going to ask you to do something that no other human being on earth has ever done. It is not overly dangerous. It is not beyond your abilities or your imagination. It is something totally within your capabilities - something that only you can accomplish. And its risks are not overly high if you follow good procedures and our instructions."

All I could think about was assassination. "It's not murder is it?" I know I asked weakly. I regretted the question as soon as I had asked it.

"No, Frieda, we are not going to ask you murder someone." Bloch smiled at me paternalistically, understandingly.

"Well, you're going to have to come up with more than that," said Hugo. "We're not just going off on a wild goose chase to Berlin on what you have told us."

Block turned to look squarely at Hugo. "Hugo, my friend. There are some things that you just have to take on a little faith. But it's just those things that, in our lives, turn out to be the real turning points." He paused. "Just think about what you can do with five-hundred-thousand-dollars. You will not have to work another day in your life if you don't want to. You can live wherever you please, raise that fine young son of yours, Donald, in whatever way you want; send him to the finest schools. The pressure will be off. In one fell swoop you will be a person of means. Well managed you can live like a king for the rest of your lives. You will never have another opportunity like this again. Think about it, Hugo."

I looked at Hugo. Hugo clearly was thinking about it.

Graff slumped in his chair lighting up a cigar. He was a despicable person, and the less he said, the better. Yet I had the feeling that what Graff was feeling was envy. His eyes drooped, and he soaked up every word. I could feel the jealousy that he was not being offered the same thing. It would be a cold day in Hell before Graff was ever offered a half million dollars. After all, we were being given the opportunity to become wealthy; an opportunity that I'll bet had never been made to Graff.

Despite our lack of details my feeling that Graff was envious of the offer gave it credibility, credence. Graff wanted the same thing, but he couldn't have it. Graff's demeanor, his sulking, his overt jealousy that we had received the offer, not him, convinced me that it was real! Hugo saw it, too. Whatever they were offering was real! I wondered how much detail Graff knew? Did he know no more than we did? Or was he privy to the full scope of the task that would be demanded?

"When do you need to know?" I heard Hugo ask. I knew from his question that Hugo had picked up on the same thing. Hugo could read Graff as well as I could. He saw Graff's envy, too. He knew the offer was for real!

"I'll call you a week from tonight - at eight o'clock. There'll be no more details about the assignment - only specific arrangements if you accept."

"We'll think about it." I had the feeling that Hugo had already made up his mind.

The waiter brought a raspberry soufflé'. Bloch had ordered it before he had ordered his entree'. Neither Hugo nor I had ever seen a soufflé'. We talked about the Cardinals and the Cubs and the World Series and ate our desserts - just four friends having dinner. The only difference was that one had offered a half-million dollars to the other for an unknown task that involved traveling to a country at which we were at war. Nothing out of the ordinary - just a routine evening at the Mayfair!

October 20, 1943

Hugo and I have been on pins and needles ever since our meeting with Bloch. What could he want? What could be so important that we had to go all of the way to Berlin to find out about it? Why couldn't they just tell us? The more we talked about it, the more we did not believe that it was real. We almost talked ourselves out of believing it.

But both of us were getting pretty good at trusting our gut feelings. We both got the same vibrations from Graff. That greasy little bastard was green with envy that Bloch was not offering him the same thing. He knew enough about the details to be green with jealousy, or at least he knew that what was going to be asked of us was attainable, and that it would result in a huge sum of money being paid to us.

A multitude of questions flooded our minds.

"How are they going to pay us five hundred thousand dollars?" Hugo was pacing up and down. "We can't just walk down to the bank with a check, and say to the teller: 'here, put this half million in our account' - there'd be a thousand questions. We don't have access to that kind of money. A policeman would be on our doorstep the next morning. They'd nab us, sure thing."

"Maybe they would pay it in cash?"

"Cash Frieda, that's the last thing we need. What do you think we could do, carry it home in a suitcase? We'd be sitting ducks to have someone take it off us - maybe even the guys who gave it to us. No cash."

"How do we go to Berlin? There's a war on, and in case anyone asks, Germany is the enemy. You don't just *go* to Berlin."

"I know, Hugo. We've never even been outside of the U.S. Just up and going to Nazi Germany is not exactly going to be easy to explain to anyone."

"That brings up another problem. How *do* we explain it? I don't think we just drift in to the Black Forest some Friday evening and announce over a draught that we are going on a vacation to Berlin. That would raise a few eyebrows; and what do we do with Donald?"

The questions kept coming. We couldn't sleep. What was worth a half-million bucks? Why couldn't someone else do it? Why us?

We made a list of questions on a newsprint tablet. Bloch was clearly not going to tell us what was going to be asked of us, but he had to tell us some of the logistical details. He had to tell us how we were going to get there. How did we go to Germany with a war on? How did we finance the trip? How long would we be gone? He had to answer those kinds of questions. The list of questions went over onto the second page, then the third.

I was writing as fast as I could. The questions kept coming. Hugo was pacing around the kitchen firing them at me faster than I could put them down.

"When did we leave?"

"Who would give us instructions *en*-route?"

"How did we know where to go and whom to talk to?"

215

"Didn't we need passports? Visas? How would we get them?"

Hugo suddenly stopped. I looked up from the paper on which I had been writing furiously. The same thought crossed our minds. It was as if we both had it at the same time. Hugo got a big grin on his face. So, did I. We had both realized that we had gone far past the question of *whether* we were going to do it; we were concentrating on the *how!* We were going for it! There was no doubt. We had run through the threshold question without even stopping, and we were already working on the details.

October 23, 1943

The phone rang at five past eight. It was Bloch. He was in no mood to discuss anything over the phone. He simply asked,

"Yes or no?"

"Yes," I said.

"Good. I'll meet you Saturday morning for coffee at the Rite-Way diner on Vandeventer and Kingshighway. I think half an hour should be enough - say, eight- thirty Saturday morning?

"Hugo opens the shop at nine. Could we make it eight o'clock?"

"Fine," said Block. "See you Saturday. Eight o'clock."

I hung up the phone. Hugo looked at me across the evening paper. "Well?"

"Eight o'clock, Saturday morning. The Rite-Way Diner; Kingshighway and Vandeventer. Half an hour."

Hugo didn't say anything. He just nodded and went back to reading the paper.

I wondered if we had sold our souls to the Devil?

October 26, 1942

It was raining when we got to the Rite-Way. It's a large white porcelain-front diner with a stainless steel and tile interior. Its plates and cups are thick white bone ware, and its waitresses chew gum and have thick asses from all of the truckers pinching them. Bloch sat in a booth and sipped coffee while reading the paper as we approached. He appeared unshaven as if he had been up all night. We later learned that he had ridden the train all night from Chicago to meet with us. He got right to the point.

"You probably have a thousand questions, so I will try to tell you enough to answer most of them."

I was ready to produce my list of questions. Block charged on.

"You'll leave January 7th by train for New York and transfer to Elizabeth, New Jersey. You will travel aboard a ship to Lisbon, Portugal, a neutral country, where you'll transfer to a train for Madrid, then Paris and Berlin. Once you start moving you won't stop until you get to Berlin. There will be no layovers. You'll be met along the way and transferred without delay. In Berlin you will have approximately one week of briefing and liaison where you will be instructed on your assignment. You will have the right to decline after you have the full details. If you decline you will be sent home the same way without further contact."

"How do we get in? I mean, you don't just go to Berlin. There's a war on."

"You will use an American Passport as you leave the United States. From there on you'll be traveling on a German passport with a clearance papers giving you priority treatment. We will prepare them for you and deliver them to you before you leave. Once you reach Portugal your route will be secure. Agents will make sure you're transported safely to Berlin."

"How long are we going to be gone?" It seemed like such a logical question, yet Bloch had not addressed it.

"You should plan on a month."

"A month! How in the heck are we going to explain that? What do I do with the shop? What about Donald?" Neither of us had even contemplated that the trip would take anywhere near that long.

Bloch seemed ready for the questions. "First, starting in early December we will circulate the rumor that you are ill. By the first of January it will be identified as tuberculosis."

"Tuberculosis?"

"Yes. It's a natural. On January 6th you will enter a sanitarium for treatment. You will not know how long you will be in, but you can estimate at least a month. The sanitarium will be in Hot Springs, Arkansas. In fact, we will actually check you into a sanitarium in Hot Springs, but you will, of course, be nowhere near the place. You'll even write a few letters, say to your parents or close friends before you leave, which we'll post from Hot Springs. Frieda you will decide to accompany Hugo."

"But my job at the Army ammunition Plant?"

"You'll ask for a leave of absence. It would be natural for a concerned wife to accompany her husband to convalescence at a sanitarium for Tuberculosis treatment. In fact, we might find it convenient for you to go for observation, Frieda. After all, you have been exposed to the disease. You live with him. Your General Hollenbeck will agree to it in a minute, particularly if you express concern that you might have been exposed to infection. We'll even have you send him a few letters from Hot Springs. The General will appreciate that."

"What about Donald?" I asked.

"I suggest that you talk to Hugo's sister, Mildred. I'm sure she might be prevailed upon to take care of Donald for a month or so."

"But will she know?"

"No, absolutely not. No one must know. You must maintain the utmost of confidences. No one will be told. Is that clear?"

It was perfectly clear. Bloch emphasized again that no one should know – "no one at all." I began to suspect that even Graff did not know the details.

"What about the cost of the trip to Berlin, and how exactly do we get paid?" said Hugo.

"We'll handle the arrangements for the trip. You'll not travel first class, but you will be treated right. We'll handle the paperwork, the documents and arrangements. We'll advance you traveling money." Bloch was rattling off details in his usual matter-of-fact way.

"And the payment?"

"Once you accept the assignment we'll make arrangements to transfer the payment to any bank of your choice. I would recommend that you consider Switzerland. There are fewer prying eyes there, and less regulation, and no IRS. The interest rates may be a little lower, but ..." Bloch shrugged his shoulders.

"Any bank?" asked Hugo.

"Of course," said Bloch. "You just need to tell us."

"*When* do we tell you?"

"When you are in Berlin, of course, and after you have decided to accept the assignment.

There was a long pause. Bloch looked out the diner's window at the rain. I looked at Hugo. He returned my gaze. I couldn't believe it. We were really talking about five hundred thousand dollars being transferred to us at "the bank of our choice."

"When do we know the details of the trip?"

"As soon as I confirm your participation I will notify Berlin. In December you will get instructions. I don't make the travel arrangements. That is done by someone else. I'll see to it you have plenty of details long before you depart."

"In the meantime, you want me to contract Tuberculosis?"

"Exactly. I suggest that you practice a cough. Make it visible, annoying to conversations. People should notice."

They had thought it out - every detail. They knew that we would accept. Was our desire for money that visible? Could they say with certainty we would do it?

December 23, 1943

November passed slowly. December followed with the same lethargic speed. Hugo and I were anxious to know more details of the trip. As each day of December plodded by we began to doubt ourselves. Was it real? Were we really doing this? Would the task be so onerous that we could not perform, or perhaps would not perform, even for a half million dollars?

Hugo began the ruse of the Tuberculosis. Friends bought onto the problem and began asking about Hugo's health. He had developed a rather convincing cough. He had perfected it down to the last wheeze. I wondered if he would be able to stop it after he had the cure in Hot Springs? Some of our friends even recommended good doctors. There was no doubt that they believed it.

On December 23 the package arrived. It was a big brown envelope delivered by a messenger boy on a bicycle. It looked like the same boy who had delivered the camera and film over a year ago. There were several other envelopes inside.

The package contained an envelope with two United States Passports - one for each of us – and visas to enter Portugal. I was not sure how they got the passport. We had not given them information or filled out a passport application. They had our dates of birth correct to the day which made Hugo and I wonder just how much they knew about us? They even had a picture of each of us in them.

The packet contained another envelope with German passports for each of us. Again, correct to the smallest detail - and with photos. They were impressive in their black leather cases with the embossed eagle on the front. Visa stamps were already affixed. We immediately noticed that the passports contained a home address for us in Solingen, Germany. "Hugo, look at this." I had found the German passports with the German addresses. "What do you make of this?"

"Something tells me we'd better read the instructions," replied Hugo.

We tore open the largest inner envelope. Very detailed typewritten instructions covered several pages – twenty-two typewritten pages. The typing was single-spaced. The instructions were minute in every detail and very specific.

Hugo read a page and handed it to me. He continued reading. It took us over an hour to wade through the exasperating details of how we were to travel, who we were to meet. There was a narrative about our life in Solingen, Germany, our jobs, our children so convincingly described that I was incredulous to realize that they were actually talking about us. Nothing was left out. Nothing except what we were to do when we got to Germany. Nothing hinted at the task that would be asked of us.

At the bottom of the last page the following was typewritten in all capital characters and then underlined with a black grease pencil:

"READ AND MEMORIZE THESE INSTRUCTIONS. DESTROY THEM BY THOROUGHLY BURNING SO AS TO LEAVE NO ASH INTACT. UNDER NO CIRCUMSTANCES RETAIN OR KEEP THESE INSTRUCTIONS."

"It will take days to memorize these instructions," I said to Hugo.

"You're right about that, but they must want us to do it for a reason."

"Hugo, it's going to be difficult with all of those German names of people and addresses." I was worried about the technical detail of the orders. The instructions were so exact, so detailed. I could see how easily we could miss just one name, a street, and address. It bothered me.

"I think we had better get started," said Hugo. We'll do a page a day."

"Hugo that will take too long. Remember we, are to leave the 7th of January."

"So? We'll just have to memorize two pages a day."

One of the other envelopes contained five hundred dollars in cash and seven hundred dollars in German marks. I knew it was seven hundred dollars even though I could not tell how many marks were to the dollar. A little brown band around the marks said '$700.'

There were tickets. Train tickets, boat tickets, tickets in Portuguese (although at the time I couldn't tell what language it was in). As we scanned the typewritten pages we saw that each of the items in the package was keyed into the instructions. We would have to read them to know what to do with each. It would take hours to memorize and correlate the instructions to the other items.

Hugo dumped the rest of the package on the table. A suede drawstring bag thumped out. It about the size of a book. I picked it up. It was instantly recognizable from its shape. I undid the string and reached in. It was a Luger. In the bottom of the suede bag were eleven shells.

I held the gun in my hand and looked at its black metal surface. I had never held a pistol in my life. It fit the palm of my hand perfectly. Its blue–black machined steel barrel gleamed in the light of the kitchen. I looked at Hugo.

I was so afraid. I was never so afraid in my life. My stomach churned with the realization that we had sold out to do something that I knew was going to be horrible. We'd done it for money.

Hugo looked at me. I could tell he was having the same feeling. I could see it in his eyes. He was scared to death. His face was white as a sheet.

We stood silent for a moment. It seemed like an eternity.

"We're not going to do it," I whispered, hardly able to speak over my fear.

Hugo nodded. "My sentiments exactly. Nothing is worth it. If they give us half a million, they'll want more from us than we can do. It's not worth it."

At that moment the five hundred thousand dollars did not seem to mean anything. It would have made us rich beyond our wildest dreams. It would have meant safety and security for the rest of our lives - probably everything we had ever hoped or dreamed of. But the truth was, it wasn't worth it.

Hugo began repacking the contents of the package. "I'll notify Graff. I don't know how to reach Bloch."

"Tell him to pick up his package. We'll leave it on the front porch for his messenger to pick up. That includes his instructions. Put it outside by the porch. It'll be safe there until he picks it up. Tell him we're out. I don't even want to talk to him."

I was sobbing. I could already feel the relief.

15
CHAPTER
THE UNWANTED VISITORS

"I don't know why," I said to Connie, "but I had a feeling of relief. Of peace. Whatever the ill-conceived plan was that would take my parents to Germany had been rejected. My parents were traitors, but at least they had called it to a halt. They had decided to get out.

I was naïve. I should have known there was more to it than that. You don't get in as deep as they were and just walk away. But at least they wanted out. There was a chance for redemption.

Boy, was I was naïve!

The more I thought about it, the more I could see what had taken them down the road to betrayal of their country. They were products of the great depression. There was no money to be had. Making money was so much more difficult then. Money didn't circulate. No one had any. They only had high school educations. Jobs were scarce to non-existent. They had a child, me, and no real way to see a future. A war was on, and God knows what after that? I don't know what I would've done given the same choices. Given the opportunity, would I have been stronger? I wondered.

Then, along comes an offer to do something to get half a million dollars. I had been trying to convert half a million to present day dollars. I had no real point of reference. Half million in 1943 could have been equivalent to two, three, four million today. I didn't know, but I knew it was a lot of money - enough to tempt even the most moral, the most loyal, among us. I'm not sure where I would have come down. It's easy to be judgmental with hindsight, but I wasn't so sure now.

"Well, I guess that explains the German passports and the Luger," said Connie as she closed the book.

I had a better feeling about my parents. Sure, they were weak. Sure, they had given in to the temptation of money. It was easy to see how they slipped into passing the secrets from Hollenbeck's office, but then along comes this offer – for a half-million dollars. That amount of money, particularly then, would have corrupted us all. At last they had finally exercised some strength against the temptations that had been offered them. I'm sure there was relief in my voice.

Like I say – *naïve*.

"But what's puzzling is if they gave back the packet why do they still have the passports?" I didn't have an answer for my own question.

Connie got up and went over to the trunk. She opened the top and set out the big photo tray. Pushing some items aside she groped for the German passports. When she found them, she stood up flipping through them to the back.

"Don, I think there is a lot more to this story. Take a look." She handed me my Father's passport holding it open to the last pages where the visa stamps went.

I looked at the thick yellowed pages in dismay. There were visa stamps - Portugal, Spain, France, Germany, Switzerland, January,1944." They were all there screaming out at me.

"They went!

"I'm afraid so, Donald."

"January 1, 1944.

Hugo left a message for Graff, and he called last week. We told him we were out. "No deal," Hugo told Graff. "Thanks anyway, but no deal." The package would be left on the front porch. It was safe there. No one would bother it. Graff's courier could pick it up. We would not be home.

Graff was indifferent. He told Hugo in a flat monotone that he should reconsider, but he made no threats. No recriminations. Hugo was firm. We were both resolute. They told us we didn't have to accept. It was our option. We were out.

Last night Gail and Tom Heberer threw a New Year's Eve Party. We had known the Heberers for only about a year, and we had many common friends with them. Hugo and I debated about going, but in the end decided to go. It would be a strange evening, and we knew it. We had lived the charade of Hugo's Tuberculosis for the last two months. We had told everyone that he would have to go into a sanitarium after the first of the year. How would we handle the questions about Hugo's hospitalization now that we were not going to Germany?

Our friends didn't disappoint us. They were genuinely concerned about Hugo. His phony cough of the last few weeks had been pretty convincing. They asked us when he was going in and pressed us for details on where he would be so that they could write. We tried to finesse the answers by saying that his recent visit to the doctor had been encouraging, and that it was even possible that he might not have to go. We should know this week. God, I hate lying! These are our best friends. They really care about us.

Despite the charade we have been living, I feel as if a load has been lifted from me. It was a good party. When the clock struck midnight and we sang *"Auld Lang Sine."* Hugo took me in his arms and kissed me more passionately than he had in months. When he pulled back I could see big tears in his eyes. I was crying, too. They were tears of relief.

"Frieda, I'm so sorry for what we've done. I should've been strong enough to keep us from getting into it. I am so glad to be out. We should have done this two years ago."

"Let's start again. Let's put this year behind us," I said. "Let's begin again. We have plenty of money, and we can have our honor if we'll just resolve to look forward, not back."

The huge bells down at Saint Raphael Church were peeling off the New Year. It was midnight. I hugged Hugo as tightly as I could. He buried his face in my shoulder and I felt myself sobbing.

"Hugo, I love you. I just want to be us - you, me and Donald. We can do without the money."

The party broke into a rousing chorus of *For He's a Jolly Good Fellow.* They were almost finished when we realized they were singing it to Hugo. They had formed a big ring around us and were clapping and offering us their best wishes for a better New Year. I was very emotional. We were touched. They were genuinely concerned for Hugo.

We broke up after 1 AM. Everyone at the party came up to us to wish Hugo the best before they left. They were concerned about his tuberculosis. He was, in their eyes, very sick. They wanted him back healthy and soon. He was their friend. He was their barber. He was one of them. We both were. I felt like a heel. I didn't have to ask Hugo how he felt. I could see it in his eyes.

January 2, 1944

I had come home from work early. Donald was still over at the baby sitter's, and I stopped by to put dinner in the oven before going over to pick him up. Hugo had received a call at the shop that there would be a special meeting of the Committee this evening at seven. He would go straight from the shop to the meeting on South Grand. Hugo went, but I could tell that he would've rather done something else. He had begun to lose interest in the National Socialist Worker's Party, but if Hugo was anything, he was loyal. As long as he was a member, he would attend the meetings. He probably wouldn't be home until after nine.

I had done a little housework and had put in a small meat loaf and some carrots with potatoes. I was going to the front hall closet to get my coat to go over and pick up Donald.

I have no idea how they got into the house.

The first thing I felt was a big burly hand around my upper body across my chest and a cloth with some chemical on it was pressed against my nose and mouth. My hands were pinned to my side. Whoever was holding me was much bigger and more powerful than I. I tried to kick but felt myself slipping away. The room was spinning. I think the cloth was saturated with chloroform. The last thing I remember was someone grabbing my flailing legs and holding them together. I don't know how many of them there were or even what they looked like.

It was dark when I awoke. I don't know how long I was out. I was naked, stretched spread-eagle on the dining room table. My legs had been spread open and folded down over the side of the table. They were tied down to the bottom of the stout legs of the table with cords around my ankles. My arms were extended upward and tied to the legs on the opposite end. A cord had been stretched under my chin and tied to the legs of the table at the same end as my arms so that I could not look down. A towel separated the cord from my chin

I remember trying to scream, but a piece of adhesive tape had been stretched over my mouth. Nothing came out. I was horrified. The first thought that I had was that I was going to be sick to my stomach. Nausea swept over me. If I vomited, I would choke to death in a minute. I fought back by trying to swallow. My mouth was dry as cotton.

I struggled against the cords that held me immobile. Whoever did it left nothing to chance. There was no play in the lines, no slack. I couldn't move. It took me a little time to realize that struggling gained me nothing. I might as well stop fighting it. I didn't feel as if I had been hurt. There was nothing to do until someone, Hugo, found me.

I didn't know what time it was. Hugo had to come home soon. What if they had done something to him? What if they killed him? I would lay there undiscovered for days. Fear again overwhelmed me.

I don't know how long I laid there. It seemed like an eternity. Horrible thoughts went through my mind. What had they done to Donald? I wondered if I had been raped?

I relaxed and tried to consciously take stock of my body. I concentrated on each limb, each part. Was there pain or evidence of injury? Was I bruised up? Had I been beaten? Except for the tight cords around my wrists and ankles I could feel no pain. My vagina wasn't sore. I didn't think I had been raped, but then again there was a feeling... What was it? Something was there. Yes, something was there in between my legs. It felt as if it had been inserted in me - not far - just inserted. I couldn't look down, but I could feel it. Something was there! Horror flowed over me. What was it? What was sticking in me?

Shortly before ten Hugo came in. I could hear him coming up the walk, whistling. I didn't know how long I had been tied to the table. I didn't know how long I had been out. My head had gone from groggy to clear. The phone had rung three times. The baby sitter had to be wondering what was going on, but she was understanding that sometimes I had to work overtime. Hugo came into the living room and began to remove his coat. The house was dark. I made as much of a sound as I could. He turned on the light.

"Oh my God!" Hugo bounded across the living room and into the dining room where I lay stretched prone on the table. I know my eyes were as big as saucers.

"Frieda!" He ripped off the adhesive tape. "What happened?"

I was sobbing uncontrollably. Hugo carried a small penknife, and he had it out in a second working on the cord that held my chin.

"Hugo, they...." I was sobbing so hard I couldn't finish.

Hugo got through the cord that went under my chin and stopped. He had fixed his gaze between my legs.

"Frieda. Don't move." He walked to the middle of the table. I could look down now even though my hands and feet still remained tied. It was a rolled-up piece of paper. Hugo removed it, unrolled it and read aloud:

> *YOU ARE NOT HURT, BUT THIS COULD HAVE JUST AS EASILY BEEN A GUN OR A KNIFE. IT COULD HAVE BEEN THE ARM OR LEG OF YOUR SON, DONALD.*
> *YOU CANNOT HIDE.*
> *THE PACKET IS ON THE COFFEE TABLE IN THE LIVING ROOM. YOUR TRAIN LEAVES ON JANUARY 7TH AT 8:30AM. NO REPLY TO THIS IS NECESSARY. WE'LL KNOW WHEN YOU ARE ON THE TRAIN.*

We couldn't sleep. They didn't rape me, but they might as well have. I felt so dirty. As Hugo and I lay in bed that night our thoughts were the same. How could we have gotten into this? How could we so stupidly believe that we could get out with just a phone call? Were we really so dumb as to believe we really had a choice?

We were at their mercy. We couldn't go to the police. It wouldn't take them long to get into our prior activities. We'd been committing treason. A war was on. It was an offense punishable by death. Graff and Bloch could do anything to us they wanted. We weren't going to call anyone. To do so signed our own death warrants! We were trapped like rats. Neither of us slept all night.

January 5, 1944

We haven't slept an hour for the past two nights. I walk around the house in fear. I can't even go into the living room without Hugo. Needless to say, I haven't been back to work. I called Hollenbeck and told him I had the flu. Hugo closed the shop for a day and stayed home with me. I was so unnerved I couldn't bear to stay in the house alone. He, too, was visibly shaken.

This morning we decided the house was our worst enemy. We were scared to death to be in it. That it could be locked was of no comfort. We never found out how they got in that night. All of the door locks worked fine, and I was sure that the only door I had unlocked that night when I came home was in the kitchen onto the back porch. Just being in the house made me feel like a canary in a cage with a cat outside who could get in at will. At least if we went to work we would be out.

We reasoned, right or wrong, that the chances of something happening to us while we were at work or going to and from were probably slight. If they were going to gun us down, they had an ample chance and didn't do it. They weren't going to kill us - at least not before the 7th. The message was clear. "Go to Germany and nothing happens to you - stay and we'll get you."

We understood it perfectly.

16
CHAPTER
FIRST TIME TRAVELERS

"January 7, 1944

Our packet contained tickets on the Wabash for Chicago to catch The Twentieth Century Limited for New York. The instructions had been precise about the train, the time, and even what to pack. 'Two suitcases and a large steamer trunk,' they had said. We didn't even own a steamer trunk, so we went to the Sears Roebuck store on South Grand Avenue and bought one. It was a big dome-topped affair, and it held lots of clothes

This morning, January 7, we left St. Louis at 8:30 after depositing Donald with Hugo's sister, Mildred. She had graciously (in hindsight, *too graciously*) agreed to keep Donald for the duration of our trip to Arkansas. The Wabash rolled out of Union Station, across the Eads Bridge and north through the winter landscape of flat, never-ending barren cornfields of Illinois. Hugo and I hardly spoke. We had memorized the instructions and realized execution of them to the very word was important. I was so scared I couldn't eat. We arrived in Chicago at three in the afternoon. Chicago's Union Station was a madhouse. Trains were coming and going every few minutes. Half the people in the station seemed to have a military uniform on.

The Twentieth Century Limited left Chicago at 5:10. Our tickets called for a sleeping compartment on one of the Pullman cars. It was dark by the time the train left the Chicago suburbs and rolled through Gary, Indiana. A Conductor came through the cabin and punched our ticket, followed by a Porter who asked us what time we wanted to eat dinner. Hugo told him 8 o'clock.

The last 48 hours have been a blur. We were correct in our assumption that getting out of the house would do us good. We had been on a treadmill getting ready right up to the time of departure. We both slept about three hours the night before we left. It was the first real sleep we had since the intrusion into our house. We were also correct in the assumption we would be left alone. We saw no one. Hugo thought they would be watching us. We couldn't tell it if they were. Someone had to watch us get on the train, but we did not see anyone watching us.

It was strange. When we boarded the train, I had a feeling of relief. The fear that they would do something to us subsided. Hugo reasoned we were safe once we got on the train because we were doing as we were instructed. There was no more danger, at least from them. I must've bought into that reasoning. I felt better, relieved would be more descriptive.

It was cold the day we left. The Gray dark skies threatened one of those big winter snowstorms that well up out of the southwest, Snow was predicted, but had not materialized before we left St. Louis.

Hugo had worn a pair of wide wale corduroy pants and a sweater. I wore a pair of gray wool slacks and a sweater. I really like the men's-styled pants that have become so popular for women with their high waists and wide pant legs. As the train rolled out of Chicago and through the Indiana countryside. Hugo opened his suitcase.

"I guess we ought to put something on for dinner besides sweaters," he said, pulling a matching corduroy sport coat out of the suitcase.

We had seen some people go by our compartment on their way to an earlier dinner seating. The men wore jackets and the women dresses. "It's a bit fancier than the Wabash," he said. It was the first thing that he had said since we left Chicago.

We pulled the blinds and began to dress for dinner. I looked at Hugo standing there in his undershirt. He looked so tired. He looked up from the shirt that he was buttoning.

"Frieda?"

"Oh, Hugo!" I rushed to him. I was in my slip, bra and panties. He held me so tight.

"Hugo, I don't know where we are going, or what for. All I know is that it must be inherently evil. But I know whatever it is - even if we do not come back - I love you."

Hugo pressed his hands into the center of my back and kissed me. It was a long, lingering kiss like the one on New Year's Eve. I got lipstick on him. He didn't mind it.

We finished dressing. Hugo looked good in the white shirt and tie, and a tan corduroy sport coat that I had bought him for Christmas. I wore a fuzzy gray sweater and a black wool skirt. I put a cardigan over my shoulders. The train was both hot and cold depending on what car you were in at the time. Hugo slipped the Luger into his waistband in the small of his back. He had carried it with him since we left St. Louis. I'm not sure why? The jacket hid it perfectly.

As we walked through the train to the dining car, we realized that it had several kinds of accommodations. There were lesser compartments - not as big as ours, and cars with seats only that tipped back for sleeping. There were sleeper cars with little berths both up and down that were made up for sleeping. Little curtains were pulled to give privacy. Our compartment was one of the largest. Our hosts had, at least, seen to it had we had good traveling arrangements.

We were seated for dinner at a table for two in a dining car with walnut paneling and starched tablecloths tended by a white-coated steward. The table was set with sparkling china, brilliant crystal and polished heavy silver utensils all bearing the crest of the Twentieth Century Limited. Around us were gentlemen and ladies in fine clothes who spoke in hushed tones. Negro waiters in short white coats glided effortlessly in the aisle serving the tables as they swayed to the rhythm of the train on the steel rails.

Wall sconces with milk glass shades cast a subdued patina light through the dining car. It was a setting I had only imagined. Our waiter asked us if we'd like wine. Hugo ordered beer for both of us. There would be a choice of steak or Whitefish as an entree, each served with "your choice of butter beans or peas and carrots," he explained. We both took steak.

"As you wish," the waiter said, and turned to the kitchen. Hugo followed him to the end of the car with his eyes. I couldn't help watching Hugo. He was fascinated with the train. Neither of us had been on a grand express train before. It was so different. We had taken the train to Okawville once or twice, but that was just a two hour ride on a local.

Hugo's gaze met mine.

"What are you looking at?" He grinned.

"I don't know. I know you are fascinated with the train. So am I. It is strange that the first ride on a big train like this is on such a clandestine journey. I mean, I always wanted to see New York, but not this way."

Hugo acknowledged his fascination - even his excitement.

The dinner was excellent. I hadn't had such a tender steak in a long time. In fact, I hadn't seen *any* steak in a long time what with war rationing and all. The waiter offered dessert - cherry pie *ala mode* or carrot cake with crème sauce. Hugo had one - I had the other, and we switched off after eating half.

"You know," Hugo said, reaching inside his jacket pocket for a Camel, "I know how scared we are. I know we wanted out, but the truth is we can't get out." He paused, leaned back, lit the cigarette and took a deep drag. I could tell he had been thinking. "We have no choice but to perform. If we don't, they'll probably kill us."

I paused. The thought was sobering, but true. "So, what have you got in mind, Hugo?"

"So as far as I can see the half million is still in the deal. Let's go for it." His eyes got wider as he looked to me for a reaction.

"Hugo, you said it yourself. We don't have a choice."

"So, that's my point. If we don't have a choice, we might as well go for the brass ring. Let's come out of this, whatever it is, rich."

"Come out of what," I said. "The big problem here is that we don't know what we're being asked to do. We're on a mission without a description," I said 'Give me one of those.' Hugo offered me one of the Camels and lit it.

"And that might just be the problem," Hugo said, blowing a big ring upward. "Maybe we overestimate the requirement. Maybe it's nothing. They might not want anything more dangerous than what we have been doing. God knows, passing out classified secrets from the plant wasn't exactly child's play, you know. Maybe it's nothing more than that. It's really not knowing that has us so nervous."

"Yes, but why us? Why can't one of their henchmen do it? Why bring us to Berlin? They've got agents everywhere. There's always the Committee. Why do they want us?"

"Think about it, Frieda. It must have something to do with the plant. It has to do with Hollenbeck, or the project out at Weldon Spring. If they really didn't think we are the only ones who could do it why would they go to all of this trouble to haul us all the way to Germany? That has to be it - it has to have something to do with the plant. Or Hollenbeck?"

Hugo was right. Otherwise, any of their thugs could do it. The real problem was not what they wanted us to do, but in not knowing what they wanted. If we knew what they wanted, we could assess it. Not knowing left us in the dark. It was the dark that caused us so much pain.

"You might be right, Hugo. Maybe we are the only ones who can do it - whatever "it" is. Maybe we only get one shot, Hugo. Maybe this is the one big chance we are going to have in our life. Maybe it's the *only shot*. We have no choice, so why not go for it."

Hugo didn't respond. He was looking out the train window, lost in his thoughts. I wondered what he was thinking. There was nothing out there but darkness and the occasional lights of a little town. The Limited didn't stop at little towns.

We ordered a couple of beers after the dessert. We were beginning to relax. Indiana was sliding by in the darkness. The window reflected our gaze. Hugo really looked great in the reflection. His dark hair, the coat and tie, the ambiance of the train. I wanted him in the worst way. Our sex life hadn't exactly been sterling since all of the pressure of the trip began. In fact, it was nonexistent. We were both so preoccupied. I could tell Hugo felt it too. His leg brushed against mine. It sent chills down my spine.

He turned and looked at me. He put his hand on my cheek. "Shall we?" Hugo snuffed out his cigarette and rose. One of the waiters backed out my chair.

The door to our compartment had hardly clicked shut before I had my sweater off. Hugo was all over me. I drank him in. This was the Hugo that I had known and wanted back. I could smell his bay rum cologne. I don't even remember taking off the rest of my clothes. I just remember him in me. I impaled myself on him urging him deeper. He pushed me back into the mattress of the lower berth. I sat, half reclining with my legs apart as he pushed himself upward and into me to his fullest extent. It was absolutely wonderful! I was so wet that he slid into me effortlessly. Hugo was back!

I remember Hugo having three climaxes over the next two hours as Ohio and then western Pennsylvania slipped by in the night. I haven't the slightest idea how many I had. It was the old Hugo. He manipulated, caressed, bit, sucked and rubbed every inch of me. And when I felt I couldn't come again, he'd find another spot and push me over the edge. He would push himself into me and somehow cock his pelvis so as to rotate himself. It felt as if he was scouring every inch of my insides. We slept enfolded in each other's arms, but not for long. It was almost morning before we finally dozed off. New York and Grand Central station would come soon enough – 11:30 to be exact. We stopped at Pittsburgh just before dawn without either of us knowing it. We both slept soundly for a couple of hours. It was our first good sleep in over a week.

January 8, 1944

Our instructions, which we had memorized and destroyed, told us to take a taxicab from Grand Central Station to Elizabeth, New Jersey and to Pier 53 at the Elizabeth docks. We went through the Holland Tunnel. The taxicab ride took about an hour.

Included in our packet was a pair of tickets, poorly printed, on the freighter Polar Star. We arrived at the pier and alighted from the cab at the foot of the gangplank of a rusting ocean freighter. It was after three in the afternoon. A cold wind blew out of a steel gray sky. Rain or snow would soon follow - probably the same storm that had followed us out of St. Louis. Hugo paid the taxi driver and we stood, our baggage at our feet, on the cold concrete pier looking up at the rusting hulk. On her stern were the words ***"POLAR STAR, LONDON."***

"Hugo, this can't be it."

Hugo walked to the base of the gangplank. A chalkboard was affixed to the railing with the inscription:

'POLAR STAR, LONDON, DEPARTS 1800 HRS'

"This is it," said Hugo. "Might as well get aboard."

"Hugo, this thing is a death trap. This boat won't make it out of the harbor, let alone to ...."

"Hello! You must be the Jurgens." A squat man in a dark blue Pea Coat was hailing us from the railing in front of the superstructure. I had seen him when we drove up in the cab. He had been supervising the loading. From his perch he could see down into the hold where large cranes were depositing nets loaded with wooden crated bottles.

"Yes, we are the Jurgens."

"Please come aboard. Leave your bags. I'll have someone attend to them." His accent was a blend of British and German.

He met us halfway up the gangplank and shook our hands warmly.

"I'm Captain Luther Altmann. Welcome aboard. We are honored to have you as passengers."

Hugo formally introduced us. It seemed superfluous. Altmann asked us if we had a pleasant journey from St. Louis. He was clearly informed of who we were and where we had come from. I wondered if he knew why we were here?

Altmann showed us to a spacious accommodation on the central port side of the superstructure. It was actually two staterooms connected with a door. Each room had an outside door with a porthole on the exterior gangway. There was also a door from one of the rooms to a central interior gangway that seemed to go down between a similar suite on the starboard side of the ship. At the end of the central gangway was a stairway leading down to another level. Smells of food emanated from the stairway, so I surmised that there must be a kitchen or dining room down there someplace.

"We sail at 6 PM," said Altmann, after showing us to our accommodations. Dinner will be at eight, but you are cordially invited to join me at seven fifteen in my quarters for a cocktail. Other officers will be there. It will be a nice time for you to meet the crew."

Hugo told him we would be pleased to accept. I got the impression Altmann would have been disappointed if we had declined. Luther Altmann was a likable sort of fellow, but there was a commanding air about him. After you talked to him for a while there was no doubt, he was captain of the ship.

Hugo and I had never been on an ocean-going vessel before. We noticed something immediately. The Polar Star was anything but a rusting scow. The outside may have looked shabby, but on the inside, it was as clean, well maintained and modern as it could be. Our quarters were exquisite. There was freshly shellacked oak paneling halfway up the walls with a quality carpet on the polished teak floors. The cabins were large and furnished with modern well-upholstered furniture. Curtains adorned the portholes and there was a bathroom that was modern in every respect with ample hot water and a shower.

The interior gangways were immaculate and well-appointed, and the interior walls and bulkheads appeared freshly painted. It might have been a neglected freighter on the outside, but her looks of rust and neglect were superficial only. This was a quality vessel.

By five thirty we had settled in. Altmann told us the crossing would take five days. Hugo suggested we put on our coats and go outside to see the cast off. I had to admit there was a certain excitement in the event. We donned coats, scarves and hats and went out on the rail. It was dark, but the lights of the docks were ample to allow us to see what was happening. Hugo and I watched in fascination as lines were withdrawn from the massive cleats on the quay and stowed in huge coils on the deck. A small tugboat waited to nudge us into open water. The wind had picked up. It was beginning to snow.

Total darkness descended as we left the mooring and inched into the channel. Commands were being given from the bridge high above us by Altmann. The massive cargo doors had been closed and bolted and the towering cranes pulled back and stowed. Smoke belched from the stack. The *Polar Star* was under way.

"Listen," said Hugo, as he leaned against the icy railing.

"What?"

"Listen to the commands on the ship."

I listened.

The commands from the bridge were all in German.

As we dressed for dinner the *Polar Star* rolled slightly to her starboard side. The lights of New York Harbor had not taken long to blur into the mist of the gathering snowstorm. It was so foggy that we had only caught a glimpse of the Statute of Liberty shrouded in mist and falling snow as we passed 30 minutes ago.

"Hugo what is it? Why are we listing to one side?" We had begun to encounter rolling seas. After all we were going into the North Atlantic, and in winter. I was already trying to get used to the forward and backward pitching of the boat as it broke through the rollers, but the list to the left was not natural.

"Were turning. Turning south. It must be a new course."

"Of course, that's it. We have to go south. Remember our itinerary takes us through Lisbon, Portugal, not London."

"You're right. But the blackboard?"

"I can't explain the blackboard, but it's something like the ship. It's not what it seems to be."

January 14, 1944

My seasickness had begun just after our dinner with Captain Altmann on the first night out and lasted for two days. The ship's doctor, a pharmacy student, gave me some pills he said would make me feel better. All they did was make me drowsy. I spent the next two days in our cabin - mostly sleeping. That was OK; I needed the rest. Hugo got a little queasy, but never really contracted the full brunt of the sea sickness that I had. He managed to move about the ship a lot. His observations were interesting. He was fascinated with the mechanisms of the ship and studied each device. He asked about every machine from the winches to the cleats. The tinkerer in him was forever asking questions.

He found out that the ship was carrying glass bottles from a plant in the Ohio River Valley near Wheeling, West Virginia. They were bound for Lisbon, Portugal and three factories that made chemicals. I was surprised that such commerce was still going on with the War and all. I had heard that the North Atlantic was full of submarines and war ships. We never saw one.

Hugo had gleaned something else from his contact with the officers and crew of the ship. We were the main cargo, and everyone on board knew it. Somehow, they surmised that Hugo and I knew more than we did. They talked to Hugo as if he were one of them. The truth was, this ship had one mission - to carry us to Portugal. The consignment of glass bottles was secondary, arranged solely so that a freighter voyage to Lisbon would be common and ordinary. We were the primary cargo!

On the morning of the fifth day dawn broke clear and cold. We were off the coast of Portugal. Our ship was ready to enter the mouth of the Tagus River which marked the harbor of Lisbon, Portugal. The red tile roofs of the little brick houses cascaded all the way down the steep hillside to the harbor. Wagons and trucks lined the docks. The sun was shining brightly, but it was cold. A cutting wind knifed in from the north and made it unpleasant on deck.

The wide channel took us to the north side of the river where we passed below the red tile roofs of the Barrio Alto, and slowly inched toward an alongside dock at the foot of the Biaxa district. The wharf was a mix of warehouses and brokerage sheds. The ship was tied off and the gangplank lowered. The Captain went ashore first.

Almost immediately a police sedan appeared from between one of the buildings occupied by a policeman and a man in a dark rumpled gray suit who spoke only Portuguese. Neither of us had ever heard Portuguese spoken before and could not communicate with either of the welcoming party. They ushered us off the ship and through a building that housed Portuguese customs and immigration without as much as a stop. A uniformed officer stamped our passports without reading them. A porter trailed behind with a dolly carrying our suitcase and our steamer trunk. Once through the building we were shown to a car and whisked off for the railroad station. It seemed only a few blocks away. Our tickets had been previously purchased by the man in the soiled gray suit. He handed them to us pre-stamped with a red emblem of the Portuguese National Railway System emblazoned on the cover, and we were asked to board the train.

The little compartment of the old train bore little resemblance to the modern Twentieth Century Limited. Its narrow-gauge track gave it a rough and herky-jerky ride down the rails leading out of the city. The little train trundled off into the hills beyond the harbor and swung east through rolling vineyards toward Spain.

Troops were in evidence now at almost every town and crossing. Knots of soldiers stood around, rifles on their shoulders, talking and smoking. Portugal was supposedly neutral on the conflict going on in Europe, but soldiers were everywhere. We had trouble making out the uniforms and could not tell if they were police or military. The train made numerous stops at small towns as passengers got on and off with old worn suitcases and sacks of belongings. They seemed poor and down trodden. The day had clouded over, and it began to spit rain.

Just after dark we reached the Spanish frontier. The train was stopped for over thirty minutes while a different engine was hooked to it. Uniformed border guards came into our compartment and asked for our papers. Hugo produced the German passports that they quickly stamped and handed back to us. There were no questions. We couldn't understand them anyway.

January 15, 1944

By mid-morning we were approaching the outskirts of Madrid. Our instructions were to transfer to another train at Madrid. It had a number and a name. Its destination would be Paris. Tickets had been included in our package.

The uniforms of the soldiers had changed when we crossed into Spain. The high peaked hats of the Spanish soldiers replaced the casual caps of the Portuguese. The uniforms were brown with big belts and shoulder straps. Some officers wore pistols. Most carried long rifles with bayonets affixed.

Madrid appeared dreary even though we only got to see the railway station. The clothes were so drab, and no one seemed cheery. Hugo asked directions to the proper train quay but could find no one that spoke English. We wandered around until we found it. By noon we were on our way again, rising across the broad Spanish hills toward the Pyrenees and the French frontier on a Spanish train.

It was a long night on the train. The ride was rough, and the tracks groaned with the weight of the narrow-gauge train as we rose into the Pyrenees Mountains. It got very cold outside, and by nightfall it had begun to snow. Darkness fell with snow pelting the windows. Our compartment was cold, and I asked the train attendant if we could have more blankets. He responded with a grunt but produced two more scratchy olive drab wool blankets from a closet at the end of the car.

January 16, 1944

We were awakened at 3:30 AM by the brakes being applied and the train coming to an abrupt stop. Steam hissed from the hoses beneath the train and curled up past the windows. It was clear outside and very cold. We were high in the mountains. There was a commotion at the end of our car as men in gray-blue uniforms entered and began knocking on each compartment door. They were speaking German.

When they got to our compartment a tall man pushed our door open without knocking. He wore the unmistakable uniform of a Nazi officer.

"Herr Jurgens?"

"Yes, I'm Hugo Jurgens." I detected a tremor in Hugo's voice.

"You will gather your belongings and come with us." The voice was authoritative and unyielding. The English was perfect.

"Everything?" said Hugo.

"Everything. You are crossing the French frontier and you must change trains. You will not be coming back to this train. Do not leave anything." He motioned for two of the soldiers with him to help us with the trunk and our bags. They entered the compartment and began tugging the bags out the door.

Approximately a hundred yards away on a track with a big barrier at the end of it stood another train. It was steaming. Its engine was emitting a large plume of white smoke as it rested on the track that headed off into the darkness in the direction we were facing. I could see that the Spanish train was at the end of the track. It could go no further. The train cars on the French side were bigger; their wheels were wider apart.

January 18, 1944

It took us 24 hours to reach Paris. Our stop there would be brief - just enough time to change trains, produce papers to unemotional guards in Nazi uniforms and depart again. The train made numerous stops and some deviations that seemed unnecessary. I got the impression that some of the track had been torn up, perhaps bombed, and recently repaired.

German Army uniforms were everywhere. They were in every railroad station, rail yard, and at the entrances to tunnels and at bridges. The French railroads were clearly the object of significant security and under the complete control of the German troops. We passed Panzer units and huge numbers of troops encamped. Some were moving along the roads in truck convoys. The French countryside seemed cold and bleak. Winter had it in its full grip. Barren trees, their sparse limbs swept upward, were silhouetted against the gray sky. Vineyards denuded of all leaves and vines clipped to the stalks stretched to the horizon. We traveled east through Reims, Sedan, and on toward the German border. The conductor said we would cross the Rhine at Koblenz. By morning we would cross the Rhine into Germany. I could feel it; both Hugo and I were getting tense.

January 19, 1944

We crossed the Rhine on a heavily fortified bridge at Koblenz. The train ran along the river for several miles beneath steep bluffs. Several tracks ran parallel here and I saw that some of them had been damaged. There had been bombing in this area. I wondered if the tracks that our train was running on had been damaged and repaired. The American and British bombers could reach this far, and the war was coming home to Germany. At Koblenz the train was stopped for over an hour. Papers were requested, checked, stamped and returned. After the first inspection of papers by German policemen, a second group came in and asked us to open our bags. A brash young lieutenant asked to see our papers again. Hugo gave him our passports. He took them and compared them with a list. He stared at each of us and then back at the photos on the passports. Satisfied, he returned them.

We waited another twenty minutes.

Three more men, this time in long military coats wearing high peaked hats got onto the train. They came straight to our compartment.

"Mister and Mrs. Jurgens?" It was not really a question. I had the feeling they already knew who we were. "I am Marshall von Boldt." He bowed slightly, a gesture I found somewhat exaggerated.

Hugo stood up and extended his hand. Von Boldt took it and shook it warmly.

"I would like to introduce you to Reichslieutenant, Joseph Bruckner."

Bruckner stepped through the compartment door into our view. He was a tall man with blond hair and blue eyes. He wore a shorter coat, black belt and the unmistakable skull and crossbones insignia of the SS on each collar point. His hat was under his arm. Bruckner snapped his heels and bowed slightly.

"Lieutenant Bruckner will be your escort to Berlin. I'm sure you will find him most acceptable and accommodating."

Bruckner spoke for the first time. His English was flawless, executed with a smooth fluid German accent. "I'm sure we will get along fine," said Bruckner. He looked at me with his blue eyes and winked. He was brutally handsome. That he was charming was an understatement.

"Thank you, Marshall von Boldt." Bruckner dismissed von Boldt with a movement of his hand. Von Boldt said something to him in German and departed the train. Von Boldt had no sooner stepped off the train and onto the platform than the train began to move.

"Well, Mister and Mrs. Jurgens, I have heard so much about you," began Bruckner as he walked across the compartment and watched the station platform slip by. He turned, opened a cigarette case and offered one to me and then Hugo.

"My instructions are to deliver you safely to Berlin. I do not think that is going to be so difficult a task. In fact, I think that I am going to enjoy it very much." I felt as if he were peeling off my clothing layer by layer with his eyes as he spoke.

"I have read your dossier. It is quite remarkable."

"How so?" I said.

"You operated for almost three years without even a hint of suspicion. Even to this day your superiors do not have any idea of the information that you have gotten out to us."

"That's over now," said Hugo.

"I know that, but your service to the Reich is not." It was a strange statement. I never looked on what we did as much of a service to anyone except ourselves by bringing in some extra money.

"Do you know why we are here?" I had to find out.

"Of course, but I am not at liberty to tell you. You will be briefed in Berlin. We will arrive tomorrow afternoon. Your briefings will begin at 1000 hours the next morning."

I was miffed that he could not tell us.

"And where will we be staying?" asked Hugo.

"I think you will be very pleased with your accommodations in Berlin. We have seen to it that you will be very comfortable." Bruckner could be very evasive when asked direct questions.

January 19, 1944

Our entry into Berlin was uneventful – a little herky-jerky as the train was switched from one track to another. Allied bombing had taken a toll on the tracks. We were surprised how quickly the passing landscape changed from rural to urban. Evidence of bombing damage was everywhere. We had arrived a little late at Berlin's Hauptbahnhof. The station had been badly damaged by bombing and only a couple of tracks were intact to handle trains. Hugo and I were met by a black-booted driver and a car. Bruckner ordered our bags and the trunk transferred to the Mercedes and slipped in beside the driver. The big silver headlights were masked leaving only slits for lights. We rode in back. Hugo rubbed his hands on the rich cowhide seats of the big Mercedes.

"Never thought I'd be riding in one of these," he said.

The hazy winter sun had dipped below the horizon as the black Mercedes Benz Grand Saloon left the Enlastungstrasse, swung west on Tiergartenstrass and drove parallel to the Tiergarten. We turned on a small street and glided the two blocks to the gravel driveway of the Limpen House.

Darkness comes quickly in Berlin in January after the sun leaves the sky. On cloudy days it comes even faster. The masked headlights of the Mercedes pierced the light fog like a stiletto and swept past the two large stone gateposts up the curving drive toward the marble steps.

The Limpen House was in a fashionable section of Berlin among several equally large town houses. Several of the houses had bomb damage. The only thing that distinguished the Limpen House from its neighbors was that it was on larger grounds than those around it with more shrubbery and a larger lawn. It was neo-Classical in design with a stone facade executed as only the Germans can do it. Grand black cast-iron railings, massive window grilles, and large globular light fixtures adorned the stucco and stone facade. The exterior lights were off. The house appeared dark except for the light that streamed from the front door that opened as soon as we entered the driveway. Bruckner explained that the windows were dark because of the blackout drapes. The interior was lit brightly.

The Limpen house had three stories. A magnificent wrought iron and marble staircase wound its way up from the polished black and white marble floor of the entry vestibule and curved along the back wall in a balcony over the entry foyer to access the second floor. Exquisite period furniture adorned the sitting rooms on either side of the entrance hallway. Hugo and I probably gawked pretty hard. It was impressive.

From a domed-top door beneath the staircase a gentleman in striped trousers followed by a very attractive young lady in a maid's uniform, emerged and approached us.

"Good evening Mister and Mrs. Jurgens," intoned the man. "We hope you had a pleasant journey. My name is Heinrik Luffendorf. You may call me Heine. I am the concierge here, and this is Ellie. She will be your maid. Welcome to the Limpen House."

"What kind of a place is this?" blurted Hugo.

"This is a guest house for esteemed visitors of the Reich," said Heine. We have only six rooms for guests, but I'm sure that you will find them very satisfactory." He almost sounded apologetic.

Bruckner motioned to the girl and she began gathering up our bags.

"Here, I'll help you with that," said Hugo, reaching for the suitcase nearest him.

"That's all right," said Ellie, beating him to the handle and snatching it out of his reach. "I'll take care of it." Her English was halting, but understandable.

"We'll have your trunk sent up to your room in a few minutes," said Luffendorf.

A cold rain had settled in before we had gotten to the Limpen House. A biting wind blew it from the north. Rain now ran in sheets down the tall windows behind the drawn blackout drapes. Our room was nothing short of sumptuous. It actually consisted of a small suite of rooms with a bedroom, sitting room and bath. A crystal chandelier hung from a plaster ceiling rosette over the bed, and wall sconces lit the high ceiling sitting room.

Ellie popped in and turned back the spacious bed bending low to stretch over its wide expanse providing a display of very shapely buttocks for Hugo's benefit. Somehow, I got the impression that Ellie made more than beds.

"I hope you have a pleasant night's sleep" she cooed, as she pulled the door closed behind her.

Hugo began to pull his shirt out of his trouser belt. "I'm bushed. That big tub looks very inviting. Want to join me?"

I had seen it, too. In the bathroom was an enormous claw-footed porcelain tub that could easily accommodate two people. It even had water inlets with bulbous white porcelain ceramic hot and cold faucets on both ends. There were no showers or baths on the trains. We had not bathed since we left the ship. We had to make do with small basins on the train – and cold water. A hot bath sounded like a grand idea.

"Can you really believe that we are doing this?" said Hugo as he sponged my back. The hot water felt so good. We were both tired and sore after over a solid week of traveling.

"I guess we find out tomorrow what it's all about. Bruckner said he would pick us up at 9:30 sharp for a meeting. I feel like I could sleep until then.

A mantel clock in the sitting room was chiming 19:30. We told Ellie that we would not have any dinner. She seemed disappointed and offered us some tea and cookies.

By 8:30 we were both in bed sound asleep.

17

CHAPTER

THE MEETING

The big black Mercedes rolled through the morning rain and fog like a ghost. We passed into the Tiergarten. In its day it must have been a lovely wooded park with dark forests of mature trees lining the roadways that converged in the center. Today it was a forlorn, barren wasteland where most of the trees had been cut to provide wood for Berliners' stoves, and it was pockmarked with bomb craters. Some of the land had been cultivated into small garden patches which now, in winter, were only barren splotches of bare earth. Bruckner commented that the Furher had authorized the planting of gardens to produce food for starved and strapped Berliners. It brought to mind the "Victory Gardens" back home that had sprouted up all across America after the start of the war.

Few people were out even though it was after nine. Our first glimpse of Berlin through the fogged windows was of a cold, rain-soaked dull and battened-down city. We passed onto the Unter den Linden which was heavily bomb-damaged. The few shops and stores that remained were blocked with sandbags piled in front of the windows to protect from the incessant bombing. Shutters were drawn. Here and there was a building completely destroyed by the bombing. There were piles of rubble everywhere. The Allied bombing had been precise. It was not an exciting place. Everything seemed gray. Not a leaf, blade of green grass or flower bloomed. A North Sea wind drove the cold rain against the windows of the car.

We passed in front of the Reich's Chancellery – a burned out hulk of a building just past the Brandenburg Gate. Neither of us would have known what it was if Bruckner hadn't pointed it out. The Mercedes swung onto Wilhelmstrasse. This was where most of the administration buildings of the Third Reich were located. It has also been a magnet for Allied bombs. The destruction was incredible with almost every building showing some bomb damage. All but one, that is. On the east side of the Wilhelmstrasse one lone building was almost unscathed. All but a few windows were intact, and the structure showed none of the massive damage of the buildings all around it.

It was the headquarters of Goring's Luftwaffe – the German Air force, and for some reason American and British bombers had left the building unscathed. Its gray stone façade stood out from around it, not for its beauty, but for its total lack of damage. We went around the side and stopped in a dead-end street that ran alongside the massive gray office building. Bruckner got out, opened the door and gestured toward a door at street level. A guard stood under a small canopy in front of the door and stood aside as we approached.

"Follow me, please," said Bruckner as he led us into the stone building and down the stairs. He held open a large thick door, and we entered another hallway. Bruckner then went ahead and stopped in front of another guarded door. He said something to the guard in German and the guard opened the door and held it open. Another flight of steps led downward. I figured that we were now two levels beneath the street. The walls were made of gray concrete and appeared very thick. It was clearly built to withstand bomb blasts. At the end of the stairs was a short hallway with two double doors across the end.

Bruckner knocked.

"Enter," came a vice from inside. It was in German, but even I understood it.

Bruckner swung the two narrow double doors open and stepped in.

Before us was a table approximately ten feet long behind which three men in Nazi uniforms sat smoking. Each wore uniforms bearing several medals and decorations. I did not recognize them all. One bore the skull and cross bones of the Schutzstaffel, the 'SS." That one I recognized.

"Ah, Mister and Mrs. Jurgens." It was the middle Nazi who spoke. "Please come in. We have heard so much about you."

Hugo took a tentative step forward. Neither of us knew what the protocol here was. Do we shake hands? We decided not.

"Please sit down." The middle Nazi gestured toward a bank of chairs that were in front of the long table. I noticed that it was an exquisite table, with thick carved round legs and polished to a high luster. Behind them hung a huge stylized eagle standing on a perch made of the world. The inference was unmistakable.

"We're so glad you agreed to come," said the middle Nazi.

We sat.

"I am Albert Speer, Minister of Armaments of the Reich. This, he said gesturing to the man on his right, is Heinrik Himmler, Director General of the *Schutzstaffel*; you may know it as the S.S." Himmler wore a decided scowl. I could see the S.S. insignia on his pointed collar. "Herr Himmler has recently been appointed by the Furher to the position of Minister of the Interior."

I felt Hugo go tense.

"And this," he continued gesturing to his left, "is Joseph Paul Goebbels, Reichsminister for Propaganda and National Enlightenment." I saw Hugo's jaw open just a little. He obviously knew who they were. I didn't.

Goebbels spoke: "Mrs. Jurgens, the entire Reich is indebted to you for your excellent work in the ordinance plant in St. Louis. Your reports have been of major benefit to us. Your perception and skill in retrieving documents and information has been remarkable. You are a legend in our intelligence community."

"Thank you, sir, but surely you didn't bring us all the way to Berlin just to say 'thanks'?"

"No," continued Speer, "but we want you to know that we respect your tenacity, attention to detail and unyielding dedication to the development of information which has helped us track the progress of Project Manhattan."

"Project Manhattan? What's that?"

"It's a program the Americans are pursuing to develop a weapon system. It's in its early stages, but your General Hollenbeck is a part of a team that is putting it together."

"What is this 'Manhattan' supposed to do?"

"I can't tell you just yet, but before you leave us you will have an understanding of why we have such a keen interest in your work, and you will know what project Manhattan is supposed to do."

"And in the meantime?" It was Hugo, inquisitive as usual.

"You will be our guests for several days. You will get to know us, and we will get to know you. We're not trying to be coy with you, but when you know everything at the end of the week you will understand why we are so cautious." He hesitated, "and why you have been chosen."

Himmler had not spoken. He got up and walked around the front of the table. He never took his eyes off us. He was a brooding man, with deep furrows in his brow even when he wasn't scowling. I could tell Hugo didn't like him; his body reverberated with tension. I felt like Himmler undressed me with his eyes and crawled around inside.

"I have my doubts," said Himmler as he circled behind my chair and put his hand on my shoulder. His hand was cold, bony.

"I have my doubts as to whether you are the right people to carry out the task we are going to assign you. I'm not sure you have the courage, the fortitude, or cunning, even though we know you are highly motivated by the offer of five hundred thousand dollars. You will have to prove to me you are capable and strong-willed enough to succeed."

"You used the word 'assign'? Are we to understand that we now have no choice?" I said.

"My dear Mrs. Jurgens," Himmler continued, "I would have thought you would have figured that out when you were strapped to your dining room table. Not only do you have no choice, but we will eliminate you if you fail." The coldness with which he pronounced the lack of options was remarkable. Himmler proceeded back to the table and sat back down.

"Thank you for coming," said Speer, rising from his chair. "You'll start this afternoon. Bruckner will drive you to Peenemunde. It's a long drive, but we know that you will find it interesting." He smiled a patronizing smile and Bruckner tapped us on the shoulder. The meeting was clearly over.

Hugo was up the steps two at a time. I followed as best I could. He was better suited to stair climbing than I. We emerged back at street level into the same gray drizzly day. Bruckner went out ahead and got the car. We waited under the canopy to stay dry until he brought it around.

"Jesus Christ!" said Hugo when Bruckner was out of earshot. "Do you know who that was?"

"Not exactly, but they seemed..."

"That was most of the German High Command. But for Hitler and a couple of others we were looking at the biggest names in the Reich!"

"So, what do they want with us? I mean, we..."

"Frieda, I haven't the slightest idea. But whatever it is it must have the highest priority. Those guys weren't just out to welcome a couple of tourists to exciting, friendly Berlin."

Bruckner drove the car to the curb and opened the rear door.

"Well," I said, trying to make the best of it, "I guess we find out soon. Where is Peenemunde?"

"Damned if I know," said Hugo as he held the Mercedes door open, and we got in.

18
CHAPTER
PEENEMUNDE

"January 21, 1944

We drove north out of Berlin through the foggy Grey day toward the Baltic Sea. Charcoal clouds spit a fine cold mist on our car. The land flattened into a monotonous coastal plain. Shuttered farmhouses dotted the horizon. There were checkpoints every few miles. At each Bruckner stopped the car, showed papers and identification, said something in German and we were off again. No stop lasted over a minute, but the frequency of the stops and the narrow roads made making any time difficult. After about three hours we topped a low sandy ridge and the Baltic Sea popped into view. Bruckner swung west and immediately encountered another checkpoint. This time one of the guards got into the car beside Bruckner and we drove on. Whoever he was, they were clearly expecting us. The fortifications in the area were heavy. Concrete bunkers and pillboxes dotted the sandy landscape. Large caliber gun emplacements were everywhere.

The big Mercedes slowed as we topped a low rise in the dunes and turned into what appeared to be a farm road that headed straight for the sea. On either side the sea oats and sawgrass came right up to the side of the road and occasionally brushed against the car. Sea birds squawked in the frigid air. The road was bumpy from sand ripples that had formed from blown sand across the car tracks.

A small, unpainted bridge appeared ahead. It had no rails or sides and was made of wood weathered to a light gray. When we got near it, I could see that it was very sturdy - built to hold more than just an occasional automobile, yet there was nothing around. Heavy trucks had made marks in the sand road leading to the bridge. In either direction the sea, sand and sea oats stretched as for as the eye could see.

We clattered across the bridge toward a spit of land that stuck out in the sea. At the end of the bridge was another checkpoint. With the passenger on board we simply slowed but did not stop. When the guards saw him, we were immediately waived through. The road veered left and over some low dunes. Squat buildings came into view. They were long and rectangular in shape and camouflaged for protection from aerial surveillance. They reminded me of barracks - low and Quonset-like. At the far end near the beach there were tee-shaped concrete pads mostly covered with sand and blown sea oats. You could see their outlines, but they looked like the wind had blown the sand and a little dry vegetation over them making them barely visible. On the other side of the road was a tall building without windows. Part of it was open and we could see a steel framework inside, sort of like a crane or lifting structure. This was Peenemunde - the secret German rocket base where Werner von Braun and a host of German scientists were hard at work on the V1, V2, V3 and V4 Rockets and flying bombs.

We were greeted at what appeared to be an administration building by our guide and interpreter, Helmut von Lumet. He was a tall man, gaunt in appearance and not very expressive. He wore a khaki shirt and pants with a web belt. Everything about him was bland. Before the war he was a physics professor at the University at Heidelberg. His specialty was propulsion, and he had been transferred to Peenemunde in 1942 to work on the "flying bomb" project. He was one of the team working on the development of a guided rocket that would change the course of the War.

"We are far ahead of the rest of the world," von Lumet told us. "Even the Americans have not recognized the potential of pilotless bombs and rockets that can penetrate air space at several hundred miles an hour. Aircraft cannot stop them, and they are virtually impossible to shoot down."

Both Hugo and I wondered why we were being shown all of this. It was impressive, but we couldn't help wondering what this had to do with the mission we were being asked to accomplish? We know nothing about rockets and flying bombs.

"Have you been successful?" asked Hugo.

"On June 13 of last year, we test-launched a twelve-ton rocket, an A4, the advanced prototype of the V2 we are now developing. The rocket was designed to reach England from launch sites on the North Sea. It's designed range was two hundred miles."

"And?"

"Thirty-five officials, many members of the High Command, came up from Berlin to watch the test. Our major supporters, Field Marshall Milch and Minister for Armaments, Albert Speer, whom you have met, came to watch the test flight."

"I suppose you didn't disappoint them?" said Hugo. Sometimes Hugo amazes me. He has a wonderful gift of gab. He was chatting with von Lumet like he was an old friend.

"On the contrary, the rocket successfully fired, lifted off the pad over there," von Lumet gestured toward one of the sand-covered concrete pads, "and it crashed into the sea out there just a mile away."

"What a disaster. What did you do?"

"Everyone was disappointed. Doctor von Braun was most depressed at the failure. But the lift off and few seconds of controlled flight convinced everyone that we were right. Speer doubled our manpower and money. The Fuhrer, when told of the flight, was skeptical, but Speer and Goring encouraged him to continue our efforts."

Hugo was intrigued. His interest in things mechanical and scientific was showing through. "Are you making progress now?"

"Very definitely," said von Lumet. "On October 3rd, after many modifications, we successfully tested the A4 and obtained a two-hundred-mile controlled flight out over the Baltic. The rocket hit within a mile of its target. Not bad for two hundred miles. The Fuhrer was so enthusiastic that he immediately authorized the mass production of the rocket. The first will be ready in another month. England will be our primary target. By late spring we will be able to deliver two hundred pounds of explosives into the heart of London from the French and Dutch coasts with absolutely no defense."

"That's quite impressive," I said, tentatively. I was out of my league. I knew it. Somehow, it seemed like the right thing to say.

Hugo was fascinated.

"And our successes continue on another front. On December 24th of 1943, just over a year ago, we successfully flew our "Flying Bomb." It's a pilotless bomb, radio controlled, and jet propelled. The first flight went a mile and a half, but we have extended its range. They can reach London from the Continent. We are producing them at the rate of three a day. As soon as they are completed, they're shipped to the coast and fired. The English are afraid of them, and their effect on morale is as devastating as their blast. When we are able to complement them with the big rockets carrying hundreds of pounds of explosives the combination will be lethal. We'll be able to reach every part of England from the coast of France. As our telemetry accuracy increases, we'll be able to pinpoint targets and destroy them at will. The English Air Forces will be unable to stop them."

We walked on through the complex of buildings with von Lumet praising the advances they had made in propulsion and guidance. He seemed to take dreary pleasure in describing his rockets and bombs. He was an academician through and through, and his delivery showed it. It was as if he were lecturing a physics class - thorough, unemotional, and calculating.

Peenemunde is a dreary place in winter. The north wind howls in off the Baltic and blows the sand around. Sea birds screech and dip against the gusts. The workers here are a morose appearing lot, too. I think some are prisoners who live in the barracks buildings we had seen when we arrived. Few talked, to us or even acknowledged our presence when we are shown into their work area. They go about their tasks like little drones. Von Lumet makes pronouncements of death and destruction on England as if he were talking about what he would have for dinner. He predicted someday they could even build a rocket that would reach New York, Washington or Philadelphia. To him it was all statistics and science. He speaks in terms of "range," "telemetry" and "payload." He is the dullest, most unemotional, man I had ever met.

Darkness had fallen. As we walked through the buildings, I got the impression that there were some areas of the compound we were not supposed to see. Von Lumet steered us gingerly away from some of the buildings and hurriedly into others. We were told we would have a dinner and be billeted in one of the bunk buildings for the night. There would be a special meeting and briefing in the morning. Darkness had consumed the compound. Shrouded interior work lights were turned on, and blackout shutters blocked all windows. From the outside of the buildings it was pitch dark. No plane or ship would ever see Peenemunde in the blackness.

Our room was stark - four walls, two metal frame beds and a washbasin. We were to share a bathroom at the end of the hall with the others in the billet. If there was anyone else there, we never saw them. The place was quiet as a tomb. After a sparse dinner alone in a little dining room we retired to our room. Rain had begun to fall in sheets. It thundered on the metal roof and ran down the small windowpane. Our room was cold.

"Hugo," I said, slipping across the four-foot space between the single beds and into his bed. "I..."

"Shhhhh!" Hugo put his finger to my lips. He put his lips to my ear. "They have to be listening."

"What do you mean?"

"Frieda, they have just shown us the biggest secret in the Reich. "Do you know where we are? This is their top-secret experimental rocket base. This isn't a busman's holiday they have us on; they're doing this for a reason. You don't just take a couple of folks from

South St. Louis and show them your state secrets for nothing." Hugo continued to whisper, very gently into my ear. His lips hardly moved. I lay still to be able to hear him over the thundering rain on the tin roof. "They have to have this room bugged. They're probably listening to every word we say. Whisper in my ear. The rain on the roof will drown out the words."

"What's it all mean?"

"First, I don't have the slightest idea what they want of us, but whatever it is it's bigger than anything you or I ever imagined. Second, Himmler left no doubt about our options. We aren't going to be given a choice. We do what they want, or they'll kill us."

"But what do they want? What are they going to require us to do?"

Hugo put his arms around me and hugged me. He was warm and the heat from his body felt good in the cold room. I could see my breath in the cold damp air. There were plenty of covers. I put my lips on his neck and kissed him. He returned the kiss on my shoulder.

"Whatever it is," he whispered, I think we're going to find out in the morning."

I was scared. I know Hugo was, too. I can read him like a book. He didn't have to tell me. We dozed off snuggled together in a tight embrace to keep warm. If the Germans were listening all they heard was two people snoring lightly under the heavy covers of a single bed.

I hope they enjoyed it.

The morning clouds seemed closer to earth than ever. They hung like wet gray cotton. Big droplets of rain continued to fall, but not in the downpour of last night. The sea had come up, and from our little window we could see the waves crashing on the beach a quarter-mile away. The wind was howling and blowing the raindrops hard against the window. Hugo said he thought that there was some snow or sleet in them. I couldn't tell. I was scared to death and almost sick to my stomach.

On top of that I started my period.

January 22, 1944

We were awakened by a knock on the door at seven. After dressing we were shown to a room in an adjacent building where two tables had been set. Breakfast was being laid out by two young men in short white smocks when we entered. The tables had starched white tablecloths and faced each other. On the wall were maps of the Baltic area, the French coast, England and the Dutch coast. On one wall was a picture of Adolph Hitler. Von Lumet greeted us and bid us be seated for breakfast. He took a seat at our table next to Hugo. The servers laid out a breakfast of herring and eggs. In a minute two men entered and took the table across from us.

One, a short balding man, wore a Nazi uniform, but I could not tell his rank. He wore little in the way of insignia, just a brown shirt and loose-fitting fatigue slacks. The other was a very handsome man in his mid-forties dressed in fatigues. Von Lumet introduced them as Doctor Otto Besserman, and Doctor Eric Storch.

Storch, the younger man, spoke first. "Mr. and Mrs. Jurgens, you have come a long way. We are sure that you did not expect to see Peenemunde, but we hope you have been impressed with what you have seen. German science has been advanced very rapidly by the things we do here. I suspect that you are the first American citizens to ever see this place, and you may be the only Americans to ever see it."

"We still don't know why we're here," I said. "You've brought us a long way and shown us a lot of things. I think it's time you tell us what you want."

Storch's brow furled. He clearly didn't like being rushed in what he had to say. My comment irritated him.

"I'll get right to the point. You are here for two reasons: first you are greedy. The offer of five hundred thousand dollars is more than you will ever see in your lives, and you are opportunistic enough to act on the chance of receiving it. Second, you are here because you now have no choice. Our uninvited visit to your home should have left you no doubt that we can get to you any time we want to. If you do not do as we tell you, we will visit you again."

"All right. You've made yourself perfectly clear," said Hugo, straightening in his chair. "But you still haven't told us what it is you want?"

Besserman spoke: "Doctor Storch and I work in Berlin, not here in Peenemunde. Our work is not in the science of propulsion as is Doctor Lumet's, but rather in an area little known to most." Besserman paused to let that revelation dangle for a few seconds.

Besserman continued. "Let me give you some background. A few years ago, two of our colleagues, Otto Hahn and Fritz Strassman along with Lise Meitner and her nephew Otto Frisch, were experimenting with uranium. Do you know what uranium is?"

Something welled up in the pit of my stomach. I swallowed hard. I had only heard that word one other time in my life. It was when General Hollenbeck told me that they were going to build a plant at Weldon Spring in St. Charles County to process uranium. My skin went clammy. I know I was white as a sheet. I must have shown some emotion.

Besserman picked up on my discomfort. "You know what uranium is, Mrs. Jurgens?" He looked right into my eyes.

"Uh, no, Doctor Besserman. I don't."

"Uranium is a relatively new element. At least it is new to the scientific world. It's difficult to refine, but when refined and processed becomes the densest heavy metal on earth."

Besserman paused and looked at me again as if to see if there would be any more reaction. I sat motionless, afraid to move, lest I give away my fear.

Besserman continued as if he were lecturing a college class. "Hahn and Strassman bombarded several different elements with neutrons to see what their reaction would be. When they bombarded uranium, the nucleus split into two pieces."

Something about what Besserman was saying rang a bell. One of the communiques that I had seen on Hollenbeck's secure Telex referred to this very thing. Even the names Hahn and Strassman were familiar. It had to do with one of the important meetings that

Hollenbeck attended in Washington. Somehow the Americans knew about the Hahn and Strassman experiment.

"I suppose this split was something revolutionary?" said Hugo.

"Not really. We already knew we could bombard some elements, and they broke down. What was revolutionary was when we measured the weight of the two masses of bombarded uranium, we found that together they weighed significantly less than the total of the mass before the bombardment."

"So, where did it go?"

"It took us a while to figure it out. But we did. The missing portion of the uranium had been transformed into energy."

"Energy? What do you mean, 'energy'?" Hugo was staying with him. I didn't understand - a condition I was beginning to get used to.

"Within a few weeks we realized we had split the atoms of the element uranium and released a huge volume of energy. We repeated the experiment again and again, each time with the same results. Each time there was a release of energy. We even figured out how to measure the energy that was released. That is where the real revelation came. To our astonishment the ratio of energy released to material used was billions to one! We had created a miniature nuclear reaction. The process is called fission."

"I'm not sure what that means?" said Hugo, "but I think you are going to tell me."

"Shortly after this breakthrough, Meitner and her nephew, Frisch, defected. We already knew that the English were theorizing that fission was possible. Even the American theoreticians were talking about the possibilities of a sustained continuous reaction. But no one had been able to do it. Meitner and Frisch took our information with them, and we are sure that the English, perhaps even the Americans, have it."

"How can you be so sure the British and the Americans have it?"

"In mid-1941 a panel of British scientists theorized that it would be possible to build a bomb using nuclear fission. It was only theory, but their theories track the experiments of Hahn and Strassman precisely. The source had to be the information carried out by Meitner and Frisch."

"That was three years ago. So why haven't the British built this bomb?"

"Theory is one thing. Putting it into practice is quite another. They don't know how to refine and enrich the uranium. The British theorized that it would take at least twenty-two pounds of enriched uranium to make a bomb. The most anyone has been able to refine has been traces. The Americans are confronting the same problem, but they are more resourceful."

I felt sick. The key was not the knowledge to *build* the bomb, but the *ability to refine* the uranium. Weldon Spring held the key! I had unwittingly played a part in supplying the missing link! I had been passing information on the building of the Weldon Spring plant including the schematics for the American processes for refinement. It was all so clear now. The United States was racing to build a plant that could refine the uranium, and I had been keeping the Germans abreast of what was happening! I had been doing it for over three years. The Germans were taking our information and building a bomb!

"Are you all right, Mrs. Jurgens? You look pale."

"I'll be all right." I sipped some coffee and broke one of the hard rolls open. It was fluffy white inside its thick crust. Steam rose from its soft center. I spread it with butter. I needed something in my stomach. Besserman watched me with some interest. The only sound was the rain on the tin roof that had now settled into a monotonous drizzle.

I nodded to him. "Please continue Doctor Besserman."

Storch cut in abruptly. "We're sure that you must know that advances in German science are not limited to the feats that have been accomplished here at Peenemunde. We are making daily technological breakthroughs in many places and in many other fields. You will recall that my colleague, Herr Doctor Besserman, said that no one *had* been able to refine enough uranium to build a bomb."

"You mean you've done it? You have succeeded in refining enough uranium to build a bomb?" Hugo was pressing Storch.

"*We have done it*, Herr Jurgens. But without the excellent help that you and your wife provided us in the form or photographs, drawings, designs and data on the design of the Weldon Spring refining plant we could not have done it so quickly. Why, we were testing the Americans' processing theory before they had the footings in the ground, thanks to you. What you provided allowed us to move far ahead of both the Americans and the British in uranium refining theory."

I was aghast! I know I must have looked surprised. Storch plunged on. "And," he said, pointing his finger at the ceiling like a lecturer about to make a point, "what we learned from what you sent us has allowed us to avoid the costly and stupid mistakes that the Americans are making in the construction at Oak Ridge, Tennessee."

"And what is that?"

"They believe that refinement using extremely high amounts of electricity will yield the necessary quantities of usable uranium. They are quite wrong, but they have yet to discover their error. True, their method will produce usable Uranium 235, but the process is slow, and the quality produced will not yield the explosive power that is obtainable using another method. We have already tested it, and it is a poor process."

"I suppose that you are going to tell us you have a better method?" Hugo seemed to enjoy baiting Storch.

"Not only do we have a better method. We have already produced a pure grade of uranium 235 that far exceeds anything either of the processes the Americans are experimenting with can produce."

Besserman cut in. "Enough Storch. We are not at liberty to divulge the process. You've told them enough." He turned to Hugo and I and spoke patronizingly. "It is well enough that you know that we have refined a sufficient amount of high-grade uranium to produce a bomb of immense proportions."

The thought made me sick. "Thanks to us, Germany has an atomic bomb!"

January 23, 1944

The ride back to Berlin the next day was quiet and somber. Hugo and I began to realize the magnitude of our acts, and, frankly, it sickened us. We had been instrumental in delivering secrets that had allowed the Germans to build a monster bomb. The ramifications were all too clear - a huge bomb, a rocket - thousands (maybe hundreds of thousands) of English were going to die! Bruckner said little as he maneuvered the Mercedes through the checkpoints and around the barriers that would stop a tank. The rain had stopped. Thick gray sodden clouds hung like a wet drape occasionally spitting an errant snowflake. It had gotten colder. I was having trouble digesting all I had learned in the last thirty-six hours. I wasn't sure I even knew what an atomic bomb was. All I knew was that Hugo and I had been instrumental in providing information that allowed them to do it - and it was clear what they were going to do with it. But we still couldn't figure where Hugo and I fit in?

We had not left Peenemunde until noon. It was early evening when we arrived back at Limpen house. We were greeted by the staff like we were long lost relatives. A pine log fire crackled in the immense fireplace, and Heine Luffendorf advised us that dinner would be at eight. The chef had prepared a special meal. Additional guests were expected. Cocktails would be in the drawing room at seven.

Hugo shaved while I bathed in the luxurious hot water of the deep porcelain tub. I just wanted to scrub the dirt off of me. We weren't that dirty - we just felt that way.

We were now both convinced our room was bugged and spoke of nothing relevant to what we had seen or what we thought. We made small talk. If we needed to communicate, we whispered in each other's ears. It was difficult not to think about what we had seen and heard at Peenemunde. It was difficult not to talk about it. Hugo made small talk. I commented on Berlin, and how it seemed shuttered. We speculated on the possibilities of an air raid and the potential of an

Allied bomb falling on us. We were free from bombing as long as this cloud cover continued.

We dressed. I had only one good dress, a black velvet ankle length gown with an Empire waist and a scooped neckline. Hugo bought it for me for last New Year's, and I knew he liked it. There was just enough bosom showing to attract interest, but not enough to show the whole store. Hugo had one dark suit. He wore it, and I have to admit, we were a pretty darn good-looking couple. Good looking, maybe, but scared to death. We had gotten in over our heads and we both knew it. Unfortunately, there was little we could do but forge ahead. The options were not pleasant.

As we descended the staircase Ellie was opening the front door. In stepped Marshall Albert Speer and Joseph Goebbels shaking snowflakes from the big fur collars on their coats. Goebbels, always the charmer, looked up at me and smiled.

"Ah, Mrs. Jurgens. You look magnificent. It will be a pleasure to have you join us tonight." He extended his hand and held mine as I descended the last two steps of the broad staircase. "I believe you know Marshall Speer."

Speer extended his hand to Hugo. "It's good to see you again Mr. and Mrs. Jurgens. I hope that this evening can be a little less formal than the meeting at the Luftwaffe Headquarters the other day."

"It is quite a surprise to see you again, Marshall Speer," said Hugo. The absence of Himmler was conspicuous. Having dinner with him wouldn't have been a pleasure. I, too, was glad he hadn't come.

Goebbels guided me by the elbow toward the drawing room where Ellie was waiting to take an order for drinks. Another gentleman stood at the fireplace in the drawing room warming himself at the fire. He had arrived earlier before we had come down. In his hand he held a brandy.

"Ah, there you are Jodl," said the affable Goebbels. "We were afraid you would be late."

"Good evening." The man was tall and dressed in the uniform of an officer of the Reich. His full frame was emphasized by the blue-gray of the tailored Nazi uniform. His hat was under his arm.

"May I present Mr. and Mrs. Hugo Jurgens of the United States. General Alfred Jodl, Mr. and Mrs. Jurgens."

Jodl placed his hat on the table; snapped his heels and extended his hand to me. He was very handsome.

"I have heard many things about you, Mr. and Mrs. Jurgens." Your work has enabled us to make many advances in a short time. The Fuhrer sends his personal congratulations."

I had no idea who Alfred Jodl was.

"Would you like a drink? I can imagine that you might like one after your journey from the Baltic coast.

"A beer for me," said Hugo. "Frieda?"

"Do you have any Bourbon?" I asked. Don't ask me what made me ask for bourbon. I almost never drink it. Somehow it sounded good with a little water.

"Bourbon?" echoed Goebbels. "Heine, do we have any American bourbon?"

"Of course," said Heine. I have a bottle of Four Roses in the cupboard. With water and ice, Mrs. Jurgens?"

"That would be nice. Thank you, Heine.

"Schnapps," said Speer.

"Zwein," echoed Goebbels.

"General Jodl?"

"No thank you. I cannot stay. I just wanted to come over and extend the thanks and appreciation of the Fuhrer."

Jodl extended his hand to Hugo and shook it warmly. Then he turned and did the same to me. His grip was warm and friendly, and he held it slightly longer than I had expected.

"Mrs. Jurgens you are a beautiful and courageous woman. The Reich is deeply indebted to you for the consistent and unyielding work that you have done in the United States. I have something for you."

He reached into the inside pocket of his tunic and produced two small black leather cases each the size of a small coin purse. He opened the first as if it held a glass ornament that might break if dropped. Inside was a silver medal in the shape of a Prussian cross, threaded through a ring from which dangled a red, black and white silk ribbon. It was the Iron Cross, First Class – Germany's highest civilian award.

He took one from each case.

"These are awarded to you at the special instance and order of the Fuhrer, Adolph Hitler, as a token of the gratefulness of the Reich for what you have done." He held the medals out and presented them to Hugo and me.

I was speechless. I couldn't move. I stood motionless. Jodl then took my medal from its case and held it by the ribbon. He unlatched the clasp and stepped close to me extending his arms around my neck to hook the clasp.

I could smell his cologne; citrus.

"From a grateful Reich, and with special thanks from the Furher," he said as he latched the ribbon behind my neck. I felt the little metal hook fall on the back of my neck. He kissed me on both cheeks, very lightly.

He repeated the little ceremony with Hugo. Even to the kiss.

Heine and Ellie had not gone for the drinks, but rather had stood motionless in the pantry doorway watching the presentation. When Jodl had finished they applauded along with Speer and Goebbels and disappeared into the pantry.

"Now, I must leave you. Good night." Jodl snapped his heels, turned for the door and was gone. No one said a word as he left. Hugo and I stood motionless with the Iron Crosses we had just been presented dangling on their delicate ribbons around our necks.

19

CHAPTER

THE PLAN

"Well," said Speer, breaking the awkward silence after Jodl's departure. I know you have seen some interesting things. Do you grasp their import?"

I was not sure what he meant.

"Import?" I said.

"Yes, you have seen and heard information in the last two days that very few people, even in Germany, know."

"Yes, but we're having trouble putting it together," said Hugo. "You have a rocket and flying bomb program, and you have a program to develop an atomic bomb."

"Yes, go on," said Speer.

Well," continued Hugo, pausing to look over at me. "I suppose you're going to put one of the bombs into one of your rockets and drop it on England. It makes sense."

Speer looked at Goebbels. Goebbels glanced at my bosom. A thin smile crossed his lips.

"You might logically reach that conclusion from what you have seen," said Speer.

"Yes," said Hugo. "Aren't we correct?"

"In fact, we expected you to reach that conclusion. It's natural and probably very logical."

"But it's not right?" Hugo sounded unsure of himself.

What else could they have in mind?

"You see, Herr Jurgens, there are some facts that have either escaped you, or that we have not disclosed to you, which might cause you to reach another conclusion."

Hugo was puzzled. "Like what?"

"First, we told you that we have a process to refine the highest-grade Uranium-235. We are far ahead of the Americans and the Brits in that area, yet we have succeeded in refining only enough of the very highest-grade product to build one bomb. It will take us another year to refine enough for a second bomb."

"So, what? It obviously just takes time."

"We don't have time, Herr Jurgens," said Speer. The Russians have stopped us and are pushing us back in the Ukraine. The Americans are producing bombers and fighters in huge quantities - far more than we could have contemplated. We are now being bombed in our homeland. You have been lucky because it is cloudy, but you'll be lucky to get out of Berlin without at least one air raid. Our intelligence tells us that the Allies are going to mass an attack on the European mainland from England sometime soon. The tide of the war is turning."

Speer's admissions were the first crack I had seen in the "Invincible Germany" front we had been shown since we arrived. To hear the scientists at Peenemunde talk, Germany was unbeatable.

"What about the rockets and the flying bombs? You're already in production we were told at Peenemunde. Aren't they your secret weapon? Don't they turn the tide back in your direction?"

"We have already hobbled Britain. We can rain more destruction on them using the V2 and the Flying bombs." Speer Paused, "but Britain is not the problem. The problem is the United States."

Speer looked at Goebbels. He was choosing his words carefully. "You see, Mr. and Mrs. Jurgens, the rockets and flying bombs cannot reach the United States. Oh, if we had years to develop them, maybe we could, but we do not have years. We have only a short time. We must figure a way to deliver the atomic bomb to a city in the United States."

"That's impossible," said Hugo. "You don't have the ability to reach that far."

Speer looked at Goebbels, and then back at Hugo. "We know that." He paused and pursed his lips, "and that is where the two of you come in."

The room got very silent. Heine and Ellie were nowhere to be seen. The only sound was the crackling fire.

"What?"

"You see, Mr. and Mrs. Jurgens, we brought you here to take the atomic bomb back to the United States - to St. Louis."

Hugo dropped his glass. The beer splattered all over the carpet and on both Goebbels's and Speer's trouser legs. Ellie rushed in with a towel to mop it up.

"You *are* kidding, aren't you?" Hugo asked meekly.

"Not at all," said Goebbels.

Hugo looked first at Speer, then at Goebbels, for a hint of a smile. It had to be a joke. It wasn't. There was no doubt; they were dead serious. We were brought here to deliver an atomic bomb to St. Louis!

"Shall we have dinner?" said Goebbels, putting on a broad smile. He took me by the elbow and guided me toward the big dining room. I saw him glance down my dress once again.

January 24, 1944

I sat by the big window of our suite. It looked out over the front drive of the Limpen House toward the street. Snow had begun to fall sometime in the night. About three inches had accumulated on the window ledge. It clung to the dark Cedars and the Junipers that lined the driveway like sugar icing. A cold wind blew the flakes at an angle. Except for the sandbags in front of the buildings and the destroyed buildings down the block the scene was a picture post card, but I couldn't enjoy it.

I was tired. The events of the night before had drained us. The dinner had been a farce. Speer and Goebbels drank too much and got sloppy laughing at each other's jokes and thoroughly enjoying our discomfort. Neither Hugo nor I had slept at all.

Hugo was in a dressing robe smoking a cigarette.

"They want us to carry a bomb back into the United States" said Hugo. "That's what this is all about."

"Not just any bomb, Hugo, an atomic bomb!"

"What the hell's the difference? It's a bomb, atomic or not, it's the same thing." Hugo was irritable. He had big bags under his eyes. He was chain-smoking.

"Why do they want us to deliver it to St. Louis? Why not New York or Washington? Saint Louis is a little improbable."

It had irritated me that Goebbels and Speer wouldn't answer any more questions last night. They made jokes and talked about racing cars and French women. Goebbels put his hand on my knee three times. I just moved it away. How could they be so nonchalant? I'm sure I hardly ate. I didn't know how to react. These two goons just told us that we were going to be transporting an atomic bomb into the United States, and they had a great meal and a good time. I hope they enjoyed our agony!

The only thing that was said about it at dinner was that we would receive complete instructions at a briefing this morning at ten.

That was three hours away.

20
CHAPTER
NEGOTIATING
WITH THE NAZIS

"January 24, 1944

Bruckner arrived promptly at 9:30. It was snowing harder now; big goose flakes drifted softly to earth on a light north wind. Everything was white. I guessed six inches had fallen. More was expected to come according to Heine.

The streets of Berlin are beautiful when it snows despite the obvious damage. No longer was there the depressing feeling as when I first saw it. The snow clung to the dark evergreens and outlined the building details. It was much prettier now. We took almost the identical route toward the Chancellery as on our first trip except we veered off just before the Brandenburg Gate and headed down a narrow street. I tried to read the name of the street on the corner of a passing building but couldn't make it out in the falling snow. There would be no Allied bombing today, or tonight either, if this cloud cover kept up.

After three blocks Bruckner swung the car into an archway that led to an inner courtyard of a red stone building. A frozen fountain was in the middle surrounded by an octagon-shaped horse-watering trough. The perimeter of the courtyard was adorned with ornate pillars and arches. Gargoyles peered down from the parapets. It looked like a college or university. Bruckner stopped the car and held the rear door open.

"This way," he said and gestured toward a doorway with a large brass knocker in the center. Two soldiers stood on either side. They snapped to attention as we approached. A small man in a gray workman's coat let us in and took our coats before retiring through a side door.

The room was large with a big oriental rug on the floor. Around the walls were books and manuscripts, some in glass cases. I surmised it was a library. A fire blazed in a massive stone fireplace

"Ah, Mrs. Jurgens." It was the familiar voice of Goebbels. "So nice to see you this morning." He was all smiles as usual. "You slept well I trust?" He ignored Hugo as if he was not there.

"I slept fine," I said. I lied.

Speer was walking down a side hallway toward us. He was dressed in a more formal uniform, jackboots, short gray jacket, wide patent belt and high-peaked hat. He had just arrived.

"Mr. and Mrs. Jurgens. Welcome." He extended his hand. Hugo shook it.

Closely behind Speer was Himmler. He wore boots and a long gray coat and the peaked hat of an S.S. officer. He did not extend his hand. I wondered if Hugo would have shaken it if he did? I really did not like that man. Hugo shared my loathing for him. He had mentioned him on more than one occasion after the first meeting, never in a complementary way. I could see Hugo stiffen as Himmler approached down the hallway.

"You remember Heinrik Himmler," said Goebbels.

"Of course, we do." Said Hugo.

Himmler snapped his heels and took my hand.

"Good morning," said Himmler stiffly. He gestured toward the room on our right.

"Shall we?"

We entered a side room where another fireplace blazed brightly.

I saw it the minute we entered the room. Goebbels must have noticed that I could not take my eyes off of it.

"Quite unique isn't it?"

"But..., but it's our steamer trunk!"

"We took the liberty of borrowing it from your room after Ellie had unpacked it for you when you arrived."

Hugo had put it into the large anteroom off the sitting room after its contents had been hung in the huge wardrobe in our bedroom. We hadn't even noticed that it was gone.

"Take a closer look."

Hugo walked to the trunk and ran his fingers along the top. He stooped and looked closely at the lock and hinges.

"This isn't our trunk. It just looks like it.

"You flatter us, Mr. Jurgens. Our craftsmen are excellent at reproductions. You are quite correct that it is not your steamer trunk. But we did borrow yours from your room, and we did reproduce it. I agree, the results are quite impressive.

"You could have fooled me," said Hugo. "Unless I got right up on it I couldn't tell."

"That's the whole idea - to look like your trunk, that is," said Speer. "You see, that is the atomic bomb!"

"Hugo drew his hand back. I heard him say "no shit?" under his breath. I was speechless.

"Sit down Mr. and Mrs. Jurgens," said Himmler. He was all business. "We have a lot of work to do today. We might as well get started."

We were positioned in puffed chairs in a rough semi-circle. Speer and Goebbels rolled the trunk into the center on the little dolly on which it had been resting. Himmler walked to a small table near the window and poured himself a cup of coffee. He didn't offer any to the rest.

"Let's begin with the question Why?" said Himmler. "I know you must be asking yourself why we have chosen you to do this."

He took a sip of the coffee. Hugo sat motionless smoking a cigarette. He didn't say a word.

Himmler began: "As you have seen we have begun the work on a rocket that can deliver a warhead very accurately up to two hundred miles away. To lift twelve tons into the sky and drop it on a target that far away is quite a feat - and we will begin doing that in about a month. We will begin using the V4 on Britain. The world will then know, if their intelligence has not already told them, that we have the capability to deliver explosive payloads by V4 rockets over long distances. We'll begin with Britain, and shortly follow with the Soviet Union. It will be a brilliant advance in the art of warfare." Himmler paused, and lit a cigarette, "but it will not win the war."

"We need to reach the United States. You see, we intend to explode the atomic bomb in an American city. But America is too far away for our rocket technology. Someday..." Himmler paused, "but not soon enough." We have considered alternates - a sea launch from off the Atlantic coast. We'd never get a ship through. The Americans dominate the North Atlantic with their Navy. They control the airspace over the North Atlantic. Besides the logistics and guidance problems of launching a rocket from a rolling ship..," Himmler shook his head.

"We even considered smuggling a rocket into Mexico through Argentina or some other South American country. We might be able to do it, but the risk is too high. In addition, we have some concerns about the accuracy of a missile fired from some point in Mexico after its transport completely across the ocean and as much as a thousand miles over land. Even if we were able to transport it undetected the odds are too great of a misfire or a guidance failure. And even if we were successful, we might reach San Antonio, or Corpus Christi, Texas, or Tucson, in Arizona, not-so-impressive targets."

"But why Saint Louis?" Hugo had asked the obvious question. I, too, wanted to know.

"I'll let Herr Goebbels answer that question." Himmler sat down and took a deep drag on his cigarette.

"To understand what we want to accomplish you must understand the power of propaganda," began Goebbels. "It's the most powerful weapon of war man has yet devised. It's more powerful than all of the bombs we can make - even this one." Goebbels rose from his chair and walked to a roll-down map of the United States. He continued: "The British and the United States have to know of our successes with rocketry, or at least they soon will. It's problematic how much they know about our knowledge of the atom bomb. At least they know we are experimenting with fission and nuclear reactions. We are far ahead of them, and they suspect so. America's Project Manhattan is just in its infancy. We believe it may be a year or two before the Americans can even think of testing a bomb."

"So, we strike now, while we have the clear technological advantage, but in a way that is designed to eliminate America from the war."

"I don't understand?"

"You must remember we have only one bomb. It will take us a year to make another. We must achieve success by maximizing its effect and its potential utilizing a brilliant propaganda coup."

Goebbels moved to a map of England stretched on a roll up screen. "First we rain a group of rockets and flying bombs on Britain to demonstrate our ability to deliver warheads over long distances at will. The Allies will be impressed with our advancements.

Then we boast that we can do it anywhere in the world, even to the United States. The Americans will not believe us, but they will be wary. Through a known double agent, we will leak the time and place – St. Louis, Missouri, ten AM, April 30. The leak will be subtle; the Americans will wonder if their information is accurate. But they will verify their source and find it reliable. What's more the leak will tell them that the bomb will be delivered by a top-secret rocket - even more advanced than those we are using on Britain. They'll scoff at the idea, but they will go berserk wondering what we are up to. They will probably put their home defenses on full alert. Meanwhile, thanks to your quite excellent facilities, the bomb, is resting quietly in a most unlikely place – the attic of your home in South St. Louis. No one will suspect.

At the appointed time you will detonate the bomb. The destruction will be spectacular, but most importantly we will claim to have delivered it, as promised, with one of our guided missiles from an undisclosed base in Europe. We'll be sure to point out there is no defense against the delivery of the bomb by our missiles!

Do you know what a panic that is going to cause in America? Do you know what the potential is for the expectation of more of these bombs to be delivered to the Heartland of the United States – or possibly New York or Washington? It is one thing for the United States to be sending its boys halfway around the world to fight a war in Europe, but when we start blowing up their homes and their cities with a single bomb the United States will quickly find reasons why it ought to get out of the war. America has no real stomach for this war. They are in it as the result of old debts to England. The thought of destruction of their homeland is enough to bring the Americans home in a rush."

"But why St. Louis? Why not a more strategic target like New York or Washington, or even Chicago or San Francisco?" said Hugo.

Goebbels went back to the map of the United States. He pointed his finger at St. Louis. "Look at the map. Is there any more central city? Is there any more *geographically protected* city in America than St. Louis? Why, it is a thousand miles in any direction to the sea. We must show America that we can reach the most remote area on their continent; that nothing is safe. The unequivocal message is: if we can reach St. Louis we can reach anywhere!"

Hugo got up and walked to the table at the window and poured himself a cup of coffee. I guess he just got tired of waiting for them to offer him a cup. He noisily rattled the spoon in the china cup as he stirred in some sugar. "What makes you think we can do it? You have but one bomb, and you entrust it to two unknowns from South Saint Louis? What's wrong with your 'highly trained agents' we have heard so much about? Why us?"

Speer spoke: "It's simple, Mr. Jurgens. Who suspects you? No one. Your J. Edgar Hoover and his band of spy-hunters have done a good job of tracking our agents. It's too risky to use any of them. Who would think that *you* would bring such a device into the country and place it in your home? No one." Speer paused. "No, Mr. Jurgens, you are so improbable that we believe you will succeed."

"You said that *we* were to detonate the bomb? said Hugo."

I had heard the same thing and I didn't like it.

"I really don't like the sound of that plan." Hugo folded his arms. "It sounds like you plan to detonate us too. That doesn't have much appeal."

I would have asked the same question. What was Speer talking about? Do they expect this to be a suicide mission?

"It's a fair question, and one we were sure you would ask," said Speer. "I think the answer to that question lies in a better understanding of the device," Speer continued and walked over to the bomb. "You need a tour of the greatest scientific achievement of the Twentieth Century."

Speer turned to the door and waived to one of the guards that had stationed themselves just outside. In a few seconds a man in a gray smock came in. He was introduced as Doctor Raul Larsen. His accent sounded Swedish.

"Doctor Larsen was one of the scientists responsible for the packaging of the bomb into this unique case – a reproduction of your trunk. He can explain its workings and answer some of the questions that we are sure you want to ask." Speer turned to Larsen. "Doctor..."

Larsen began with a tour of the trunk exterior. "It is a lightweight titanium –lined case; a relatively new metal that is lighter and stronger than steel. We used it because we must be absolutely sure of the integrity of the shell. The seams have been double folded and riveted together. The rivets of the trunk are exact duplicates of those used by the manufacturer of your trunk, but if you look closer you will see they are stronger and thicker. The handles and hardware are exact duplicates of those on the original trunk, but, again, if you'll look closely you will see that these are much stronger, reinforced at the points where they are attached to the body of the trunk, and designed to carry much more weight. We cannot trust the conventional hardware. This trunk is much heavier."

Larsen opened the latch and lifted the lid. We strained to look inside. It appeared to be full to the brim with a dull substance, gray and metallic looking. Directly in the center was a gleaming brass timing device countersunk into the gray substance and held down with a metal plate with four acorn-shaped nuts that screwed into embedded bolts in each corner. The timing device looked like an alarm clock without the case. Next to the timing device, and countersunk, so that the top was flush with the metallic surface of the timer, was a battery. To the right of the battery was a bright red switch with a hinged protective cover. You had to flip up the protective cover to access the switch. He began a verbal tour:

"The gray metallic substance you see is conventional explosive - TNT based in a plastic form, but of a very high grade. It has been shaped and honed to fit exactly in the trunk as you can see. The exact weight of the explosive is eighty-six pounds."

Hugo moved closer by sliding his chair up further into the circle. He was interested in the mechanics of the device. This horrible thing was right up Hugo's alley, and the technology of it fascinated him. I could tell that the timer had caught his eye.

"Where's the uranium?" he asked.

"The conventional explosive has been molded around twenty-six pounds of high-grade Uranium-235. It's a much higher quality than the Americans have yet been able to produce. You can't see it, but it is deep in the core of the explosive shell. If you lift out the timing device the bottom of the hole in which it is countersunk is just one fourth of an inch above the Uranium-235."

"So, the explosive detonates the uranium?" said Hugo.

"Not exactly," said Larsen. "We actually squeeze the uranium by exploding the conventional explosive around it. What we are really doing is forcing the atoms together by imploding the conventional explosive. The blast crushes the fissionable material. It is a theory that the Americans have not figured out yet. They are still theorizing that forcing the elements together with a shotgun-like device is the way to initiate the reaction. Their method will work, but it is crude and highly inefficient. implosion is the key to the detonation. It gives a much higher efficiency to the compaction. You must force the molecules together just like you would squeeze a grape and force out the seed. It was the implosion issue that caused us much difficulty. You see, the force on the uranium core must be equal on all sides if we are to achieve the perfect reaction. We achieve this by creating 'lenses' out of the conventional explosive material so that when it explodes the concave shock waves force the uranium molecules together on all sides with the same force. The combination of this 'lensing' and the one hundred percent pure uranium allows us to achieve a complete detonation of all of the fissionable material. The Americans would have to use three hundred pounds of their refined material to achieve what we can do with twenty-six pounds of our pure Uranium-235 refined with our superior process, and we have assured a perfect implosion."

"I want to hear more about the detonation," I said. The idea of detonating this thing scared me.

"It's very simple, Mrs. Jurgens." Larsen laid his hand gently on the timer. "This is a mechanical timer. It works pretty much like your alarm clock. It is, of course a much higher-grade mechanism, but the principle is the same. Once you turn this dial on top, it starts the clock in motion." Larsen made a rotating motion with his hand as if he were winding the timer. "See these calibrations. There are twenty-four - one for each hour. Once you turn the dial past twenty-four you have twenty-four hours to get away. At the end of the twenty-four hours the clock winds down and trips a little lever which allows two contact points to connect and the circuit with the battery is completed. The conventional explosive is detonated by the spark and the chain reaction begins. It all takes less than a second."

"What's that red switch?" said Hugo pointing at the red toggle that was under the hinged red cover.

"It's the master switch. It allows the spark to go through the timer and on to the TNT for the detonation. After you turn the dial past twenty-four you must arm the device by switching on the red switch. The timer then winds down just like an egg timer until it hits zero. Then the connection is then made with the battery.

"What's really going to happen when this thing goes off?" said Hugo. "You've never tested it have you?"

"No," said Speer, "it has never been tested. We would love to have the opportunity to take it so some remote spot and try it out, but we have but one bomb. We cannot quickly manufacture more so we'll have to give you our best speculation. Doctor Larsen, will you give Herr Jurgens our projections."

Larsen unfolded a piece of paper with some notes. "The explosion will be the equivalent of twenty to thirty thousand tons of TNT. That's roughly the equivalent of all of the bombs that we have dropped on England to date, perhaps a little more. From ground zero, which will be your home, there will be total destruction of all structures in all directions. 360 degrees."

"What do you mean 'total'?" said Hugo.

"Leveled, disintegrated, gone." Larsen replied. "We cannot be exact about the size of this area, perhaps four or five miles outward. We refer to the total destruction area as 'Sector A'. From there, in an area we call 'Sector B', every window of every building all the way to the Mississippi river on the east and to the rail yards on the north side of the city, will be blown out by the shock wave. The destruction to the west will extend to the City Limits. Damage in some of this sector will be heavy, but not total. Some buildings will still be standing. You might equate it to a major hurricane or a major earthquake in force and destruction. There will be numerous fires in this sector. Beyond Sector B the damage will be minimal - an occasional blown out window, power lines down, minimal force damage." Larsen paused, as if to invite questions. He was clearly enjoying his position as forecaster of the Apocalypse.

"How many people is this thing going to kill?"

"Our best estimates are from one hundred fifty thousand to two hundred thousand people will be killed instantly or die within forty-eight hours from injuries, burns or radiation poisoning.

Another one hundred thousand could die from radiation poisoning within a few weeks. We are not confident of our estimates here because we have not been able to measure the radiation from the detonation. In theory, and in the laboratory, the radiation is quite high."

"Good God! You want us to carry back and explode a bomb that is going to kill a quarter of a million people. It's inhumane." Hugo was out of his chair, jabbing his finger in the air.

"Sit down Mr. Jurgens." It was Goebbels. "Look at yourself. You are demonstrating the correctness of our theories. The result is too horrible for you or the rest of America to contemplate. The horror is its virtue. Your sentiments are exactly why our bomb will end the war. The Americans will not be able to tolerate the thought that Germany can bring this kind of destruction through our technology."

"If you think this will cause America to surrender you are..."

"Who said anything about surrendering?" Speer interrupted. All we want them to do is withdraw from Europe. We have no reason to be at war with America. It is another country in another hemisphere. We just want them to abandon England. We just want the Americans to go home and abandon England and the rest of Europe. America has no business here. We are the rightful rulers of Europe. We are the pure race. In the long run many lives will be saved. Far fewer people will die than if we continue this war. You might even say that this bomb will save lives."

There was a long silence. No one spoke. I kept visualizing St. Louis in ruins after the explosion.

"What about us?" I said. "What happens to us?"

"You have several options," Mrs. Jurgens. "Remember you are going to have five hundred thousand dollars at your disposal, so you have several choices you do not have today."

"Like what?"

"You have twenty-four hours to get away from your house once you have activated the timer. If you wish you can just be away for the weekend. You'll have plenty of time to simply drive yourselves and your son, Donald, to a safe location, say, on a fishing trip, or on a weekend excursion. Don't you like to go to a place called Okawville and take the baths?"

God, what didn't they know about us?

"In such case you will just be considered lucky. Your home, of course, will be destroyed, but you will be financially able to recover with little effort."

"Another option," continued Goebbels, "is that you simply do not return, but rather disappear. You have a substantial bank account with which to reestablish yourselves somewhere else, Europe, Mexico or South America. You could live like royalty in any of those locations with that kind of money."

"But won't they figure out the bomb was in our house?"

"Not a chance. The assumption will be that there is where it fell. You are going to place it in your attic before detonation. Everything around it will be disintegrated. Do not detonate it from your basement. It must be placed as high in your house as possible so that the explosive pressure is unimpeded or diverted by earth or foundation structures. If so placed, it will be impossible to determine it was not dropped from the sky - particularly with our previous leaks that it will be delivered by a missile. No one will be able to tell that the explosion originated inside your house. Of course, the optimum would be that we could explode it several thousand feet in the air from an airplane, but we cannot. The destruction would be much greater. Your home and the area for several blocks around will be vaporized. No one could be certain where the center of the detonation originated."

The room was silent for a few seconds as everyone was contemplating the magnitude of the explosion.

"Our money?" said Hugo. "How do we get our money?"

"When you leave here," said Himmler, "you will be presented with a bank draft for one hundred thousand dollars drawn on the Banque de Credit Falmer, in Zurich. You may go out through Switzerland if you wish and draw out the money. You can leave it in the Banque de Credit Falmer or move it to another bank. It is strictly up to you."

"Yes, but that's only a part of..."

"Let me finish, Herr Jurgens." Himmler put up his hand in a mock 'stop' gesture. "When the apparatus is safely delivered to your home in St. Louis and placed in your attic you will send a telegram to an address we will provide you in New Jersey. It will say simply 'the egg is in the nest'. Within twenty- four hours we will deposit an additional one hundred thousand dollars into your account in Switzerland, and the bank will wire confirmation of receipt to you. Again, you can do anything with it you wish."

"And the remaining three hundred thousand?"

"The event of which we speak will, of course be of world-wide notice. We will know when the mission is completed. Upon receiving word of the detonation, we will deposit the balance into your account and provide confirmation."

There was again an awkward silence. I could tell that Hugo was thinking. His brow was furled up, and he stared at the floor. He was silent for several seconds.

"No deal," said Hugo, standing up. He even startled me.

"What do you mean, 'no deal'?" Himmler said. Himmler was not used to being countermanded.

"I said 'no deal'. You want us to take all of the risk, carry the bomb through Europe, across the Atlantic and deliver it to St. Louis, detonate it, run, hide and never be heard from again, and you want to pay us as we go? You aren't paying enough, and you aren't paying it right!" Hugo hit is fist on the top of the trunk.

"Herr Jurgens, it is we who dictate the terms, here, not you."

"I don't think so, 'Herr Himmler'. You need us badly. Your little scheme is all in place except for a courier. Your rockets really don't have the range. We're the only thing you have. Your American agents are worthless. And you're right about the odds of us succeeding because we're so unlikely. We are your only entry into St. Louis, Missouri, USA with the bomb. If Mr. Goebbels' theory is right, you have to reach America's heartland to make this thing work. You have to get right in the middle to demonstrate that you can reach anywhere. And..." Hugo paused. "We're all you have. It will take months, maybe a year to recruit another reliable courier to take this thing to St. Louis, particularly an unknown and unsuspected courier like us. You can't get it in with your agents because the U.S. knows who they are. Even less likely are your odds to get it to St. Louis. You have to get it in through unknown channels. Your regular spies can't do it. The Americans are closing in on you, aren't they? The risk of failure by any other delivery method is too great."

Hugo was leaning into Himmler's face, and Himmler clearly didn't like it.

"The price, Herr Himmler, is one million dollars - five hundred thousand now and five hundred thousand on detonation. Take it or leave it."

"My, my," said Goebbels. "You certainly have this thing figured out, don't you?"

"You've taught me something, Herr Goebbels." Hugo was up, pacing. "You've taught me that spying is not an ideology or a blind adherence to dogma. Spying and international treachery is a profession. The smart, careful and attentive do a good job, survive and get paid well. The slow and careless become irrelevant by getting caught and either wind up in a prison or get shot for their deeds. The good spy who doesn't get top dollar is a fool. The penalty for failure is the same in all cases, and the rewards for success should be to those who produce."

Hugo walked over to Speer. "The truth is you have only one delivery system - it's us. Your V4s and flying bombs just can't cut it. You have to rely on us to pack your prize into the United States and detonate it in St. Louis. It's an attainable task. You know, and so do we, that we can do it. The price is simply one million dollars - probably less than it takes to build one of your little rockets."

Himmler was silent.

"You can threaten us, torture us or even shoot us. It still doesn't get your bomb to St. Louis. You've got only one choice - us and one million dollars, U.S."

I was watching Goebbels and Speer. They were looking at Himmler. The next move would clearly be up to him. No one spoke.

"Will you excuse us?" said Himmler. He stepped toward the hall door.

"Of course, but don't plan to go out there and come back with a figure less than a million. You'll have to shoot us first, and none of us wants that." Hugo was calm as a monk. Himmler was clearly irritated. Goebbels led them from the room.

Hugo Jurgens never ceases to amaze me. As a barber he is good; but as a negotiator he is brilliant! There wasn't a doubt in my mind, or his, that they were going to pay it. He winked at me as they went out the door and into the hallway. He put his finger to his lips to make sure I didn't say anything. We sat for ten minutes saying nothing.

Hugo poured another cup of coffee.

21
CHAPTER
ZURICH

"January 27, 1944

We sat in the ornate high-ceilinged office of Klaus Frederich, Director General of Banque de Credit Falmer in Zurich. We were two blocks off the Lake. We had been driven to Switzerland by Bruckner rather than to take the train from Berlin. It had been a long ride. Hugo had demanded we be driven to Zurich. The trunk and our packed luggage had been loaded into the trunk of the Mercedes and we had driven all night after our meeting with Speer, Himmler and Goebbels broke up. Bruckner drove all night from Berlin. He seemed indefatigable.

As we wound through the narrow streets of Zurich and on to the Paradeplatz we passed several ornate doors each with a brass plaque on the wall next to it announcing its name.

"Look at these," said Hugo. "The street is full of them. They are all banks!"

"They don't look like any bank that I've ever seen," I said. "Look at that beautiful carved door on that one, right there." I was pointing. "Heller bank."

The Bank de Credit Falmer was on a little side street just off the Paradeplatz. The Mercedes turned right and rolled to a stop just a few yards further in front of one of the ornate doors. The brass plaque announced: *"Banque de Credit Falmer."*

We went in.

I'd never seen a bank with no teller windows and no lobby where people could transact business like checks, payments, deposits and withdrawals sitting at a desk or ornate table.

Klaus Frederich greeted us at the door. "Mr. and Mr. Jurgens, welcome to Zurich. We had received notice that you would be coming." His English was perfect with a creamy German accent, typical of educated Swiss. He escorted us into his office and gestured toward a small Louis XIV table where a silver service held coffee, fine china, and an assortment of little cinnamon rolls wrapped in white napkins. "Please, have some coffee. You must be tired after your long trip from Berlin."

"Thank you, sir," said Hugo, stiffly. "We need to be about our business."

"Of course," said Frederich, "Please be seated.

"Frieda," Hugo held out his hand to me, and I pulled the draft for five hundred thousand dollars from my purse. I had actually tucked it into my bra after we left Himmler and Goebbels and retrieved it with much difficulty in the car as we entered Zurich."

The draft was on soft pink paper, with an embossed eagle on the upper left- hand corner. It simply said:

> *"Berlin,*
>
> *January 21, 1944*
> *Account 248431-234*
>
> *To: Banque de Credit Falmer, You are directed, on sight, to pay to Hugo and/or Frieda Jurgens, from the above account, the sum of Five hundred thousand and 00/100 Dollars (US)."*

To Hugo and me the most unusual aspect of the draft was the signature. In scrawled, almost unreadable script, written with a pen, on the dotted signature line was the name *"Adolph Hitler."*

Hugo handed the draft to Frederich. Frederich handled it nonchalantly, read it twice, and turned it over and put his initials on it. Then he dropped it into a drawer of the big leather top desk at which he sat.

"Now," he said putting his elbows on the desk and leaning forward. "How do you want these funds?"

Hugo and I had discussed the money several times on the drive from Berlin. We had decided that if the Swiss banking system was as inviolate as we had heard that the best thing to do would be to leave the funds in a numbered account in the same bank. Bringing it back to the United States was not an option. When we advised Frederich he seemed pleased.

"A wise decision," he said. "I'll see to it right away." He reached beneath his desk and apparently pushed a buzzer. A thin gaunt man with pasty white skin in a dark blue suit appeared at the door.

"Trochner, will you see to it that an account is opened in a numbered mode. We will not need any further information. Let me know when you have completed the paperwork." Frederich retrieved the draft from the drawer and handed it to Trochner who simply bowed slightly and retreated saying nothing.

"How about a little coffee while we wait, eh?" said Frederich. "I understand that you are heading on a long journey from here. Take some refreshment. It will just be a minute."

Frederich rose from behind the big double desk and excused himself. Hugo and I were left alone in his office while half a million dollars was being transferred into a numbered account to which we, alone, would have the number.

In about twenty minutes Frederich returned holding a small slip of paper on which had been typed a number: *542069 - 001*

"You'll need this whenever you make any deposit or withdrawal. Nothing else will be required; however, you must be aware that if you do not produce the number, we cannot transact any business. No statements will be issued, and the funds will gain interest at the rate of three percent. Likewise, if anyone else has control of the number they, too will have access to the funds. I suggest you memorize it and destroy this number."

"Can we make a transfer by the telephone or telegraph?"

"Of course; but you will need the number. We can only execute your orders only if you give us the number."

Something Frederich said bothered me. How did he know we were going on a long journey? How much about us did he know?

Frederich thanked us and graciously showed us to the door of the bank where Bruckner was waiting to take us to the Swiss-French frontier to catch the train for Madrid. To say that we were excited would be understatement. We had just had half a million dollars deposited to our account! Hugo grinned a little grin as we sped through the Swiss countryside in the shadow of the Alps. Nestled in the trunk of the Mercedes Benz Grand Saloon was an atomic bomb!

It had begun to rain.

We backtracked through Spain and into Portugal on trains. Our destination was, again, Lisbon, where we were to be met by the freighter <u>Polar Star</u>. We wondered if it had been here all of the time we were in Berlin, or had it left and come back to get us? Porters and stewards complained of the weight of our trunk. We were told, by Speer, that it weighed one hundred twenty-seven pounds. An extra tip always seemed to lighten the load and reduce the grumbling to a minimum.

February 2, 1944

Both Hugo and I had wondered how difficult it would be to get the trunk through Customs at New York. As the entry into the United States approached we became more edgy. It was here that we were sure the game would be won or lost. By the time the Statute of Liberty came into view I was as jumpy as a cat.

As it turned out, it went without a hitch. After the ship docked Captain Altmann came to our cabin and instructed us to leave the ship at the pier taking with us only our hand luggage and to leave our bags and the trunk. He was very precise. Our luggage, including the trunk, would be delivered to us on the other side of Customs and Immigration. We were to show our United States passports at Immigration and state that we had been in Portugal on business – selling industrial needles to the textile industry. He provided us with a sample case of fabrics and industrial needles as a backup in case we were questioned.

There was, in fact, little questioning. We were only asked what we were doing in Portugal to which Hugo replied "Business." The immigrations officer asked nothing more. He stamped our passports and walked us through without so much as a second look. I had been sweating bullets. As we went out through the high doors of the big pier building and onto the street a man led us to a waiting taxicab. He opened the trunk of the cab to put in our sample case and our hand luggage. There was the trunk, safe and sound somehow passed through customs. We were off to New York City, Grand Central Station and St. Louis.

March 10, 1944

We have been at home over a month. We got the bomb home to St. Louis without incident. Hugo and I had struggled to get it up the ladder and through the narrow passageway in the bedroom closet into the attic. Hugo rigged a block and tackle from one of the roof rafters right over the opening for the ladder that allowed us to lift the trunk to the attic. Still, it was still difficult to get it up there, but we made it. By the time we got back home we realized how heavy and difficult to move the trunk really was.

What's it like living in a house with an atom bomb in the attic? It's a strange question, yet one that would be legitimate to ask. The perverted answer is you get used to it. We know there resided above us the power to destroy ourselves, our house and everything around us. The omnipresence is always with you, and I noticed that it even follows me to work. I assume it was the same with Hugo. We don't speak about our feelings on the matter often. A sort of grim silence has fallen over us. Hugo has lost nine pounds. I can't sleep either, and I often find myself waking in the night only to find Hugo sitting in the big overstuffed chair in the living room smoking a Camel and staring at the floor.

Both of us are having difficulty resolving the destruction that will happen upon detonation of the bomb. Many of our friends will be killed. Much of the area that we call home will be destroyed. Yet, we are strangely deadened, almost numbed, to the emotion of loss. It's as if a screen has been pulled over our conscience, and we go about our lives without really noticing either the effect or the devastation we are about to inflict on our city. We have resolved it by not speaking about it and compounding upon ourselves a numbness of spirit and a deadening of our emotions to cover it up

Despite the repression of our feelings we have begun to make preparations for the instructions that we know will inevitably come to arm the bomb and then get away. Hugo has begun to talk more about fishing. Our plan is to arm the bomb and get away for a fishing trip to the Black River. We feel that a cover story is necessary. It will just be a three-day trip - at least that's what we're telling everyone. We can arm the bomb and leave. The twenty-four-hour delay on the timer will give us enough time to simply drive to the Black River, register in a cabin and sit tight until the bomb is detonated. Hugo devised a plan to withdraw all of our money from the bank safe deposit boxes before we leave. There is no need to have our savings destroyed by the blast even though it is a pittance compared to what we have deposited in a Swiss bank.

In all candidness, I think we silently acknowledge we are driven by the riches that have been promised us. Speer was right; the money has blurred all conscience and all visions of the consequences. We have dedicated ourselves to the mission, and we are determined that nothing will stop us."

Connie is upstairs purring away. I can't sleep. I haven't been sleeping well since we got into that part of the diary where my parents went to Berlin. It's after midnight, and I have just come downstairs into the kitchen. I know that I cannot go back to sleep. I sat straight up in bed just a few minutes ago. The thought of my parents as killers of thousands of people, murderers of innocent men, women and children, destroyers of the city sickened me. Somehow, I thought that the events chronicled in my mother's diary would resolve themselves in a benign scenario in which the war ended and everyone lived happily ever after. Diaries are supposed to have happy endings, aren't they? In the end all problems are resolved, aren't they? It wasn't going to happen. My parents were traitors of the highest degree, motivated and lured by the promise of riches, and hell-bent on accomplishing a result that invoked the Apocalypse. They were killers of the worst sort - without conscience or remorse. They were going to kill for money.

Connie comes downstairs into the kitchen in her robe. She says nothing to me. I look at her blankly. She has long sensed my shock and despair and understands without saying so. She sits cross-legged on the sofa under the glow of the light on the reading table and works her way through the book behind me. We might as well keep going. I'm not going to sleep until it's over. We have developed the routine of me reading a book and then passing it to her; after which we would discuss the notebook's content. I could hardly wait for her comments on this one. Until now she had said nothing about my parent's odyssey to Berlin.

She watched me for a while without talking and then said: "I don't believe it, but the truth is your parents are 'guns for hire'. It's despicable," she said.

"You know Connie," I said. "You think you know someone, and then everything you believed is shattered, and they become someone else. It's like reading about a character in a play or a novel. You think you know them and then the author turns them into a monster." I must have looked pale. I felt it in my face.

"C'mon on Donald. It's not you. Your parents have just turned out to be something other than you thought they were. It doesn't reflect on you. You aren't to blame."

"I don't care. It is shocking. I'm ashamed. My parents turn out to be Nazi spies. It is disgusting. I don't even want to be known as their child."

Connie was sympathetic as she always was. She understood, but something was troubling her.

"Donald," she said. "Obviously the bomb was never detonated. The fact that St. Louis is still intact proves that. So, your parents never detonated the bomb."

"Yeah, so what?"

"So, what happened to it?"

"What are you talking about?" I stared at Connie, not completely grasping the import of her statement.

"Donald, what's wrong with this picture? Your parents have half a million dollars in an account in Zurich. There has never been an atomic bomb exploded anywhere in the United States except at the Nevada Proving Ground Sites when they were testing them years ago."

I looked at her, blankly. "So?"

"So, there is a lot more to this puzzle we don't know. What happened to the bomb? What happened to the money? What the Hell happened at all?"

I didn't have any answers. I had sat down on the sofa. I reached forward into the trunk and picked out the second to last book

22
CHAPTER
INTERNATIONAL BANKING

"April 5, 1944

It is Sunday morning. Hugo is sitting at the kitchen table reading the *St. Louis Star Times* Newspaper in his bathrobe. His pajamas are sticking out the bottom under his robe. Bright sunlight spills in through the window and splashes on the table strewn with breakfast dishes. He is unshaven.

"Frieda. Listen to this." Hugo was peering at a story on the third page of the first section of the paper. He folded the paper backward so as to isolate the page with the article, and began to read:

'NAZIS CLAIM TO HAVE SECRET WEAPON.

'Reuters. London. British Intelligence announced that it had intercepted messages between German High Command Staff that indicated the Germans were working on a secret weapon that', they claimed, 'could swing the tide of the war.' Details were sketchy, but the intercepted report alluded to a bomb and delivery system that could not be defended against by any known plane or aircraft defense system.

The report was greeted here with significant skepticism. The Germans have already been utilizing the V1 and V2 "flying bomb" against Britain. Even the buzz bombs seem to have limited range and accuracy. If the Germans had such a system, it was speculated that it would have shown up in the flying bomb technology that they were currently employing.

It was noted that the Nazis had made similar claims before and nothing significant had materialized.'

"Hugo, it's the beginning! I know it is. Goebbels has begun the groundwork for the propaganda campaign!"

"It has to be, Frieda. That was no more an intercepted transmission that I am. It had to be a plant. Goebbels wanted it to be intercepted. It's the beginning, and it won't be long now.

It would be the first of several such 'intercepted' releases hinting at a secret weapon and a delivery system. Indeed, the messages were intercepted by British Intelligence, but the boys in Berlin knew exactly what they were doing.

April 16, 1944

This morning an ominous event occurred, and it left no doubt in our mind what was coming. Germany publicly announced the successful flight of an unnamed rocket from an unknown location in Germany to a target a thousand miles north in Norway. The report was carried by all of the news services and made the front page of both Saint Louis papers. Even Hugo and I were startled. When we were at Peenemunde no one talked about ranges of over a few hundred miles at the most. A thousand miles was incredible, unless...

"Unless it is just a lie," said Hugo. "Maybe they just didn't make that flight. Maybe the truth is that the best they can do is two hundred miles. Maybe the story is just part of the overall propaganda scheme."

I wondered? Could they have improved the rockets that much since we were there? I doubted it too, but it gave credibility to the "secret weapon" theory.

Two days later another story appeared. This time the "intercepted dispatch" talked of a strike on the United States "sometime in late April."

April 19, 1944

Today, three days after the announcement of the thousand-mile flight the first rockets rained down on London. We heard it on the CBS Evening News. They carried warheads of two thousand pounds. While they were not very accurate and missed the center of the city by several miles. Their launching sites were not known. The event struck absolute horror in the minds of the Brits. Hitler, indeed, did have a weapon that could not be defended against. It came out of the sky and rained death so fast that no plane could catch it, let alone bring it down. Anti-aircraft could not shoot it down. It was equally horrifying because no one knew the launching site, and no one knew how far it had come. Still, a thousand miles...? Hugo and I both wondered.

The significance of the event did not escape General Hollenbeck. He knew that the Germans were working at break-neck speed to develop an atomic bomb. He knew that the ability to build a bomb was one thing, but the ability to deliver it was quite another. If the V4 had been perfected as the Germans claimed they had one part of the equation completed. It was clear that Hollenbeck was worried. He spent most of the time on the telephone with Washington. The Weldon Spring plant was all but finished and scheduled to begin to produce small amounts of refined uranium. I had not seen all of the reports, but I surmised that the initial results were disappointing. I know that the project at Oak Ridge, Tennessee had everyone up in arms. It was, to judge by the reactions of General Hollenbeck, a failure. Weldon Spring was apparently critical.

April 21, 1944.

Hugo has grown more irritable. He hardly sleeps. His eyes are sunk into his head like two dark coals and he is drinking more than usual. Living beneath the device is taking its toll. We haven't had sex since we got home from Germany, and frankly, I am not in the mood either. Hugo smokes a lot and sits up late at night looking at the floor. He had gone up to the attic three times and repositioned the trunk each time. Once I climbed up the narrow stairs from the bedroom closet and found him just sitting on the floor staring at the trunk, his arms folded over his chest. I wondered what he was thinking. He never told me. We don't talk much.

I too, have had my personality altered by the device. I wonder what will become of our friends. Most of them will be killed by the blast. Those who aren't killed will be sickened or injured. There is a great temptation to warn those that we dearly love. That, of course, is impossible. No one can know, or everything is for naught. It's a secret that Hugo and I alone must share, but not reveal.

Hugo and I decided that on the day before our departure we'll take off work in the early afternoon and make the rounds of the banks in which we have placed the money we have been paid over the years for passing the information to the Nazis. We have spread the money between six banks, and we believe that, even though at least three of them are outside the sectors that Speer described as having severe destruction, it's a good idea to get the money out. We'll just visit the banks and take the currency out of the safe deposit boxes. It's just that simple. No one knows it's there so the removal from the boxes, all at different banks, won't raise any inquiries. Hugo suggested that we should not cancel the safe deposit boxes, but rather leave them in place. The rent is just under two dollars per year for each, and to cancel the safe deposit box contracts would be a tip off to anyone who might look, particularly if they found we closed all of them on the same day. So, we have just decided to remove the money and leave the boxes intact.

We played our story over and over. We are going to announce a fishing trip to the Black River the last of April. It is important that others know we will be gone on the fatal week-end. Hugo has already been talking it up in the shop even though we have not announced the exact date yet. A couple of our friends even asked if they could be included. Hugo sort of finessed it by making up a story about "having to get away what with the Tuberculosis and all." The truth is that he really looks terrible. He has lost some weight and looks drawn. The story is entirely plausible. Surely, a fishing trip would do us good. Spring is in the air. The weather is breaking; the days are warming up; we need the weekend away. Naturally, Donald is coming, too. Lies. Lies.

We have devised a pretty simple story to disguise our plan. We are going to tell everyone that we are going to go to the Black River fishing. In fact, we intend to just keep going. If the bomb is everything that Speer and Goebbels have said it was the whole area around us will be annihilated. No one will remember what we had told them. Half of Saint Louis was going to be blown away. No one will recollect that we had said that we were going to go fishing. In fact, most, if not all, of everyone we tell it to will be gone - dead. Our house will be vaporized; our neighborhood, all of South Saint Louis, and everyone in it blown to bits. If we do not return they will presume us vaporized – blown away if we did not reappear. We have no intention of coming back. There will be nothing to come back to. We have half million bucks in the bank in Zurich and another half million on demand after the detonation. We can lose ourselves, create another identity and live happily ever after.

We have decided our destination is going to be California. We've made plans to change our names, our identities, and our future. The bomb has already made us rich, and with the second five hundred thousand we'll have over a million dollars. We can do anything that we like. On Friday morning we'll just set the timer, climb into our car, and head out U.S. Highway 66. Instead of swinging south to the Black River, we'll just keep on going. We will reach Joplin, Missouri by nightfall, stay overnight, and be well into Oklahoma by the time of the blast on Saturday morning. We can read about the bomb in the paper, but we will be long gone, dissolved into the mist, or presumed vaporized at ground zero.

To avoid any suspicion, we aren't going to pack anything except a few things that would not be missed - just in case the bomb didn't explode or anyone came snooping around. We're only taking fishing clothes and supplies. No sense letting people know that we were leaving for good. We'll have the money from the safe deposit boxes readily accessible. There's no reason to leave the money in the boxes when the blast hit. It would be destroyed anyway. It's almost thirty thousand dollars, and while we had much more in the account in Zurich, this will provide us with easy traveling money until we can make a withdrawal by wire using the code for the Swiss account. In fact, the safe deposit boxes contain enough money for us to live comfortably for at least a year if we had to.

Despite our elaborate, well thought out and discussed, plans I'm just plain frightened. Even Hugo frightens me. He is near despondency, and I fear that either he, or I, or both of us, are going to have a breakdown. I can't eat, and I have lost eleven pounds. I can't sleep either, and I often find myself waking in the night usually to find Hugo sitting in the big overstuffed chair in the living room smoking a Camel and staring at the floor.

April 22, 1944

Last night was Saturday night. Hugo and I had gone to a little restaurant down on Morganford for dinner and returned home about nine. We had just settled into the living room. The telephone rang:

"Mrs. Jurgens?"

"Yes. Who is this?"

"Bloch"

"What is it?"

"Listen carefully. D-Day will be a week from today, Saturday, April 29, at ten o'clock in the morning. Arm the timer twenty-four hours before and leave."

"We understand."

Hugo looked up. He was sitting in a big overstuffed chair reading the Saturday evening edition of the Sunday Post-Dispatch paper we had picked up on our way back from dinner. He folded the paper into his lap. His face was white as a sheet. He didn't need for me to tell him what the call was about.

"When?"

"Saturday, a week from today. Ten o'clock in the morning."

Hugo buried his face in the paper, again. I knew he was not reading.

Thursday, April 27, 1944

We've made the rounds of the banks with time to spare. Hugo took three and I took three. At each we checked ourselves into the safe deposit section and presented our identification and duplicate key. The attendant would require us to sign the little register book and then show us into the vault. The attendant would then insert the bank's key into the lock on the box and we would insert our key into the other lock on the box. We could then withdraw the box. With the box in hand we would go into one of the little private cubicles where we could be alone and take out the cash.

Hugo and I had resolved to wear big coats with many pockets so that we could empty the contents of each box into our pockets. I took a large purse with nothing in it. We would depart without the attendant knowing we had removed anything from the box. We would put the box back in the vault space so that the attendant could not feel that it was empty, lock it with our key and tell the attendant to lock it with his key. There was no reason to leave a trail for anyone snooping. Hundred- dollar bills are light and could be tucked easily into the purse and coat pockets without a bulge.

I arrived home a little after six. Both Hugo and I had taken the bus and streetcar on our rounds of the banks, and Hugo was just a few minutes behind me. The removal of the money from the safe deposit boxes had gone smoothly. Neither of us had anyone pay any attention to us. Donald was still at the babysitters. We drew the shades and spread the bills on the dining room table. Hugo counted the money, and then I did too. There was over twenty-nine thousand dollars - all in hundreds. Cash. Untraced, unknown, and our ticket to California until we could get our money from The Banque de Credit Falmer in Zurich.

Tonight, would be our last meal in the house. Tomorrow morning, Friday, at ten o'clock, we would set the twenty-four-hour timer and leave. Hugo went to pick up Donald from the babysitter. I started dinner. I had vowed to make a good last dinner for us before we left. We were a family, although it was hardly the highest priority for the past few weeks. We are going to start anew. The horrible act that we are about to commit has to be put behind us if we were to be a family again. We'll begin tonight. I had bought a roast and had left it simmering on low in a pot on the Magic Chef with carrots, onions and potatoes before I left for work this morning. We would feed and bathe Donald and put him to bed. Then there would be a candlelight dinner with roast and vegetables and a piece of lemon pie for dessert. We are starting anew - tonight. I'm going to see to it. We would be a family again.

Hugo had declared that there would not be any beer or wine with dinner. We needed a clear head. No mistakes. No fuzziness. After all, tonight we eat a good meal, and he's going to set the timer in the morning, and we will be off. We had done what little packing that was necessary on Wednesday night. Our departure time would be at about ten in the morning – right after setting the timer. We could let Donald sleep until nine.

Hugo had used all of his gas ration coupons to fill the car and had gotten another supply this afternoon from a friend who comes into the shop and always seems to have some extras to sell. We knew they were black market. He never told us where he got them, and we never asked. After all, a fishing expedition to the Black River is a worthy use of gasoline ration coupons.

By nine thirty I was clearing dinner dishes. Hugo had turned on Edward R. Murrow and the news. I thought it ironic that I was standing at the sink washing dishes, and that, on Saturday, at this time, this house would not exist. Old habits do not die easily. I thought that we were really organized for a family whose life was about to change completely. Hugo sat at the kitchen table and listened to the radio. There was another story about the 'Nazi Secret Weapon'. Hitler was now threatening a demonstration of its power against the Allies. No one seemed to take him seriously according to Murrow. I wondered how they would feel on Saturday afternoon?

There was other news of the war, too. There had been a discovery of a spy ring in the United States with several arrests. They read the names of the spies that were arrested. Among those arrested were Bloch and Graff.

"Hugo, did you hear that? Bloch and Graff have been arrested. What does that mean?"

"I'm not sure, Frieda," said Hugo as he got up and paced around the kitchen. "Remember, they told us that the FBI knew who the spies are." He lit a Camel and rubbed his hand together as if they were cold. "I don't know," he repeated, "but it doesn't change our plans." He walked back and forth and blew smoke up to the ceiling.

Hugo decided to go upstairs to the attic. I haven't the faintest idea what he had in mind. After just few minutes he came back through the kitchen on his way to his workbench in the basement.

"The acorn nuts on the timer have worked loose. I'm going to get a wrench and tighten them."

"The timer on the bomb?"

"Yes, what other timer do you think," Hugo snapped. "I guess the vibration of the travel worked them loose." He disappeared down the steps to the basement and soon returned with the little portable toolbox he used to carry his basic tools around the house for fix-it projects. He passed through the kitchen without speaking - a determined look on his face. I heard him mount the ladder stairs to the attic.

The dishes had been scraped and washed and were drying in the rack at the sink. I was wiping off the table. I heard Hugo come bounding down the attic ladder.

"Jesus Christ!" he yelled, before he had reached the hallway. "Frieda, come here, now!"

I met him in the dining room. "What is it Hugo? What's wrong?"

"Frieda, look at this. Look!" Hugo held the timer in his hands.

"Hugo, what is it? What have you done?"

"I was just tightening the nuts. I couldn't resist it, so I just lifted out the timer to see how it worked."

"Hugo, you shouldn't ..."

"Frieda, look! Look at this." His hands were trembling.

"Hugo you shouldn't have taken that out of the..."

"Frieda that is not the point. Look." Hugo turned the alarm timer handle to twenty-four hours by twisting it. The ratchet made a little clicking sound – just as they had said. When it reached "24" there was an immediate "click." Hugo looked up at me and said: "See?"

"See what?" Frieda hesitated, "What does that mean?"

"Frieda, it means that there is *no delay* on the timer! The circuit is closed when the timer is set! The bomb is designed to go off just as soon as the arming switch is flipped!"

"You mean there is no twenty-four-hour timer? The bomb goes off immediately when we set the timer?"

"That's it, exactly. You set the 24 hour timer, flip the switch, the bomb goes off instantly. Frieda, they intend to blow us up with the bomb!"

"Oh my God!"

"Those dirty bastards." Hugo sunk down in one of the dining room chairs, staring at the timer. "They intend to get rid of us with the explosion - gone; no trace."

"Hugo, that can't be. What about the money?"

"Jesus, Frieda, don't you see. They don't intend for us to have the money. They don't intend to give it to us. It's all a set up."

"Hugo, how can they do that? The money is in our account in Zurich. We know that. We put it there. We have the number!"

"Somehow, they must control the bank, or they have some way to..." He waived his hands. Hugo stopped. I could tell his mind was racing.

"What is it Hugo?"

"Or someone else has the number!"

"How can that be? Frederich said we, alone, had the number."

"He could have been lying, or maybe he was telling the truth, but somehow they got the number later. One of those bastards could be double crossing the others, and he'll draw out the money as soon as the bomb is detonated."

"Which one?"

"I don't know, Frieda. Maybe they are all in on it. I don't know. But they clearly don't intend for us to have the money. They intend for us to be dead!"

"Hugo, what do we do?"

"Frieda, it's almost eleven o'clock."

"So?"

"The banks in Zurich open at nine. That's two AM our time."

"Yes?"

"We've got to get that money out of that account before the time for the detonation."

"The detonation is not to be until Saturday morning. We have plenty of time to do that Hugo. It's not yet midnight Thursday."

"No, Frieda. We just have a few hours. Remember, they know there's a direct no-delay trigger on the timer. They know it'll go off when we set it. That means that they expect the blast to be twenty-four hours earlier. That's _Friday_ morning. _Friday_ morning – tomorrow! That means whoever goes after the money will be after it right after the blast on Friday morning. We've got to get it out tonight!"

"How, Hugo, and to where? How do we transfer it, and where do we transfer it? We can't just have them mail us a check!"

"Remember that little bank on the Paradeplatz in Zurich, just down the street? We saw it when we drove past on the way to the Banque de Credit Falmer. Remember, you remarked how the banks didn't look anything like they did back home?"

"Sure, it was the Bank Heller or Heller Bank, something like that."

"Heller Bank; that's it."

"How are you going to transfer the..."

"If these guys are as secretive as everyone says they are, and really do jealously guard their clients' accounts. We can try to move it. If the identities are really inviolate, we just need to get it moved to the Heller Bank before nine AM, our time."

"Hugo, that's risky. It's just down the block from the other bank."

"I know, but we don't have many choices. We sure can't bring it into the United States. If we leave it where it is, you can bet it'll be gone by noon." Hugo was putting on his jacket.

"Where are you going?"

"C'mon on Frieda." Hugo was heading for the door. I was in a daze. "Come on" he repeated and held the kitchen door. "We're going downtown – to Western Union. I'll explain in the car.

"But, what about Donald..."

"Don't worry about him, Frieda. He sleeps all night. Wild horses won't wake him until morning.

Hugo drove down Market Street to Twelfth Street and swung east onto Olive. The yellow lights of the Western Union office splashed out onto the sidewalk through big dirty plate glass windows. Even though it was near Midnight the place was a beehive of activity. Several clerks worked behind wooden desks. Tickers could be heard in the background.

A clerk with a green visor met us at the big counter. He was thin and pimply- faced. A Lucky Strike dangled from his lips.

"Yeah?"

"We want to send a telegram to Switzerland. Can you do it?"

"Sure. Cost ya plenty, though."

"How much?" Said Hugo, as if he really had a choice to send it or not.

"Depends on how many words." He slid a pad toward us. "Ya got a pencil?"

Hugo took a Scripto mechanical pencil out of his shirt pocket, hunched over the counter and began to write.

"Heller Bank
Paradeplatz,
Zurich, Switzerland

    Please open numbered account in the name of the
undersigned. Expect transfer of funds from Banque de
Credit Falmer to the account today. Please acknowledge
opening of account and receipt of funds to my credit,
and forward new account number to the undersigned
at the following address via telegram upon receipt.

Hugo Jurgens
6334 Vienna Av.
Saint Louis, Missouri, USA"
Phone: FL 1262"

Hugo tore off the sheet and handed it to the clerk. The pimply-faced clerk counted the words, forming each number with his lips. He looked up once at Hugo. I wondered what he was thinking.

"We can't put punctuation in a telegram, ya know," he said as if imparting some knowledge of great importance.

Hugo ignored him. He was writing on the pad again.

Banque de Credit Falmer
Paradeplatz
Zurich, Switzerland

    Transfer immediately all funds in account number
542096-001 to Heller Bank, Zurich office, Paradeplatz,
to the account of Hugo Jurgens.
    Close account.

Hugo Jurgens"
542069-001
Phone: FL 1262"

He slid the pad across the counter and the clerk again counted the words.

"How much?" said Hugo.

The clerk was looking at a chart. "Nine dollars and seventy cents."

"When will they arrive in Switzerland?"

"We'll get it out in the next few minutes. It'll be there within the hour. Has to go through New York. We can't guarantee it'll go through, though, what with the war and all."

"Do many not go through?"

"Well, the big problems are in France and Germany and the Netherlands, but most everything to Switzerland makes it sooner or later."

Real reassuring, I thought: 'Sooner or later?' 'Later' wasn't good enough.

As we turned to leave, I turned toward Hugo. He looked so tired. Everything depended on the wires getting through.

Neither of us would have bet on it.

Friday, April 28, 1944

We drove home through the night. It had begun a fine cold mist. It was Spring, but the evening was chilly. I scooted across the seat and snuggled next to Hugo. I hadn't done that in a long time. He put his arm over my shoulder and I curled into the crook of his arm.

"Frieda," he said, "don't go to sleep. I need to tell you something." Hugo sounded wide awake, alive.

"What is it, Hugo?"

"Frieda, think for a moment what's just happened." He pulled back his arm. I sat up squarely on the car seat. "We may have just transferred half a million dollars out of the Nazi's bank into our own account."

"You mean, if we are lucky, we got it out? Sure, Hugo, what do you think the odds really are that we got the money out?"

"Well, maybe not big; but let's assume we did. Indulge me for a minute."

"O.K. we got it out."

"Then, we have the money, and we don't have to detonate the bomb."

"Hugo are you nuts?" I turned and looked at him. He was dead serious. "What are you going to do with the bomb? Are you going call up the police and tell them it was just a big joke? I can hear it now: "excuse me, Officer, I happen to have one of Germany's atom bombs in my attic, and I'd like to give it to you?"

"No, Frieda. We don't have to give it to anybody. No one knows that we have it."

"The Nazis know. You think they aren't going to come looking for it?"

Think about it, Frieda. None of the local boys know about it. They are still around. They are still in town. In fact, they probably had a Committee meeting last night. If they knew about the Plan, they would be out of town – not hanging around to be blown to bits. They're still here. They don't know a thing. They were to be sacrificed with you and me when the device went off."

"Yeah, but Bloch sure knows about it."

"Of course, he does, but I think he's really high level. No one else has ever contacted us except Graff, and never about the bomb. I'll bet he does not know any details. He is clearly not on Bloch's level. No one else but Bloch knows about what we have, and he is under arrest as a spy. He was arrested. Remember? He's going to be deported or sent to jail; maybe even shot. He isn't going to bother us."

"Hugo, that's naive. You don't think that those guys are going to let us get away with stealing their bomb, do you?"

"I don't know, Frieda. Those guys have got a heap of trouble over there now, and it sounds like their American operatives are being rounded up. Their world is crumbling. The war is getting awfully close to home. They're pretty busy trying to save their own skins."

"I don't know, Hugo."

"Look, Frieda. Let's face it. We've been in a living Hell ever since we got back from Germany. Look at us. We've lost weight. We're nervous as a couple of junkyard dogs. Neither of us has had a full night's sleep for two months and we're both smoking like a chimney. The truth is, that no matter how hard we rationalize it by the thoughts of the money neither of us wants the blood of two hundred thousand people on our hands. We're going to become the greatest mass murderers the world has ever known. Neither of us likes it, and we are both sick about what we are supposed to do."

I began to cry.

"Don't cry, Frieda. We've just been presented the greatest opportunity of our lives. We might just get the money out and not have to set off the bomb."

"And be hunted down by that pack of wolves?"

"I don't think so, Frieda. They took a shot. We were it. A last desperate try. It's is going to fail. We're going to make it fail. Their prime operative, Bloch, is in custody. So is Graff. Maybe those others that were arrested were his back up. They might not have a secondary plan. Speer and the boys just might not have a game plan for this one. And if we got the money transferred, we win, and they lose."

"I don't know, Hugo. I just don't know." We had reached the driveway. It was just two in the morning. The banks in Zurich would just be opening.

Hugo locked the door and told me to go and get the Luger. We went into the bedroom. He put it on the table by the bed and laid down on his back, fully clothed. I laid down beside him. Neither of us spoke.

I saw the dawn lighting up the sky. Hugo had fallen into a fitful slumber. He mumbled and groaned in his sleep while pitching around on the bed. I got up and put on a pot of coffee. Hugo came in, rubbing his eyes. He looked terrible.

"Want some coffee?"

"No. What time is it?"

"Seven fifteen."

"One o'clock in the afternoon in Zurich - plenty of time to have made the transfer."

"Hugo, get serious. You really don't think that money is going to be transferred out of that account to an account for us at Heller Bank on just that telegram, do you? That account has to be watched. There's a high probability they never even got the telegrams. There's a war on. Remember, for it to work *both* telegrams have to go through, and *both* had to be acted upon. Do you know what the odds against that are?"

Hugo looked dejected, like a kid who had realized that Christmas was going to be canceled this year. He looked up at me with those big eyes that years ago charmed me at the Casa Loma. There were wrinkles around those eyes and bags under them now. The weeks of no sleep had taken their toll. He was so defeated. I wanted to hug him. What had we done to ourselves? We had sold out everything we ever stood for. We had agreed to be killers for money. We didn't care. Watching Hugo stand there, rumpled, with his head bowed, made me cry. I couldn't help it. I cried for me. I was so ashamed.

It was Friday morning. We were supposed to be fishing on the Black River. In Berlin there were a bunch of thugs huddled around news wires waiting for word of a giant blast in America's heartland. I took my coffee and went out on the back porch. Hugo laid down on the sofa in the living room and promptly fell back asleep.

I fell asleep.

I was awakened by the telephone.

"Yes?"

"Is this the Jurgens residence?"

"Yes. This is Mrs. Jurgens. Can I help you?"

"This is Western Union. Is Mr. Jurgens there?"

"I'll get him." I looked at my watch. It was eight thirty.

"Hugo! Get up. It's Western Union." I put my hand on his shoulder and jostled him awake. "Hugo, get up. Telephone."

Hugo stirred and sat up. "What?"

"Get the phone. It's Western Union - a telegram."

"Western Union?" Hugo was still in a fog.

"This is Hugo Jurgens."

"I have a telegram for you sir. We can deliver it if you'll be home, or we can read it to you."

"Please read it."

"It says:

'To Hugo Jurgens Stop Confirm new account opened Stop Number 75245-09839 Stop US five hundred thousand-dollar deposit received Stop Will hold await further instructions Stop'

It's signed, 'Heller Bank, Zurich'

Hugo's jaw dropped, then curled into a soft smile. He winked at me.

"Do you want us to deliver the printed copy?"

"Sure," said Hugo, "but take your time. There's no hurry. We'll be home all day."

"They did it! The money transferred! We got it out!" I rushed forward to hug him. Hugo held me. I could feel the tension flowing out of him. I, too, felt as if a burden had been lifted from me.

Donald padded into the room in his pajamas with the little feet.

"Hi fella. Were we a little noisy?" Hugo said. He picked him up. "I guess we were. We're sorry." Donald just rubbed his eyes and clung to his father.

"Hugo. Will they come?" I said, as we walked down the hall and into the bright kitchen.

"I don't know, Frieda. I just don't know."

23

THE PILE OF OLD CLOTHES

"September 22, 1945

It has been a year and four months since the Allied armies landed at Normandy, and over a year and a half since we were supposed to detonate the bomb. After that fateful day 17 months ago, we followed news accounts of the Normandy Landings, the liberation of France and the fall of Germany. It was an exhilarating day when the armies of the United States, Great Britain and their allies crossed the Rhine into Germany. Not once since that night of April 1944, have we heard one more account of Hitler's boast of a secret weapon. More buzz bombs have fallen on Britain, and even a few errant V2s. The "secret weapon" talk has no longer been heard.

Hugo and I have lived a different life since that night in April. On that Friday afternoon we actually did drive down to the Black River. We stopped at Dohack's and got catfish sandwiches to go. In the evening we made love under an open window after Donald had gone to sleep. We slept twelve hours on Saturday night and drove to Steeleville for church on Sunday morning. We never put a hook in the water, but to the world it was a great fishing trip – we were at ease with ourselves.

It took a while, but Hugo and I began to talk openly about what we had almost done. It was several months before we could admit that we were driven by greed and the astronomical amount of money we were supposed to get, and we were willing to commit a horrible, unforgivable, act to get it. At first, we were both surprised by the lack of remorse that we exhibited during that period. As it was unfolding, we really had very little guilt.

As the months rolled by, we attempted to reason through our actions and to talk openly about our feelings. Occasionally, we rationalized our actions, but in the end, we could find no excuse that played well. We came dangerously close to committing an act of immense proportions that no one, not even God, could have forgiven. We were both surprised that we could contemplate performing such an act. The truth was we almost did it. We had journeyed to the edge of the abyss, but we did not fall in.

But as we thought it through in the cold light of reason, we couldn't see punishing ourselves for something we didn't actually commit. Little was gained by torturing our souls ruminating over what never happened. Nothing was accomplished by revealing our "almost crime" or flailing ourselves for the unseen consequences. At least we had each other. We could talk to each other about it, but no one else. We were a club of two persons, but at least it was *our* secret.

For a long time, there was a nagging fear that we would have a visitor. Surely, those madmen in Berlin would not let us go unpunished. We had their bomb! We had their *only* bomb! It was hard to believe that they would let us get away with the double cross that we had pulled. Hugo slept with the Luger under his pillow.

No one ever came. We heard from no one. Not a soul. The Reich had crumbled. The Allies had advanced on Berlin and overrun it. The Nazis were too busy trying to save their souls to worry about us. The bomb is resting quietly without its timer in our attic. Hugo had thrown the timer on top of the trunk and covered it up with a pile of old clothes. We never ...."

Donald stood straight up. "Oh my God! Connie, the old clothes! The pile of old clothes! Remember the pile of old clothes in the attic over under the eaves? You made fun of them when we were looking for the photo trunk - the ones with all of the dust on them. It has to be there!"

Connie looked at me blankly. "I think so," she said.

"There is an atomic bomb in my parents' attic! It's under the pile of clothes!

I was putting on my shoes and a jacket.

"Where are you going?" Connie was at the kitchen door.

"Where do you think."

"Don, it's eleven o'clock at night! It can wait until morning."

"Connie, you've got to be kidding. Neither of us would sleep a wink tonight."

"Donald. Haven't you forgotten something?"

"What?"

"Donald, there might be an atomic bomb in the attic of your parent's home. In fact, from what we've just read, I'll bet you're right."

"So?" My mind was racing.

"So, what about the money?"

"Holy Cow! The money! You don't think..."

"Why not? Your parents didn't live an extravagant life. They never flaunted anything like a half million dollars around. Least of all, they never mentioned it. I'll bet that money is still in the Heller Bank in Zurich."

"And it is in the name of *Hugo Jurgens*!"

"Your name is Donald Hugo Jurgens, and you have the account number."

"Connie, you don't think we could get it, do you?"

"Why not?"

"Jesus, Connie. If it's still there it has been compounding interest since 1944. How much would it be?"

"I hear that Swiss banks maintain secret and numbered accounts with unyielding security, but they don't pay much interest on deposits. Didn't your Mom mention three percent?"

"That low?"

Connie was pounding on the calculator. "Let's see, five hundred thousand compounded at three percent for fifty years. She continued to punch. When the numbers appeared she held the calculator up for me to read.

"*Three million six hundred thousand dollars!*" She looked up and smiled. "I can handle that."

"Donald, we need to call Zurich first thing in the morning. The banks don't open for three more hours, but if the money is there, we should be able to transfer it."

"To where?"

"To our own personal accounts here in St. Louis? We didn't steal that money. We haven't done anything illegal to get it. You're their only heir. It's yours."

I couldn't resist. "Yeah, but Connie, if we get it I might quit teaching and be around the house and under foot all the time!"

Connie got the joke. She screwed up her nose like she had just detected a foul smell. "That's when I go to back to work!" She swatted me on the shoulder with the calculator.

"Come on." This time it was Connie who was putting on a jacket. "Let's go see what's hidden under that pile of clothes."

My parent's house was dark. The electricity had been turned off for a month. We had cleaned out most of the furniture after the sale. The few items we couldn't sell were strewn about. We had the house under contract with a nice young couple buying their first house. They were very excited. They reminded me of Hugo and Frieda Jurgens. They were waiting on a loan approval from the S & L so we could set a closing date. I had the electricity and the gas turned off since there was no necessity to heat the house.

It was after midnight. The bells over at Francis of Assisi Catholic Church chimed the quarter hour. I held the flashlight. Connie followed closely behind. She was not a fan of the dark. I could feel her holding on to the back of my jacket. I stumbled on a rolled-up rug in the bedroom that not yet been removed. The big closet was empty except for empty clothes hangers that rattled as we brushed past them. We ascended the wooden ladder-stairs to the attic. A faint light from a street light outside came through the ventilator slits in the end of the gable and cast a dim blue mercury vapor glow in the attic.

I swept the empty attic with the flashlight. There were still stray pieces of furniture that we were not able to sell, but not many. The floorboards creaked as I stepped off of the ladder onto the planked floor. Connie was right behind.

"It's over there," she said and gently prodded my light to the right. I swept the area and took three steps in the same direction. Pushed back under the eaves was an old horsehair overstuffed chair, its cover stained and worn. Behind it I could see the edges of the pile of clothing.

"Over here." Connie moved ahead of me and began wrestling with the big chair. I held the light, and the chair slid with a grating sound across the hardwood floorboards exposing the big pile of dusty clothing.

"What do we do now," she said.

"Well, if what Mom wrote is accurate, it's not going to explode. The panel with the timer and the arming switch are out of it. Even if they were still in it the batteries would be dead."

"Yeah, but isn't there something about radiation?"

"Connie, my parents lived under this thing into their eighties. If this thing was giving off lethal doses of radiation, I doubt they would have made it that long. Remember, dad died of a heart attack, not Cancer."

We pulled away dusty clothes. A brooding form began to take shape in the beam of the flashlight.

It was the trunk.

"That's it!"

I put the flashlight in my mouth and used both hands to help her uncover the balance of the trunk. It was dark brown with black bands and wooden strips on the side, just like mother had described it - well constructed. The quality of its latches and hinges was immediately apparent, but it looked just like an old American sea trunk. On the top sat the timer and arming switch with the bare wires dangling over the side. Just where Mom said Dad left it. The flat round latch of the trunk had been shut and locked. We saw no key. It would take a big screwdriver or a bar to pry it open. I didn't have either one with me. I had a tool box in the car. I turned to go back down the stairs to get it.

"Don't move!" The voice was definitely not Connie's. Two bright hand-held spotlights shone into our eyes. It was impossible to see beyond the lights.

"Don't move, or we'll blow you away." It was the same voice - familiar - but I just couldn't place it.

"Move over there," the voice commanded. "Now!" The light gestured to my right.

"Mildred?"

"Shut up, Donald. Turn your light off and move over there." The light gestured to my right again, this time with more authority.

"Mildred what the hell are you doing here?"

"Shut up, buddy boy, and move over there like she said." It was a different voice. This time it was masculine - thick with a heavy German accent. I was being pushed in the direction I was supposed to go.

"Mildred, what are you doing?" It was Connie. "You have no right to..."

Connie was hit in the side of the head with the butt of a gun. She went down like a limp rag. I bent to help her.

"Don't! Leave her alone!" The steel barrel of a gun was forced into my forehead. I straightened up instinctively.

The gun stayed at my forehead. "The light. I said turn it off!" The thick accent was edgy. I turned off my flashlight and put it into my pocket. One of the two lights went to the bomb. It was the light of the person that had hit Connie.

"All right. Let's move it." It was Mildred again. "C'mon on, Donald you take one handle." I felt the barrel of a gun. This time it was in my ribs. The other person moved to the other side of the trunk and took the handle. Mildred's light stayed on me.

"You thought we'd never come, didn't you Donald?"

"Mildred I really don't understand."

"Pick up the trunk handle, Donald. We're moving it downstairs."

"Mildred, you knew about the bomb in the trunk? My parents told you about it?"

"Your parents? Hah!" Mildred spat on the floor. "Your parents were a pair of idiots! They couldn't tell me anything. They were worse than idiots; they were traitors."

"Well, then how did..." It came all of a sudden. What a dummy I had been. Mildred was one of *them*!

"Let's get going," said Mildred. "Donald, lift your end. Eric, you lead."

"Eric? That can't be Eric Muller?"

There was an unusually long silence. Mildred obviously didn't intend to call him by name. But it was too late. She had used his name, Eric. I hadn't recognized the other voice, but it impressed me as that of an older man, perhaps in his seventies or even eighties.

"Eric Muller, is that really you?"

"I did my time, my friend," said the thick accent. He had lifted up the end of the trunk by its handle and began pulling the trunk toward the opening in the floor where the ladder stair came up. It made a scraping sound as it slid across the floor.

"Donald, you always were a little shit. I hated you even when you were a kid. You were a little brat when I baby sat you, and you are a big brat now." Mildred's voice was dripping with contempt.

Connie was stirring. She tried getting to her feet, unsteadily. "Donald, I..."

"Shut up Connie, or I'll have Muller put you out for good."

Connie stood up, wobbling, still trying to focus her eyes. She was having trouble contemplating what was going on.

"Donald, your dear Hugo and Frieda told you about the money, I'm sure?"

"Money? What Money?" I thought I feigned ignorance of the money pretty well.

"Oh Donald, don't give me that bullshit," said Mildred, shining the light directly into my eyes. "You have to know about the money. Nothing you can say will make me believe otherwise."

I said nothing.

"Your parents somehow succeeded in getting the money out. Do you know that money was supposed to be for me and the other operatives in the United States?"

"You? The money in the account in Switzerland was destined for you?"

"Donald, sometimes I wonder how you ever got a college degree. It shows how mediocre the Americans are if a dummy like you can get a Ph.D."

"Why you? I mean..."

"Donald, who do you think was directing the espionage activities in the United States for Wartime Germany?"

"Bloch?"

"Donald you *are* a jerk. It was me you dumbass, I was Bloch's controller. I made the decisions. It was I who made the decision to send your parents to Germany!"

"You?"

"Surprise, Donald. Well, that was then, and now I want the money!"

"Mildred, I honestly don't...."

"Cut the crap Donald. You will never make me believe you didn't know about the money."

We were inching the trunk toward the hole in the floor through which the ladder - stairway dropped into the bedroom closet. Muller had swung around in front of the trunk and was trying to pull me along. I pushed it along the floor halfheartedly, then I lifted my end. I sensed that it was all Muller could do to lift his end of the heavy trunk. He was clearly past his prime. He was trying to get it to the hole under the rope and pulley so he could hook it up to the block and tackle in the rafter above.

"Mildred, what if I did know about the money? Would it change anything? I mean, what is it you really want?

"Donald, the money doesn't mean anything. The money is a commodity, obtainable in many ways."

"What are you talking about?"

"Donald, you are dumber than a stone. The value is in the *bomb*, not the money! Why do you think we've been watching you for the past few weeks?"

"What!"

"Donald, we've been tailing you ever since your parents died. We knew sooner or later you would lead us to the bomb. When you headed for this house tonight - after midnight - we knew you had located it. We were willing to wait. We have waited for fifty years. It was just a matter of time."

"Mildred, what in the Hell are you going to do with an atomic bomb?" I could feel my grip on the handle slipping. My hands were wet. I needed to put the trunk down or I was going to drop it.

"Sell it, of course. There are people who will pay handsomely for an atomic bomb."

"Sell it? You? Mildred, who are you going to sell an atomic bomb to? This is the nineties. You don't just put a 'For Sale' sign on it and put it in the yard."

Connie was moving around more steadily now. Mildred ordered her to my side so that she could watch both of us with her light. Muller was at the edge of the stair ladder. He was breathing heavily and started to put the trunk down on the floor to rest his hands and hook up the block and tackle. I felt it too. My hands were aching from the weight. I, too, needed to relax my arms. I sat my end down.

"Mildred, I can't get over you wanting to sell this bomb."

Connie could see her better than I. She was closer. "Don't Donald," she injected. "Don't egg her on."

"Let him," said the old lady. "It's going to all be over soon. I get a kick out of his eternal baiting. He thinks he's this brilliant college professor. He's really the stupid one." She pointed the gun right into my face. I could see her now in the faint light of the street light shining through the ventilator, "If we didn't need you to get this thing out of here I would blow your brains out right now."

I felt my face flushing. I hated that old lady. I had hated her from the time she babysat me. She was always intimidating. Despite my disdain Mildred's last statement struck terror in me. I had no doubt she meant it. Connie and I could probably expect a bullet in the head as soon as we got this thing downstairs - or at least into her car. She needed us only to get it out. The frail Muller couldn't do it alone.

"You think you're going to sell this bomb?" I heard myself continuing. "You're a wacko, Mildred." It was as if someone else was talking. "You think you can get a lot of money for this thing? You're nuts!" I continued to bait her. I'm not sure why. I had no plan. I only knew it irritated her. She hated me more than I hated her. It was easy to get her mad.

"It's already sold, you asshole." Mildred's voice had an edge on it. I knew I was getting to her. "We've sold it to Iran for twenty million dollars. That's why I don't care if you found the money your stupid parents stole from us. It's a drop in the bucket. The bomb is worth much more!"

"Iran?" I was stunned. I just blurted out the word. Did she mean it?

"You got it, buddy boy. You think you are a hot shot, but you got nothing. What'd ya think, I was just doing this for - old time's sake?"

"Iran? Mildred you don't have ...."

"C'mon asshole. You didn't know your Mommy and Daddy fucked up our playhouse in 1944? You don't think that we would just go away did ya?"

"But Mildred, That was fifty years ago. What in the Hell do ...."

"Donald you are such a simpleton. Just because the Third Reich went to Hell in a hand basket doesn't mean the Organization went away. The Committee is just as strong now as it was then - maybe stronger."

"But Iran?"

"Why not Iran? They have money. They want a bomb. The International Community won't let them build one. We know where one is. It's a natural, Donald. Only you're too stupid to see it.

She poked me in the ribs with the gun. "Now let's get it moving. Eric, get up!"

Muller, who had been sitting on the top step breathing heavily, stood up. He was standing on the second step of the ladder stairs contemplating the block and tackle above.

"Muller, get it under the pully and hook it up. You go first. Keep your light on the stairs so little Donald here doesn't fall."

We inched the trunk across the floor toward the hole. Muller pulled the trunk from his position in the well of the ladder stairs and stepped down one rung. Only his waist was now above floor level. The trunk made a scraping sound as we scooted it across the wooden plank floor like when you ran your fingernails on the chalkboard in school. Muller stepped down another rung, tipped the trunk slightly and reached for the rope hanging from the pulley. I held firmly to the upper end handle of the trunk and took as much weight as I could. I felt the weight shift to Muller below me.

I'm not sure what happened next. I felt a boot in the rear. It was a firm sure shot that sent me sprawling across the hole and to the other side. Instantly I lost my grip on the trunk and my falling weight on its upper end pushed the trunk downward through the ladder hole with terrific force as I fell across the hole. The trunk careened downward taking Muller with it for seven or eight feet. There was a wicked cracking sound as Muller hit the floor below and the trunk caught the sprawling Muller across the face and chest. I could swear I could hear bones breaking.

Mildred cursed, "Donald you assho..." She was cut short by a blow to her abdomen administered by Connie with a broken touchier lamp base. The gun went flying. Connie was on top of her, before I could extricate myself from the spread-eagled position I occupied across the ladder hole in the floor. I looked down through the well of the ladder stairs. Muller lay on the closet floor below. He did not move.

"Get the lamp cord!" Connie yelled.

I pulled the flashlight from my pocket and retrieved the lamp cord from the base of the touchier. I yanked it free with a firm jerk.

Connie had rolled the writhing Mildred onto her stomach and pulled her arms behind her. She was a wiry little bitch, but her strength was no match for the two of us. I tied her hands firmly with the lamp cord. I stretched it to her feet, folded up her legs behind her and made two loops around her ankles before tying it off.

Connie stood up. "What about him?"

I went to the edge of the hole and looked down. Eric Muller did not move. I shined the light in his face. The corner of the trunk had hit him squarely in the face and broken his nose to one side. Blood was all over the floor of the closet below. The corner of the trunk looked like it had gone into his face about two inches. His temple was caved in. I speculated that he might have had a fractured skull.

"He's out. Maybe dead. I can't tell."

"Well, husband." Connie put her hands on her hips. I could see her face puffing up from the blow. "What do we do now?"

I dropped back into the big overstuffed chair to think. Mildred glared at me from her prone position on the floor of the attic. She was swearing.

I sat in the big overstuffed chair trying to sort out what had happened. Connie slumped to sit on the top of the ladder. She looked down at Muller. I could see her face was swollen up, and her left eye was black from the blow Mildred had struck.

"Connie, my parents carried a horrible secret to their deaths. They were spies, but worse, they smuggled an Atomic Bomb into the United States. No one knew about it except these two, Mildred and Muller. All of the others are dead."

"This thing has got to stop. Here. Now."

"Donald, I don't know where you are going with this." Connie dabbed her puffy cheek with her sleeve.

"I think it's time this terrible secret came to an end."

"You're going to the police?"

"Not a chance. Connie, do you know what would happen if we went to the police with this story? Think about it. First, they wouldn't believe us. When they found the bomb we'd be in big trouble. It's a federal Crime to possess a weapon of mass destruction, and they'd never believe us when we tried to explain how we got it. We'd have to show them the diaries to get them to believe it. If they did believe it, my parents would be branded as spies. It would be sensationalized all over the media. I don't want my parents defiled in public - and for all purposes it would rub off on us. We'd be pariahs. I'd probably lose my job at the University."

"We'd lose the money too," said Connie. "If the police saw the diaries they would trace the money."

"Connie, we don't have the money. We may never get it, but if we did, once the word got out the United States Government would seize the money as funds of the War Criminals." We wouldn't see a red cent.

24

THE VIEW FROM
THE BRIDGE

The Jefferson Barracks Bridge spans the Mississippi River just south of St. Louis. It is the bridge Interstate-255 uses to connect Missouri and Illinois. It's a high bridge - high enough for the huge barges and tows that ply the nation's biggest waterway to pass under. Its superstructure is a high steel arch from which the roadbed is suspended across the river. It took us twenty-five minutes to drive from my parent's home to the bridge.

The big wires on its huge suspension cantilevered arch howled in the night wind as we drove onto the span from the west - the Missouri side. There were no cars in sight. At 3:30 in the morning even I-255 gets quiet.

We drove onto the bridge slowly. I'd been over it before, but I really wasn't that familiar with it, and I wanted to cross all of the way to the Illinois side. It was Connie's idea to reconnoiter the bridge first. No one was in sight as we crossed the center of the span and proceeded toward the Illinois side on the divided highway. We'd have to go about a mile into Illinois and circle back at the first exit where we could turn around. A half-moon was peeking from behind a blanket of clouds. Stars hunted for openings to shine through.

"We've got to move fast, Connie. Once we stop, we have to move quickly."

"I know. I know." Connie rested her bruised face in the palm of her hand.

On the middle span of the bridge returning back toward Missouri we were two hundred feet above the river. We could see in both directions along I-55 for a long way if a car was coming from either side. The Illinois side is flood plain and very flat. I judged we could see three miles to the east. On the west I-255 tops a hill as it approaches the bridge, so a car could be hidden behind the hill until it came over the crest. I estimated we could see only a mile and a half to the west.

The plan was simple. Turn off the lights and get out of the car. The bomb would be tied off to the bridge railing with rope and pitched over the side. It would take both of us to lift it over the rail. A line would be attached to each end handle and then to the railing using a slipknot. After we dumped the trunk with the bomb over the rail we'd let it hang by the ropes. As we left Dad's house I went out to the garage and got a large nylon rope he kept on a nail. The plan was to pitch the bomb over first. It was to be the weight. Connie and I wouldn't have the strength to lift Mildred and Muller together with the bomb and throw them over the bridge rail. The bomb would be tied off with slip knots with about ten feet of rope tied to the trunk handles on each end. It would dangle from the bridge with the heavy rope until we got Mildred and Muller tied on to the end lines. Then we would pull the slip knots and all three would fall the two hundred feet into the river. With the weight of the bomb they would go straight to the bottom. In my mind I rehearsed tying the rope to the bomb with slip knots holding it to the railing. That would leave plenty of line on each end to tie Mildred and Muller to the remaining line before pulling the slipknots.

We approached the bridge from the east. I had rolled my window down. All I could hear was the wind in the bridge cables. I looked over at Connie. She looked pale in the moonlight.

"You OK?"

"No Donald, I'm not OK. We are about to dump an Atomic Bomb, an old lady and a body into the Mississippi River. I don't do this every day!"

Muller had not moved after his fall from the ladder stairs with the bomb on top of him. We did not know if he was dead or alive. When we climbed down from the attic, I could see that the damage was more than I had even expected. His whole head was caved in on the underside that faced the floor. The full weight of the bomb must have come down on his head. He had stopped bleeding and I stooped to feel his pulse. There was none. As far as I knew Eric Muller was dead. We had loaded him in the trunk of the car with the bomb.

"Connie, do this right and all traces are gone. We are closing the book on a horror story that began fifty years ago."

Connie didn't respond.

"See anything to the east?" I said.

Connie twisted around in the seat and looked east toward Illinois.

"Nothing," she said. I saw her look down at the horrified Mildred who lay tied up in the back seat. Mildred knew what we were up to. She had to hear us talk about it on the way from the house.

"Mildred," I said, "the way I look at it, I am only doing the job that should have been done on you years ago. You probably would've been executed if you had been caught during the War. You were part of a plan to kill thousands in St. Louis. Do you know how many people your little plan would have killed?"

Mildred didn't respond.

"I know the answer, Mildred: If that bomb would have gone off two hundred thousand people would have died. Maybe more. Many more would have been sickened." I hated that old woman. I was only glad that it was my parents who had the bomb. Mildred and her Committee would have set it off.

We slowed to a stop at the highest point on the center of the bridge, and I cut the headlights leaving only the running lights on. I left the motor running. Connie was out of the car and to the back lifting the lid of the car's trunk. It popped open. The bomb rested on the body of Muller. The handles made it possible for two to lift, from each end but it was very heavy. I secured the line to the handles of the trunk and tied the slipknots to attach it to the bridge railing. Connie and I heaved the trunk over the rail. The two lines that I had secured to the handles went taught and held firmly. The trunk swung ten feet below the rail with two hundred feet of air between it and the water below. We looked in both directions along the bridge - still no cars.

Muller was heavy. His dead weight was all Connie and I could handle. We dragged him to the rail and tied one of the slipknot lines around him in a harness, passing the line under his arms and crisscrossing over his shoulders. We heaved him over the rail. The knots held. Muller joined the trunk dangling from the bridge railing.

Mildred was kicking and squirming as we pulled her from the back seat. The electrical cords with which we had tied her in the attic made a nice handle and we carried her to the rail and tied on the ropes. The wind was whining in the wires of the bridge. I could see Mildred's eyes. She had stopped whimpering for some unexplained reason. All I could see was the hatred and contempt that she held for me.

A car crested the hill to the west of the bridge as I was tying Mildred to the other slipknot line.

"Donald, we've got to hurry. A car is coming," said Connie.

"When I say 'now', pull the slip on your line. I'll do the same on my end."

Connie grasped the line that held Muller. "Now!" We both pulled the slip lines. Connie's end released. Mine had been tied tighter, and it did not release, The Trunk and Muller swung free below the bridge suspended only by the line on my end. The trunk and Muller dangled from the taught line on my end. The slipknot would not release.

I was frantically trying to release the slipknot on my end of the trunk. The weight of the trunk and Muller had only made the knot tighter. Mildred was gyrating wildly. She began to scream and curse. The slipknot would not release. The eastbound car was within a half a mile of the bridge.

"Donald, pull your line, quickly!"

Somehow Mildred broke her hands free from the cord. She hit me in the groin with all her strength and I fell backwards writhing in pain. Connie was on her. Mildred scratched her in the face and dug her fingers into Connie's already swollen cheeks. Mildred's feet were still tethered to the cord and the trunk, but she held on to Connie with both hands. She released one hand and brought her fist crashing onto the side of Connie's head. Connie released her grip on the old lady and was momentarily stunned. Mildred saw her chance and hit her again - in the same place even harder. Connie's head snapped to the side and she fell to one side against the railing.

The old lady was fishing into her fanny pack. She had trouble getting the zipper free. I got up and started for her. My groin was throbbing. She found what she was looking for. "That's far enough, buddy boy," she said in a scratchy cackle. She held up a straight razor. The moon glinted off its shiny blade. She grabbed Connie and put the blade against her neck."

"One step and I cut her!" Connie was groggy and did not stir.

"The gun, asshole! Get the gun out of the car or she's history!"

I stood immobile, stunned. How did Mildred know that we had her gun in the car? I could only speculate that she was guessing. Connie and I had not talked about it since we left the house.

"We didn't bring the gun, Mildred. It's still at the house." I knew the gun was on the front seat of the car. If Mildred got it we were finished.

"You're lying, asshole! Get it or I'll cut her."

"Now!" Mildred slowly drew the blade across Connie's throat just enough to break the skin. Connie offered no resistance. Her eyes were droopy, and I couldn't tell if she was even conscious.

"OK, OK, I'll look. I took two steps to the car. I was still holding the line of the slipknot that I had been unsuccessful in pulling loose. The car's engine was still running. I walked around the front of the car to the driver's side. The driver's side door was still open. I slid into the seat. The gun glistened on the seat. I knew Mildred wouldn't do anything to Connie until she had the gun.

I picked the gun up off the seat and waived it so that Mildred could see it. She beckoned to me to bring it to her by waiving the razor. Its steel glint flashed in the moonlight of the clear cold night. Connie was a limp as a rag. Mildred began sawing at the electrical cords that bound her feet with the razor. She easily cut through the insulation on the wire, but the copper wire would not yield.

I don't know how the idea came to me. There seemed to be no time between the idea and the action. I pulled the transmission knob into 'Drive' and stomped the accelerator. The car door slammed shut from the acceleration, wedging the rope between the open door and the jamb. The rope snapped taught instantly and the force of the car pulled the slipknot free. I had only gone about ten feet, but to my right through the open window I heard a sickening thwack as the knot broke free and the weight of the trunk and Muller jerked Mildred from her crouched position holding Connie and smashed her into the top of the rail as she went over.

I stopped the car. Mildred had been upended and was hooked on the top of the rail. One of her legs was obviously broken from the force of the falling trunk slamming her into the rail. Her body flopped over the rail and she dangled over the other side of the railing as she grasped at the railing with both hands. She was suspended for just a second, but she was no match for the weight of the trunk and Muller's body pulling her downward. As I stepped from the car she released her grip. I could see her eyes through the grillwork of the railing as she went down. She was staring at me. The hatred was still there as she slipped into the blackness.

The splash below was muffled by the sound of the oncoming vehicle. It was a Ford F-150 pickup with a camper-top in the bed. It slowed and stopped opposite me across the bridge in the westbound lanes.

"Hey! You alright, buddy?" A man in a plaid hunting jacket and a John Deere cap was shouting out of the window.

"Yes. Thanks. We're all right." I was helping Connie to her feet. "My wife has just had a little too much to drink. She got sick and we had to stop."

"You're not going to jump or anything like that, are you?" yelled the driver.

"No, nothing like that. She just needed to toss her cookies over the side." What a stupid thing to say, I thought.

I waived him on.

The plaid jacket and green cap pulled back inside the window and the truck drove away. I got Connie to the car and helped her inside. The side of her face was swollen up and turning blue - black. I left the window open as we drove away. I thought the cold air might do us both good. Connie began to stir.

"It's over?" Connie said, as we turned into our street. I tried to calculate the odds of anyone ever finding the bomb and the bodies of Mildred and Muller at the bottom of the river. No one saw us. No one knew they were there. The trunk would hold them on the bottom unless someone just happened to drag the area on the bottom where the trunk had sunk. The chances were about zero. I agreed with Connie. It was over - all but one thing.

"Not quite, Connie. There is the money."

"Donald, get serious. You don't really think the money is still there, do you?"

"I certainly intend to find out." It was five AM in St. Louis, but in Zurich it was noon. "The banks in Zurich are open. I think we need to make a call, don't you?"

We put the car away and went into the house. Connie made a pot of coffee while I got the notebook where Mom had put the name of the Heller Bank in Zurich and the number of the account. I found it and brought it to the kitchen table with the phone.

The operator gave me the Country Code and City Code for Zurich information, and after telling us how to reach Zurich information she asked if she could help me dial. I wrote down the numbers down and told her, "no, thanks." The last thing I wanted was a nosy operator with nothing to do at five in the morning listening in on our call.

I dialed the number of Zurich Information. There was a lot of clicking and switching as the signal shot through the circuits, and via satellite found its target on a small street in Zurich. It began to ring.

"Ya, Information."

"Do you speak English?"

"Hello. May I help you?" came a crisp reply in English with a creamy Swiss-German accent.

"Yes. Can you give me the number of the Heller Bank in Zurich?"

I could hear the name being typed into a computer.

"Yes, that number is 92582543."

I pressed the "hang up button" and dialed putting in the country code and the number Zurich Information had given me. With amazing speed the telephone began to give me the distinctive ring tone of European phone systems.

"Allo, Heller Bank, Zurich." The voice spoke German.

"Yes, I wish to check on the status of an account."

"One moment please," the reply was in clear English. I looked at Connie while the call was being transferred. She was beat and looked it. The swollen bruises on the side of her face had deepened, and her eyes drooped. She held a coffee mug with both hands as if it would get away. Her elbows were on the table. Steam was rising from the cup into her eyes. She managed a weak smile.

"This is Hans Franckel, Principal Cashier. How can I help you?" The voice was stern - all business.

"My name is Hugo Jurgens. I have an account in your bank. I want to check on its status."

"The number please, and the date and amount of your last deposit?" The voice was cold, unyielding.

"The number is 75245-09838. There have been no deposits since the original when the account was opened except your interest credits." It was a calculated risk. I didn't think that my mother and father had made any more deposits. I didn't know for sure.

"That's quite an old account. We don't use that numbering system anymore. One moment please."

I didn't have time to respond. The comment didn't require a response anyway. The line went dead as if I had been put on hold. Music played. God, I thought, must everyone have Music on Hold?

"Herr Jurgens?"

"Yes?"

"Do you want the balance in Francs, Dollars or Marks?"

I knew I had hit the Mother Lode!

"Dollars please."

I could hear an adding machine in the background as Franckel calculated the balance in dollars.

"The account has a current balance of three million seven hundred eighty- one thousand six hundred seven dollars and fifty- five cents as of the close of business yesterday. We do not credit today's interest until tomorrow morning.

Are there any instructions?"

"No. No instructions. Thank you. I just wanted to know the status."

"Is that all, Herr Jurgens?" The Swiss stiffness was still there.

"Yes. Thank you. That's all I needed to know."

"At your service, Herr Jurgens." The phone went dead.

I pushed the "off" button and leaned back against the chair.

Connie held her coffee to her lips with both hands and winked over the top of the cup at me.

EPILOGUE

Hugo and Frieda Jurgens lived in the house on Vienna Avenue in St. Louis until their deaths. Hugo continued to barber until his retirement at age seventy, and Frieda remained as secretary to Avril Hollenbeck until his employment was ended by his retirement in 1947 at which time Frieda retired to stay home and raise their son, Donald. They were active Lutherans attending church almost every Sunday. Hugo coached a Little League baseball team for ten years. In every way they were exemplary citizens. They carried the secret of their activities during World War II to their graves, never mentioning it to a soul – not even their son. The deposit in the bank in Zurich was never touched. Frieda died in 1984 of congestive heart failure. Hugo died of a heart attack in 1990.

In the spring of 1992, two years after Donald and Connie Jurgens had dumped the atomic bomb and the bodies of Mildred and Muller into the Mississippi River, the stern wheeler dredge, *Sainte Genevieve*[i], operated by the U.S. Corps of Engineers, was assigned to dredge the channel of the Mississippi from the Jefferson Barracks Bridge south to Caruthersville, Missouri. By Corps of Engineers' Standards, the depth of the channel was to be maintained at a minimum of nine feet to facilitate barge traffic on the river. The *Saint Genevieve* was the primary dredge of the Corps of Engineers' St. Louis District and was assigned this task.

The dredging began at a point thirty feet south of the center abutment of the Jefferson Barracks Bridge and continued southward in the center of the marked channel down river toward Caruthersville for several weeks. Had the dredging begun 18 feet closer to the bridge the intake scoops of the dredge would have encountered the trunk and the remains of Mildred and Muller in the mud at the bottom of the river. It completely missed them.

The Sainte Genevieve, however, was equipped with a Geiger counter that began reporting radioactivity immediately on positioning the dredge south of the bridge. A notation was made in the ship's log of the location, time and place of the Geiger counter activity, but it was devoid of any other details other than the elevated level of radioactivity.

No one followed up on the log entry. The *Saint Genevieve* was decommissioned in 1992.

The whereabouts of the logbook are unknown

Acknowledgements

No book is solely, the product of its author. Whether intentional in inadvertent, a finished book, fiction or factual, contains words, thoughts phrases, research and information gleaned from a myriad of sources, including experiences of the author. This book was no different.

The primary time covered by this novel was 1929 to 1945. I was born in 1940, and even though I grew up in South St. Louis, I have no significant recollection of the events of the Thirties or the first half of the Forties. World War II was just a little blur on my infant memory, but I had a resource. A resource that lived through the Thirties, who remembered the war, and who willingly recounted the conflicts in the German-American community to me, his only child. He was a barber with a busy shop on Morganford Road in South St. Louis. He was a model for the 'good' side of Hugo Jurgens, and he had a fantastic memory. It was my Dad.

It was in his barbershop that many of the debates between those sympathetic to the rise of the Nazis, and those patriots, convinced that America should intervene with the Allies, took place. Dad clearly differentiated between those who strongly believed, and those whose commitment (to either side), were sincere. And it was Dad who instilled me the thought that one, just one, of the antagonists could just be actively working as an agent for the other side.

Neither was Dad an uninterested observer. He had skin in the game with seven brothers and sisters enlisted in the US Armed forces on *active* duty in World War II in both the European and Pacific theatres. That's right, I said "SEVEN" dwarfing (but in no way diminishing) the sacrifices of the Ryan family, and no one was sent in to rescue any of them. The good news is, that they all returned home after active combat, to live long and exemplary lives.

He related to me the conflicts, the rationalizations, and the uncertainty that was rampant in South St. Louis, and, as I look back on it, his recall of events and attitudes were conveyed to me clearly, cogently and very factually. What a resource for an unusual time in our history!

And on the technical side, I had the advice and counsel of a great proofreader, and patient teacher, in Kristine Rollings. Kris would patiently mark-up my copy and correct my English pointing out where additional (or less) punctuation was required. That she was a former teacher was evident, and her patience was duly acknowledged and appreciated. I'm sure I was, at best, a reluctant student. Oh yes, she is my daughter-in-law, and I take full credit for instilling in my son the perception to find, meet, and marry this intelligent lady.

Finally, a big "thanks" to the people of South St. Louis, with whom I grew up, went to school and will never forget. They are the epitome of flyover-country - committed, hard-working, conservative, respectful. Despite the conflicts, and some might say "unpatriotic attitudes," of some of the "South Siders" of the late Thirties, after Pearl Harbor and the Declaration of War with Germany, and later, the discovery of the atrocities of the Holocaust, the doubters of American policy faded into history.

We had become one united and determined nation.

More from Dale Rollings, Author

Coming soon, Dale Rollings' third book, *"At the End of the Day,"* explores the life of one person, one of the millions, who comprised "The Greatest Generation."

It opens on Utah Beach, Normandy, in June of 1944. But this is not a "World War II" book. There are no "Private Ryan" heroics, no sweeping battlefield panoramas, but rather, a story of the life and times of an ordinary person who was drafted into an active Army support role as the Allies swept from Normandy to Berlin, and was forced to adapt, (perhaps some would say 'endure') circumstances he had never before encountered.

Michael Poulos was the son of Greek immigrant parents, He saw almost no direct combat, but was moved, shaped and transported by his experiences, and the wartime scenarios into which he was thrown. The war brought about an introspection of the experiences of his youth and propelled him into Post-War achievements and success.

He returned home after the war with no education past high school, but he had the inner spark that propelled many of his generation to take hold of their lives, and he succeeds beyond his wildest dreams.

It's a love story, but not what you think. Poulos' relationships with family, lovers and those around him call forth the lessons learned while in Europe during the War. He suffers losses and setbacks yet returns to the table of life more eager to play. And play he does, with a life of contribution, joy, sadness and rebirth.

"At the End of the Day" promises great reading. It's an "All American story" of a common man with an uncommon life, and an uncommon legacy for us all to enjoy.

More information at www.dalerollings.net.

ABOUT THE AUTHOR

Dale L. Rollings grew up in St. Louis, attended Washington University (B.S. 1962) and Washington University Law School (J.D. 1964). On graduation he practiced law in Springfield, Missouri before being appointed Principal Trial Counsel of Green County Prosecuting Attorney's office, and then Chief Counsel of the Criminal Division of the Missouri Attorney General's Office.

His first extensive writing came as manager and overseer of appellate briefs and arguments of criminal cases for the State of Missouri before the Missouri Supreme Court.

Upon returning to private practice Rollings assumed the position of Executive Director of an international trade association, and continued writing by producing numerous trade association articles, educational materials and conducting courses and seminars on business subjects, points of law and matters of legislative interest.

His law practice migrated toward corporate transactions, mergers and acquisitions, tax and family business succession planning, and his firm managed transactions in all but three states and several foreign countries. With his practice requiring extensive travel Rollings produced his first book, *Exit Laughing*, a primer for those considering selling, retiring from or passing a family-owned business to the next generation.

Commencing in the Eighties Rollings began writing fiction, and produced several drafts of historical and current fiction which were "shelved" as his business demands grew. On his retirement from the practice of law he "dusted off" the drafts and began finalizing several novels that he intends to bring to print, the first of which is *The Trunk*.

He is the father of two sons, Mark and Matt, and he and his wife, Linda, live in University City, Missouri, a suburb of St. Louis.